The Fall of a Sparrow

The Author

The Fall of a Sparrow

*. . . there's a special providence
in the fall of a sparrow.*
Hamlet, V.ii.232–3

SÁLIM ALI

DELHI
OXFORD UNIVERSITY PRESS
BOMBAY CALCUTTA MADRAS

Oxford University Press, Walton Street, Oxford OX2 6DP

NEW YORK TORONTO
DELHI BOMBAY CALCUTTA MADRAS KARACHI
PETALING JAYA SINGAPORE HONG KONG TOKYO
NAIROBI DAR ES SALAAM
MELBOURNE AUCKLAND
and associates in
BERLIN IBADAN

First published 1985

Paperback edition 1987
Second impression 1988

Phototypeset by Taj Services Ltd., Noida, U.P.
Printed in India by Mohan Makhijani at Rekha Printers Pvt. Ltd.,
and published by S.K. Mookerjee, Oxford University Press
Y.M.C.A. Library Building, Jai Singh Road, New Delhi 110001

To 'Hawk' (R.E. Hawkins)
for first instilling the thought that
my story might be worth telling

Prologue

Living three-quarters of a century with no thought of writing one's memoirs and then suddenly deciding to do so is a bad business, I realize. With practically no archival material by way of preserved correspondence, diaries, etc., and only tricky memory to fall back on, the task is unsatisfactory. In the circumstances it took considerable persuasion from friends and 'fans' to evoke in me the courage to write an autobiography. This is, however, a useful way of letting curious people know how and whence I contracted the germs of ornithology at a time when the disease was practically unknown among Indians, and of showing the development of my scientific interest in birds. The writing of this narrative, under duress as it were, began eight years ago without any proper planning or chronological sequence—more or less in the nature of random recollections and reminiscences jotted down lackadaisically in bits and pieces, as the spirit moved. But for the kindly though merciless nagging of well-meaning friends and relations it would have floundered in the mire of procrastination.

To the many—too numerous to identify individually—who have helped to recall long-forgotten happenings and who have helped in other ways, I am deeply grateful. Most of all, my thanks are due to R.E. Hawkins (Hawk) for agreeing so cheerfully to sort out the jumbled narrative and reduce the chaos to some semblance of order. Among the others to whom I feel specially beholden are J.S. Serrao, possessed of an enviable memory, who has been my indispensable aide and archivist for over three decades; and to the enthusiastic Archna Mehrotra who did all the tedious typing and retyping of drafts, and who by constant prodding and helpful suggestions was largely responsible for bringing to a close a venture that had begun to seem unending. I am aware that under the circumstances many incidents and personalities that should have found a place in the story may have inadvertently been overlooked. But eighty eventful years is a long time to pack into these few printed pages, and all I can do at this stage is to deplore their non-inclusion.

SÁLIM ALI

Contents

APPENDICES

PLATES

Frontispiece: The Author

(following page 92)

1 Father and Mother with five. Four more to come! *c.*1889.
  (*Photo by Ibrahim Ahmedi*)
2 Two of the five plus the 'four more to come', 1902. SA on
  stool at right. (*Photo by Shamsuddin Lukmanji*)
3 'Gathering of the Clan' at Uncle Badruddin Tyabji's
  Somerset House estate, Warden Road, Bombay, 1902. A
  traditional annual fixture. SA in middle of front row in
  black *sherwani*. Tehmina seventh from right in second
  row from top: the little girl in cap and curls.
4 At Khetwadi, with brother Hamid and sister Kamoo. *c.* 1905.
5 Tehmina and her brother Sarhan in London, *c.* 1905 or 6.
  (*Photo by W. Whiteley Ltd., photographers*)
6 SA, *c.* 1910, in Hyderabad (at Hashoobhai's).
7 Amiruddin Tyabji (father/uncle), August 1910. (*Photo by
  Shamsuddin Lukmanji*)
8 Amir Manzil, the family house, at Khetwadi, Bombay, *c.*
  1912. Window (top right) of 'maternity ward' where the
  entire series of us, five brothers and four sisters, were born
  between 1878 and 1896.

Contents

FACSIMILES (*following plates*)

1

Special Providence

Until a few years ago the question of how my interest in birds originated never bothered me or anyone else. I grew up with it and the oddness was taken for granted—that was that. It was only much later, after the question was put to me by an inquisitive press reporter, that I began giving thought to the matter. I then realized that, considering my early background, his query was actually less irrelevant than it first appeared. Eighty-seven years is a long time to remember details, but I vividly recall our rambling family house in Khetwadi, a middle-class residential quarter of Bombay, in the now overcrowded area between Girgaum and Charni Road. Here I lived as the youngest of an orphaned family of five brothers and four sisters: my mother Zeenat-un-nissa had died when I was about three and my father Moizuddin two years earlier. We grew up under the loving care of a maternal uncle, Amiruddin Tyabji, and his childless wife, Hamida Begam, who were more to us all than any parents could be. They were guardians as well to a miscellaneous assortment of other orphans and children of absentee friends and relations of different ages, and very variable—sometimes even dubious—quality. There was no one in that very mixed ménage who, as far as I can remember, was at all interested in birds, except perhaps as ingredients of an occasional festive *pulao*.

'Nature conservation' was then a phrase only rarely heard. Partridges and quails were abundantly and freely sold in the market, and six to eight birds per rupee of the former and sixteen to twenty of the latter made them cheap enough as a variant, on high days and holidays, of the eternal *murghi*, costing perhaps 6 to 8 annas (35 to 50 paise). The birds used to be brought alive to the Khetwadi house, crowded in round flat bamboo baskets with a burlap flap on top, and 'lawfully' *halalled* (had their throats slit). I well remember how, when about ten years old, Suleiman (a nephew two years my junior) and I used to rescue a few of these unfortunates on the sly and keep them as pets in a rough-and-ready open-air pen, made from wire mesh and old packing cases, with the help of Nannoo, the trusty old cook and factotum of the family and us children's unfailing friend, abettor and accomplice in all such enterprises. It is a wonder to all of us who knew him, and increasingly so in the context of current servant problems, how Nannoo ever found time to volunteer for all these 'extra-curricular' activities, and always with so much zest and cheerfulness. He ran the kitchen single-handed, cooking two full meals a day for seldom less than ten people, mostly children and teenagers with healthy appetites. This involved scraping and cleaning pots and pans (for he had no kitchen help), kneading the *ātā* and baking a pile of *chapatis* which, in a sporting mood, he would challenge us to finish faster than he could produce while squatting on the ground at a smoky wood fire *choola*. The 'aviary' was run in partnership by Suleiman and myself and it gave us immense joy to sit beside the enclosure and watch the behaviour and action of the birds—among which our favourites were named—for hours together. On school holidays it was certainly a far pleasanter way of passing time than doing homework.

We made as frequent excursions as our pocket money of Rs 2 per month would permit to the bird section of Crawford Market to see if any new birds had arrived which could be added to our collection. In the early days our interest was confined chiefly to game birds, and our collection consisted of Grey and Painted Partridges, and Grey, Rain and Bush Quails. Occasionally when feeling particularly flush, as after a birthday celebration, we would acquire a pair or two of Grey Junglefowl or Red Spurfowl. But I never was nor have been successful in keeping captive birds and other animals or pets alive for long. After repeated disappointment and failure I finally gave up trying; and though I have from time to time in later years kept birds for various experimental purposes, I have always released them thereafter.

About this time, when I was about nine or ten, the father-uncle with whom we lived and whom we boys greatly hero-worshipped for his shikar exploits presented me with an air gun. I well remember that it was a nickel-plated 500-shot repeater 'Daisy'—a popular make in those days, more toy than gun. Through a hole behind the front sight you had to drop up to 500 round lead pellets of BB size into a hollow cylinder round the barrel; after each shot you worked a hand lever to compress the spring which at the same time automatically slipped the next pellet into the breech. It was not much of a weapon as air guns go, extremely inaccurate and temperamental in its performance and needing a good deal of manipulation and allowances in aiming before you could hit a mark at 30-feet range. However, a repeater air gun was an innovation and as such was the envy of my little companions, some of whom possessed equally innocuous single-shot affairs. To own such a 'sophisticated' piece of weaponry added greatly to my ego and I loved to show it off. In spite of its shortcomings I soon acquired enough cunning with it to shoot house sparrows, of which a colony used to be in permanent residence in the stable. Spilt grain from the horses' nose-bags, sundry holes in the ceiling and walls for nests provided them with bountiful living. We boys, being correctly brought up as god-fearing Muslim children, knew that although the sparrow fell within the category of lawful meat it could only be eaten provided the birds had been *halalled* in the ordained manner. Under fear of dire consequences in the hereafter, and with timely warning from our elders, we were usually scrupulous in observing the ritual, but even at the risk of purgatory were sometimes tempted to cheat by cajoling Nannoo to cut their throats even after the birds were long dead and cold. Nannoo taught us how to deal with the sparrows after the correct obsequies had been performed, and some of us little boys became expert at transforming them, with *masala*, a blob of ghee and a frying-pan, into delicious morsels.

The very first bird note I ever made was during this era, at the age of nine or ten. It concerned an incident in the course of one of those sparrow hunts in that Khetwadi stable. Wooden pegs had been driven into the wall, on which harness was hung. One of these pegs had come off, leaving a hole in the wall which became a coveted nesting place for the sparrows. The observation made was on a female sparrow nesting in that hole. Crude and incomplete as it was when rediscovered nearly sixty years later, the gist of the note seemed relevant enough for publication in *Newsletter for Birdwatchers*, more or less in its original form, thus:

> 1906/7. The cock sparrow perched on the nail near the entrance to the hole while the female sat inside on the eggs. I ambushed them from behind a stabled carriage and shot the male. In a very short while the female acquired another male who also sat 'on guard' on the nail outside. I shot this male also, and again in no time the female had yet another male in attendance. In the next 7 days I shot 8 male sparrows from this perch; each time the female seemed to have another male in waiting who immediately stepped into the gap of the deceased husband.

I am rather proud of this note because though intended as a record of my prowess as a hunter and made long before I was conscious of any possible relevance, it has proved more meaningful in the light of present-day behavioural studies.

Each year when school vacations began in summer the entire Khetwadi ménage migrated to Chembur—now a noisy part of metropolitan Bombay but in those days a delightfully quiet sylvan haven of secondary moist-deciduous jungle set among outlying hillocks of the Western Ghats. The highest of these, Trombay Hill, just over 300 metres and the venue of our youthful mountaineering exploits, now forms part of the Bhabha Atomic Research Centre's estate. It was thickly wooded in parts till uniformly denuded into a veritable Rock of Gibraltar by the relentless fuel-hunters of the janata colony which was established round its base after the Second World War. The Chembur of those days is memorable for its peaceful jungle flavour and the considerable wildlife it held despite its closeness to the city. The nearest railway station, Kurla, was three miles by foot or bullock cart. There were no industries, shopping facilities, schools or other social amenities in the neighbourhood. Motor cars and buses had not invaded the scene and practically no commuters resided in the locality. Such rare townsfolk as one occasionally met were, like ourselves, vacationing visitors or absentee landholders on weekend trips to their farms or mango orchards, of which there were a flourishing number around. The Chembur area has long enjoyed a well-deserved reputation for the excellence of its mangoes, especially alphonso and pairi. Unfortunately, such orchards as have not already succumbed to housing or industrial development are fast disappearing in the wake of rocketing land values with the growth and expansion of the city. The mango trees, once so lovingly tended, have vanished or stand gaunt and neglected spectres, overrun by the parasitic growth of *bandha* (loranthus) and awaiting the vandal's axe. Most of the animal sounds, so evocative of our schoolboy vacations, have been long since silenced one by one with the inexorable encroachment of 'civilization'. The familiar howling of jackals at dusk and all through the night, inseparable from my Chembur memories, ceased years ago, and hyenas, scarce even then, have completely disappeared. The spirited song of the Magpie-Robin which regaled us at daybreak as we lay half awake, reluctant to leave our cosy beds, is one of the earliest and most cherished of my ornithological memories. They bring back those matchless, carefree school vacations in Chembur every time I listen to a Magpie-Robin's song, no matter where.

Like idle and thoughtless schoolboys everywhere, with no notion of the ethics of sport (whatever they be!) or conservation instilled into us either at home or in school—on the contrary with a certain Victorian aura attached to hunting and shooting as a manly sport—we roamed the countryside with our air guns, making a target of every little bird trusting enough to permit a close approach. I recall my juvenile elation if I managed to drop a honeysucker or similar small bird in this vandalistic sport. Happily, such occasions were rare. Part of a more regular hunting programme of us gangsters was to visit the tiny neighbouring hamlet of Deonar near sunset when large numbers of House Sparrows collected to roost among the stacks of rice-straw, piled up in trees to keep it out of reach of hungry

cattle. The sparrows came just as it was getting dark and
hurriedly tunnelled their way into the straw, and our strategy
was to keep ready for their arrival and sportingly pot only the
males before they disappeared within. The forays to Deonar
often served a dual purpose since the family supply of eggs,
vegetables and milk came from this village, and we were commissioned to bring back the hut-to-hut egg collection along
with our own bag of 'game'. (Eggs cost one *phadia* or 4 pies or
1/48 of the old rupee!) As far as I can recall it was at this point,
and as a fortuitous offshoot of one of these sparrow-hunting
expeditions, that my first 'scientific' interest in birds was born.

While one of my victims was about to be *halalled* I suspected
something was wrong with the bird: it looked like any other
female sparrow I sometimes got except that it had a yellow
patch on the throat, like a curry-stain. My main concern at this
moment was whether this sparrow was lawful meat for a
God-fearing little Muslim or not. Unwilling to jeopardize my
prospects in the hereafter, I prevented the *halalling* and instead
carried the corpse back to the house to obtain an authentic
pronouncement (*fatwa*) from Uncle Amiruddin, the shikari of
the family. He examined the sparrow carefully and agreed that
it was a different bird, apparently not having noticed one like it
before. Uncle Amiruddin was one of the earliest Indian
members of the Bombay Natural History Society (BNHS),
having joined it soon after its founding in 1883, and became an
active participant in its work. He gave me a letter of introduction
to the then Honorary Secretary, Mr W.S. Millard, the head of
Phipson & Co., Wine Merchants, asking his help in identifying
the bird. My very first contact with the Society, then housed
in the premises occupied by Phipsons, came about in this way.
That visit was a thrilling experience and is still fresh in my
memory.

Incidentally this building at the corner of Forbes Street and
Apollo Street was the former residence of the Chief Justice of
the Bombay High Court. In those days there was practically
no social contact between English people and Indians, much
less so for boys of my age. The sahibs lived in the insulated little
Englands they had created for themselves; their exclusive clubs

were defiled by no black man's shadow, excepting only the 'bearers' who poured out their *chhota* and *bara* pegs. They had built around themselves a mythical aura about their nobility and greatness and superior virtues, about carrying the black man's burden and all that. This myth took such firm root that even after forty years of independence it still survives. It was a rare occurrence for a middle-class Indian to meet and talk to an Englishman, official or otherwise, except purely on matters of business. A schoolboy's only contact with the English was perhaps when his classroom was visited annually by an educational inspector who, of course, always had to be a sahib.

I remember the feeling of nervousness—almost of fear and trembling—at the prospect of meeting a full-grown sahib face to face with which I entered the quaint old single-storeyed building through its magnificent solid teakwood portal. After due checking of my bona fides I was led up the shallow coir-carpeted steps by a supercilious khaki-liveried sepoy, the flanking walls covered with mounted heads of shikar trophies in terrifying profusion. Upstairs, in a corner of the wooden-floored room chock-a-block with desk showcases displaying seashells, butterflies, birds' eggs and miscellaneous natural history bric-à-brac, the walls were still more crowded with skulls and mounted heads of tigers and leopards staring glassily down at the intruder, or snarling with bared fangs more ferociously than they ever did in life. I was piloted to the sanctum sanctorum through this welter of animal remnants, stumbling over stuffed crocodiles and hoofs of sambar floor-rugs. In a corner of this congested junk shop, which was the Society's museum in those days, and partitioned off by swing doors, sat, leaning over his desk, the genial bald-headed Walter Samuel Millard, the Honorary Secretary.

This must have been somewhere in 1908, and my first contact with the BNHS was later to become such an important element in the shaping of my life and career. All my nervousness vanished completely in the face of the charming kindliness and consideration of Mr Millard. I then realized that perhaps *all* white men were not the ogres our youthful fancy had painted them from stories of unsavoury incidents on tea plantations and confrontations in railway carriages. As Mr Millard peered at me over his reading glasses I fumbled out my credentials and the little paper packet containing the mystery bird. He identified it at a glance as a Yellowthroated Sparrow (*Petronia xanthocollis*) and bid me follow him to the reference cabinets, from one of which he produced several stuffed specimens for confirmation. There were numerous other species of sparrows in the collection, which he took great pains to show me, and explained the differences and points for identification. He patiently opened drawer after drawer for me to see the hundreds of different birds found in the Indian Empire, and I believe it was at this moment that my curiosity about birds really clicked. Mr Millard gave me a few bird books from the small library to read, and this is how I made my first acquaintance with Edward Hamilton Aitken's (EHA's) inimitable classics—*Common Birds of Bombay* and *A Naturalist on the Prowl*. They spurred my interest, and I have since read them again and again over the last sixty years or more with undiminished pleasure and admiration. At the request of the publishers I had the rare privilege of annotating the first for a new edition brought out in 1946 under the altered title of *Common Birds of India*, which carries a short biographical sketch of the author by my friend Loke Wan Tho.

Mr Millard encouraged me to make a collection of birds as the best way of learning about them, and offered to have me trained at the Society in skinning and preserving specimens and keeping proper notes about them. He introduced me to a young Englishman in the next room who had lately been recruited as the first paid Curator of the Society. This was Norman Boyd Kinnear who, later, after World War I, joined the Bird Room of the British Museum (Natural History) and ended up as Sir Norman Kinnear, Director of the Musuem, in 1947–50. Kinnear, a dour Scotsman, appeared to me rather stand-offish and reserved, and therefore outwardly at least more like the *pukka* sahib of our youthful conception. Behind this facade of stand-offishness, however, he was rather shy, but kindly and helpful, and did much to encourage and foster my new-born enthusiasm, both during his curatorship of the

Society and later from the Bird Room of the British Museum. He put me under the training of two young assistants, S.H. Prater and P.F. Gomes. They showed me over the entire bird collection and initiated me into the art of skinning, stuffing, preparing and labelling bird and mammal specimens for a study collection. Both these persons remained in the Society's employ to the end of their working lives. Prater, of whom I shall have more to say later, distinguished himself in several ways: as the Society's Curator in its most consolidative years, as a leader of the Anglo-Indian community in Western India, and as its elected representative in the Constituent Assembly and Bombay Legislative Council till his retirement and emigration to England in 1948. P.F. Gomes, a rather stolid pachydermic Goan, was in charge of the Society's insect collection in his later years, a function which he discharged with phlegmatic efficiency. I remember him chiefly for his neat handwriting, which can still be seen in the old accession registers of the Society, and on many of the labels in the reference collections. I remember Gomes also for invariably referring to tendons (while teaching me to skin) as 'nostrils', and that with a soft Portuguese 't' which was puzzling at first but continued to amuse me the rest of the time.

The fortuitous incident of the Yellowthroated Sparrow opened up undreamt vistas for me. Thenceforth my reading tended progressively towards books on general natural history, and particularly birds. Illustrated books on Indian birds were virtually non-existent in those days, and indeed for many years later, and there was little available to help a beginner in identifying and learning about the birds around him. The absence of illustrated books was in my opinion the most serious obstacle to the development of bird-watching as an outdoor hobby among Indians generally. Thus, most people who contributed to bird study in India in the early years were foreigners—mostly Englishmen—who had grown up in their home country in the time-honoured British natural history tradition and were already familiar with bird lore—if only as egg-collecting schoolboys—before they came out to India. Spurred by the wealth of bird life around them here, and perhaps by the opportunities as well as the social constraints in the lonely life of a district officer in the backwoods, some of them took to sport shooting and natural history as a serious pastime, or to collecting bird skins and eggs. Many blossomed in course of time into scholarly naturalists or highly competent ornithologists who helped to lay the foundation of scientific natural history in India. Jerdon's *Birds of India* (1864) and later the four-volume publication on Indian avifauna by Oates and Blanford (1898) were adequate for identification, provided you had an elementary familiarity with birds, the necessary ferreting zeal and a specimen in hand. The lack of illustrated field guides and good field glasses, however, seriously inhibited the cult of birdwatching as we know it today. There is no doubt that I owe the beginning of my serious interest in birds to that enigmatic Yellowthroated Sparrow and the chain of events it brought in its train.

2

Schooldays

Till I was eight or nine I attended with two of my sisters (Akhtar and Kamoo) a mission school for girls at Girgaum with a mouthful of a name—Zanana Bible Medical Mission Girls High School (ZBMM for short), since rechristened Queen Mary's High School for Girls. Little boys were admitted but, as in my case, had to leave when they ceased to be girls! Later my greatest joy at being entered in St Xavier's, where all my brothers have been in their time, was the prospect of being able to commute to school (at Dhobi Talao; in those days the locality was known as Money School) and back by horse tram, which held a special romance for children. There was always keen competition among us schoolboys to capture the front bench, just behind the driver, to watch the fascinating operations, and we envied the driver for all the fun we imagined he was having. Horse trams came in two sizes, drawn by a single horse—in which case it was a huge Waler imported from Australia—or by a pair of Arabs, mostly from Iraq. They were always kept in beautiful condition, the former being fitted with enormous pith topees, like the white sahibs, for protection from the tropical sun, with the ears protruding through two holes. The trams had rows of long benches of five or six seats one behind the other and facing front, each bench entered from the side. The driver stood in front of the first bench and urged the horses by tapping the metal-ferruled end of his whip, held upright in a bracket, on the wooden floor. He had a revolving brake arm (lever) regulated by a ratchet arrangement for stopping the tram while drawing in the reins. There were no

fixed halts as far as I remember, but the tram slowed down or
stopped whenever a passenger wanted to get on or off. Pedestrians and handcarts were kept off the track by a clanging bell
under the driver's heel. For supplementary horse power
required on gradients, as when going over a bridge, an extra
horse with attendant was kept ready at the foot of the bridge
and was skilfully hitched on by the attendant while the tram
was in motion. The attendant then jumped on next to the driver
till the top of the rise was reached, when he jumped off the
running tram, unhitched the extra horse and led it back to the
foot of the bridge to await the next tram, and so on.

I used to get 2 annas (about 12 paise) every day for the tram
fare to school (Money School Terminus) and back to Grant
Road Junction (Play House, locally better known as 'pila
house'), which was the tramhead for our locality, Khetwadi.
There was a single-horse shuttle service every fifteen minutes
or so between Money School Terminus and Crawford Market,
past St Xavier's High School where one had to change to the
Main Line into a two-horse tram for Grant Road via Pydhoni.
Horses were usually changed at Pydhoni where a number of
fresh relays were kept ready harnessed. It frequently happened
in my case that the tram fare was misappropriated for *bhelpuri*
during the tiffin break, leaving me the unpleasant prospect of
walking home after school through a short-cut of back lanes
and byways, perhaps a couple of miles. On one such day I
absent-mindedly got into the tram at Money School Terminus,
and realized only when I put my hand into my pocket for the
fare that it was empty! The kindly, bearded old conductor, a
UP man—as were many employees in the Bombay Tramway
Company—who knew me as a daily customer must have
noticed my embarrassment, for instead of putting me off the
tram as I feared, he quietly issued a ticket and consoled me
paternally saying not to worry and that I could pay him
tomorrow! True, the risk of an anna was not about to break his
back, but which conductor in this mercenary age of rush and
endemic incivility would ever be so considerate to an impecunious and frightened little schoolboy? It was a gesture I can
never forget. It developed an almost filial relationship between

us and I was not slow to cash in on his good nature by falling to the temptation of mid-day *bhelpuris* more often thereafter!

In my school career there is little to boast about and perhaps the less said about it the better. I was average in most subjects, somewhat above in geography and games and considerably below in maths. I was said to be good in English and sometimes had the satisfaction of having my essays read out aloud to the class by the teacher. Later in life, in 1934, I found to my astonished disbelief that I had been included in an anthology of English prose by Indian writers, selected and edited by an Englishman, E.E. Speight, Senior Professor of English at Osmania University in Hyderabad. The book, meant for supplementary reading by college students, bears the grandiose title *Indian Masters of English* and has among my 'co-masters' such distinguished names as Rabindranath Tagore and Sarojini Naidu! I managed to take all the school examination hurdles as they came, but uniformly without distinction; the only school prize I ever got being for 'Good Conduct' when I was in the fourth class—prophetically enough a book entitled *Our Animal Friends*. The outdoor games I liked best were hockey, tennis and badminton, at which I was perhaps slightly above average. I also enjoyed football, and although I sometimes did play cricket I never got into the spirit of the game. However, I enjoy watching good, fast cricket in moderate doses, not a full five-day Test! I love riding but have not had as much opportunity to ride as I would have wished, except for a short period in Dehra Dun. Perhaps the sport-shooting of birds and big-game hunting have always been my No. 1 favourites, and I like to think that in these my performance has been somewhat better than average. It is not so much the killing or the size of the bag that matters with me, but the lure of the outdoor and wild places and the general atmosphere of thrill and excitement with the occasional spice of danger that makes the overall experience so enjoyable. However, to get back to school.

Around the time when I was thirteen or fourteen years old (1910) I suffered from chronic headaches, the cause of which was never diagnosed. But the doctors thought that a change of air might help. A half-year's break in school terms was prescribed

to my undisguised delight and my brother Hamid and his wife
Sharifa sportingly offered to take charge of me as the dry
climate of Sind, it was thought, would be beneficial. At that
time Hamidbhai was Superintendent of Land Records in Sind
and head of the Tapedar (land surveyors) school in Hyderabad,
an assignment that involved extensive touring throughout the
province in winter. They lived in a picturesque castle-like
house of sandstone on the edge of the town of Hyderabad
known as Jacob Castle, for it was built by General Jacob in
1840 or thereabouts, soon after the annexation of Sind. The
building had two round towers or battlements at each end, on
either side of the main entrance, connected by an open terrace.
My living room was on the first floor with the bathroom in the
tower at the same level. The castle was situated on slightly
raised ground, hardly a hillock, in a mud-walled compound.
This compound was a thin, rambling jungle of *kandi* and *babul*
trees and an ideal habitat for warblers and other small birds.
Although I had seen *baya* nests when holidaying in Chembur,
they were usually on tall date palms and tantalizingly out of
reach. I remember my joy on finding them on low *babul* trees
in this compound, where they could be reached and robbed
without much difficulty, I being an avid egg collector in those
days. One of Hamidbhai's *chaprasis* was a *hubshi* giant named
Oors. He was the one who acted as 'staff shikari' and looked
after the guns and shikar equipment, and whose self-appointed
job it was to gather local information of where game—especially
partridge, quail, duck and snipe—could be had, collect beaters,
and make all the necessary *bandobast* for his master's shoots
when on tour. Oors was my constant companion and instigator
in matters of shooting, and particularly helpful in nest-finding
and collecting birds' eggs.

One of my vivid memories of this period is driving out one
morning with Hamidbhai in his tonga for a partridge shoot at a
place called Tando Hyder, a few miles out of Hyderabad, in
the starry dark of an early dawn with Halley's Comet looming
brilliantly overhead, and wondering if any of us would be alive
when it made its next scheduled appearance in 1986. At eighty-
nine 1986 still seems a long way ahead, but considering the

toughness and durability of the Abdulali breed (grandfather 114, uncle 103, an aunt 100, a sister 97), I begin to suspect that this may not prove as improbable an event as it then seemed.

After missing one year of school because of those mysterious headaches I managed, but only just, to scrape through the matriculation examination of Bombay University in 1913, with the distinction of ranking perilously near the bottom of the list of something like 3,000 candidates who appeared that year.

But to go back a little earlier, in the years around 1908 one of my cherished ambitions was to become a big-game hunter, and a famous one if possible. Much of my reading, which admittedly was never very avid or profound, consisted of articles and books on natural history and shikar adventures such as Sanderson's *Thirteen Years among the Wild Beasts of India*, and later, Capt. A.I.R. Glasfurd's *Rifle and Romance in the Indian Jungle*, Theodore Roosevelt's *African Game Trails*, and others by the veteran British hunters in India during the nineteenth century. 'Two or three rhinos or tigers before breakfast' seems unbelievable at the present time. This kind of remark, common in such books, gives an idea of what the forests and wildlife in those days must have been. As I have said before, we greatly hero-worshipped my uncle Amiruddin, who to us was *the* authority on Indian shikar. Most of his exploits, however, were as a guest of sporting rulers of various Indian states, conducted in royal style, and I am not sure if he ever organized any shikar trips on his own or was particularly knowledgeable about the animals he shot, or of jungle lore. His armoury was rather antique by modern standards. It consisted of a double-barrel 12-bore vintage English-made hammer gun, a combination double-barrel 12-bore/450 black powder rifle made for the Army and Navy Co-operative Society, an elegant but old-fashioned 16-bore double-barrel hammer rifle with Damascus steel barrels, made to order by a well-known French gunmaker of the period around 1870 with gold inlay and monogram, and a military Martini-Henry cavalry carbine 577/450 with adapter tube for .25 ammunition. In addition there was a walking stick pin-fire gun 410-bore, a 32 gauge so-called 'rook rifle' rim fire single-barrel smooth-bore hammer gun for short ball cartridges. It was loaded by turning sideways a thumb lever under the barrel, pulling the barrel forward an inch or two and pushing it back after inserting the shell into the breech. This was the gun some of us older boys were allowed to use for killing stray cats and crows. Considering how irresponsibly we often handled the gun in that fairly crowded Khetwadi neighbourhood, it is fortunate and indeed surprising that no accident occurred. Hammerless guns and magazine rifles had not become popular, and the former were decried by the older and more conservative shikaris as positively dangerous since there were no visible hammers to tell you when they were ready to go off.

Arms licences to Indians, except to rajas, big zamindars and such like title-holding and proven loyalists, were very restricted. They were regarded as status symbols and there was much jockeying to get a licence. They were issued very sparingly, and only after a good deal of scrutinizing of character and the financial stability of the applicant, even though these were often acquired only for the purpose of 'display', which was one of the reasons printed on the official form, beside sport and self-defence! As a Justice of the Peace, Uncle Amir was entitled to keep any reasonable number of firearms free of licence or fee. Indian arms dealers were likewise few and restricted, the business being mostly in the hands of British concerns like Army & Navy Stores of Bombay and Calcutta, I. Hollis & Son (Bombay), R.B. Rodda & Co. and Manton & Son of Calcutta. All of these had JP's and the like on their mailing lists for catalogues of firearms and ammunition and shikar and camping requisites, such catalogues being issued every year before Christmas. I, along with some like-minded boy cousins, lay in wait for and devoured these catalogues avidly. We studied the specifications of each new gun and rifle in detail—the calibre, the muzzle velocity, the striking energy in foot/pounds, the powder of different types and weights of the various bullets, and so on, and, as a sort of window-shopping, there would be endless discussion and argument about the superiority of this or that make or action. We had many of the vital statistics of our favourites by heart and could reel them out freely for long periods afterwards. In later years in my own case the same sort of infatuation was transferred to motorcycles and I enjoyed the exercise immensely.

The firearms I have myself possessed from time to time, commencing with 1917, were a BSA single-barrel .410 gun in Tavoy, with which I did most of my bird collecting and sport shooting in Burma and India till 1927. For my thirty-first birthday my wife Tehmina presented me with a double-barrel hammerless ejector 20-bore shot gun by Lincoln Jeffries. This gun has been my field companion ever since, now fifty-six years, and most of the several thousand birds collected during my regional bird surveys in the intervening years have been shot with this well beloved weapon, besides a good deal of shooting for sport. Of rifles, I had presented to me from his own armoury by my brother Hamid in 1918, a Winchester .351 calibre semi-automatic repeater. It was an excellent weapon for non-dangerous medium game but had the disconcerting tendency of jamming at unexpected moments—not often, it is true, but enough to make it not completely dependable in a tight corner. In 1922 I replaced this with a .423 (10.5 mm) Mauser bolt action magazine rifle, with which I did most of my big-game shooting in Tavoy (bison), and subsequently in India (two tigers, two panthers, several sloth bear, sambar, cheetal, nilgai, blackbuck, etc.). In 1927, after getting the Assistant Curator's job with the BNHS I added to my armoury a 6.5 (.256) Mannlicher-Schoenauer magazine carbine, a handy little weapon accurate and pleasurable to use. With a soft nose bullet it was effective enough against such tough customers as nilgai and sambar, while with nickel-coated solid bullets no more damage was done to specimens of large birds out of shot-gun range (cranes, raptors, etc.) than with a .22.

One truly remarkable piece of weaponry I acquired in exchange for my .32 calibre Colt automatic pistol during later years in Tavoy was a Mauser pistol of a model that was in use with the German cavalry in the First World War. It was rather a bulky weapon compared to a conventional pistol, with a barrel about 12 inches long. But attached to the wooden holster in which it was slung from the saddle or waist it could be aimed like an ordinary carbine and fired from the shoulder. It was semi-automatic, with a 10-shot magazine, and sighted up to 1,000 metres. It was accurate and though perhaps less useful as a pistol for self-defence at close quarters, I found it very effective at ranges up to 150 or 200 yards. Back in Bombay my cousin, lifetime friend and one-time fellow shooting enthusiast Asaf Fyzee, presented me with his .366 (9.5 mm) Mauser magazine rifle, which was also a remarkably versatile weapon.

Among boys more or less my own age who used to flock together for games and other activities in the Khetwadi days— 1909 or thereabouts—was a distant cousin, Iskandar Mirza, the story of whose sudden and fortuitous rise to power and then ignominious downfall in the first military takeover in Pakistan holds a moral and a warning for all upstarts of this genre. As a boy Iskandar was certainly very good company, resourceful and devil-may-care, and acknowledged leader in all the pranks to which we mischievous boys were prone. He was an enviable marksman with his 'Gem' air gun when we had our pigeon-shooting forays among the rooftops and garrets of the Khetwadi neighbourhood, better than average at most other games, and particularly good at cricket. In our schoolboy cricket matches, played on most Saturdays and Sundays in an open plot beside Sandhurst Road (not far from where Harkishandas Hospital now stands), I remember how Iskandar was always in great demand as a bowler for the special quirk he had of suddenly sneaking in a yorker which took the batsman off his guard and often his wicket as well. This same cunning device of sneaking in unexpected political yorkers seems to have served him in good stead in after life—for example while he was British Political Agent in the North West Frontier Provinces during the Khudai Khidmatgar movement of Khan Abdul Ghaffar Khan. It won him many a troublesome wicket which was loudly applauded by his masters. May it have been one too many of these same political yorkers, delivered on a different field, that finally cost him his own wicket as President of Pakistan? Cricket is what originally brought Iskandar Mirza to the notice of Lord Willingdon, himself a reputed cricketer in his day. It was through the lord sahib's influence and patronage that he was selected among the first batch of Indians to be sent to

Sandhurst for training as King's Commissioned Officers in the Indian Army around 1924, an innovation stubbornly opposed by British diehards in India but grudgingly yielded to by the English parliament under mounting pressure from Indian nationalists.

3

Burma 1914–17

From the early bird-keeping days in Khetwadi I had dreamed of taking up zoology, particularly ornithology, as a profession when I grew up, and of becoming an intrepid explorer and big-game hunter—a respectable appellation in those days, and even somewhat of a status symbol. My reading, such as it was, consisted mostly of books about birds and general natural history, and about travel, exploration and shikar, particularly big-game hunting with all its thrills and derring-do. But in order to reach the stage at which formal biology began in the university curriculum in those days, one had to get through the Previous or First Year course following matriculation. After struggling hopelessly with logarithms and suchlike evils in the first few months at St Xavier's College it did not seem that I would ever be able to cross this formidable barrier. I was thoroughly miserable and scheming for some way of escape. Providentially, a rescue letter to Uncle Amiruddin from brother Jabir in Burma came just then. After obtaining a Cambridge diploma in Agriculture, Jabir had returned to India in August 1910 full of hope, but after trying unsuccessfully to get a job in the Agriculture Department—or some other suitable appointment—he had in desperation decided to join a cousin, Salah Tyabji, in business in Rangoon. Salah had recently acquired an interest in a wolfram mine in the Tavoy district of Tenasserim.

Tavoy had lately shot into prominence as a tin and wolfram mining centre and was attracting to itself adventurers and shady characters of the Gold Rush type. 'Mongrel, puppy, whelp and hound and curs of low degree', they were all there, struggling, jostling and elbowing, not necessarily honestly, to get rich quick. Salah's business in Rangoon consisted chiefly of hardware and engineering stores for the flourishing rice and saw mills, and I remember his mainstay at the time was the selling agency for Burma of 'Gripoly' belting, 'leather-edged' as the advertisement boasted, which was then a popular brand. He was short-handed and had asked Jabir if he would care to come and join him in his Tavoy wolfram mining venture. Jabir, who was by this time pretty sick of unsuccessful job-hunting for a year or more, readily agreed, and his having done some geology at Cambridge was expected to be of help in the technology of mining. But Jabir's foremost love was agriculture and farming. He was sorely frustrated at not being able to find a congenial occupation, but decided to take up the Rangoon offer, hoping that in due course he would make and save up enough money to start farming on his own.

The wolfram mine in which Tyabji had a share with the concessionaire, a Burmese named Maung Lu Pe, was situated at Talaingya, a night's journey by sampan up the Tavoy river. Side by side with organizing and supervising the working of the mine, which necessitated frequent visits of several days at a time, Jabir had started a business in Tavoy town—the headquarters of the district and centre of the mining industry—in building material, mining tools and other articles in demand for the growing wolfram mining industry. The stock, consisting of sledge-hammers, picks and shovels, mining drill steel, corrugated iron, cement barrels, nails, coir ropes and suchlike dismal miscellanea, was stored and displayed on the ground floor of a house in Bazar Road near the central market, rented from one Maung E Cho—a Burmese Muslim (Zerbadi). The landlord, with his numerous and often noisily quarrelsome family, lived above. The front part of the ground floor served as the shop, the back part as our living quarters, which included an indoor open well for the water supply. I still remember the musty smelliness of this unlovely abode quite vividly, though it is now over sixty years ago.

Jabir was a born and incorrigible optimist, a man who had no inhibition or false pride in putting his hand to any honest occupation, however incongruous or undignified it may seem to more 'sensitive' or snobbish natures. I have no doubt that it was the dream of the farm in the nebulous future and the compulsion to make it come true that impelled him into hardware shopkeeping. The prospects of achieving his purpose looked promising enough while the mining boom lasted, but it needed uncommon stubbornness of character for a man of his upbringing, education and intellectual background to weigh and wrap and exchange half a kilogram of iron nails or coir rope for a few annas—as the retail business often entailed.

It was under these circumstances that Jabir had written to Uncle Amiruddin suggesting that, unless I was particularly keen to pursue my college education, he could offer me a partnership in his newly-opened business if I was prepared to join him in Tavoy immediately. From childhood I had somehow held a low opinion of shopkeeping and shopkeepers, as distinct from business and businessmen, though I doubt whether I would have been able to define either. My ranking business within a higher category derived no doubt from the fact that many of my own revered elders happened to be businessmen, though by forgetting that their evolution to respectability from itinerant peddling was only through petty shopkeeping.

However, Jabir's letter arrived at the psychological moment when I was looking for a strategic escape from logarithms and higher algebra, and I was only too happy to bid goodbye to college education and prepare to launch myself in 'business'. That this might also mean the end of my dream of becoming a professional zoologist did not bother me at all, at least for the time being, so desperate had I become with college mathematics. All this happened in 1914 when I was about eighteen years old, and after I had struggled hopelessly for eight uneasy months with the university's first-year curriculum. I left for Rangoon via Calcutta in September 1914. The First World War had broken out a month before, and India had been dragged willy-nilly into it by our British masters, by illusory promises of self-government as a reward for loyalty to the King Emperor in his time of need. The legendary German cruiser *Emden* was playing chivalrous pranks with shipping in the Bay of Bengal, saving passengers and sinking ships. Wireless telegraphy was in its infancy, radio had not appeared on the scene, and radar had not even been thought of. All this added vastly to the excitement of a sea voyage to Rangoon at that period, and fresh rumours and fantastic tales erupted every day of the near-magical exploits of the *Emden*—suddenly appearing at two or three far-flung places simultaneously and miraculously vanishing after doing her fell work—bombarding coastal towns, sinking ships after gallantly saving their human cargo. Such tales improved considerably in the telling and soon a store of the most unlikely legends gathered and snowballed round the *Emden*. At the same time it must be conceded that her commander, Capt. Schmidt, was a remarkably audacious, gallant and chivalrous enemy. Although the *Emden* was believed to be operating in the Bay of Bengal at the time of my crossing, and in spite of the alarmist rumours once or twice of suspicious ships being sighted from aboard, our passage was uneventful though unpleasantly rough, it still being the tail end of the monsoon. I saw the hand of the captain in these false alarms and excursions as a ploy to induct more serious attendance at the daily boat drills; it certainly worked.

The veteran B.I. (British India) mail steamer, which had been on the Calcutta-Rangoon run for over a generation, was boarded by a pilot at the mouth of the tidal Rangoon river, and we slid up it slowly, hooting steam launches, sampans and paddy barges out of the way, through a succession of corrugated iron-roofed rice and saw mills with enormous teak logs rafted down from the forest, lying sprawled helter-skelter and half buried in the squelchy mud at low tide along the banks, waiting to be hauled out by elephants for conversion.

The voyage from Calcutta, which took about forty hours, was a new adventure for me. My only experience of 'sea-faring' till then had been crossing Bombay harbour by steam ferry on occasional holiday visits to Kihim, and the experience of living, eating and sleeping on board was a novelty, albeit not a particularly memorable or luxurious one since I was travelling

'European deck'.* Sister Akhtar and brother-in-law Salah who received me at Tseekai Maung Taulay wharf had lately lost all their belongings in a fire which engulfed their rented bungalow, and were now living rather skimpily in a tiny makeshift flat in Brooking Street—a typical Anglo-Indian quarter—with one of their twin sons, Nadir, about one year old. His sibling Ahsan was being cared for in Baroda by his grandparents Abbas and Amina Tyabji, and only joined his parents in Rangoon two or three years later when they moved into a less cramped residence in a more respectable locality.

The little backwater town of Tavoy in Lower Burma was to be my domicile from 1914 to 1923, with an eventful break of some fifteen months back in Bombay (October 1917 to February 1919) which proved to be perhaps the most momentous period of my life and career. After a few days of acclimatization—or 'orientation' as is currently the more fashionable term—I sailed from Rangoon by an antiquated paddle steamship of the BISN Company—perhaps the last of its breed on this weekly Penang service—to the mouth of the Tavoy river for about twenty-four hours and thence upstream about two hours, by a smaller but more modern shallow draft steam launch, the *Yengyua*. We went through a maze of muddy tidal creeks lined on both banks with mangroves, *nepa* palms and wide stretches of paddy fields beyond. Until some years after the British occupation of Tenasserim in 1870 or thereabouts Tavoy was a criminal settlement like the Andamans, with a mixed lot of prisoners, chiefly Burmese, Chinese and Indian, many of whom married Burmese women and settled there after release from prison. Some had become reformed characters and respectable citizens while many continued to provide living evidence of their past history, creating a perfect setting for the scum of humanity—the crooks, scoundrels and charlatans that were to follow in the wake of the mining boom.

After the first few months of apprenticeship in hardware

---

* This was a space on the deck—chiefly in coastal steamers of the British India Steam Navigation Company—reserved for 'pore whites', 'eurasians' and others with westernized habits. Its fare was cheaper than that for IInd Class passengers, slightly more than ordinary deck fare.

shopkeeping, learning office routine, typewriting and other tricks of the trade under brother Jabir—senior partner in our newly established firm of J.A. Ali Bros. & Co. and an extremely conscientious worker and hard taskmaster—I felt freer, especially on weekends, to move around and explore the surrounding countryside. Jabir had a handsome white pony which I frequently rode out three or four miles after the shop closed on Saturday afternoons, to various rubber estates and fruit gardens of friends where enjoyable and rewarding birding could usually be had. At that time I possessed no binoculars, but as the eyes were young and my birdwatching rather dilet-tante, that was not such a serious handicap. In those early greenhorn days I was even less familiar with the commoner Burmese birds than with Indian. Their identification was a knotty problem since none of the people around could help, and the only reference book I possessed was Murray's *Birds of India*—an inept publication made more inept by the lack of proper illustrations. However, learning the hard way is fun, and, in spite of the inherent frustrations, far more satisfying and enduring in the end. The richness and diversity of the animal life, especially birds, in the forests of Tavoy district, was fascinating, much of it of course new to me, and I started making a small reference collection of my own. The abundance of woodpecker species was particularly striking, one of the first to catch my eye being the Black-and-Buff (*Meiglyptes jugularis*), so similar in 'jizz' to our Heartspotted (*Hemicircus canente*) and yet so different. The multicoloured Broadbills were also an exciting novelty. But my best remembered excite-ment was the first sighting of the Whitewinged Black Jay (*Platysmurus leucopterus*), quite different from anything I knew in India. It is strange how some insignificant trifles stick in one's memory: to this day I can vividly recall in minute detail the exact location, the tree, the branch and the stance in which that bird sat sixty years ago.

I had casually discovered a good samaritan and helpful mentor in J.C. Hopwood of the then Imperial Forest Service, the Divisional Forest Officer at the time. Hopwood was very knowledgeable about Burmese birds and was himself busy collecting specimens and nests and eggs of birds of this area for Stuart Baker, then working on the second edition of the *Fauna of British India—Birds*. I was in occasional correspondence with Charles M. Inglis, a tea and indigo planter of Bihar, an authority on Indian birds, particularly of the north-east region. I frequently exchanged notes and specimens with Inglis. Some of my Tavoy specimens are probably still in the Inglis collection which was widely dispersed after his death in 1954, a large part of it being purchased by Dr Dillon Ripley for the Yale University Zoological Museum when he was Professor of Zoology there. However, during my first innings in Burma, between 1914 and 1917, and till I resumed in 1919 after doing the formal zoology course, my birding activity remained rather sporadic and dilettante.

In addition to retailing hardware and machinery, and mining for tin and wolfram, J.A. Ali Bros.'s business consisted in purchasing small lots of the ore and smoked raw rubber sheets from small hand-to-mouth producers and building up stocks for sale to larger operators. In a fluctuating wartime market the last was often a somewhat speculative undertaking.

In November 1915 I was left in sole charge of the Tavoy business for two or three months while Jabir was away in India getting married. Before he left for Bombay, and in preparation for receiving his bride and setting up a home, we had shifted from the dingy back part of the shop in Bazar Road to a rented single-storeyed wooden-walled and shingle-roofed house in a pleasanter locality on the fringe of the town. Although it lacked a compound and had its entrance directly from the street, it overlooked extensive paddy fields with wooded hills on the distant horizon and was a welcome change indeed from our previous musty 'stable'. When sister-in-law Safia (née Badruddin Tyabji Sr.) came, the womanly touch soon transformed it into a snug and comfortable abode. My wife Tehmina and I continued to live happily in this place till after Jabir and his wife left Tavoy for good in 1921 to establish a branch of the hardware business in Rangoon in partnership with our would-be financier, Osman Mustikhan & Co., a well-established firm of Baluchi P.W.D. contractors. (This step had become necessary in order to offset the declining prospects of the hardware trade in Tavoy since the slump in the mining industry).

Soon after returning to Tavoy with his bride, Jabir left again on a business trip to Britain, accompanied by his wife and one of our newly acquired partners, to establish business contacts for the Rangoon branch in Europe and the USA. Jabir was accompanied by young Yusuf Khan, the pleasantest, most educated and rational brother of the Mustikhan trio, who was to be directly associated with us in the Rangoon business. As kismet would dispose, within a few days of their arrival in London Yusuf Khan suffered a fatal heart attack, completely upsetting all their plans, and Jabir returned to Rangoon with little achieved. With Yusuf Khan gone the Mustikhan brothers lost heart and interest in the hardware partnership, which really never did get off the ground. Jabir found the brothers uncooperative and difficult to deal with, and, after a year or so of trial and frustration, gave up. He retreated to India in 1923 and got back once more to his agricultural dream, which, through unflagging optimism, dogged determination and relentless self-flogging, he did—all honour to him—finally manage to bring true.

A couple of years after Jabir and Safia had left Tavoy to settle in Rangoon my wife and I found and moved into a pleasant and more comfortable cottage with a large compound and some shady cashew trees, in a more 'genteel' locality known as the Civil Lines on the outskirts of the town. The cottage was pretty and well designed, but of a semi *pukka* nature, raised off the ground on posts to fight the damp, with the walls of asbestos-cement sheets and roof wooden-shingled. Full advantage was taken by Tehmina of the opportunities here for kitchen-gardening and poultry-keeping on a domestic scale, and we were soon enjoying our own roast duck with tender home-grown green peas! We also had opportunities for raising a few Burmese Silver Pheasants from wild collected eggs, and nursing from babyhood such other interesting pets as a Leopard Cat (*Felis bengalensis*), a Tree Shrew (*Tupaia glis*), a Flying Lemur (*Galleopithecus volans*) and a Great Pied Hornbill (*Buceros bicornis*), in addition to the lady-dog 'Gyp' and the gentleman pie, 'General Dyer', named after the 'hero' of Jallianwala Bagh, whose behaviour towards his fellow pets was singularly evocative of the original. Brother Hamid (on furlough) and his wife Sharifa spent a delightful week with us at this cottage, and Tehmina returned with them to Rangoon en route to Bombay for good, since after the collapse of the timber venture we had decided to close down the business in Tavoy. It was the practice of BISN Co. to announce in the Rangoon dailies the names of the first-class passengers on their mail boats to Calcutta, and I was much amused to find in the passenger list one morning a 'Mr Hamid Ali and 3 Mrs Alis', which must surely have convinced doubters that here was a true Muslim! It seems that for the voyage Sharifa and Tehmina had been joined by Jabir's wife, Safia, thus making up the covey.

Till our affairs could be wound up I moved into the Tavoy Asian Club premises, whose ownership had unsolicitedly fallen round my neck on my clearing its hypothecation to the bank. For some time, and till finally leaving Tavoy, I was the Secretary of the Tavoy Athletic Association—actually an internationally made up football club—started by a few of us some years before. One of the most enthusiastic players in the team I had assembled was a friendly, totally untypical and eccentric ICS Englishman, F.W. Scott, the Sessions Judge of Tenasserim division at the time. He was a fanatical self-appointed guardian of the football field against encroaching pedestrians, mostly milk vendors short-cutting across the turf who were liable to be furiously chased and manhandled by Scott if caught. One morning, before the court sitting, he rushed almost breathless into my living room to inquire the cost of ten seers of milk. In spite of being familiar with his eccentricities I couldn't make out what this was all about. It seems that, driving past the football ground on his way to work, Scott had seen a milkman taking a short-cut through the field with a pail in his hand. He had stopped the car suddenly, jumped out and given chase. The man had dropped his bucket in terror and fled for life, where-upon Scott had emptied the milk on the ground; he now wanted to compensate the man! Another time, on his way home after the court had risen, Scott barged into my room looking pale, nervous and thoroughly miserable, and flopped into an easy chair to relax. He was almost shivering with emotion and explained that he had just sentenced a Burmese dacoit to be hung for murder. Before being taken away by the police the man was asked if he had any last wish to make. The murderer, who seemed completely unshaken by the sentence, replied quite coolly that he would like to eat a durian! The contrast in the reactions of the sentencer and sentencee, he said, was a revealing commentary on human nature.

4

Interlude at Bombay and Marriage

Having thrust myself into business at the early age of eighteen with my formal education incomplete and without any sort of training or natural aptitude for the job, I began to realize after a couple of years how unsatisfactory the situation was. My home leave was due towards the end of 1917 and in consultation with the Senior it was decided that I should prolong my leave in Bombay to undergo a year's formal course in Commercial Law and Accountancy at Davar's College of Commerce. This decision proved an indirect blessing in disguise, because with the considerate goading and encouragement of Reverend Father Blatter, Director of the Biology Department at St Xavier's College, who had soon discovered where my true interest lay, I was able in the same year to complete the B.Sc. (in those days B.A. Honours) course in Zoology under the stimulating tutelage of Professor Jal P. Mullan—a remarkable man and admirable teacher who remained a valued friend till his death in about 1953.

My introduction to a formal zoology curriculum at St Xavier's came through a slim textbook of the crammer sort entitled *Animal Types for College Students*. It opened with a thundering broadside which could have laid low for all time a greater enthusiasm for biology than mine, were it not that the author himself was initiating us in the course. The opening sentence of the very first chapter, on the Amoeba, ran (how well I remember it!): 'The Amoeba or "*Proteus Animalcule*" is a Protozoon belonging to the Order Lobosa which includes simple forms with blunt psuedopodia which do not anastomose.'

Wonderful news! It is to the credit of Professor Mullan that in spite of this terrifying barrage he succeeded so well not only in sustaining my interest in biology but in fanning it till it grew to a lasting and radiant flame. Mullan was a quiet man, an exceedingly keen observer of human nature with a dry humour and sound common sense, an incisive commentator on men and matters.

The daily schedule of attendance at Davar's was from eight to ten o'clock in the morning, which left just enough time to pick up Stanley Prater from his miniature terrace flat at Elphinstone Circle on the pillion of my little Douglas and dash off to St Xavier's before the zoology class began. Prater, an Anglo-Indian, had joined the BNHS as a callow youth just out of school as a 'bottlewasher' ten years or so before, and had shown great promise during his apprenticeship as museum assistant and field collector under the Society's first stipendiary curator, N.B. Kinnear. I had corresponded with Prater fairly regularly from Tavoy on natural history matters, chiefly birds, in course of time spilling over to other matters of wide common interest. Close friendship and understanding had developed between us, which continued to grow during the many years of subsequent personal contact we were destined to be colleagues in the Society. But before his claim for consideration as a scientific member of the staff could be entertained, the Society's Executive Committee had required him to undergo a formal course in biology under Father Blatter.

My admiration and regard for Prater's intellectual versatility was profound. Though perhaps he cannot claim any *original* contribution to science, he read voraciously and managed to keep himself abreast of all the latest developments in natural history. Apart from possessing a remarkably retentive memory, he had a gift for digesting complicated technicalities and reducing pedantic professional jargon into simple language a layman could understand. Indeed this was Prater's forte—the popularization of zoological knowledge. Most of his writings bear witness to his mastery of the art. He wrote in a pleasing and often humourous style. For our zoology practicals at St Xavier's we had to work in pairs, and I well remember how convenient it was for me to use him as the working partner whenever unsavoury jobs, such as dissecting a cockroach, had to be performed.

It was a sincere regret to me—and later I suspect also to himself—that with Independence Prater allowed himself to be virtually stampeded to emigrate out of India by an irrationally panicked wife and doubting Anglo-Indian friends. I have a conviction that he never really felt at home in England, having being born and having spent the major part of his life in India. In unguarded moments one could sense his longing to be back among the people and surroundings with which he was more familiar, but having burnt his boats his pride obliged him to keep up the facade of being happy in exile. It depressed me beyond words to visit him in his London home a few years before he died. I found him a partly paralysed cripple in bed, all alone with a radio by his side to allay boredom. His wife and daughter were away at their respective wage-earning jobs, with no servant or any other person within call to attend to his wants or to talk to all day, except for a kindly old lady tenant upstairs who peeped in occasionally to see that all was well. To one of Prater's dynamic temperament and alertness, physical as well as mental, and accustomed in his native environment to servants at beck and call all hours of the day, I can well imagine how galling it must all have been.

After the zoology class at St Xavier's we would rush back to the Society's rooms, which in those days and up to 1953 were in the premises of Phipson & Co., Wine Merchants. I spent many hours several times a week in the library or rummaging among the bird collection to familiarize myself with Indian birds and in trying to identify with the help of Prater or Kinnear some of the species that had puzzled me in Tenasserim.

By lucky coincidence I found that another fellow-student in the zoology class was my distant cousin, a childhood and lifelong friend, Asaf Ali Asghar Fyzee, popularly known as AAA, a brilliant intellect and habitual winner of prizes throughout his career, who, to my sorrow and disappointment, forsook biology after securing a First Class Hons. degree in favour of law at Cambridge. Here, as was to be expected, he

likewise won a number of coveted scholarships and distinctions.
Asaf was, besides, an excellent all-round sportsman. In his
younger days he was more than ordinarily good with shot-gun
and rifle and played tennis and cricket for his college, St John's,
at Cambridge, being at one time captain of the college tennis
team and proving thus a worthy disciple of his well known
uncles, Azhar and Athar, the 'Fyzee brothers' of international
tennis fame. Asaf distinguished himself as an Arabic scholar
and prizeman at Cambridge, and thereafter also in real life. The
mastery of Arabic enabled him to go direct to the grassroot
sources of Muhammadan law, especially that of the Ismailis,
and to interpret it critically and rationally. He has published a
number of books on the subject, some of which have been
prescribed as manuals by universities in India and abroad, and
which have received wide acclaim in Muslim countries. It is
tragic that a career of such outstanding brilliance and versatility
should have got so clogged in later life by family misfortunes
which turned him into something of a recluse and a misanthrope.

Back in Bombay, September 1917, I lived with my eldest
sister Ashraf-unnissa—Ashraf for short—and brother-in-law
Shums, the shikari-solicitor, in their Khetwadi flat above the
stable, the venue of my boyhood sparrow hunts. This was an
annexe of the old Amir Manzil belonging to uncle Amiruddin
Tyabji who had died in February 1917 while I was still in
Burma, after which the property was dismembered and sold.
Unbeknown to me, Ashraf and my younger sister Kamoo had,
in secret collusion, been scheming, like all loving sisters, to get
me engaged to an attractive relation who had taken their fancy
and evidently charmed them off their feet. In their letters to me
in Tavoy, and in personal conversation later, this apparition
was being subtly brought in somewhat oftener than the occasion
would seem to demand, though I thought I had made it sufficiently clear that at that point of time I was not interested in
women at all. Tehmina and I, it seems, had been together as
kindergarten pupils in the ZBMM Girls High School at Girgaum
in 1904 or 1905, before her father, C.A. Latif, migrated to
London with his family to extend his pearl business to Europe.
I did not remember the little girl at all till shown an ancient

group photograph of the school, years later. After passing her London matric from a somewhat élite boarding school in Surrey, Tehmina was discouraged by her father from continuing at a university, and instead she was entered into a Finishing School for young ladies to learn the correct socialite airs and graces. Tehmina often described with much amusement the inanity of some of the tenets of genteel behaviour taught there. For example, one which I remember was that before you stirred a pot of weak tea at a party you had always to say 'excuse me' to the company with a sweetly apologetic smile. The Latif family repatriated itself to India in 1915, as World War I was hotting up over London and there seemed little likelihood of an early end, and settled in an elegant rented flat in Adenwala Mansion at Chowpati, before their own building, 'Latifia', just across the way in Harvey Road, was completed. My sisters artfully contrived a supposedly impromptu meeting between us at this flat, and in due course the train of events followed according to their plan. At first I was rather nervous as to how a girl brought up and educated abroad in an entirely different milieu and used to the sophisticated amenities of life would respond to the prospect of a rough-and-ready existence in a backwater like Tavoy, with its primitive conditions and practically no entertainments or social life.

Kamoo and Tehmina had taken to each other from their very first meeting after the latter's return from Britain, and remained the closest of friends even after Kamoo's marriage to cousin Hassan F. Ali in 1918 and their departure to settle in Japan, right up to Tehmina's death in July 1939. It was evident that Kamoo had started the preparatory softening process well in advance of my coming from Burma, because Tehmina seemed to know a great many things about me that I would not otherwise have expected. On closer acquaintance with Tehmina I was relieved to find that her tastes and interests and likes and dislikes were almost identical with my own. Despite her sophisticated upbringing and background she remained a country girl at heart. Luckily the finishing school had not finished her completely. Like me she was ever happy to escape boring social parties, specially of society ladies and small talk.

She liked informal friendly company in small doses and people of kindred interests and outlook. Tehmina also despised hypocrisy, cant, and pomposity, and could stomach no ostentation. She loved the wooded countryside and jungle walks, good books and poetry, both Urdu and English, and flowers and gardening, and later, during my ornithological surveys, she became seriously interested in birds. In short, most of our interests overlapped as much as one could wish, a discovery that gave me a little more confidence about the future. Later, while we were living in Dehra Dun, we had frequent opportunities to attend good *mushairas*. Tehmina, with her alien background, felt a pang of regret at missing all the fun and took up the study of Urdu with ferocious dedication, aided and abetted by a professional *munshi* and a good two-way dictionary. She soon developed a passion for the language, specially for Urdu poetry, and spent many hours of her spare time each day, at home and in camp, with her favourite *intekhabs* (anthologies) and the Urdu-English dictionary ever at the ready.

It was lucky for me as much as for Tehmina herself that, thanks to her lively temperament and friendly disposition, she was so well loved by all my sisters and brothers and got on so well with the family. Kamoo and Farhat were her special favourites, and I feel she was never so relaxed and happy as when living in their company. Farhat, my second-oldest sister, who in turn had grown particularly fond of Tehmina, was two years younger than Ashraf, and the fourth in the family series. She had finished with her elementary English education at the ZBMM Girls School long before I joined, and thereafter had shared with aunt Hamida Begam some of the housework and responsibilities of the Khetwadi establishment, as well as her care for the developing family brood. Farhat was in fact a surrogate mother to me: she gave me my first lessons in Urdu as a child and remained in many ways my favourite sister till her end in 1982. Being the 'baby' of the family I could wheedle many special privileges and concessions denied to the older children, and was not slow to take undue advantage of her indulgent mollycoddling whenever possible. She was gentle and cheerful by nature, possessed a lively sense of humour, and, like Hamid, had an amazing knack of creating enduring friendships at all levels, which made her remembered even by casual acquaintances ever after. In 1911 she married Shuja-ud-din (Shujoobhai to us), a younger brother of Shums, the shikari-solicitor, who was the eldest son of uncle Abbas (Tyabji).* I recall her delightful house visits to us—first at Kihim and Kotagiri while I was marking time for the assignments in Hyderabad and Kerala, and then at Dehra Dun at the time we were living there—and how immensely we enjoyed her cheerful presence and witty conversation, and her reading aloud to us *Musaddas-e-Hali*, Ghalib and Iqbal, and some of Premchand's well-known novels. In later years Tehmina and I spent several happy weeks at a time holidaying with Farhat and Shuja in the various back-of-beyond Hyderabad districts where Shuja was posted as a revenue officer in the Nizam's service, and then again in their delightful home at Daulatabad after his retirement.

Harking back to the time I got engaged to Tehmina, I am reminded of that telegram which, by the perfection of its mutilation, was for me more embarrassing than funny under the particular circumstances. Many may recall the murderous epidemic of influenza that swept across the continents in 1918 and carried off in a few short weeks many times more lives than the total killed in the four years of World War I immediately preceding it. I happened to be in Bombay then, doing my training in commerce and zoology. Tehmina's elder brother, Hassan Latif, was a district engineer in the Nizam's service, and news came through that his entire household, including his wife, several children and servants, were down with the fever with none at home to attend to them. Being newly engaged to the sister in the face of a mild domestic reservation and anxious to cut a dash with the family, I gallantly offered to go to Hyderabad and help with the nursing. No wonder Hassan felt somewhat alarmed, on receiving the telegram, at my beginning to scrounge on inlaws-to-be so early in the day! Actually the telegram which had left me as SHALL I COME AND HELP

---

* Three of uncle Abbas's sons married three of my sisters, thus almost cornering the market, as it were: Shums—Ashraf, Shuja—Farhat, and Salah—Akhtar.

had read on arrival at its destination as SMALL INCOME
SEND HELP. This is the most perfect example of telegraphic
mutilation I know of and deserves to be immortalized.

We got married in December 1918. Though I was only
twenty-two at the time and perhaps rather young to marry, I
was persuaded to do so since there was no knowing how soon I
would be able to return to India next. In the event it proved just
as well I didn't put it off, because economic conditions for our
business worsened steadily with the end of the war and would
have remained impossible for me until many years later. Brother
Aamir, four years my senior, had also married the charming
and accomplished Leila Hydari a year earlier, and, getting
disenchanted with the Nizam's Police Service, had decided to
try his luck in business as one of the bros. in J.A. Ali Bros. &
Co. He decided to leave his young wife behind with her
parents at Hyderabad as she was then expecting a baby. Aamir
was tragically destined never to see her again. He died in
Burma a few months later in unfortunate and strange circumstances which I shall recount later. However, in January 1919,
unaware of what the future held, Aamir sailed along with
newly-married us from Calcutta to Rangoon.

5

Memories of Burma

The popularity of the diminutive couple, sister Akhtar and Salah Tyabji, particularly with the Indian community in Rangoon, was amazing. It extended not only to what may be called high society—professional men like lawyers and doctors and the top brass of government officials, High Court judges and the like—but also to those of humbler status, down to rickshaw-pullers and hack *tikka gharry* drivers. Their popularity was sustained and continued to grow during the thirty-five years or so they lived in Burma, and at one stage or another Salah was President or Secretary of the various labour and political unions, leader of the Indian National Congress in Burma, representative of the Indian community in the pre-Independence diarchical Burmese Legislative Council, and a thorn in the side of the colonial administration. Akhtar was the moving spirit in the education of girls, specially Muslim, domiciled Indian and Zerbadi. When the Japanese overran Burma in 1942, Salah and his son Nadir (later Captain N.S. Tyabji, I.N.) played an outstanding and heroic role in the evacuation of Indian nationals from Burma along the murderous overland route through Nagaland with superhuman courage and physical exertion. As the cumulative result of all this and the black-water fever he had contracted on the disastrous trek, Salah collapsed upon reaching Mussoorie and for several days teetered alarmingly on the brink under the hospitable roof of 'Southwood', the home of Hamid and Sharifa. The circle of their friends and acquaintances was remarkable. Almost every Indian of consequence and many without, who had resided in Burma, specially Rangoon, during the period, or who merely happened to pass through, was familiar with the Tyabjis. They kept open house, entertained freely, and were ready to help everyone in any sort of trouble and in every way they could. Indeed it is astonishing how well and affectionately they are remembered by the older generation of expatriates even thirty-five years after they left Burma. There are few 'refugees' who have not at one time or another come across one or both of this remarkable couple and who do not recall some little kindness or friendly gesture from them.

My introduction to Big Game really came in Burma after the diversification of our declining wolfram mining business on the ending of World War I into leasing government forests for exploitation for sleeper supply to the Indian railways. The species in greatest demand for railway sleepers was the hard-wood known in Burma as Pyinkado (*Xylia dolabriformis*). Within the magnificent moist-deciduous forests in the upper reaches of the Tavoy river, in the Natkyzin and Heinze basin areas where this species occurred in workable quantities, large tracts had to be surveyed from the viewpoint of availability, gregariousness, extraction and the transport facilities of logs to depots and saw pits, and of shipment of sleepers to India. The lack of roads and communications in this remote and un-developed area proved a serious bottleneck. The difficulties of shipping the product in specially chartered tramps and auxiliary-engined junks (dhows) from out-of-the-way places without proper docking or loading facilities ultimately forced the abandonment of the timber venture. On paper, and on the irrepressible optimism of my partner, it had seemed a maker of our fortunes. This enterprise, known as Tavoy Timbers, was started in partnership with a Parsi friend, Jamshedji Manekji of Rangoon, an extraordinarily energetic and resourceful indi-vidual, but given to wild over-optimism in all circumstances—a weakness that had originally sucked him into the vortex of the short-lived tin and wolfram mining boom in Tavoy a few years earlier. Financially our timber concern never really got off the ground as a business, but in other ways, for me personally, it proved highly congenial and rewarding from the sport and natural history angle. It gave me excellent opportunities for visiting remote and undisturbed forest areas and of camping out in the wilds for several days at a time in sequestered forest bungalows, sometimes sharing isolated huts of the Karen 'taungya' (shifting cultivation) cultivators for night halts, thanks to their friendly contacts with my Karen guide. A cheerful Madrasi cook-bearer carried the 'Icmic' cooker in action, with a hot meal available from it on tap. The bedding was carried in a rucksack on my back and the trusty Mauser slung across my shoulder. The ration of rice and *dal* in bags and miscellaneous extras travelled on a hired camp follower. The guide, U Kyan Tha, a christianized Karen, was an elephant owner as well as our dragging contractor for logs from the forests to the saw pits. His intimate familiarity with the terrain proved invaluable in the prospecting for eligible forest blocks. Moreover, U Kyan Tha was an excellent and knowledgeable jungle man and a veteran hunter to boot. He was inseparable from his rusty Belgian-made 12-bore single-barrelled gun, with which he claimed to regularly kill sambar, barking deer, pig and even gaur. He claimed also to have shot a tiger with it, and a rhinoceros, and once to have destroyed a rogue elephant. 'Let the credit rest with the relater', as the Emperor Babur would say, but U Kyan Tha was certainly quite knowledgeable about his native wildlife and trees in general, and I learnt a good deal of the local jungle and folk-lore from him. He knew all the swamps in the Heinze basin area that were frequented by the then (1922) fast-vanishing Lesser Onehorned Rhinoceros (*Rhinoceros sondaicus*), an animal I was specially keen to see and photograph if possible. He guided me to several of its typical haunts but unfortunately we never came across the beast, although in one swamp a recent wallow and fresh spoor did provide positive proof of its existence. A short while before, the colonial government of Burma had imposed a total ban on the killing of rhinoceros, but, as elsewhere, poaching by horn hunters was continuing and by now the species has probably vanished.

Looking at the Heinze basin on the map of Lower Burma today brings back nostalgic memories of those uncomfortable yet exhilarating nomadic days in the jungle. And at this distance of time, when one has forgotten the mosquitoes and the leeches, the constant monsoon drenchings all day and the wet, soggy bedding all night, they even seem romantic. In any case it was all very good fun sixty years ago.

The story of the Burma epoch would be incomplete without the introduction of a rather curious and enigmatic character who fortuitously breezed into my life and affairs during the early and more optimistic mining days. Bert Ribbentrop, who had himself drifted to Tavoy with the flotsam on the wave-crest of the mining boom, was an inexplicable and in some ways remarkable, even admirable, character. But though'I was closely associated with him for over three years during our disastrous mining partnership, often spending three or four days at a time together in his primitive raised-on-poles palm-leaf and bamboo hut at our Mechoung concession, I was able to discover precious little about his life-history and antecedents. He was a son of Mr Berthold Ribbentrop, C.I.E., one of the forestry experts imported from Germany by the British Indian government in 1866 on the advice of Sir Dietrich Brandis, to organize scientific forestry in India and establish the Provincial Forest Service. Bert talked a good deal about Simla, where his father had spent the last few years till his retirement in 1900 as Inspector-General, and of many of his father's contemporaries in government services. However, I never learnt if he himself was born in India or had spent any part of his childhood in this country. He never mentioned his mother, whether she was German or not, nor anything about her—and only in passing did he refer to a sister living in London with whom he seemed to be on affectionate terms. I gathered he also had a wife living in London, from whom he was either estranged or divorced, and a daughter. He spoke very little indeed about his private life and connections, and to my knowledge he certainly never wrote to or received any letters from his relations during the years I knew him; neither did he ever express a longing to go back home to England; nor did he receive from or send home any remittances during that period. The latter is easily under-standable because the poor man never had anything to send.

I often wondered how he himself managed to survive, considering that the Mechoung mine hardly ever showed any profit despite Bert's unflagging and perhaps baseless optimism. I suppose it is possible to exist at least for some time on an unvarying diet of *dal* and rice if generously spiced with optimism and hope. Bert was a congenital optimist but the basis of his optimism was hard to detect; the output of the mine certainly never justified it.

After three years of the mining partnership, when I 'retired hurt' from Burma—a thoroughly disillusioned but wiser businessman—leaving Ribbentrop as the sole 'beneficiary' of the mining enterprise, he was still struggling heroically with undiminished hope and faith, but now interspersed with unaccustomed fits of deep despondency. A few months afterwards I heard the pathetic news that in one of these fits of depression Bert had removed himself to spend the night in an unfrequented dak bungalow and there shot himself with a pistol. This was the disastrous culmination of my mining venture and also that of one who, true to the traditions of the mining profession, must surely rank among the world's most unbending optimists. Ribbentrop had received his mining engineer's training at the University of Freiburg in Germany and had put in a few years gold mining in British Guiana, apparently with no better luck. He was inducted into tin and wolfram mining in Tavoy by a friend of his, J.W. Donaldson-Aiken, who owned a rubber estate up the river at Egane and a wolfram mine at Pagaye—afterwards sold to Burma Finance and Mining Co. Ltd. Ribbentrop was a happy-go-lucky, kind and friendly individual, well liked by the mine labourers and villagers who often came to him for help and advice in their domestic and official troubles and scrapes. Among his many lines of versatility, one, oddly enough, was his competence as an amateur midwife. He had acquired a reputation in the surrounding countryside and was in great demand, prospective fathers coming to call him from long distances in the jungle and from outlying villages, sometimes in the middle of the night. He kept at hand a Gladstone bag with all the medical and even surgical requisites ready, and I never knew him refuse to attend a call, however inconvenient the hour. In return his patients occasionally brought him bananas or freshly caught fish, or eggs or chickens, but these were all grateful voluntary offerings, for his services were all gratis.

The name Ribbentrop is apparently uncommon in Germany. Thus, in later years (*c.* 1937), when one of that name became Hitler's ambassador in London, I was rather intrigued and asked my ornithologist friend, Colonel R. Meinertzhagen, who knew the ambassador personally, to find out if he was connected in any way with the once Inspector-General of Forests in India. At the next opportunity Colonel Meinertzhagen tackled von Ribbentrop on this and wrote to me as follows: (London, 16.12.38) 'I remember your telling me of your Ribbentrop and I asked, but our VON (and the VON is a lie) denied all connection with commerce (he would, being a super snob and one of the worst men in Germany) or ever having had a connection with the timber trade.'

6

Bombay 1924–9

On the retreat from Burma in 1924, Tehmina and I lived for a while with my sister Kamoo and brother-in-law Hassan, who had kindly offered to let us be nominal paying guests in their spacious, newly-built bungalow on Pali Hill in Bombay. Hassan had done well in business in Kobe, Japan, as Manager of Samuel, Samuel & Co.'s Indian department, but was keen to return and settle down in India. Here he went into partnership with an old school friend, Rattanchand Talakchand Master, a flourishing share and bullion broker, but the partnership was short-lived as Rattanchand turned out to be a reckless speculator who soon came to grief and insolvency. After trying his hand unsuccessfully at share brokering on his own, Hassan decided to return to Japan, leaving Kamoo and three children—Saad, Laeeq and Aamir (born 1923)—to follow when he had found his feet again. The Pali Hill bungalow was to be let thereafter to the manager of Burmah Shell. Pali Hill and the area around its base, from the fishing village of Danda eastward—Khar, Vile Parle, Santa Cruz, etc. and south to Bandra were paddy fields interspersed with large mango and tamarind trees and palmyra (*Borassus*) palms. Most of Pali Hill, including the golf links up to Danda, was the private property of Mulraj Khatau. It was an extensive grove of grafted mango trees, mostly alphonso and pairi. Plots were sold for residential bungalows chiefly, and preferably to Europeans, and on the whole the locality was more or less an exclusively European preserve. The bungalows were of attractive single-storeyed, colonial-type architecture, with tiled roofs, and mostly surrounded by well-kept lawns and flower beds. In fact there was a municipal ruling up to the time of Independence and later that two-thirds of every plot was to be maintained as open space and only one-third could be built upon. At that time there were no pukka roads, no electricity, no municipal sanitation, and only a restricted and undependable water supply. The most important landmark of the locality was the Petit Parsi Orphanage—now the Avabai Petit Girls High School. Happily, the place had not then been discovered by movie stars.

The hill slope from the golf links and up Carter Road, from where the bottom paddy fields and golf links ended, was well wooded—shrubbery of *karwanda*, *ber*, *babul* and wild date, with large shady trees of *imli* (tamarind), banyan and others characteristic of the South Konkan landscape. It was an excellent venue for birding and it was while living on Pali Hill in 1924 that I did most of the collecting and study for a paper I hoped to produce titled 'Birds of Bombay and Salsette', as a pendant to Prater's very useful *Snakes of Bombay and Salsette*, which had recently been published by the Society. The paper on birds was actually published in the Society's journal many years later, jointly with Humayun Abdulali, who had also gathered a lot of additional material while doing zoology at St Xavier's College for his B.A. degree, with encouragement from Father Palacios, a Spanish Jesuit who was then Director of Biology in the College. Commuting to office between Bandra and Churchgate was done by steam-engined trains. Cars were few and the roads dusty and untarred. The first local electric trains started at about this time. There were frequent interruptions and stoppages due to short-circuiting caused by the iron wire in crows' nests built in overhead brackets, until a special crow-proof bracket was designed. Besides the Pali Hill area, most of my bird collecting in Salsette was done in the well-wooded areas around Powai, Tulsi and Vihar lakes, the Trombay hills, Mulund, Vikhroli, Bhandup, Ghodbunder, Bhyndar, etc. On Sundays and holidays, Prater, McCann and Jacobs (Secretary of the Prince of Wales Museum) often took part in these collecting forays and many unexpected species figured in the collection, such as the Malabar Trogon and the

Three-toed Forest Kingfisher—two that I remember vividly. The Mulund hills backdropping the present Godrej complex at Vikhroli were densely forested and the entire catchment area of the lakes and all that is now Aarey Milk Colony and Borivli National Park was one continuous stretch of fairly thick jungle and palmyra palms. Pig and barking deer were common, and also sambar. Panthers frequently strayed in, and the last stray tiger was shot in 1929 near Vihar Lake.

After Kamoo and the children left for Japan and the Pali bungalow was let, we moved over to Tehmina's father, C.A. Latif, in the top flat of his apartment building, 'Latifia', on Harvey Road behind Wilson College at Chowpati. Tehmina soon got a part-time job as Secretary of the Bombay Presidency Women's Council with its office in the south wing of the Town Hall. A post of ornithologist was advertised by the Zoological Survey of India at that time, for which I applied with Father Blatter, Dr Stresemann and the BNHS as my referees, but, having no university degree, stood little chance against M.Sc.s and Ph.D.s. This post actually went to M.L. Roonwal, who retired in 1965 as Director of the Zoological Survey of India, having succeeded Sundar Lal Hora. I felt greatly dejected at the time because it seemed unlikely that there would soon be another opening for an ornithologist elsewhere in India. My advice to all young aspirants for government jobs is: never fail to arm yourself with a university degree, for whatever it is worth. However, in retrospect I feel it was the luckiest thing that could have happened to me as it saved me from ending up as a fossilized bureaucrat.

One elderly Mrs Dracup had been an Inspectress of Schools in Bombay Presidency and had become friendly with Kamoo when Kamoo was teaching in the Parsi Girls' School in Broach (1917). After retirement Mrs Dracup was living with her son, a Secretary to the Government of Bombay around 1925/6, in the charming English villa-type bungalow built as a model dwelling for the proposed 'Garden City' of the Bombay Development Committee at Chembur—a plan which was later given up. Mrs Dracup invited us (Tehmina's father Camruddin Latif, Tehmina and myself) to tea one day to have a look at the bungalow which the government was trying to dispose of, and which Uncle Camruddin was interested in buying for Tehmina. The idea was to give up the Chowpati flat and live in the suburbs, where we could have a garden and grow our own vegetables and flowers, for which Tehmina was pining, as was I for the open countryside and birding rambles.

The bungalow was charmingly situated and designed and beautifully kept, and surrounded by greenery and well laid-out lawns. All three of us fell for it immediately. So much so that Uncle Camruddin—a very shrewd and cool-headed businessman—started negotiations with the government for its purchase the very next day and offers and counter-offers were in progress, with a good probability of the deal being concluded. We were both greatly excited and impatient, and Tehmina lost no time in starting to plan the furnishings and other details— what the upholstery would be, what the *purdahs* and hangings, and so on, and I the experimental aviaries I had long dreamed about. We had realized that it would be rather inconvenient and tiring for both of us to commute to the city daily since there were no buses to Chembur in those days, the railway station three miles away and the local train service leaving much to be desired. But the overall prospect was so alluring that we didn't worry too much about the disadvantages.

However, fate decreed otherwise. Just when the government accepted Uncle C's final offer, he died—in fact the government's acceptance letter was actually received the day after his death. As it would have been impossible for us at the time to run the new establishment on our joint income and without her father's major contribution, we regretfully did not pursue the matter further. And that was the end of one dream.

After I got the job at the BNHS, Tehmina and I continued to live with her father in the 'Latifia' flat at Chowpati. The annexe was occupied by Saif and Badr as paying guests. They had been left behind in Bombay for their education in the Law College and St Xavier's respectively, while their parents, Faiz and Salima Tyabji, had moved to Karachi on his appointment as Judicial Commissioner in Sind. After my father-in-law's death in February 1927, we had to shift for ourselves and moved into a comfortable little two-bedroom flat in a very well maintained building named 'Unity Hall' in Rebsch Street, Byculla, overlooking the maidan used as a cricket field by the YMCA two buildings away. It was a pleasant, quiet and respectable residential locality in those days, and must not be judged from the disreputable shabby slum it has become today, with the maidan buried under the lower-middle-class *chawls* crowding cheek by jowl.

In a letter of 23 June 1927 to my sister Kamoo, then in Japan, after we moved into this flat, Tehmina says

a dear little flat—everyone who comes to see me falls in love with it. It is on the first floor and in such a nice locality. There is a maidan in front so that we don't feel all closed in, and it's the next best thing to a garden. There is one big room in front which we have divided by a screen into drawing and dining rooms and then there are two other small rooms and a nice bathroom. One of the rooms is our bedroom and the other is Sálim's 'den', where repose his gun almirah designed by himself, his desk and our book cases and some comfy chairs. He is ever so happy in his room and hates to be disturbed! I have some lovely china and other things as my share of Father's property and this gives the flat such an air! We have bought and had made some very good furniture too, Jacobean period, and really 'though I says it as shouldn't', it looks very pretty. We don't have table cloths on our table in the dining room but have mats and d'oyleys. The table is a good one and has lovely polish and is oval . . . Mrs Naidu and Padmaja dined with us last night and we had such a nice time. They are both charming and such good talkers, so witty, we laughed and laughed till our sides ached . . .

Fortuitously, I discovered that a class friend from my schooldays, Osman Sobhani, occupied the top floor of this three-storey building. Though less directly involved in the Khilafat and Non-Co-operation Movements than his elder brother Umar, Osman was still very close to the inner circle of political big guns like Maulana Shaukat Ali, Mrs Sarojini Naidu, Shuaib Qureshi and others of the day, many of whom used to visit him frequently at his elegant, tastefully appointed bachelor's apartment. We could not help soon getting sucked into the political vortex, but managed to cling only to the outer fringe because both Tehmina and I had some very dear friends in the 'opposition', both Indian and British, with whom we were anxious to maintain our friendship. Also, I did not want to be sidetracked from my main interest—natural history and birds.

Thus we managed to get the best of both worlds, such as they were. Mrs Naidu used to live in the Taj Hotel in Bombay during those days of high political drama so as to be on tap for the frequent snap meetings of the Congress Working Committee, of which she was President at the time if I remember rightly, or, in any case, a very close associate and confidante of Gandhiji. With her remarkable intellect and sense of humour—sorely lacking in politicians as a species then as now—she always managed to pour oil on troubled waters and restore calm among the factions. Mrs Naidu was not only gifted with a delightful sense of humour but was one of those rare politicians who can laugh at themselves and are not obsessed by their own importance. She was perhaps the only one of the inner circle who joked and traded banter with Gandhiji, who could himself enjoy a good joke even at his own expense. Among informal friendly company Mrs Naidu often referred to the Mahatma as Mickey Mouse, and Gandhiji accepted the compliment with lighthearted toothless gaiety. Even from her pre-political days Mrs Naidu had close friendly ties with the Tyabji family, particularly the Baroda branch, of which the patriarch, my maternal uncle Abbas, later became her comrade-in-arms during the Bardoli and Salt Satyagraha in 1930. On one of her visits to Osman Mrs Naidu discovered that Tehmina and I lived below him, and thereafter she frequently dropped in at our flat on her way up or down with delightful informality and much mutual pleasure. She was a delightful conversationalist, raconteur and mimic, and regaled us with recitations of her latest poems, or with current and past anecdotes and remembrances with inimitable humour. Her assessments of her political contemporaries and their foibles and eccentricities were particularly incisive and entertaining.

It was on one of these impromptu visits that she brought in

with her and introduced us to a panting Maulana Shaukat Ali, the leader of the Khilafat Movement in Bombay, and his co-worker, the handsome and lovable Shuaib Qureshi, who soon became a close friend and constant visitor to our flat. He had a deep, sonorous voice, and often entertained us with his chanting of many of the moving, patriotic and pro-Islamic verses of Iqbal, of whom he was an ardent admirer, both as a poet and as a champion of Islamism. One of his recitations, the beauty and sonorousness of which still rings in my ears, is the touching *shikwa* (panegyric) of the vicissitudes of the island of Sicily, once an important Muslim stronghold in Europe. Shuaib was an ardent Turkophile and hero-worshipper of Enver Pasha. He had been a volunteer with Dr M.A. Ansari's medical mission to the Turks in their war in the Balkans (1912) and won high praise for his courage in rescuing the wounded from the battle-field under fire.

In 1927 frigidaires were a recent innovation in India and I am reminded that Tehmina and I were the first in the family to acquire one. The Kelvinator was a particular joy in the mango season because an ice-cooled alphonso is a thing apart. And this reminds me of a day when some kind friend had sent us eight of the best from his garden, justly famed for the excellence of its mangoes. Presently there was a knock on the door and in walked the breathless biomass of the ponderous Maulana en route up the stairs to Osman's flat. In an effort to seem hospitable Tehmina made the mistake—never repeated again—of asking if he would care to try an ice-cold mango. Of course the great man was ready to oblige, as he said he had never tasted a refrigerated mango before. The great mistake Tehmina made and realized too late was to place for gentility's sake the entire bowlful before a hungry guest of that size. To our suppressed consternation the mangoes disappeared into that capacious paunch one after another at astonishing speed, with an approving exclamation or two after each, until we were left staring at the empty dish. This was the price of a valuable lesson well and truly learned.

At one time a staunch Gandhiite, nationalist and Congress-man, Shuaib unfortunately found cause to turn a complete somersault later and become a hundred per cent anti-Congress, pro-Jinnah and pro-Pakistan. He migrated to Pakistan when Bhopal State—where he was a minister in the nawab's government—was taken over in the Indian Union, and in due course ended up as a minister in the central Pakistan cabinet.

One of the first things we did on shifting to a flat of our own, after my father-in-law's death, was to purchase a small car. It was a seven horse-power Baby Austin, the collapsible canvas-top model with wire-ribbed (cycle) wheels. It cost Rs 1700 brand new, shock absorbers and screen wiper extra. It did forty-five miles to the gallon when the price of petrol, thanks to cut-throat competition between the two main oil companies, Burma Oil and Shell, was 11 annas per gallon. Roadside pumps were few and far between, and petrol was available mostly in two-gallon cans—green for BOC and red for Shell. An entry in a tattered pocket notebook of the time reminds me that petrol for a shikar trip to Lonand, beyond Poona, and back to Bombay, three-hundred miles plus, cost Rs 13 and 8 annas.

We usually drove to the Fort together and I dropped Tehmina at her office (Women's Council) in the south wing of the Town Hall on my way to the Prince of Wales Museum. 'Jane' (as the car was named by Tehmina after one of her favourite authors, Jane Austen) was driven up parallel sloping planks and parked for the day on the raised open verandah outside the then Natural History gallery. The little car provided great fun on Sundays and holidays for picnics and for bird collecting or small game shooting trips in the Bombay neighbourhood—in Salsette, and on the mainland, and beyond. It also provided thoroughly enjoyable leisurely motoring holidays to Poona, Aurangabad, Nasik and other places within 200 miles or so of Bombay. The roads were untarred, usually full of pot-holes and very dusty, which inhibited venturing further afield. With such a lightweight car one had to pick one's way slowly and carefully and there was the constant nuisance of trucks and heavier vehicles overtaking and covering one in a pall of dust. Many of the rivers and nullahs were unbridged and impassable for the little car during the monsoon. I remember our once getting badly stuck in the sandy bed of the unbridged Bhima river on the main Poona-Aurangabad road, the engine stalling mid-stream when half under water and being dragged out quite casually, without any apparent effort, by a supercilious pair of bullocks being led back to the village after the day's ploughing! The lightness of the car had another great advantage: if it ran out of petrol in the city it could easily be perambulated single-handedly to the nearest filling station or depot.

From a little beyond Poona, and up to Sholapur and beyond, blackbuck were plentiful and hardly ever out of sight on both sides of the road, constantly crossing and recrossing in front of the car. One could stop almost anywhere and do a short cross-country stalk of a shootable trophy. No shooting licence was necessary and it was normal practice for weekend 'sportsmen' to 'rail off' extra animals killed to any one of the bigger hotels in Bombay, for instance the Taj, without previous intimation, way-billed by the railways as 'Dead deer' and 'Freight to pay'. The hotels gladly took delivery and paid the sender Rs 5 per animal with thanks. During the open shooting season several such consignments, even from so-called bona fide sportsmen, reached the various hotels every day, and venison was freely advertised on the menu. In such black-cotton-soil country the antelopes were highly vulnerable in the monsoon, when the heavy clay hampered speedy escape and professional hunters took full advantage of their helplessness. Small wonder that this sort of commercialized slaughter, aided and abetted by four-wheel-drive jeeps, powerful spotlights, the free issue of firearms ('crop protection') and relaxed law-and-order conditions after World War II, especially since Independence, have completely wiped out blackbuck from this area.

In the Unity Hall flat we were often visited by Sarojini Naidu and her daughter, Padmaja. They frequently stayed on for pot-luck and we drove them back to their hotel in 'Jane' afterwards. Four well-grown adults made a snug fit in that tiny frail-looking car, but never so snug as on a memorable occasion when the ponderous Maulana Shaukat Ali overflowed the front bucket seat, with me driving and Sarojini and Tehmina jammed against each other in the rear. Loaded thus the car presented a comically Maulana-oriented tilt. But the sight would have gladdened the heart of its makers; it demonstrated what the midget could do at a pinch.

7

Jobs 1923–9 and
Germany 1929–30

While unsuccessfully job-hunting and marking time for some congenial natural history assignment, I was accommodated by kindly cousins with a temporary clerical position in their cotton exporting firm of N. Futehally & Co., where I arrogated to myself the grandiose designation of 'Extra-assistant sub-deputy head clerk, *pro tem*'. The salary, euphemistically called 'allowance', commenced with Rs 150 per month, but soon back-slid to Rs 100 when the firm sustained a serious financial reverse in Japan through the failure of an important textile-mill client.

I had gratefully accepted the job under pressure of circumstances and without enthusiasm, but having had some training in office management had hoped all the same to be able to instil a semblance of order into the chaos that pervaded the office routine of my kind-hearted employers. It seemed a wonder to me that this old firm, established as long ago as 1870 or thereabouts, had managed to survive the violent vicissitudes of the intervening years with so little regard for any sort of methodical system in its business affairs. I regret to admit that after the first flush of optimism and reforming zeal I soon gave up trying, because my impact seemed obviously too feeble, and their will to change too half-hearted to last in that happy-go-lucky atmosphere. That N. Futehally & Co. had endured so many serious crises is due entirely to the admirable unity and spirit of reasonable accommodation which all five partner-brothers maintained through thick and thin.

At this time I was offered a business job by another relation who was then opening a branch office in Aden. It sounded attractive enough financially in my state of joblessness, but I am happy to have resisted the temptation and declined, because from the antecedents and clever practices of this sanctimonious and highly successful businessman I would doubtless have been expected to do similar clever things that, squeamishly enough, I would not have enjoyed.

As luck would have it, after a protracted palaver the BNHS had just succeeded in persuading the Government of Bombay to budget the appointment of a Guide Lecturer in the newly opened Natural History Section of the Prince of Wales Museum. Reverend Father Blatter happened to be Chairman of the selection committee for the post and supported my candidature strongly. My being appointed was largely due to him and to Prater, the Curator, under whom the Guide Lecturer would have to work. Fate had decreed that the selection committee should hold its meeting during the fortnight in which my brother-in-law Shums and I had planned a shooting holiday in the Utnoor forests of Adilabad district of Hyderabad State, then some of the finest tiger country in the peninsula. With great disappointment I had to back out of this venture (ill-fated as it later proved) since I was a candidate for the post. A few days after I had begun work in my new appointment, the very sad news came that Shums had been fatally mauled by a tiger that he had wounded and was following up without sufficient caution. His plucky young companion, Azeem, who had beaten off the animal, was also badly clawed and bitten, but was fortunate enough to be removed in time to better medical care in Bombay, where he recovered after weeks of grave anxiety.

Shums, who had married my eldest sister Ashraf, was in his own way a remarkable, curiously conflicting but lovable character, and very good company, especially in camp. He was good natured and talented and better than average at doing most things that took his fancy, so long as they had nothing to do with his profession or family responsibilities. For example he could fritter away endless effort and time in activities like

stamp collecting, amateur theatricals, music, and days on end
of cricket umpiring and club-going; but dearest of all to his
heart was big game hunting in which, ironically, he never had
much luck. *The* great ambition of his life was to shoot a tiger:
he lived for it and, as it happened, died for it. Shikar was such
an obsession with him that wags had named him Nawab
Hărdăm Shikār Jung.

Planning the syllabus and organizing the work of the new
Nature Study Department was enjoyable. In the comparatively
short life of the scheme I think a marked increase of intelligent
interest in natural history in pupils and teachers of the participating schools, and in the Museum Natural History section's
popularity with the general public, was clearly discernible. To
begin with only a few secondary and high schools were selected,
which sent classes by appointment and in rotation for simple,
informal talks on animal life, illustrated with lantern slides,
models and museum specimens. I particularly enjoyed talking
to pupils from the School for the Blind, because of the lively
interest they showed, and I never ceased to marvel at their
almost magical aptitude for grasping anatomical details merely
by passing their fingers over the exhibits of skulls and bones
specially prepared for them. The usefulness and success of the
Society's Nature Education Scheme was so gratifying that it
seemed sacrilegious of the Bombay Government to have dis-
continued it after only a three-years' run on the dubious pretext,
considering the paltry expenditure involved, of financial
stringency. Thus, as soon as possible after Independence,
during the sympathetic Chief Ministership of Bombay State of
the friendly B.G. Kher, Prater and I as Curator and Honorary
Secretary of the Society respectively, pressed for and succeeded
in getting the Nature Study Scheme resuscitated, with M.R.
Raut as its organizer. With a widening of its scope and activities
it has been functioning satisfactorily since about 1949 and is no
doubt responsible, at least in part, for the noticeable increase of
awareness and interest in wildlife and nature conservation
among the youth and general public of Maharashtra in recent
years.

However, two years of guide-lecturing were enough for me.

I realized that my real metier was birds and decided to undergo a course of training in systematic and field ornithology before settling down to it, hopefully as a whole-time occupation. As to how I would keep the wolf from the door thereafter did not worry me then. Ornithology has always been the Cinderella of Indian zoology and there was no university or institution in the country where such training could be had. I had therefore written to the British Museum (Natural History) and to the Berlin University Zoological Museum to ask what facilities were available there. The political atmosphere between India and Britain at that period, 1929—when, according to a scandalized Churchill a half-naked fakir had the temerity to parley on equal terms with the representative of His Majesty the King Emperor—was charged with so much bias and bitterness that, as was apparent from the discouragingly lukewarm response I got from the British Museum, conditions of work in Britain would have been uncongenial. On the other hand, although I was not personally known to Professor Erwin Stresemann till then, his response was so cordial and welcoming that I immediately decided to go to Berlin.

As part of the practical training in taxonomy, Stresemann had suggested my bringing a collection of Indian birds to work out under his guidance. A collection of about 200 birds had just been received from Burma, collected by J.K. Stanford, ICS, a keen ornithologist member of the BNHS, with the assistance of the Society's skinner, E. Henricks, in I think Henzada district. Stanford had undertaken this collection at the instance of Dr Claud B. Ticehurst, who was evidently meaning to work it out himself. Ticehurst was so outraged at the thought of an obscure greenhorn Indian trying to do so, and that too with the help of a naughty *German* (so soon after the Kaiser's war) that he wrote a nasty official protest to the Society behind my back saying that the collector, Mr Stanford, would never condone this slight. Both Sir Reginald Spence, then Honorary Secretary, and Prater, however, had faith in my competence and agreed that with Stresemann's help and guidance the collection would be well served. History does not record whether Mr Stanford did in fact feel any serious resentment at the Society's action or whether it was merely Dr Ticehurst's solicitous imagination. Mr Stanford himself never expressed it officially or openly at that time or afterwards, nor was he anything but most friendly and cordial to me when we met at the 1950 International Ornithological Congress in Uppsala in Sweden, or at subsequent meetings, or in correspondence.

There is no doubt that Berlin proved for me the luckiest turning at the crossroads of my ornithological career. Considering that I was only an unknown and aspiring ornithologist at the time, and an entire stranger to him personally, the warmth of Stresemann's welcome and the painstaking cooperation and guidance he gave me from the first day—and throughout the entire period I was privileged to work with him—were heart-warming. His simplicity and modesty, his unassuming erudition, his lively, almost boyish humour, and the vastness of his scientific knowledge have left in me a vivid impression and admiration for the man, the scientist, the mentor and the friend, that has endured and grown with the years. I considered him my guru to the end. Appeals to him for advice and assistance in knotty problems of taxonomy, ecology or zoogeography never failed to elicit prompt and detailed replies, all scribbled by hand, the lines often running diagonally across a sheet and none too easy to decipher until the code was broken, yet meticulously reasoned, documented and free from all ambiguity. Considering that I was only one of his numerous worldwide proteges, it is a standing wonder to me how Stresemann ever managed to keep abreast with his correspondence and up-to-date with the increasing spate of scientific literature, and at the same time still found time to continue his own research and discharge the other responsibilities inherent in his acknowledged position as the doyen of world ornithologists.

Kinnear, who had himself been one of the people who, as Curator of the BNHS, had helped to kindle my youthful interest in birds in earlier years, seemed a changed personality in the vitiated Indo-British atmosphere of the Gandhian era, and in the aura of the British Museum. In August 1929 one of the prominent Indians we found settled in Berlin since before and all through World War I was Champakraman Pillay, a 'fugitive' member of the revolutionary group which called itself the Provisional Government of India and had some sort of recognition from the Kaiser. Its President was a curious simpleton, though a completely serious and dedicated visionary, Raja Mahendra Pratap, a dispossessed *taluqdar* of UP. M.N. Roy, another revolutionary member of the Provisional Government, had shifted his activities to Moscow, I think, and I did not meet him. Pillay claimed to have had frequent meetings with the Kaiser during the progress of the war in Europe to apprise him of the subversive propaganda (anti-British) conducted vicariously by the Provisional Government in India. Like Raja Mahendra Pratap, Pillay was a sincere and serious activist, but, unlike his leader, a more practical and pragmatic revolutionary. After the defeat of Germany both had a price put on their heads by the British Indian government and so found it more prudent to continue living in Germany. Pillay, we discovered, was an excellent cook and gave us delicious Indian meals from time to time prepared from ersatz *masalas*. He visited his native Kerala after umpteen years of exile once India attained independence, but later returned to Germany and died there. Raja Mahendra Pratap also returned to India from Japan, where he had moved after the Kaiser's eclipse, and settled down in Dehra Dun. He must have felt seriously disillusioned by the comparatively scant fuss made over him by the Nehru government of the day, as well as by the public at large; but this was not surprising to those who knew him, though everyone will concede his integrity and dedication and the personal sacrifices he had made for the cause.

It was while working at the Zoological Museum of Berlin University that I first made the acquaintance of Bernhard Rensch, a brilliant young zoologist who had been making methodical collections of birds and other animal groups in the Sunda Islands. His special studies were about the problems of geographical variation produced by climatic factors in the context of the origin of species and evolution. He had been newly appointed on the museum staff in the Department of Malacology (the science of molluscs), another field of his specialization, for lack of an immediate vacancy in ornithology.

Bernhard and I took to each other immediately, as did Tehmina to Bernhard's friendly and charming wife, Ilse. They have been among my closest foreign friends through the intervening years of peace and war. After a varied career in learned zoological positions, including the directorship of Prague Museum after the 'liberation' of Czechoslovakia by Hitler, he retired a few years ago from the directorship of the University Zoological Institute, Münster. I have a very great regard for Rensch as an interpretative biologist and as a sensitive, artistic and cultured intellectual.

In the bird room of the museum I also had my first meeting with Ernst Mayr, another brilliant and upcoming young protege of Stresemann who had just returned from a major bird-collecting expedition in the New Guinea region, and whom I met again in the USA only after World War II. He had emigrated from Germany just before the War and had been working extensively in New York on taxonomy and speciation problems with the Rothschild bird collection purchased by the American Museum of Natural History. Ernst Mayr is currently Emeritus Professor of Zoology at Harvard University and undisputably among the topmost biologists of the world today. Unfortunately—in marked contrast to his mentor Stresemann's unassuming modesty—Mayr makes you feel he is not unaware of the fact.

Here I also had the pleasure and privilege of meeting for the first time (and thereafter frequently at the Berlin Zoo and Aquarium, of which he was the Director), the jolly and indefatigable biologist Oskar Heinroth and his remarkable wife, Magdalena, dedicated pioneers of the modern scientific cult of bird behaviour study. Indeed, Heinroth can rightfully be called the Father of Ethology, a discipline which has in many ways revolutionized the old concept of establishing phylogenetic relationships between bird groups solely on the basis of anatomy and morphology, and helped to bridge the yawning gulf between systematics and biology. Heinroth's studies of living birds opened my eyes to problems and possibilities that had received but scant consideration before. They helped to provide a direction and strong ecological bias to my subsequent work on Indian birds, which has drawn complimentary comment from reviewers.

The working out under Stresemann's guidance of the collection of Burmese birds I had brought from Bombay gave me a good idea of the techniques and procedures of taxonomical work and also of the pitfalls with which they are beset, including the danger of hasty conclusions based on slender 'eye of faith' premises. Apart from working in the Museum, the highlight of my study-leave in Germany was the coveted opportunity of visiting the island of Heligoland with Stresemann, and participating in the bird migration studies being conducted there under the direction of the enthusiastic Dr Rudolf Drost.

Heligoland is a barren rock, standing abruptly out of the North Sea at the mouths of the rivers Elbe and Weser, about thirty miles from the German mainland, and directly on the route of migratory birds from the north. It is triangular in shape and with sheer rocky sides 200 feet high. The top of the island—or the Oberland—is an undulating tableland, beautifully turfed with green but practically treeless due to the heavy gales that ceaselessly sweep over it. Therefore, in order to tempt the migrants down, a sunken trapping garden—the Sapskule—about 120 metres long and 15 wide has been constructed at the northern end of the Oberland, thickly planted with shrubs and bushes and provided with little pools of fresh water for the birds. The shrubbery helps to hide the cleverly designed tapering chicken-wire traps, ending in small glass-fronted boxes into which the birds can be driven and concentrated and removed for ringing. The depth of the sunken garden is increased by a concrete wall 2.5 metres high all round the basin, which affords further protection from the wind to the fairly tall shrubs within. It was at Heligoland that I had my first practical demonstration of the ringing techniques that have since been so widely and successfully employed by the BNHS in its various field projects.

In addition to the trapping garden, Heligoland possesses a powerful lighthouse of some 42,000 candle-power, whose beams, on certain cloud-overcast nights in spring and autumn, act as a magnet for tens of thousands of migratory birds. The birds dash against the glass panes round the turret and fall dazed and fluttering on to the surrounding balcony, whence they are gathered in gunny sacks in enormous numbers and taken for ringing. This attraction of the migrating birds to the lighthouse is essentially the same as what happens on similar cloudy and starless monsoon nights at the Meghalaya village of Jatinga in north-east India, sensationally reported by some of our newspapers as 'mass suicide' by birds! During the spring and autumn migrations the Biological Station on Heligoland is thronged by university students and amateur bird-watchers, not only from Germany but from many other European countries as well, and there is no dearth of willing and experienced hands. On a night like this the lighthouse is alive with enthusiastic young people running up and down with sackfuls of birds so collected. The 'reigning' lighthouse keeper and his family lived on one of the floors through which the winding staircase ran. His wife was a dreaded termagant and a terror for the volunteers as she was wont to burst in on them in the middle of the night, ranting violently about being disturbed in her slumber. It was comic to see big hefty toughs wilting so abjectly under her thunderous assault and tiptoeing sheepishly up and down the stairs; but anyone who has experienced such a riotous night at the lighthouse will readily sympathize with the harassed female.

Under the right meteorological conditions as many as 1,200 or more birds may be taken in a single night for ringing, in addition to the hundreds upon hundreds gathered by the local Heligolanders, who turn out in force on a god-sent night like this, to replenish their larders. The meadows for many metres around the base of the tower are pulsating with exhausted birds or with those that have fluttered down to the ground, dazed or dying after dashing against the light. The holocaust is further aggravated by the ravages of the swarms of stray cats, protected like our holy cows by popular sentiment, for which Heligoland was as notorious as was old-time Constantinople for dogs. All this was before World War II. Since then conditions may have improved, with the general adoption of the international convention for fixing nets of soft material around the lanterns of lighthouses to prevent mortality among migrating birds that dash into them.

8

Hyderabad State
Ornithological Survey

It was while refugeeing at Kihim as an unemployed and unsuccessful job-hunter after my return from Germany in early 1930, and pondering how I could utilize what little expertise I had acquired abroad, that the idea of the regional ornithological surveys first came to me. There were vast tracts of the Indian subcontinent, particularly the Princely States, whose avifauna had been little explored and studied. I offered the BNHS to carry out systematic field surveys of the bird life of these areas on a voluntary basis, provided they would raise the necessary funds to cover the actual working expenses, transport, etc., arrange for camping facilities and local assistance from the state forest and other government departments, and loan me the services of one or two of the Society's field collectors and taxidermists. Hyderabad State represented the largest gap in our ornithological knowledge; it was the obvious first priority, considering the important results recently obtained by the Vernay Scientific Survey in the adjoining area of the Eastern Ghats. At that time many of the key positions in the Nizam's administration were held by British ICS or Political Department officers on loan from the Government of India. Most of them were sportsmen-naturalists and members of the BNHS, keenly interested in birds and therefore sympathetically responsive to the Society's appeal. Also, the Finance Minister, Sir Akbar Hydari, a distant connection, and some other well-wishers in the state who had a good regard for my work, lent their personal support to the BNHS proposal and appeal. Thus, after seemingly endless ding-dong correspondence with the nizam's government authorities, a grant of Rs 3,000 for three months of field work was finally sanctioned, and soon thereafter the Hyderabad State Ornithological Survey began. As the entire state could not be covered within the stipulated period, the government sanctioned a renewal of the grant for a further two months.

Hugh Whistler, the foremost British student of Indian birds in his day, was, like E.C. Stuart Baker, also an officer in the Imperial Police Service. He served the entire sixteen years or so before his premature voluntary retirement in Punjab. During his tenure in India he collected and studied birds in the field so thoroughly and perceptively that one unfamiliar with his professional efficiency would suspect police work to have been for him merely an occasional spare-time occupation. By the time he left the country he had acquired an unsurpassed knowledge not only of the ornithology of Punjab but also of neighbouring Kashmir and the NWFP, and, in the process, of the entire British Indian Empire as well. After settling down at Battle in Sussex he continued to develop his expertise on birds, particularly Indian and Palaearctic, but now more on the taxonomic side with only periodical forays for field collecting.

My relations with Whistler, strangely as with so many of my English friends, started on a somewhat jarring and acrimonious note. In an admirable serial article he was writing in the *Journal* of the BNHS around the year 1928, 'The Study of Indian Birds', Whistler had made a statement concerning the structure of the elongated tail feathers of the Racket-tailed Drongo which I contradicted. I did not know Whistler personally at that time, and he had possibly never heard of me as having anything to do with birds. He was obviously peeved at being openly contradicted and wrote a rather snooty letter to the editors, Sir Reginald Spence and S.H. Prater. However, after re-examining his specimens and being convinced that I was right he corrected himself in a subsequent issue of the *Journal*. After years of close and fruitful collaboration in my various regional bird surveys, Whistler reminded me of the drongo's tail incident in a letter (dated 24.10.1938), thanking me for some bird skins I had sent him, thus: 'So now I should like to thank you properly and most heartily for what is merely an addition to long years of help and kindness which I have already experienced at your hands. It has been a very great benefit to me that we drifted into collaboration largely in its beginning as an accident when you pointed out my mistake over the webs of a drongo's tail feathers—and the mistake has proved to me well worth while.'

Up till that time I had no practical experience in running a methodical bird survey of this kind, so I approached Whistler for advice and suggestions and asked at the same time if he would be willing to undertake the taxonomical work on the Hyderabad collection, since that would be merely an extension of the excellent study he had just finished on the birds collected by the Vernay Scientific Survey in a contiguous area of the Eastern Ghats. Whistler seemed only too eager to collaborate, and I soon received from him a list of excellent suggestions on how such a survey could be carried out. These suggestions, together with the helpful tips received in the field from time to time from my guru, Stresemann, proved invaluable during this and subsequent bird surveys. Whistler's prescriptions are so pertinent and excellent that, though it may be questionable whether this is the right place, I have included them as an appendix, as a model for all who may hereafter chance to engage in similar field work. That the results of the regional bird surveys have received such generous acclaim and comment must be attributed in large measure to my following Whistler's admirable prescriptions and to his energetic participation through the running correspondence he maintained with me throughout the Hyderabad survey, and during all the subsequent ones as well, right up to the time of his untimely death in 1944.

Mist nets had not appeared on the scene till then, nor indeed until considerably later. But after using them in the last few years I am convinced that no field collecting can be regarded as thorough where mist nets have not been employed to supplement shooting and visual observation. The unsuspected presence of many shy and skulking birds of dense shrubbery—especially of tropical jungle as in the East Himalayan foothills—is revealed only when they fall into nets suitably deployed or in the dark hours of dawn and dusk, or during the night; otherwise they are easily missed. Japanese mist nets first came into use in India only in 1959 with the inception of the WHO/BNHS bird ringing project. They have somewhat shaken my confidence in the comprehensiveness of my own collecting before that time. Their use has already added several species, unnoticed earlier, to the bird lists of various surveyed areas, and doubtless more species could be added by further intensive netting.

I have always been an admirer of good handwriting. To me it is an indication of a tidy mind and of a striving after meticulousness and perfection. This generalization is perhaps too simple to hold, and there are far too many exceptions to prove the rule, e.g. Stresemann, Roy Hawkins, *et al.* But in the case of Whistler it was clearly demonstrable. He wrote all his letters, comments and taxonomical notes, including tables of measurements and suchlike things, in a bold, clear manuscript, neatly aligned. In days when general devaluation has touched even calligraphy, and legible—leave alone good—handwriting has become old fashioned, it was a refreshing experience to see letters from him. I don't know how he kept track of what he wrote because there was no sign of carbon copies having been made. Yet he seldom repeated anything or forgot what he had said before.

Many of the areas I selected for the specimen collecting in Hyderabad State (Oct.–Dec. 1931, Mar.–Apr. 1932) had primitive communication facilities. Their remoteness, partly, was my rationale for selecting them. They could be reached only on foot or by unsprung bullock carts known as *khachars* over dusty, deeply rutted and bumpy cross-country tracks, or *kutcha* forest roads cut up by unbridged rocky nullahs, mostly dry in that season—roads that would nowadays be euphemistically termed jeepable. However, that was long before the jeep was born. Such nullahs were crossed by the cart storming down one steep boulder-strewn bank and up the opposite one, to the frantic shouting, stick-waving and tail-twisting of the bullocks by the cartmen. I usually preferred to walk behind the cart (and so did Tehmina) for part of the way in the shady bits, and when the sun wasn't too hot, or when the cart ride got too painful. The wooden axles frequently gave way under this violent treatment, but apart from the time lost in repair this presented no problem because the cartmen were excellent rough-and-ready carpenters and well used to such minor calamities. They would just walk into the jungle, hack down a suitable hardwood sapling with their handy all-purpose *koita*, fashion it into a serviceable axle, and we would soon be on our way again. I recollect that, once, when the moon was nearing full, in order to avoid the midday heat we started in the late afternoon by foot and *khachar*, hoping to reach our next camp at a forest hamlet by seven or eight. A broken axle and some other unforeseen hold-ups delayed us on the way, so that we reached our destination only at 1 a.m. instead, hungry and dead beat. Luckily it was bright moonlight all the way. We decided to turn in at once and leave the eating till morning as it would take too long for Rahim, our admirable cook-bearer—one of the best of his tribe that UP produced before the days of Partition—to open up the kitchen things and prepare a meal. But Rahim was scandalized at the suggestion and would have none of it. He could not bear to think of our going to bed hungry, insisted on making a hasty wood fire and unpacking the barest essentials. In a few minutes we were served with sizzling grilled kidneys and liver of a chinkara I had shot on the way, with some cold *chapatis* he had brought for himself. Not much of a meal, but only then were we allowed to go to bed. Such faithful and considerate servants as Rahim belong to a bygone age and to an extinct species that we shall never have the good fortune to see any more, alas.

Often these localities were also off the few and far-between bus routes. Public motor transport in the state was still poorly developed, and privately-owned buses were rare in the *mofussil* towns and out-of-the-way stations. Usually, they were ancient Ford or Chevrolet cars converted by local talent into rattling bone-shakers, with sides of 3-ply wood or galvanized iron sheeting and no restriction on the number of passengers they could carry. Even these were often difficult to hire without some coaxing, or various degrees of official pressure from the local police sub-inspector or other official to whom orders for rendering assistance to the survey party had trickled down from above. That the private buses were truly independent left little doubt in one, from the behaviour and business methods of their owner-drivers, who, by and large, were a sorry tribe. In spite of repeated exhortations to them to be punctual, and solemn assurances from them to come for loading up at six in the morning, there would be no sign of the bus till seven or eight, while you sat on your pile of baggage all packed and ready, or paced up and down muttering curses. The unabashed justification was invariably the same—driver 'taking tea' or 'taking food'. After much haranguing and noisy argumentation and disarranging and rearranging the baggage and equipment—specimen boxes, hurricane lanterns, galvanized iron buckets, bags of rice and *ata*, ghee and kerosene tins and the various other odds and ends inside the bus and on the roof (the latter usually surmounted by a dome-shaped openwork bamboo basket of live chickens for progressive transfer to the menu)—the driver would suddenly remember that petrol had to be filled and off we would go to the petrol pump. No electric power, so pumping by hand, so further delay. With many or all of these routine obstacles it was seldom before nine that we could strike the road, when the day would already be warming up nicely. Thereafter, arrival at destination depended on many imponderables—the condition of the road, the health of the wheezy, asthmatic engine, and the wear of the ominous-looking much-retreaded tyres. Camp sites varied between a PWD Dak Bungalow, a Forest Rest House, and sometimes a vacated *chauri* or disused cowshed. At that time, before Independence, dak and forest bungalows, specially the less frequented out-of-the-way ones, were poorly appointed: a couple of the standard iron bedsteads (without mattress or pillow) and a few wooden chairs and tables, etc. were usually all they could provide; you had thus to travel fully self-contained. Bedding, towels, sheets, buckets, cooking utensils, lamps, crockery, cutlery, etc., all had to be carted round—plus folding camp beds for unexpected cowsheds. Tehmina had a flair for transforming even the dilapidated *chauris*—to which we were sometimes driven at a pinch—into cosy liveable 'homelike' places when a longer halt was involved. On arrival at a camp, while the others were out collecting, she went into action, getting the place swept and tidied up and giving it little womanly touches with the colourful curtains, counterpanes, flower vases and suchlike trifles that she always insisted on carrying around with her: they made all the difference.

With bullock carts or manual porterage, where motor buses were not feasible, it was necessary to fix short distances between camps, perhaps eight or ten miles; with motor transport they seldom exceeded thirty to fifty miles. The process of opening up the specimen boxes, arranging the work tables and general settling-in took a couple of hours, and it was therefore usually late afternoon by the time we were ready for the evening round of specimen collecting. My strategy, refined by experience and circumstances, was to brief my assistant, the taxidermist, and leave to him the job of collecting the commoner birds around the camp. One of the BNHS field assistants who accompanied me on most of my later bird surveys was a young East Indian Christian—as a point of honour his confreres insisted on differentiating him from a mere Goan in those Portuguese colonial days. His name was John Gabriel, a quiet, dependable and amazingly fast bird skinner who turned out excellent bird skins. Only one who has tried skinning a small bird like a Flowerpecker or Leaf Warbler, often badly shot up to begin with, and stuff it not only as a presentable study specimen but also show the minute details of plumage so necessary for subspecific diagnosis, can appreciate what a tricky, patience-trying and time-consuming business it is. Yet I have known Gabriel sitting down to skin after the morning's round of collecting, and finish up to twenty-six clean and excellently prepared small to medium-sized skins before dinner. Gabriel also could be trusted to correctly identify the birds he was told specially to look out for, which made things very satisfactory in every way. Every forenoon when we returned from our respective collecting rounds it was a ritual for me to ask Gabriel what luck he had had, and all too frequently the answer would be the same—his own picturesque and invariable formula—'I tried and tried to get some goodgood birds but saw nothing except this', (dejectedly pulling out the mangled remains of a myna or some other common bird from his haversack) 'so I said "Let's take" '. In the absence of 'goodgood' birds I must confess sometimes having had recourse to the same pragmatic procedure myself, since for subspecific determination common birds are also of importance. By temperament and deportment Gabriel was as satisfactory a field assistant and camp follower as one could wish. His one great drawback was at meals: each time he shovelled in a mouthful his spoon would rattle metalically against his teeth in a way that was normally irritating, but which could become positively maddening to frayed nerves.

From a study of large-scale Survey of India topographical sheets for diverse and promising physical features, and after discussion with local forest staff and village shikaris, areas within a radius of ten miles or so, which could be conveniently investigated on foot, were identified. This general plan worked satisfactorily on the whole during my other regional surveys as well; few biotopes or facies escaped attention and few bird species got away uncollected or unrecorded. This at least is what I had hopefully imagined at the time; it was only years later, after mist netting came into general use, that I realized that a few nocturnal or exceptionally unobtrusive species possibly did manage to evade the reckoning.

The opening gambit of the Hyderabad ornithological survey of October 1931—itself the first of the series of such regional surveys—was Mananur, a largish, sprawling village situated on the Amrabad Plateau at an altitude of 2,000 feet in the Nallamalai Hills—a *taluka* headquarters town in Mahboobnagar district. The excellent reserved forest around was of the mixed moist-deciduous type, with an abundance of teak and *nallamaddi* (*Terminalia tomentosa*)—my first experience of many such sylvan paradises explored subsequently in so many different corners of the country. The Mananur locality stands out vividly in my memory for its wealth of wild animals, including a greater number of tigers than I had ever experienced before.

I recall the thrill of seeing the forest roads covered with the
fresh pug marks of tiger, panther, bear and other wildlife each
early morning as I tramped along them behind the local Chenchu
tracker, and the greater thrill on sighting some of the beasts
themselves, as frequently happened in the course of a morning's
collecting. The second camp, Farahabad, twelve miles to the
south and on a higher plateau (2,800 feet) was earmarked by the
State government for development as a hill station, but the plan
never materialized. It was the home of an Adivasi tribe, the
Chenchus, so well studied and documented by the anthropologist, Fürer-Haimendorf. There was no road up to the
little rest-house on the hill, only a foot track, so the baggage
and equipment had to be carried in head-loads by Chenchu
tribals—men, women and children—*begar* (forced labour) I
fear, raked up by the local *tahsildar*. Their official daily hire, as
I recall in disbelief, was one seer (*c.* 1 kg) of jowar per head.
Payment was in kind, since even up to that time the Chenchus,
living so cut off from 'civilization', had little use for money, so
we were told, and preferred to receive their wages this way. To
pay for services during camp we had brought up a goodly
supply of jowar from the plains. The price of jowar at the time
was Re 1 for twelve seers, which made it easy enough on the
budget.

The atrocious system of *begar*—actually a form of slavery—
persisted in the nizam's state in practice long after it was
abolished by law elsewhere. The *patel* or village headman was
bound to provide manual labour for government work whenever called upon. Therefore he would just pounce upon any
able-bodied male in the village, regardless of whatever he might
be engaged in at the time, and press him into service. The daily
wage of the labourer was fixed by the government, as described
above. In one instance my survey party arrived at an out-of-
the-way forest village, where a relay of porters was to be
available. It was rather late in the morning and the menfolk had
already left for their fields. The *patel* ransacked hut after hut
and found them all empty, till he came upon one where a small,
tired group was lying fast asleep. He roused the men and
promptly collared the lot for our service, in spite of their

protests that they were only professional musicians who had
been hired from a distant village for a wedding here, and were
sleeping off their tiredness after playing music all night. Their
pleading fell on deaf ears; the *patel*, who had had orders from
his *tahsildar*, dragged the men out and they were soon loaded
up to follow us. Fortunately for them, a fresh relay was available
at the next village some five miles away, and I was glad to
release the musicians to go back and resume their slumbers.

Another *tahsildar* had provided me with the official printed
schedule of rates, fixed by the nizam's government some years
before, for supplies to government servants on duty tour—goat
Re 1, chicken 2 annas (= *c*. 12 paise), other things in proportion, and eggs almost for the asking—and all that in Hali (the
nizam's) currency, which was equivalent to two-thirds of the
British Indian. Though no longer wholly valid in 1931, the
price of everything was low enough to make the survey possible
well within the Hyderabad government's subsidy.

At Nelipaka, a backwoods cluster of dilapidated hovels on
the bank of the Godavari river, a few miles from Borgampad,
we were encamped in an abandoned cowshed on the outskirts
of the village. Walls had been improvised from old bamboo
matting which partly kept out the fierce afternoon sun. Word
had gone round that a party of queer Bombayites had come
with the object of shooting every kind of bird found in the
locality and noting down how they tasted. Thus, soon after our
arrival we were besieged by a motley crowd of urchins and
other inquisitive village folk, some of whom offered themselves
as local shikaris and who were in fact well known to be unabashed professional poachers. I was told that a large crocodile came
out every day to bask on a little islet in the river, a few minutes'
walk down the bank. They would inform me when it was next
sighted in case I was interested in shooting it, as in those days I
was indeed ever keen to do. Two days later, as I returned from
the morning's collecting at about noon, a village shikari was
waiting with the news that he had seen the crocodile an hour
before, and he offered to guide me to the spot. Of course, true
to pattern, there was no crocodile when I arrived on the scene,
but while scanning the precincts with binoculars, and the

vegetation along the river's edge, I noticed a black object partially hidden among the marginal reeds, about 200 metres upstream, which could well be the head of a partly submerged crocodile. Closer approach revealed this object to be a bloated human body which was later identified as the old woman who had left her hut in the village after a violent quarrel with her daughter-in-law, and been missing since. To my horror I then realized that the point from where the washing and drinking water for our camp came was directly below this, so that we had obviously been living on the unsavoury decoction of this old lady all the time. The stinking cadaver was fished out by the loudly wailing relations, but it had to await police investigation and a clean report before it could be disposed of. Due to the urgency of the matter, and the 'blue haze' already gathered around the putre-fying carcass, the relations trudged nine miles in the burning sun to the nearest police station. The sub-inspector in charge, however, decided that it was too late in the evening for him to bother: therefore it was not till 7.30 or so next morning that he turned up, mounted on a miserable *tattoo*.

The sub-inspector, no doubt smelling a heaven-sent oppor-tunity, seemed determined to be as difficult as possible, in spite of the piteous pleadings of the bereaved relations and my own remonstrances. He said that Duty made it imperative for him to have a post-mortem conducted and a thorough investigation undertaken before permitting disposal of the remains. And the man was so ostentatiously adamant about this absolutely mandatory procedure that it looked as if the body would have to lie there and befoul the neighbourhood for at least another twenty-four hours. As the officer seemed so righteously bent upon upholding the letter of the law, and finding my arguments of no avail, I set out for the morning's collecting. When I returned three hours later I found the body and its wailing attendants vanished, along with the sub-inspector, and every-thing in the village unexpectedly quiet and normal. It seems that soon after my back was turned the deceased woman's son had been able to make the self-righteous official see reason, and all for fifty rupees, scraped together with great difficulty by the mourning relations. Thereupon, the matter was closed abruptly and to the satisfaction of all concerned. I was reminded by this of the reply a Bombay municipal milk inspector gave to the kindly inquiry of an upcountry friend: 'the pay is small but the income is good'. And this was the general pattern of the processes of officialdom in the dominions of 'His Exalted Highness' the Nizam of Hyderabad in those days. Perhaps not *only* in that state, and maybe not in those days alone.

Every couple of weeks or so, depending on how remote and off-beat the survey localities were, we were obliged to surface from the wilds into 'civilization' and Hyderabad city for refitting—laying in provisions and supplies not procurable in the backwoods. During these breaks we usually stayed with brother Hasham and his family in their pleasant Saifabad home. Hasham was my eldest brother, eighteen years older than I, and the father of Suleiman, my bird-keeping partner in the early Khetwadi days. He had got married-off by our elders to the only daughter (Dilber-un-nissa) of a well-to-do family friend in Hyderabad at the early age of nineteen or so, while still studying law at Bombay. Soon after receiving his law degree he moved over to Hyderabad and set up a precarious legal practice, and the Khetwadi ménage lost personal contact with him thereafter. Suleiman was born a couple of years later and long before Hasham (Hashoobhai as we called him) had found his feet. Thus when Suleiman reached schooling age he was packed off to Bombay to the care of aunt Hamida Begam and uncle Amiruddin, who had more or less adopted and brought up Hasham himself as their own child. Hasham was a deeply religious man in the best sense of the term, never preaching to others and eloquent only by his own silent example. His reputation for honesty and integrity had become a byword in Hyderabad officialdom, and it is to his lasting credit that inspite of walls having ears—residences of important government officials were planted by aspiring or malicious rivals with snooping domestics—his record as a district judge, and later as a judge of the Hyderabad High Court, remained impeccable and unsullied throughout his service. He was not unsociable by nature, but he reserved his intimacies chiefly for the family circle and seldom had much intercourse with

outsiders except at a formal official level. For his own sake this
was perhaps just as well, considering how luxuriantly the
grapevine flourished in the Hyderabad climate of the time.
Indeed so widely and well was his character known and appreciated—his unapproachability as a judge, and his integrity,
uprightness and impartiality—that he was honoured by the
Nizam, Mir Osman Ali Khan, with the title of Nawab Hasham
Yar Jung during his lifetime, and by a self-composed poetical
panegyric after his death, lauding his character and virtues—a
mark of very exceptional royal favour. With the unorthodox
qualities he possessed it was hardly likely that Hasham would
ever have made a materially successful lawyer in the prevailing
nawabi atmosphere of Hyderabad. Thus it was fortunate for
him to get sucked into the nizam's judicial service fairly early in
his struggling legal career.

Because of the great disparity in our ages and the fact of his
being cut off so early from the Bombay household, I had less
rapport with Hasham than with the rest of my brothers and
sisters. Except for occasional school vacations spent in
Hyderabad as children along with Suleiman and his younger
brothers (two) and sisters (four), I hardly had occasion to
know him at that juvenile age. But even then, and later as a
grown-up, there was plenty of occasion to know a great deal *of*
him. Hashoobhai was verily one of God's Good Men, and
though our temperaments and beliefs and outlook on life were
diametrically different, I have deep affection and the highest
admiration and respect for him.

In 1931, at the time the Hyderabad survey was in the field,
the *Journal* of the BNHS was publishing a series of articles on
'The Preservation of Wildlife in the Indian Empire' dealing
with the different provinces and princely states individually. I
was requested by the Society to contribute the section on
Hyderabad State, since I was on the spot and had the opportunity and facilities for collecting first-hand data. Up to 1897
there was, it seems, no restriction as to tiger or any other
shooting. According to the game regulations, introduced only
in 1914, no hunting could be done by anyone in the state
without a government permit, except by the nizam and his

family, and the Paigah nobles and *jagirdars*. But up till 1933 there was no Arms Act in the nizam's dominions, and the state was bristling with guns of every description. They were mostly vintage muzzle-loaders, it is true, but good enough for slaughtering animals at waterholes, which seemed to be the approved method of the poacher, judging from the number of rude *machans* on trees, and pits in the ground near the water's edge, wherever one came across a pool in the forest. I recalled that Captain A.I.R. Glasfurd in his book *Rifle and Romance in the Indian Jungle* (published about 1905)—a favourite and evocative reading of my youthful shikar days—had already remarked on the disastrous effect the unrestricted use of these unlicensed muzzle-loaders was having on the wildlife of the surrounding Deccan country even at that time. In spite of the belated game regulations, therefore, and with no regard by the poacher for season, age or sex of the quarry, the larger animals were disappearing rapidly, a trend that has unfortunately been accelerated by the advent of the jeep since World War II, the change from feudalism to democracy and the consequent all round loosening of control of arms and forest regulations.

My investigations showed that, by and large, the *muntazims* (game wardens) and watchers of the *shikargahs* or royal game preserves were a thoroughly corrupt and 'measly' lot. The information they supplied about local conditions and wildlife was seldom reliable, and it seemed conceivable that a good deal of the poaching—much of it by government officials, high and low—was tolerated by them either actively or through indifference and neglect. No wonder then that Hyderabad State, which in the early years of the nineteenth century included some of the finest tiger and other big-game areas in the country, had been reduced to such a sorry plight a mere hundred years later. A large majority of the state officials—from the taluqdar down to the lowly sub-inspector of police or revenue, including foresters themselves, as well as the numerous *vakils* (lawyers) that thronged the district courts, local businessman and the more prosperous shopkeepers—all claimed the status symbol of having shot at least one tiger, and many two or more. Even with a generous allowance for bravado and idle boasting, an estimate of the enormous population of tigers the state must have held as recently as forty years ago makes comparison with the situation today depressing. Although the nizam himself did not hunt, the two elder princes were accomplished butchers. Around May 1935, soon after my survey, the then heir-apparent, Azam Jah Bahadur, and his party, in the course of thirty-three days' shooting from sybaritic *machans* fitted with a variety of 'home comforts'—including field telephones to report minute-by-minute progress of the tiger during a beat— killed thirty-five tigers, in addition to numerous bears, sambar, and other game in proportion, in the *shikargahs* of Pakhal, Mulug and others.

9

Interlude in the Nilgiris

The Hyderabad State Ornithological Survey was completed in April 1932. Having no fixed abode to retire to while awaiting the result of the negotiations between the BNHS and the Travancore–Cochin governments for a bird survey, we were happy, and indeed lucky, to have been offered by a family friend, Mrs Nundy of Hyderabad, her delightful holiday cottage, 'Mon Abri,' at the quiet little hill-station of Kotagiri in the Nilgiri hills. Till then I had had no experience of the South Indian evergreen rain and shola forests, and the opportunity of living in the Nilgiris for a few months by way of an orientation course for Travancore, as it were, was doubly welcome. The quiet interlude also permitted me to finalize my report on the birds of Hyderabad State which, in turn, helped materially in inducing other unexplored states to follow suit. Kotagiri fifty years ago was a charming but sleepy hill-station, the chosen habitat of a variety of Christian missions, of sects like the Seventh Day Adventists, and others, such as 'One by One Band,' whose names even we had never heard before. Many of the 'civilized' people one came across on walks were retired European missionaries of one brand or another, male and female, most of them old and doddering, who seemingly came up here only to die in comfort. In spite of all its sylvan peacefulness and alluring natural attractions of climate and scenery, Kotagiri was altogether too dull and lifeless a place for active young people to live in, except on a short holiday and for escape from the heat and dust of the plains.

The lack of stimulating, intellectual contacts had begun to

pall on both of us by the end of the second month; it was therefore providential that a chance visit to the government hospital for some minor complaint brought us in touch with the pleasant young medical officer-in-charge, Dr K.M. Anantan, a Keralite who had volunteered as an army doctor in Mesopotamia during World War I. He had retired as a Captain in the Army Medical Corps at the end of the war and gone back into the civil medical employ of the Government of Madras. The amusing doctor and his charming, active young wife—they, like ourselves, had no children—soon became our inseparable companions, and thereafter there was hardly any activity or pleasure that we didn't share together—jungle walks, bird-watching, picnics, motor drives, indoor games, and merry-making. At the end of each month Dr Anantan had to go to Ootacamund, some twenty kilometres away, to draw his salary. He had an ancient two-seater Morris Oxford with a dicky seat into which we squeezed ourselves. The drive to Ooty over the hill road involved many gradients too steep for the tired little car to negotiate without a great deal of coaxing, and at times even some physical aid. We made this an occasion for pleasurable birdwatching and picnicking in and around the beautifully laid out and maintained Botanical Garden, and for listening to the many funny stories and experiences of which the doctor had an inexhaustible supply. All the same, I was not at all sorry when intimation came from the BNHS that the Travancore Durbar had sanctioned a bird survey of the state and wanted to know how soon it could begin.

It was while living at Kotagiri that I had my first meeting with Ralph Morris, a coffee planter in the Biligirirangan hills of the then Mysore State, a first-rate naturalist and big-game hunter, and—later in life—a dedicated wildlife conservationist. His highly readable and perceptive accounts of shikar and natural history experiences in the South-Indian hills, which for some years around the period 1920–40 appeared regularly in the Society's *Journal*, were widely appreciated. Ralph and his very attractive, physically tough and highly competent wife, Heather, were frequent visitors to Kotagiri, to the latter's widowed mother Mrs Kinloch who lived in a lovely bungalow

on the edge of Longwood Shola. Tehmina and I and the
Morrises took to each other from that first meeting at Kotagiri,
and they remained among our dearest and most treasured
friends till they made their respective exits—Tehmina herself
in 1939, Ralph in 1977 and Heather two or three years later.

Ralph and I had long known of each other's interests and
activities through the *Journal* and by personal correspondence.
When he heard of the impending Travancore bird survey, both
he and Heather warmly invited us to spend a few days with
them at their coffee estate prior to commencing the field work.
He suggested Maraiyur in north Travancore as the most convenient point of entry from Kotagiri. That week or ten days at
Honnametti enabled me, with Ralph's intimate knowledge of
the South-Indian jungles, to work out a promising programme
and itinerary for the survey covering all the various physiographical features of the state fairly comprehensively. That
delightful time in the Morrises' comfortable patrician home in
the heart of more or less primeval tiger and elephant-infested
jungle is nostalgic, and also memorable for the intimate insight
it gave us into the life style of a cultured European coffee
planter in South India, and what it took in those near-pioneering
days to make a successful and contented one: physical toughness, unrelenting hard work, dedication to a lonely jungle life
cut off from social contacts and amenities, and complete self-
sufficiency as jack of all trades—carpenter, mason, plumber,
electrician, motor mechanic and general handyman. In addition,
of course, Morris had to be a practical horticulturist with a
good basic knowledge of field botany, plant diseases and insect
pests. He had to have a good command of the local lingo, and
have the ability to control a large labour force with tact and
understanding to keep it ticking happily. Heather had all that it
takes to be a good planter's wife—toughness, pride in her
elegantly appointed, comfortable home, and complete self-
reliance for the multifarious domestic chores, which included a
working knowledge of home medicine, care and management
of infants and milch cows, growing vegetables and gardening,
and a genuine concern for the welfare of labourers and their
families. She, like her husband, was enamoured of the peaceful

'care-free' (as she called it!) jungle life, and earlier on had also been a keen and adventurous big-game hunter—a sport for which the Biligirirangan and associated hills were famous.

Remembering Ralph Morris brings to mind a mystifying and inexplicable episode concerning him that occurred much later. In 1953 the Government of Jammu & Kashmir requested the BNHS to depute a team of two or three experienced conservationists to study the status of wildlife in the Dachigam and other sanctuaries (then 'game reserves') in the state, and advise them on their proper management. An obvious choice was Morris, but he was then suffering from a troublesome slipped disc, which brought on crippling, excruciating pain from time to time. However, he was greatly tempted by the opportunity to see the country and its wildlife and had haltingly agreed. We started from camp in Srinagar one morning on ponies when he was already in some pain, and I was wondering how he would stand the long and bumpy ride. We were walking our two ponies abreast when his horse put one foot into a rat-hole and stumbled, vaulting Ralph over its head and sending him flat on his back on the hard ground. I feared he had broken his back and that would be the end of the survey. Wonder of wonders! Ralph soon got up, rather shaken but with the pain completely gone and never to return!

Of all my regional bird surveys between the years 1930 and 1950—which I regard as the most productive period of my career—perhaps the one that gave me the greatest satisfaction both as to the fieldwork and writing up its results was the ornithological survey of Travancore–Cochin which later provided the basis for my book *The Birds of Kerala*. Apart from the matchless beauty of the South-Indian hills, the southern extremity of the Sahyadri or Western Ghats, and the lushness and grandeur of their primeval evergreen forests, there was something special in much of their animal and plant life that stood out distinctly from the rest of the peninsula. The curious similarity between the fauna and flora of the higher hills of Kerala forming part of the southern Western Ghats complex (Nilgiri, Palni, etc.) on the one hand and the Eastern Himalaya, West China, Burma and Malaysia on the other, had been remarked on by earlier naturalists. The two end-populations are separated often by more than 2,000 kilometres of very different terrain ecologically, and the problem is to explain this anomaly. The case of fish species inhabiting rivers and mountain streams in the two areas and nowhere in between is the most puzzling of all, since fish obviously could not have reached here without some kind of water interconnection. To my mind the most plausible explanation seems the one postulated after a critical study of the fish fauna and geology, geomorphology and climatology of the peninsula by the renowned biologist Dr Sundar Lal Hora in his 'Satpura Hypothesis', which assumes a one-time connection of the Eastern Himalayas with south-west India, westward over the Rajmahal hills gap and the Satpura mountain range, then southward down the Western Ghats to their southern extremity, and on into Sri Lanka before it was severed from the mainland. The connecting highlands have been worn down through the ages and the South-Indian populations are thus the residue of a once continuous distribution, now living in a sort of refugium. This problem lent a special fascination to my bird study in Travancore/Cochin.

The report of the ornithological survey, published serially in the *Journal* of the BNHS, drew gratifying reviews and comments in scientific periodicals and from individual scientists whose opinions I specially valued. Hugh Whistler wrote (8.1.1936): 'I was glad to see the tribute to your excellent field work in Travancore in *The Ibis*. Ticehurst is a very critical editor, and if he praises a thing it is praise worth having.' Ticehurst's favourable review was particularly gratifying to my ego because, since the Stresemann and Stanford Burma bird-collection episode in 1929, he had never been overtly cordial to me. Ernst Mayr, then Curator of Birds at the Natural History Museum, New York, said (27.1.1936): 'The most valuable part of your report is the notes on the life history and ecology of the observed species. I would like to congratulate you on your admirable treatment of the subject which I hope will set a standard for similar surveys.' Professor Kenneth Mason of the Geography Department, Oxford University (formerly Surveyor-

General to the Government of India) wrote back to Whistler, who had sent him the Introduction to my account of the ornithology of Travancore and Cochin, saying:

> I found it of very great geographical interest, for the author has gone out of his way to base his conclusions on geographical factors 'influencing the bird life'. As far as I know the geography of southern India, he has all the salient points—and has used them to the best advantage. A minor point is that geologists, I believe, now consider that the crest of the old watershed lay to the west of Penisular India, somewhere in the neighbourhood of where the Laccadive corals are now built, and that the Ghats are faulted by the subsidence of the whole range crest. Southern peninsular India is therefore less than an eastern half, and the present waterparting is east of the ancient one. It does not, of course, affect Sálim Ali's argument, but in fact enforces it.

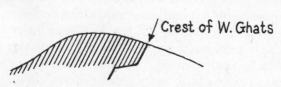

I have included this very useful information here since it may be new to many interested in the geotectonics of peninsular India, as it was to me.

E.C. Stuart Baker, the author of the second edition of the bird volumes in the Fauna of British India series, who was the Secretary of the British Ornithologists' Union at the time, after acknowledging receipt of 'the copies of your very excellent work on the Travancore birds', said: 'I must say I was very grieved at your little note about "inaccuracies being typical" of my work in the Fauna. I am afraid Whistler and Ticehurst have imbued you with their personal antagonism to me. . . . In 12 years I wrote 8 volumes, but I had to average 10 to 12 hours work daily to get it done.' In reply, after expressing great admiration for his achievement, which I truly felt, and regretting the grief inadvertently caused, I assured him that my criticism was made independently and in perfect good faith and not prompted by others. I added 'There can be no advance in scientific knowledge unless this [criticism of work] was so.' All of which shows that ornithologists are also human.

One of the prize specimens obtained in Travancore which was casually misidentified by me at the time as a Crested Hawk-Eagle, and at first sight by Whistler as Jerdon's Baza, proved on closer examination at the British Museum to be a Feathertoed Hawk-Eagle (*Spizaetus nipalensis kelaarti*), according to Whistler 'one of the rarest birds of prey in the world in collections, I suppose. The bird was quite new to me. Curiously enough Baza is a sort of miniature of it.' The specimen had come into my possession quite fortuitously: the bird was killed with a faggot of wood stacked as engine fuel by a fireman of the Cochin Forest Tramway at the hill-top terminal station, Parambikulam, as it swooped on some of his chickens. As I happened to be camping at Kuriarkutti a few miles down the line, and the man knew we were after birds, he just stopped the train in passing by our camp and handed the bird over. I must admit that because I thought it was just an ordinary Crested Hawk-Eagle and I was short of packing space for large birds, I was not exceedingly pleased at the time. However, it was too good a specimen to lose, and since the survey collection was particularly weak in birds of prey, I managed somehow, after much inward grumbling, to accommodate the skin, though it was a thorough nuisance each time it came to packing and repacking for a camp shift. I was therefore specially pleased that it had justified itself so well.

For richness and diversity of bird life Kerala stands, in my estimation—at least stood at the time of the survey fifty years ago—as undisputed No.1. There were certain localities in particular, for example Thattakad on the Periyar river in nothern Travancore, which linger in my memory as the richest bird habitat in peninsular India I have known—comparable only with the Eastern Himalaya. Since the survey, and particularly since our Independence, I have visited Kerala every few years and been more and more depressed and scandalized each time by the mindless vandalism being perpetrated by successive state governments and crooked politicians in the devastation of virgin evergreen forests to settle repatriates, or for so-called 'development' projects such as dams for hydro-electric power and raw material for wood-based industries. Thattakad has become a travesty of its former self, with most of the superb natural forest replaced by monoculture of commercial species to pander to industrial development, or drowned in the huge reservoir created by the damming of the Periyar river. Continuingly, some 1,500 hectares of virgin evergreen forest are being clear-felled every year to give way to eucalyptus, rubbber and oil palm. Thousands of hectares of prime evergreen and moist-deciduous mixed forest in the Parambikulam area, memorable for the romantic Forest Tramway, have been clear-felled for teak plantation or drowned under the water-spread, while the ding-dong battle between conservationists and the Kerala government to save Silent Valley, imminently threatened with a similar fate, may only be temporarily over.

From an old household account book of my wife's, salvaged from miscellaneous junk, in which she had kept detailed figures of the Travancore–Cochin survey expenses, I notice with much astonishment and a sense of utter disbelief that for the entire five months of fieldwork in the two states the total expenditure came to Rs 2,458. This included two separate return train journeys from Bombay for the two of us and one servant, and considerable excess luggage. It also included meals for four people, the servant's pay, private bus transport for camp shifts, the daily wages of shikaris and jungle guides, and all other odds and ends. The salary, field allowance and train travel of the bird skinner, the cost of ammunition (Rs 9 per hundred .410 dust, and Rs 10½ of 20-bore short cartridges), preservatives and postage of specimen parcels, etc. were borne by the BNHS. The two state governments had together contributed Rs 4,500 towards the survey, so that on completion of the work I still found myself Rs 2,000 to the good. It seems truly unbelievable how much it was possible to accomplish in those days and with how little, and it is fortunate for Indian ornithology that so much unworked ground could be covered by the various regional surveys while I was available gratis, and time was not of the essence. With the present level of field researchers' salaries and the rocketing cost of goods and services, such unhurried in-depth surveys are unthinkable, and would be completely beyond the means of an unendowed institution like the BNHS.

10

Dehra Dun and Bahawalpur
1934–9

Four years after the return from Germany, when I still remained without a permanent job and home, we thought it was time to stop living like gypsies or inflicting ourselves on friends and relations, and to look out for a pleasanter, quieter and less expensive place to live than Bombay, yet not an entirely social and intellectual backwater. My brother Hamid, who on retirement from the ICS had settled down in Mussoorie, suggested Dehra Dun at the foot of the hill-station as just such a place, and we accepted his suggestion with alacrity. To the attractions I had dreamed of earlier there would now be the added one of living close to Hamid, who was not only my favourite brother but also my *beau ideal* of a rational, this-worldly human being, and one I greatly admired.

From my boyhood days, and long before I had ever set eyes upon them, I had a romantic craving for the Himalaya and often day-dreamed that in later life, if I ever got the option of choosing a place to settle in, it would most certainly be somewhere among the foothills of the Himalaya where I would have at my doorstep, as it were, all the things that mattered most to me—beautiful forests, magnificent scenery, good birding, trekking in the mountains and plenty of opportunities for game shooting and 'naturalizing'. What could be more idyllic? A business trip to the Forest Research Institute, Dehra Dun in 1925, on behalf of my employers' match factory at Bombay for information about suitable matchwoods, had given me my first sight of the Himalaya and revived that cherished dream with redoubled longing. Through a kaleidoscopic shuffling of fate my dream had now come true, at least partially. Tehmina and I had spent five of the happiest years of our lives in Dehra Dun among loving friends and stimulating intellectual company and enchanting surroundings, and with a sense of fulfilment in my own case. These good times were cut short by a great personal tragedy in my life. After a comparatively unrisky surgical operation Tehmina developed blood poisoning and died in July 1939. Now that she was gone I had a hard decision to face: to stay on or to migrate. My youngest sister Kamrunnisa— Kamoo for short—two years my senior—and her husband Hassan (son of my father's elder brother Faizulhussain) lovingly insisted on my giving up living alone, and very kindly invited me to come to Bombay and share their beautiful home at Pali Hill, Bandra. Even up to that time Pali Hill was a quiet and delightfully green residential suburb.

I had never been enamoured of city life and the idea of my voluntarily returning to Bombay after our near-idyllic years in Dehra Dun was not appealing. Yet without Tehmina life in Dehra Dun had not been, and could never be, the same. The main considerations that decided my fate were, firstly, the loving offer of Kamoo and Hassan, who had always been particularly dear and close to us both, and the presence in Bombay of the Natural History Society with its excellent bird collection, library, congenial colleagues and other facilities for the continuance of my work. Leaving Dehra Dun was a painful wrench, but in retrospect I feel it was the correct decision and it has been largely responsible for whatever success I have achieved since then. The cloistered seminary-like atmosphere I enjoyed in the smooth-running and cheerful Hassan Ali household, and freedom from housekeeping and other tiresome chores and headaches, allowed me to devote all my time to ornithological work. I cannot thank Kamoo and Hassan enough for the affection and forbearance I unfailingly received from them. I hope that they will accept the resulting recognitions it has brought to me and the family, and to the country, as a slight recompense and as a token of my gratitude to them.

It was in August 1934, while living in Dehra Dun, that I drew up a modest project proposal for research in Economic Ornithology. From quite early on I had felt that there were immense possibilities and potential for detailed studies on the food and feeding habits of birds in their bearing on our two basic industries, namely agriculture and forestry. This feeling was encouraged by the researches and publications of, and by my correspondence with, workers like Forbes, McAttee and Cottam in the Bureau of Biological Survey, USA, Collinge in the UK, and others in Germany, Japan and elsewhere. The proposal was submitted through Dr W. Burns, the Director of Agriculture, Bombay Presidency, for the consideration of the then 'Imperial' (now Indian) Council of Agricultural Research (ICAR).

In the prologue to the scheme I pointed out the vitally important role of birds in agriculture, horticulture and forestry in India which had not been recognized or appreciated; that their impact was of a dual nature, meaning that while birds could on the one hand be highly destructive to cereal crops and orchard fruit, they could on the other be highly beneficial in controlling the ravages of insect pests and other vermin such as rodents, since these largely constituted the food of many species, and exclusively of some. I suggested that in a country like ours, which leans so heavily on agriculture and forestry, their impact was of a very special significance and that since the economic status of one and the same species often fluctuated between beneficial and harmful—from hatching to adulthood and from season to season—it was essential for a meaningful assessment of a bird's economic status to study its entire life history and bionomics. In the case of species whose diet consists partly of vegetable and partly of animal matter, this was particularly important. Apart from the nature and quantity of the food consumed, which can usually but not always be determined by analyses of stomach contents in the laboratory, it is quite as important to know the bird's feeding habits, food preferences and behaviour, and its population dynamics, by methodical field study.

Soft-bodied insects are usually so mashed up inside a bird's stomach that it is seldom possible to identify them. This difficulty can be substantially resolved by field observation of the feeding behaviour of the bird and the nature of its prey. Similarly, many species of birds are adapted for a diet of flower nectar, in the process of procuring which they effect cross-pollination by transferring pollen adhering to their head feathers, and are thus of great usefulness in the propagation of plants. Stomach examination of such birds will show no more than some colourless liquid and is unlikely to disclose the identity of the source (species of flower), unless the bird has been observed actually feeding from a particular flower. To establish the overall economic impact of a bird species in a given area it is also necessary to take periodical censuses of its local population—its biomass—and to acquire precise knowledge of its ecology, breeding biology and population dynamics.

All this implies a comprehensive co-ordinated study of the life history of the bird by a trained field ornithologist, assisted in the laboratory by an experienced entomologist, and a botanist capable of identifying seeds and plant remains. It also implies the ready availability of a representative seed collection and other comparative reference material of this type. Such research had been and is still carried out extensively in the UK and many other countries of Europe. In the USA the erstwhile Bureau of Biological Survey—a branch of the US Department of Agriculture—has accumulated a vast amount of information of sterling pragmatic value to agriculture and forestry, besides the purely scientific aspect. Mr W.L. McAttee, the Principal Biologist of the Survey, whose opinion on my scheme was sought, considered it 'very well conceived', and among other useful suggestions mentioned that rather than trying to show the controlling influence of birds on specific insect pests, which is seldom spectacular or clear-cut enough to be demonstrable, the economic argument for the protection of birds should rest on the known tendencies of their feeding habits in relation to the organisms.

How naively optimistic I was in imagining that the scheme would materialize shortly, or ever, became clear only when efforts had to be finally abandoned after two years of a seemingly interminable ding-dong correspondence and statements and clarifications before individuals and committees galore. And this in spite of the strongest support the scheme had received from the BNHS and from Dr Burns and other influential members of the Bombay Provincial Agriculture Research Committee. The procedure in those days (it may be so today for all I know!) was chiefly on the principle of judicious 'back-scratching', or what may be regarded as a refined form of horse-trading. The various provinces each put up their various development or research schemes to the ICAR (the central Imperial Council of Agricultural Research) for funding. These were then scrutinized by an Advisory Committee representing the various provinces and miscellaneous 'experts'. If Bombay supported a Punjab scheme—in other words if Bombay scratched Punjab's back—there was a reasonable chance of the compliment being returned, and vice versa. This was the general plan of operation. My economic ornithology research scheme, after being tossed about a couple of times on various pretexts, finally got approved *in principle* but found seventeenth place on the priorities list of ICAR. Dr Burns, who had zealously supported and piloted the scheme from its conception through all its vicissitudes, wrote in disgust and after much previous bitter experience that since under the circumstances it was unpredictable when the scheme's turn for funding might come, if ever, it would be just as well for me to forget about it and start chasing a different hare. It was a sad disappointment, but not entirely unexpected from the way things had begun to look. The experience was an object lesson to me of the role of politicking in public affairs, even those of scientific and national concern. It is a wonder how any such schemes ever manage to scrape through the tortuous official corridors and legalistic hurdles, and past the manoeuvrings of the inevitable 'opposition' and all the tangled skeins of red tape at every step in their progress.

Hugh Whistler and I were both anxious to follow up the gratifying collection made in Jodhpur State in 1933 by one of the BNHS field collectors, V.S. Lapersonne, with a more comprehensive survey of the entire Rajputana desert, the bird life of which was imperfectly known. My sights were set on

Bahawalpur State as the next target. I was eager also to revive my association with the desert, remembered from the school vacations with my brother Hamid on his duty tours in Sind. The bird survey of Bahawalpur State in early 1939 was made possible through the personal interest of the British Resident of the Rajputana States Agency and one Mr Atkinson, a retired British Indian policeman, then employed as 'Shikar Officer' in the Ameer's government—both of whom were active members and supporters of the BNHS. Incidentally, Bahawalpur was the last of the field surveys in which Tehmina participated. Sadly, she died only a few months after it was completed.

The fat young Ameer had the reputation of being a consummate playboy, with all that it implies in the context of Indian princes. On being asked what had impressed him most during his 'finishing' grand tour of England as heir apparent a few years previously, he was reported to have answered 'The actresses' legs'! Some of his courtiers and hangers-on seemed to be around solely to pander to his extraordinary whims. One, who apparently held the portfolio of Pornography, upon learning I was interested in Mughul miniatures, specially of animals, drew me aside and as a mark of special favour to a special guest produced from a locker a number of Mughul and Rajput miniature paintings of which he said H.H. was particularly fond. As paintings they were exquisitely executed and finished, but they all depicted half-dressed princes (though still with bejewelled 'dastar' on their heads) and their ladies appropriately unclad, in ingenious and impossible positions that would put even Khajuraho in the shade.

It was the hospitable practice of the Bahawalpur government to treat all announced visitors to the capital as state guests for the first three days. After that they were expected to abide by the Guest House tariff. However, a uniquely naive feature of the state's hospitality was that guests were classified as First Class and Second Class. You remained in the dark about your status until you saw what was on your breakfast plate next morning. For, prominently displayed on the wall opposite the dining table, was the Key to the diagnosis. The notice had two columns listing clearly what a First Class guest should expect for his meals, and what the other of lower status: items like 'Ist Class guest 2 eggs, 2nd Class guest 1 egg. Ist Class guest 2 toasts, 2nd Class guest 1 toast'—and so on down the menu. It was an unambiguous but rather brutal way of making you see yourself as the state saw you. It was therefore some relief to find two eggs each on our tray next morning!

The Bahawalpur survey provided excellent opportunities for looking a bit more closely into the problem of the camouflaging coloration of desert animals—a subject that has always fascinated me. Meinertzhagen, who had made a special study of desert birds and life conditions in African and Asian deserts, had postulated with sound supporting evidence that the density of humidity in the atmosphere controls the amount of ultraviolet radiation penetrating to the earth and all life thereon. The very low humidity in the desert allows a higher percentage of ultraviolet rays to come through, whereas saturated air greatly impedes this process. Thus the greater the exposure to ultraviolet radiation the greater the paleness (as in the desert soil and the animals on it); conversely the less the ultraviolet radiation the darker the soil and the animal inhabitants thereon. It would seem that the same factor or factors that make the desert soil pale coloured are also responsible for making its inhabitants desert coloured and less visible in their surroundings. After drenching in a chance rain shower, I observed that the sandy coloration of desert birds, like the Desert Finch-Lark and the Desert Courser, darkened to exactly the same shade of brown as the sodden soil upon which they found themselves. The birds, whose pale sandy coloration was of obliterative value to them in an environment of pale dry desert sand, now enjoyed the same advantage when the soil was rain-sodden and considerably darker. This tends to support Meinertzhagen's suggestion that it may be the same common factor that is responsible both for the similarity in coloration of desert animals and their environment. I felt gratified when, after reading the Bahawalpur report, Meinertzhagen wrote to me: 'I was much interested in your observation on the effect of rain on plumage. It is curious how these obvious little truths get overlooked, and I think there might be a great deal in what you say. I hope you will allow me to use the idea in my Morocco paper.'

1. Father and Mother with five. Four more to come! *c.* 1889.
(Photo by Ibrahim Ahmedi)

2. Two of the five, plus the 'four more to come', 1902. SA on stool at right.
(Photo by Shamsuddin Lukmanji)

3: 'Gathering of the Clan' at uncle Badruddin Tyabji's Somerset House estate, Warden Road, Bombay, 1902. A traditional annual fixture. SA in middle of front row in black *sherwani*. Tehmina seventh from right in second row from top: the little girl in cap and curls.

4. At Khetwadi, with
brother Hamid and sister
Kamoo. *c.* 1905

5. Tehmina and her brother, Sarhan, in
London, *c.* 1905 or 6.
(Photo by W. Whiteley Ltd., photographers)

6. SA, *c.* 1910, in Hyderabad (at Hashoobhai's).

7. Amiruddin Tyabji (father/uncle), August 1910. *(Photo by Shamsuddin Lukmanji)*

8. Amir Manzil, the family house, at Khetwadi, Bombay, c. 1912. Window (top right) of 'maternity ward', where the entire series of us, five brothers and four sisters, were born between 1878 and 1896.

9. On the 'Zenith' motorcycle, with Jabir (pillion) and N.P. Gandhi (sidecar). Tavoy, July 1916.

0. Tehmina at her father's rented flat in Adenwala Mansion, Chowpati, Bombay, 1917.

11. My biology teacher at St. Xavier's College, Prof. J.P. Mullan, 1918.

12. Rev. Fr. Ethelbert Blatter, S.J., an inspiration to biology, 1918.

13. Hugh Whistler, *c.* 1917.

To dear J. S. with
much love from S. T.
27. Decem. 1920.

14. Tehmina, Jabir, Kamoo, SA, Saad, Safia. Tavoy, 1920.

15. Royal Lakes, Rangoon, 1919. Tehmina, Aamir, Akhtar with Nadir and Ahsan (aged *c.* 6)

16. At the cottage in Civil
Lines, Tavoy, 1922.

17. The evergreen optimist,
B. Ribbentrop. Tavoy,
1922.

18. Timber camp hut,
Kyaukmedoung, Tavoy, 1922.
Jamsetji (on pony), Ribbentrop, Haq
(manager).

19. BNHS's taxidermy laboratory at Phipson's. McCann at work, 1926.

20. Bullocks extricating 'Jane' from difficulties, October 1927.

21. Tehmina and 'Jane', the Austin Seven, 1927.

22. Tehmina and 'Jane' with 'dead deer'. Solapur, 1928.

23. My guru—Prof. Erwin Stresemann. Heligoland, October 1929.

24. 'Latifia', Kihim. Tehmina and Farhat, *c*. September 1930.

25. Hyderabad Survey. Camp Teppal Margoo, Utnoor, Adilabad district, 1930.

26. Collector's duty tour, camp in Kolaba district, 1931. Hamid, Sharifa, Tehmina.

27. Jungle transport. Hyderabad State Ornithological Survey, 1931.

28. V.I.P. Coach, Cochin Forest Tramway, 1933.

29. Eldest brother Hasham Moiz-ud-din—Nawab Hasham Yar Jung Bahadur, *c.* 1946. On retirement as a judge in the Nizam's High Court, Hyderabad.

30. Abbas Tyabji (uncle). Mussoorrie, *c.* 1935. *(Photo by Nadir Tyabji)*

31. At the Ghana, Bharatpur, March 1937.

32. Sahebzada Saiduzzafar Khan on 'Noorunnissa', with his daughter Hamida on 'Noorkhan'. Dehra Dun, 1936.

33. On the head of the big Buddha, Bamian. Looking south towards Koh-e-Baba, Afghanistan, April 1937.
(Photo by R. Meinertzhagen)

34. Bivouac by Surkhab River after the lorry accident. Afghanistan, May 1937. *(Photo by R. Meinertzhagen)*

35. The Mehmandar buying cotton in the weekly bazaar, for stuffing birds. Dana village, Afghanistan, May 1937. *(Photo by R. Meinertzhagen)*

36. Bound for tern breeding islet off Gorai, near Bombay, 1943.

37. Wild Ass *vs.* Domestic(s)—DeSouza, Laurie Baptista, Ibrahim—weighing in the field. Pung Bet, near Adesar, Kutch, *c.* 1943.

38. Sir Peter Clutterbuck, mounted for Flamingo City. Great Rann of Kutch, 1945.

39. Arthur Foot and his wife, Sylvia—'The Feet'—were among our closest Dehra Dun friends ever since Arthur came as the founding headmaster of the Doon School in 1935.

40. Bastar Survey, 1948. Before the days of the four-wheel drive. The station wagon in trouble.

41. Greeted by David and Elizabeth Lack on arrival at the 1950 International Ornithological Congress, Uppsala, causing wonderment among some delegates at my timing, having 'ridden out all the way from India'.

42. With house guest Dillon Ripley, at 46 (then 33) Pali Hill, 28 May 1947.

43. On top of Lipu Lekh pass, 16,700 ft., W. Tibet, 1945.

44. Gelong and Lappha loading yak. Tugging with teeth and heaving
with body weight. W. Tibet, 1945.

45. With Narayanswamy at his ashram, Sosa, Almora district, 1945.

46. Crossing meandering stream, Barkha Plain, W. Tibet, 1945. (Mt Kailas in background)

47. A 'jongpen' (local governor) on tour with bodyguards, Barkha Plain, W. Tibet, 1945.

48. With Loke Wan Tho above Pahalgam, Kashmir, 1951. Note my plastic raincoat, nibbled by a cow when hung up to dry!

49. R. Meinertzhagen, Theresa Clay, E.P. Gee. Doyang Tea Estate, Assam, 1952.

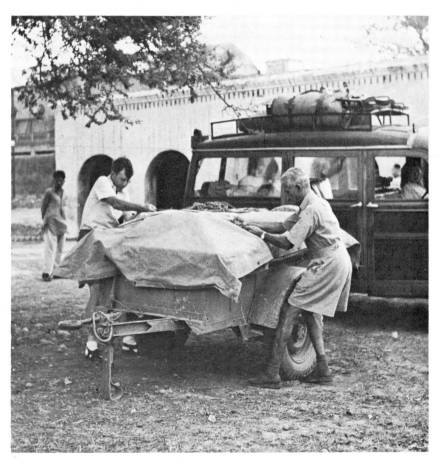

50: Loading up at Pathankot. Birding trip to Kashmir (1951) with the Lokes and 'Hawk' (left). *(Photo by Wan Tho Loke)*

51. On the trail in Sikkim—Loke Wan Tho recovering breath, 1955.

52. Birding in Keoladeo Ghana (Chris in punt), Bharatpur, January 1957. *(Photo by Wan Tho Loke)*

53. In the early days of bird ringing: nestling waterbirds and hand punched rings. Bharatpur, *c.* 1958.

54. Sea turtle egg-laying on a beach in Trengganu. E. Coast, Malaya, *c.* 1960. *(Midnight photo by Wan Tho Loke)*

55. 'House-hunting' female Baya (lower nest) on inspection visit. Chembur, July, *c.* 1956.

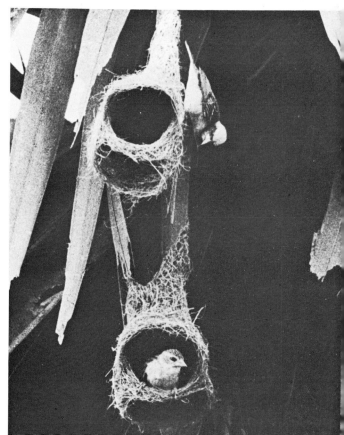

56. Nesting colony of Edible-nest Swiftlets in Loke's garage, Fraser's Hill, Malaya, 1962. *(Photo by Wan Tho Loke)*

57. Collecting swallows, Assam, 1963. *(Photo by E.P. Gee)*

58. Brig. J.E. (Jack) Clutterbuck, R.E.—a kindred spirit and inestimable jungle companion in pre-Partition days—and his wife Mary. Yeovil, 1966. He retired as Chief Engineer, G.I.P. Railway, in 1948, married, and settled down to farming in Somerset.

59. R.E. Hawkins in his office (O.U.P. Bombay), late 1969.

60. The survivors in *c.* 1970. SA, Farhat, Kamoo.

61. The Hassan Ali's, No 46 Pali Hill, my shared home for forty years. (*Photo by Shabid Ali*)

62. William Shakespeare's a master of words
And a tusker a leader of herds
But wherever you fare
Over land, sea or air

R.E. Hawkins (left) amuses an audience gathered to celebrate the release of *Handbook*, Vol. 10. Among the amused listeners of the limerick are SA (right), Ravi Dayal (centre), and Mrs Gandhi.

63. Being presented the Padma Vibhushan by the President of India,
3 April 1976.

64. With Mrs Indira Gandhi after investiture of the Padma Vibhushan. *(Photo by Anant S. Desai, press photographer)*

65. Conversing with Mrs Gandhi after the release of *Handbook*, Vol. 10.

THE INTERNATIONAL JURY FOR

The J. Paul Getty Wildlife Conservation Prize of the World Wildlife Fund

HAS SELECTED FOR 1975

SÁLIM A. ALI

Creator of an environment for conservation in India, your work over fifty years in acquainting Indians with the natural riches of the subcontinent has been instrumental in the promotion of protection, the setting up of parks and reserves, and indeed the awakening of conscience in all circles from government to the simplest village Panchayat. Since the writing of your own book, the Book of Indian Birds which in its way was the seminal natural history volume for everyone in India, your name has been the single one known throughout the length and breadth of your own country, Pakistan and Bangladesh as the father of conservation and the fount of knowledge on birds. Your message has gone high and low across the land and we are sure that weaver birds weave your initials in their nests, and swifts perform parabolas in the sky in your honor. For your lifelong dedication to the preservation of bird life in the Indian subcontinent and your identification with the Bombay Natural History Society as a force for education, the World Wildlife Fund takes delight in presenting you with the second J. Paul Getty Wildlife Conservation Prize. • February 19, 1976.

J. Paul Getty
J. Paul Getty

His Royal Highness
The Prince of The Netherlands

66. Citation of the J. Paul Getty Wildlife Conservation Prize, 1976.

67. Alfresco taxidermy. Shamgong, Bhutan, 1967. With Mary and Dillon Ripley. (*Photo by Peter Jackson*)

68. With Dillon Ripley and Mary at I.I.T. Powai—BNHS centennial symposium. December 1983. (*Photo by T.N.A. Perumal*)

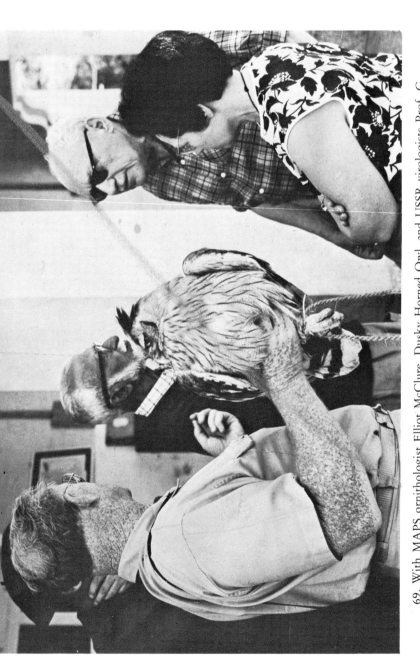

69. With MAPS ornithologist Elliot McClure, Dusky Horned Owl, and USSR virologists Prof. G. Netsky and Dr Vera Obukhora. Bharatpur, 1967. *(Photo by Peter Jackson)*

70. Prince Philip, International President, W.W.F., with Executive Committee members of BNHS, 1984. (*Photo by Liberty Photos*)

71. BNHS team birding in Keoladeo National Park, 1980.
(Photo by Peter Jackson)

1 Facsimile of a letter from Hugh Whistler to the author, dated 31 March 1936. (cont'd overleaf)

Calder House.
Battle.
31.3.36.

My dear Salim Ali:

Meanwhile a few more notes on the Travancore birds which now brings them up practically to as far as I have got in the E. Ghats survey. Some more will be ready as term as the fearful moving will allow me to work is here again. We are now shifting the Cabinets where I used to work. I have been struggling with the Terns — which as far as the marine species are concerned are very difficult as many races have been named as so few specimens from breeding colonies are available.

1 (cont'd from overleaf) Facsimile of a letter from Hugh Whistler to the author, dated 31 March 1936.

Did I tell you that on examining critically my Tibetan Tern from highest Kashmir on of them proves to be the Arctic Tern — near to the Indian list. It is in full breeding plumage (July) with flight enlarged organs, but it must have been a lost vagrant — All the same an interesting record.

Your account of the Satara feat sounds interesting and it will be excellent if the Survey can any come of.

Please forgive a hasty letter. With kindest regards

Yours very sincere
Hugh Whistler.

2 Facsimile of a letter from Erwin Stresemann to the author, dated 14 April 1956. (cont'd overleaf)

2 (cont'd from overleaf) Facsimile of a letter from Erwin Stresemann to the author, dated 14 April 1956.

3 Facsimile of the author's field notes on *Anthus rufulus* (cont'd overleaf)

④

Anthus rufulus (contd.)

Cochin State (contd.) Mr. Kall's shooting - box (above Travellers' Bungalow); Trichur,

22.-23. xii.'33 On lawns re Palace grounds!; Manjaddana (S.L.) 24.12.'33!

25.xii.33 Sp. No. 1004 ♂ (t=7×5) Pairs on wet grassland by backwater paddy fields!

Dehra Dun (2500') 15.VII.'34 Pairs occasionally in stubble & short grass oft. cultivation. Not abundant!; 24.VII.34 One viciously chasing a ♀. of Hirundo smithii on bank of stream at 'Robbi ghat' Nesting!; 25 Aug.'34 One on grassland nr Rajpanna. Apparent resident in small numbers!; 25.5.35 Pairs on scraggy grassland by Rajpanna!; 29.7.35 Apparent-ly the only pipit now present. Pairs or 3s & together occasional in grass & short grass patches in Rajpanna bed! Resident species; 17.3.'36 One tugging at & pulling out blades of dry grass from path in compound & gathering a

wisp - mouthful. before flying off! Early morning. Nestlings
commenced!; 10 Apr.'36 On ploughed fallow there treads. Rufanula, a
large half-fledged chick, fluttering but unable to fly. Stub tail;
long tufts of down above & on central & behind each eye. Iris brown,
mouth bright orange, gape yellowish cream - colour! Concern of parents
expressed by flying about such feeble chip. chip - chip re! fluttering in air ca 15-120 ft. up, sailing down to ground & moving & held
low! tail raised thus ✏, rising again; 'ejaculating'!

Bhopal State. C.J. Jaitkari (ca. 1300') 2.2.'38 ♂ 249 ♀ (wailei!) in farm field!; Bhopal Lake
    4.2.'38!; Chanderi (ca. 1450') 9.4.'38 ♂ 635 ♂ (5×4 n.n.) wailei!;
                                                                    (wailei!)
Indore State. C.J. Mandleshwar 5.9.38 Choti Tank, ♂♀ 789 ♀, 790 ♀ - No more!
Gwalior - Sardarpur (ca. 1650') 16.9.'38 ♂ 863 ♀ (wailei!); 17.9.'38!;
Bihar: Raxaul (ca. 1000') 11.3.37! (wailei!?)

(Contd. over)

Anthus rufulus (contd.)

Mysore State: Bardipur (ca. 3800') 28.11.39 Spp. 151 ♂, 152 ♂ (rufulus) Several solos / loose pairs on wet, grassy margin of Kargala tank!; Antarsanté (ca. 2500') 28.11.39 Sp. 190 ♂ (rufulus); 30.11.39 Sp. 205 ♂ (rufulus); 1.12.39 Sp. 230 ♀ (rufulus)

*thermophilus On sparse scrub fallow nr. Begür; Kārāpūr (ca. 2500') 4.12.39 Spp. 258 ♀, 258 *, 259 ♂ Dodballāpur (ca. 2900') 26.12.39 Spp. 453 ♀, 454 ♀ (A.t. trivialis), 27.12.39 Sp. 470 ♀ (A.t. trivialis); 28.12.39 Sp. 483 ♂ (5x5mm. ~ rufulus); Saklespur (ca. 3000' - Hassan Dist.) 16.1.40 Spp. 650 ♂ 5x5mm., 651 ♂ 8x6mm. (rufulus), Bābābudan Hills (Kemmangūndi, ca. 4500') 23.1.40 Sp. 722 ♂ (rufulus); Kolār Gold Fields, 21.2.40!; Biligirirangan Hills (ca. 5000') 5.3.40!;

Bombay Presy: Trombay Hill (Salsette) 14.2.42 Solo on bare patch at ca 1000 ft.!; Khandala (ca.1800')21.3.43!

Kutch: Godsar (Bhuj environs) 12.8.43 Sp. 51 ♂ undev. (wader), W 85, B 16.5, Tar. 28, T 58 Hind-claw 13. In heavy general moult, wings, tail, body. The first and only

3 (*cont'd from overleaf*) Facsimile of the author's field notes on *Anthus rufulus*.

in Kutch during a whole week!; Chaduva (Bhuj Dist) 19.8.43 2 pairs by Pragsar Tank! White outer restrices at once diagnostic from larks; Ratnal (Bhuj Dist) Sp. 194 o? imm. skull soft, W 84, B 15, Tars. 24, T 63 (*Avaijei*); Khari-Kchar - Anjar, 13.9.43 2s and 3s occasional!; A n j a r, 14.9.43 About Shinai Reservoir and towards Tuna: Apparently becoming commoner!; 15.9.43 In open country about Bhadreswar village and along Mundra road: Com!; R a p a r, 20.9.43 Nilpar Reservoir environs: Sp. 249 o? juv., skull soft, W 85, B 17, Tars.25, T 68.5 (*Avaijei*); 21.9.43 F. com. & general!; 23.9.43 In open sandy semi desert towards Gedi & Desalpur, much fewer than campestris!;

Kathiawar: D w a r k a, 12.10.43 F.abundant on flat stony ground near D.B.!; 13.10.43 Mithapur!; A m r e l i, 17.10.43 F.common!;

K u t c h: B h u j, 5.3.1944 Sp.332 ♀ undev., W 85, B 17, Tars.25, T 65 (*Avaijei*) Solos, occasional. Not common; M a n d v i, 11.3.44 Solos or pairs occasion al. Not common or abundant; J a k h a u, 14.3.44 Occasional solos or pairs!; C h o b a r i (Bhachau Dist., Wagad) 23.3.44 Occasional solos;;

Gujarat: B o d e l i (ca 250' - Baroda Dist.) 9.11.45 Sp. GS 195 ♂ W 84, B 16.5, Tar. 26.5, T 60 ( ); GS 196 ♀ W 86, B 17.5, Tar. 25.5, T 68 ( ); P a t a n (Mehsana Dist.) 24.12.45 Sp. GS706 ♂ W , B , Tar. , T ; D e e s a (ca 500' - Palanpur state) 9.1.1946;;

Kathiawar: K o d i n a r, 12.3.1946 Common!; D a l k h a n i a, 14.3.46;;

A s s a m: Sadiya (ca 400') 1.12.1946 Several on Golf Links!;

11

Afghanistan

Some time in 1935 my ornithologist friend Hugh Whistler wrote to me from England that Colonel R. Meinertzhagen, the noted British ornithologist, was planning a collecting trip to Afghanistan and was on the lookout for a companion to help him with the birds. Whistler asked if I would be prepared to go. I said I would be only too happy, since Afghanistan was an adjoining area to our own, yet so little known ornithologically. However, I said that as my own particular interest was ecology and I would not enjoy skinning birds etc. all the time, additional help would be needed. Whistler cautioned me: 'He is a great stickler—and rightly so—for the perfect preparation of all specimens in whatever branch of science, so you would need to keep a careful eye on the skinners.' The expedition didn't come off till 1937 as Meinertzhagen was preoccupied with another one in Kenya in 1936.

Richard Meinertzhagen was one of the most colourful, original and, in many ways, likeable characters that ornithology introduced me to. As an officer in the British army he had spent most of his military service in East Africa. His exploits as a soldier and big-game hunter and ornithologist make fascinating reading in his *Kenya Diary* and the several other books he wrote about Kenya and Tanganyika under colonial rule. He had a passing acquaintance with India, where he had done temporary stints of service and convalescence during the First World War. When asked if he had managed to pick up any Hindi or Urdu while in India he replied that he had only learnt the useful term *sooar ka bacha* (swine), which he had encoded as 'SKB' and frequently used in private conversation when referring to 'opposition' folk. He was a man completely devoid of sentimentalism and impervious to personal danger, and almost so to physical pain.

In one of his exploits in Africa while a young lieutenant, accompanied by six askaris against the rebellious Nandi tribe, he crawled into the Laibon's (chief's) village at night and captured the Laibon. He was removing the chief when a large force of warriors attacked. Meinertzhagen warned them that unless they withdrew immediately he would be compelled to shoot the captive. As they continued to advance threateningly, and there was imminent danger of himself and his small force being overwhelmed, he coolly raised his revolver and shot the man dead, an action that won him a DSO for gallantry and led to the unconditional surrender of the tribe.

Another of his oft recounted daredevil exploits was during the Middle East campaign in World War I. He rode out all by himself to a Turkish camp that was reported to be preparing a massive attack on a thinly defended British position which would most certainly have been overwhelmed. According to a deliberately planned strategy to mislead the enemy, Meinertzhagen carried with him a despatch case containing a fake plan of a major British offensive in an entirely different sector. As he came in sight the sentries raised the alarm and a fusillade started. He spun round and started the retreat at full gallop, with the Turkish bullets whizzing by, raising the dust all around. In the hasty retreat he contrived to drop the despatch case containing the 'secret' document. He managed to get back safely to the British lines but the ruse worked and the Turks were successfully foxed. They redirected their forces in accordance with the intercepted secret intelligence, and the British position was saved from being disastrously overrun.

Meinertzhagen narrated to me how at one stage in the Middle East campaign his job was to fly over Mesopotamian villages along with a pilot and drop propaganda leaflets to the 'oppressed' local population, assuring them of British altruism in fighting the Turks for *their* liberation. The aircraft used for the purpose was a frail looking single-engined two-seater biplane with linen-stretched wings. At the air base the young devil-may-care pilot started piling into the plane bundle upon bundle of the propaganda leaflets until even RM, silently watching, felt slightly perturbed. Finally, when perturbance began to give way to mild alarm, he casually enquired of the man how much load they were supposed to carry. The pilot looked back amused and nonchalantly quipped 'O they will decide that at the inquest' as he merrily continued stacking bundle upon bundle till the plane could hold no more!

Meinertzhagen seemed to be as indifferent to physical pain as to personal danger. While we were collecting in a reedy marsh near Kabul, he, wearing khaki shorts with legs uncovered, accidentally stepped on a barb-pointed reed which broke off, leaving about three-quarters of an inch of its length within his flesh. Regardless of this, he continued splodging through the marsh while his blood flowed freely. Finally, after some persuasion, he agreed to return. As he was limping back to the car to get back and have the barb removed by the embassy doctor, he noticed a Bearded Vulture—a wanted species—some 300 yards away in a different direction. Ignoring the projecting reed and the flowing blood he limped up to the bird and shot it before getting back to the car.

Following our first meeting at Bombay where he arrived on 11 February 1937, Meinertzhagen's meticulously kept diary, which he kindly permitted me to read 'At your risk(!)' shortly before his death, when our earlier shaky contact had ripened into abiding friendship, says 'I then went on to the Bombay Natural History Society where I met Prater and Sálim Ali. I was favourably impressed by the latter and liked what I saw of him. It is as well if we have to travel together for the next few months. He seemed intelligent, but is hideously ugly, not unlike Gandhi.'

For the additional help in skinning birds I selected N.G. Pillai, who had been seconded to my Travancore bird survey in 1933–4 by the Trivandrum museum. Pillai was a competent zoologist, a good worker, and above all a soft spoken, gentle-mannered individual who I knew would get on well in a mixed party of imponderables. His only failing was that he was perhaps too meek and mild for this Afghanistan set-up, on account of which he had sometimes to pay in petty humiliations. Besides Pillai, I had hired as skinner a local Christian scamp named Dyson from Dehra Dun. I knew Dyson from several previous expeditions as a congenital shirker and malingerer. But he was a useful drudge and a good worker if one kept twisting his tail, which I was sure Meinertzhagen was capable of doing, and more. In addition to these two we had with us a burly, handsome Pathan 'bearer', picked up en route in Peshawar. He was a competent man who had worked with foreigners before and knew the ways of the sahibs (for which he undisguisedly didn't much care!). Meinertzhagen had asked me to look out for a suitable botanist to take along with us on the Afghan expedition. A competent young student, K.N. Kaul, was recommended by my friend Birbal Sahni, F.R.S., then Professor of Botany at Lucknow University. Meinertzhagen interviewed Kaul, was well impressed but finally turned him down, I couldn't understand why. I know the reason now. The relevant entry in his diary says: 'Lucknow 8.3.1937. A young Hindu student, Kailash Nath Kaul, geologist [sic] wanting to accompany me to Afghanistan. He is a young man, nice mannered and intelligent, but I am a little doubtful whether I can stomach two seditionists for three months all day and every day. Sálim is a rank seditionist and communist, so is Kaul (a brother of Jawaharlal Nehru's wife) and it would probably end in disaster.'

We had hired a rickety old open Chevrolet truck in Peshawar for the journey to Kabul, and into it we piled our tents and camping gear, specimen boxes, stores, rations and personal baggage. The Sikh driver, Meinertzhagen and I sat on the front seat; Pillai, Dyson, the Pathan bearer, the cleaner, and one or two nondescript hangers-on, rode with the luggage behind. It was early April and the winter snow had just started melting. The untarred mountain road was slushy and with numerous hairpin bends and fearsome vertical drops of hundreds of feet on the *khud* side. The Sardarji at the wheel turned out to be a veritable Jehu. He revelled in cutting corners at speed and skidding his vehicle round greasy bends in spite of repeated remonstrances, and kept our fingers crossed and hair on end. We got to Kabul after dark, rather shaken but thankful that the ordeal had ended. The journey through the Khyber Pass to Jalalabad and on to Kabul took two days. Thanks to the hospitality of the British Minister in Kabul (Colonel Sir Kerr Fraser-Tytler), we were lodged in the luxurious Legation Building (built with Indian government money) which, at that time, must surely have been one of the grandest of its kind anywhere in the world (all to uphold the prestige and majesty of the Raj, no doubt), and it was perhaps more lavishly appointed than any international 5-star hotel today. Our entire expedition in the country north of Kabul as far as the Oxus river (the boundary of the USSR) lasted about eight weeks. It happened during the regime of Nadir Shah who had displaced the legendary upstart Bachcha-e-Saqqa who had earlier displaced the all-too-hastily reforming zealot king Amanullah. The Afghan government was hospitably co-operative throughout, and had even assigned a *mehmandar*—a sort of liaison officer—(easy-going, comfortable-shaped) to travel with our party and help clear all official and other hurdles, procure local assistance and supplies, and generally to see to it that we had complete freedom to move about in the countryside. And, as Meinertzhagen so aptly put it later, 'these many duties he carried out with indolent efficiency'.

My experience of the type of Englishman one normally came across in the heyday of the Raj was that he was a bully where one lower in the 'peck order' was concerned. Indians as a rule are too mild and submissive and thus lend themselves readily to being bullied. Another peculiarity of the British character I have found is that if you stand up to the bully and hit back, you command his respect. So it has been with me and so it was with Meinertzhagen. One of his biographers has described him as 'physically a powerful, violent and ruthless man'—a description which, happily, is only partly true. Though possessed also of many admirable qualities, he had a distinct streak of the bully in his make-up and could be unreasonable to the point of brutality at times. Due to his excessive meekness, Pillai was a perfect foil for a bully and he lived in obvious terror of

Meinertzhagen because, in the latter's estimation, Pillai could do nothing right or in the way it should be done—neither could I, as I later discovered from his diary—and I had often to intervene when the hectoring got too far.

As it happened, Meinertzhagen had brought out with him two small tents of green Willesden waterproof canvas which had evidently been his camping companions for many years in Kenya, and which he loved dearly. So dearly indeed that he would trust no one to put them up or take down but himself. One day, on a greasy road after a rainstorm, our expedition truck driven by the Flying Sardarji skidded and turned over on its side, catapulting all the kit from the roof into a roadside canal. It had all to be fished out as soon as we managed to extricate ourselves. Among the lot were the precious tents which got thoroughly soaked. As it was late evening and help to straighten the truck was not available, we decided to bivouac in an adjoining meadow and the tents were opened up and pitched. It continued drizzling all night so that the wet tents were wetter in the morning. The *mehmandar* who had gone off at dawn to fetch help from a village a couple of miles away had returned and the truck was back on its wheels once more. The wet tents were hurriedly taken down and rolled up in that condition and we reached our next dak bungalow, where they would not be needed, at 9 on a fine, sunny morning. Meinertzhagen and I set off immediately to explore the area and collect, leaving Pillai and the rest to set up camp. When we returned after a couple of hours Meinertzhagen found his beloved tents opened up and spread in the sun. The morning's collection may have been disappointing or the hurriedly bolted breakfast may have disagreed with his inside, I cannot tell, but the sight of those tents suddenly sent him off the deep end into a paroxysm of insensate rage.

Pillai was called up and mercilessly barked at: Who asked him to meddle with his tents? Why did he touch them without instructions? And so forth and so on. I could no longer remain a silent spectator of this extraordinary exhibition of unjustified bullying and felt compelled to protect the poor terrified Pillai who was struck dumb with fright. I told Meinertzhagen that he was being thoroughly unreasonable and unfair, and that in Pillai's place I couldn't imagine myself or any other sensible person doing anything different. Here were two tents that had had to be rolled up in a hurry when soaking wet, and here was a warm, sunny morning for drying them. If Pillai, sitting in camp, hadn't had the sense to spread them out to dry Meinertzhagen would surely, and with justification, have pounced on him for his stupidity in not doing so. So how had he deserved all this blame and shouting? Meinertzhagen fretted and fumed at my intervention, but then perhaps realized the absurdity of the situation and soon calmed down.

Our daily routine of work was for Meinertzhagen and I to start out after breakfast, around 7.30, in different directions, accompanied by a local shikari as guide, and collect and bird-watch till about noon. Back in camp the specimens were sorted out and readied for delousing. Meinertzhagen's special interest on the expedition, in addition to birds, was to collect the mallophaga (or feather lice) infesting them. These insects are not blood-sucking like the vulgar little creatures we know by that name; they live within the plumage of a bird and feed on the decaying portions of the feathers. They are so narrowly host-specific that a species found on an oriole, say, will not be found on a myna. Thus if the same species of mallophaga is found on two different species of bird, that indicates their probable phylogenetic relationship. In this way mallophaga are of great importance for the study of evolution and taxonomy.

Our indoor activities commenced after lunch and often continued till after dark. To collect mallophaga the bird is wrapped in a piece of white muslin and put into a tightly closing box along with a swab of cotton wool soaked in chloroform. The bird is taken out after a few minutes and the dead mallophaga picked off the linen wrapper and shaken out of the bird's plumage, forcepped into vials containing alcohol and carefully labelled as to host, date, locality and other relevant particulars. While Meinertzhagen was busy with this I weighed the birds, made notes of the moults and colours of bare parts, and dissected the skinned ones for sex, stomach and crop contents and internal parasites. When finished with delousing Meinertzhagen joined the skinners while I wrote up my field notes of the morning. Here I am reminded of an amusing incident which was rather typical of Meinertzhagen. Before the expedition started, looking over the list of stores and equipment I had brought, he was jeeringly contemptuous about my having been so sybaritic as to bring two Petromax lamps when he himself had managed well enough without this luxury and with only hurricane lanterns all the forty years or more he had been collecting. I said that the Petromaxes were really meant for myself because I was used to them and could not work at night in poor light. He made some snooty remarks about people getting soft and so on, and there the matter ended. When we got going in our first camp and the Petromaxes were lit, what did I find on return from the evening round of collecting but that Meinertzhagen had calmly monopolized both the lamps for himself, one on either side, seeming to enjoy their brightness rather than missing his old accustomed hurricane lanterns. This set the pattern; thenceforth, and all through the expedition, if I wished to work after dark I had to nestle up to the Petromaxes which had become inseparable from him.

The expedition party consisted of two Christians, one Hindu, one Sikh and three Muslims of two varieties. Doomsayers had prognosticated that none of us, particularly the *kafirs* (unbelievers), would come back alive: the Afghans were such bigotted Muslims and the country so overrun by brigands that we would be looted, murdered, etc., etc. In the event not once in the entire trip were we ever asked our religion, and we found the Afghan country folk extremely friendly and hospitable. Frequently, when out collecting, villagers working in the fields would run up to us saying, 'You are our welcome guests: you must come to our house and drink some tea.' The open truck with all our personal belongings, rations and even ammunition was left on the roadside wherever we were camping, and we never lost a thing and no one ever bothered us. Except the flies! So much for the prognostications and their perpetrators: it was perhaps the frontier tribesmen our well wishers were thinking of.

Much time was lost in travelling. From Kabul we drove north, camping in six to eight localities for five or six days each. We sometimes stayed in tents, but mostly in sheds, as there were usually no proper dak bungalows except for the fairly posh one at Bamian. Bamian, a centre of ancient Buddhist civilization, is a place of great archaeological and historical interest, with a colossal Buddha, some fifty feet or more in height, carved out of living rock. The place is visited by large numbers of foreign tourists. In the matter of accommodation the *mehmandar* was a great help. When necessary he would go in advance and fix up a place for us to stay in. Communication between two camps was maintained by telephone through police stations and outposts, or other government offices, which were all interconnected by an official network, and with Kabul, the 'nerve centre'. Thus the *mehmandar* could send information beforehand of our movements and get arrangements made.

It was in the Danaghori plain of north Afghanistan that we had our first meeting with the Common Pheasant in its ancestral Central Asian homeland, and I was surprised to find that its natural habitat here was the extensive swampy reed-beds, with practically no trees to roost in. Our Afghan bird collection was especially interesting for me as it contained several species which, till then, I had never come across in my life, such as Snowcock and Seesee Partridge. However, for me the highlight of the whole expedition was the spring (northward) migration that was in visual progress all the time we were in the country, like that of the Redlegged Falcon (*Falco vespertinus*) and Lesser Kestrel (*Falco naumanni*) from Africa to East Asia, and the unbelievable hordes of Rosy Pastor from the Indian plains to their nesting grounds in Turkestan. It was at Danaghori that we struck their main migration. Many thousands of these birds, known as *Saach* in Afghanistan, were feeding and resting en route between 4 and 10 May, their numbers being constantly added to by arrivals from the south. Meinertzhagen estimated that on 6 May they were arriving at the rate of 15,400 in seven hours. During the first week in May there must have been close on half a million Pastors on the Danaghori plain, most of them roosting in the marshy reed-beds. There were no crops available at the time and the birds seemed to be subsisting entirely on beetles and other insects. The Afghans recognize the *Saach* as beneficial to agriculture and do not molest them even when little other 'lawful meat' is safe from the pot. Another spectacular instance of visual mass migration of Marsh Harriers (*Circus aeruginosus*) was encountered at Bamian on 24 April. The birds, all adult males, suddenly commenced arriving at 6 p.m. from a south-eastern and southern direction, which could mean from the Indian subcontinent. They were obviously exhausted, for they came down and settled in a ploughed field for the night. We counted some sixty-six birds, and more were still arriving when it got too dark to see. One rarely sees more than one or two adult male Marsh Harriers during the course of a day on a large marsh in India, therefore to see such a concentration, and all adults of the same sex bound for their northern breeding grounds, was a truly memorable and thrilling experience. These Harriers must have moved on early, for there was no sign of them in the valley soon after daybreak. On the following day and at the same time about ten adult males arrived from the same direction, roosted in the identical ploughed field and were gone again next morning.

I recall another couple of incidents during the Afghanistan expedition which will round off the record. One morning as usual I went out collecting, accompanied by a local man provided by the *mehmandar*. On a cliff nearby I found the nest of a Rock Nuthatch that was new to me. So I climbed up to a ledge within photographing distance and focussed the camera on the nest. After a long and patient wait the bird returned, but just as I was about to click the man said photography was forbidden there and stepped in front of the lens. I angrily pushed him aside and got my picture all right. However, I felt this man's behaviour was extraordinary, so when we returned to camp I related the incident to the *mehmandar*. The *mehmandar* listened without a word, only looked rather annoyed. I was speaking to him in Urdu, so the Persian-speaking guide had not understood what was being said. When I had done, the *mehmandar* casually asked the man to fetch some paper and a pencil. Without uttering a word he wrote a couple of lines, folded the sheet and gave it to the man to take to the police station. In half an hour the man was back weeping and wailing, and fell at my feet begging forgiveness. At first I couldn't make out at all what this meant, till I learnt that what the *mehmandar* had written was, in effect, 'This man has insulted our guests. Deliver unto him three of the best.' The scamp weepingly begged pardon and explained that he was only trying to save the *dargah* from desecration. It seems there was a holy shrine half a mile away in that direction which I hadn't even noticed.

Another time the whole bungalow at Haibak was stinking to high heaven. Dead rat we thought. We looked around everywhere for dead rats—under the carpets, behind the cupboards, in the corners of every room and all sorts of improbable places. No rat, but stench continuing. Then I suddenly remembered that three or four days earlier we had got a surfeit of specimens and Meinertzhagen had unstrung one bird from the carrying stick and stuffed it into his breast pocket. When I reminded him of that shirt he scornfully pooh-poohed the suggestion and the search continued. A couple of days later (we didn't change our shirts too often) when he went back to that shirt he felt something wet on his chest. Apparently that Bluethroat had been 'seasoning' in the pocket and had now reached prime condition. Meinertzhagen came up to me sheepishly and said 'Sálim you were right. Here it is!' as he pulled out the stinking mangled little carcass. And all the while he had been grumbling and cursing at the *chowkidar* and everyone else and turning the establishment upside down!

12

Ornithological Pilgrimage to Kailas Manasarovar 1945

While living in Dehra Dun I had plenty of opportunities for mountain-trekking in the Western Himalaya—chiefly Kashmir, Himachal Pradesh, Garhwal and Kumaon—often in the stimulating company and under the tutelage of Arthur Foot, an enthusiastic mountaineer with considerable climbing experience in Cornwall and the Swiss Alps. This was chiefly during the long summer vacations of the Doon School of which he was the founding headmaster, as it were. Having a poor head for heights I was never tempted by anything that could be called serious mountaineering, and our ceiling on these treks hardly ever exceeded ten or twelve thousand feet. But the treks did provide opportunities for acquiring a working familiarity with the Himalayan environment—the forests, vegetation and fauna, especially birds.

One of the most exhilarating experiences for a trekking naturalist in these mountains is the kaleidoscopic change that he notices in the vegetation and bird life as he climbs higher through the succeeding life zones. These altitudinal zones or climatic belts are of absorbing interest to the student of ecology, inasmuch as each of them harbours a more or less characteristic vegetation and bird life of its own. The changes are sometimes so dramatic that after a little practice one can guess the altitude fairly accurately from the species present, even without the help of an altimeter. Indeed, for me this is one of the joys of trekking in the Himalaya, particularly the section east of

Nepal—Sikkim, Bhutan and Arunachal Pradesh, where the climate is much more humid and the life zones more abruptly telescoped into one another, from almost tropical in character at the base of the hills to arctic near the tops. Growing familiarity with the southern aspect of the Himalayan range strengthened the urge to see what there was on the other side of this lofty wall. Plans for an ornithological expedition to Tibet in 1939 were thwarted, first by ominous sabre-rattling by Hitler and then by the actual outbreak of World War II, which, as the months and years dragged on, began to look as if it would never end. In spite, therefore, of the increasing difficulties in the supply and transport position and other wartime constraints, I decided that the expedition *had* to be now or never. With promises of official help from friends at court to the extent possible, I started planning for a modest expedition to Western Tibet—from whence there had come tantalizing reports earlier of the breeding of Barheaded Geese, Blacknecked Cranes and other exciting birds, many of which are seen in India only during the winter months and of whose nesting habits and ecology little was known. I was particularly anxious to study some of these. In fact the expedition was to be—as I described it later—an ornithological pilgrimage to Mt Kailas and Lake Manasarovar.

The normal pilgrim route from Almora was chosen not only because it provides the least rigorous access over the Lipu Lekh Pass (16,750 ft) but because it was the only pass free of snow at this time of the year, May. The regular pilgrim traffic does not commence till the end of June or the middle of July. In fact, for the return journey too we were obliged to recross the Lipu Lekh since even in the first week of July all the other passes were snow-bound. Starting from Almora in Kumaon (5,200 ft) the pilgrim route switchbacks up and down, sometimes quite steeply, through fascinating forested country constantly in and out of a succession of life zones, with the snowy ranges hardly ever out of sight. Fifteen marches of an average 13 or 14 kilometres each bring you to Garbyang, the last village within Indian territory. My party was to have consisted of five members: Sucha Singh Khera (ICS) who retired as Cabinet

Secretary in 1965; a lawyer cousin, Saif Tyabji, from Bombay; a fellow ornithologist and expert bird photographer, Loke Wan Tho, of Singapore (refugeeing in Bombay from Japanese-occupied 'Shonan'); Pritam Sen, a young astro-physicist and bird watcher lately back from the USA; and I. For one reason or another the first three had to back out—Saif for failing in the preliminary self-imposed test of physical fitness, Loke for last-minute dysentery, and Khera for some similarly compelling reason. Finally, only Pritam and I were left. We started from Almora on 14 May 1945, the day after enormous bonfires on the surrounding mountain tops for miles around proclaimed the final collapse of Germany in Hitler's war, and amidst noisy fanfare and worked-up public rejoicing. Besides Pritam and myself, our party consisted of seven Dotiyals and one Kumaoni porter, laden with tents, personal baggage and food—chiefly the all-purpose 'tsampa' (roasted gram flour). As *sardar*, cook and factotum we had hired Khem Singh, a youngish Kumaoni from Almora. The sole non-Dotiyal porter was a docile stooge or fag of Khem Singh and was meant to discharge the same leadership function as a goat does among a flock of sheep. In the context of today's soaring cost of Himalayan treks it is interesting to recall from my diary that the daily wage of a porter carrying over a maund (c. 40 kg) was Rs 3 per day (all found) when marching, and Rs 2 when halting. He provided his own rations and their transport. The distance to Garbyang, the last village on the Indian side of the border—c. 237 km— took us fifteen days, involving a series of murderous ups and downs, often of a thousand feet or more each day and all the way. Being younger and sillier in those days, I prided in weighing myself down by stuffing my rucksack with all sorts of inessentials which needlessly added to the discomfort on the 'ups'.

I vividly recall one little incident on a particularly tough and sultry section of the trail which constantly switchbacked steeply several hundred feet up and then the same or more down, then higher up again and so on and on seemingly without end. At the bottom of one of these back-breaking 'saw-teeth,' fully exhausted, and before facing the next one, I sat down for a breather on a rock, unharnessed the unnecessarily overloaded rucksack and peeled myself an apple. The nickel-handled pocket knife had been my field companion for many years and I had a sentimental attachment to it. After resting a while the march was resumed—a quarter mile of comparative flat followed by another rise of disconcerting steepness. Stopping breathless on the summit to admire the view I casually put a hand in my pocket and found the knife missing. A thorough rummaging of the rucksack produced no knife, so I thought it must have slipped out somewhere along the route. I felt sad at losing an old friend but was unenthusiastic about going back to look for it. However, after a short rest and before resuming the march I idly trained my glasses on the spot where the apple was peeled, now half a mile away and several hundred feet below. Lo and behold, there lay the knife fully exposed and glistening in the morning sun, heliographing its SOS to me. How I cursed it then! But I didn't have the heart to deliberately abandon it though it meant an exhausting and most unenjoyable rescue operation, and a delay of over an hour in the day's programme. But that knife was retrieved. It lived with me for another thirty years, but was evidently destined to be stolen, and that is how we finally parted.

Pritam was the son of an old family friend, Lala Ugra Sen, a prominent landlord and businessman of Dun. I had known Pritam initimately as a bright and gentle-mannered school and college lad before he went to the USA for higher studies, and had been much impressed by the competence he developed in bird-watching in my company around Dehra Dun and in the Mussoorie hills. Thus when he expressed his keenness to accompany me on the Tibet jaunt I gladly accepted him as a potential asset. It all went well for the first few days, but then I began to notice a certain queerness in his behaviour and a marked falling off in his interest in the surroundings and scenery that had driven him so ecstatic earlier. Soon he seemed not to be enjoying himself, marching mechanically behind the porters, looking neither right nor left, engrossed in a book of Hindi verse by the well-known poetess Mahadevi Varma, which he held open before him as he trudged along. I suspected it might be the altitude, but we were still in the range of seven or eight thousand feet, which is surely not high enough to worry most people. However, the position got worse day by day until, when we were camping on the Barkha plain at about 15,000 ft, it became positively unpleasant for me. Pritam grew morose and would hardly utter a word even when squatting face to face on the tent floor across a box which served both as work table and for meals. While I was skinning a bird or writing up my notes or pressing a plant specimen he would order food for himself directly, bolt it down hastily and hunch himself in a corner or walk out with Mahadevi. After suffering this unpleasantness for a few more days I had at last to suggest to Pritam that since he was obviously not enjoying himself and also ruining my fun in the process, it might be a good idea for him to take some of the yaks with him and return to Almora, leaving me to complete my plans and study by myself. He was so vehement in rejecting this suggestion that, after suffering the situation for a few days (after completing the *parikrama* of Mt Kailas), I decided to cut short the programme and turn back. The other higher passes (Anta-dhura, Jayanti La, *et al.*), by one of which I had meant to return, were still snowbound and impassable, so that there was no option but to retrace the same route. Luckily the intervening five weeks, with the melting of the snows and the approach of summer, had renovated the scene so magically that it was like entering a brand new country. I had learnt from past experience, my own and that of other mountaineers, how important it is to have the right companions at high altitudes, when a small group of assorted temperaments has to live in a huddle day in and day out, maybe for several weeks on end. Murder is seldom away from one's thoughts! However, one would have to be a fortune-teller to know beforehand who will be affected at what height, which makes it difficult to choose the right companions at sea level.

On the return trek, half way down the Indian side of Lipu Lekh Pass, I came across a pathetic party of four Gujarati *jatris*—one male and three females—on their way to seek salvation at Manasarovar and Kailas, followed by a straggly band of Dotiyal porters laden with bedding, tiffin carriers, *lotas*, and kerosene tinfuls of *chewda, gathias* and such like sustenance for the journey. It was early July but summer hadn't set in as yet, and on a cloudy day it could still be freezing cold with the piercing wind blowing all the time. The man had the look of a typical Gujarati sharebroker from Bombay's Dalal Street, returning from business. He wore a loose whitish cotton shirt with a sleeveless woollen pullover, a cotton dhoti pulled up almost to the haunches on one side, thin nylon socks held up on his calves by elastic suspenders, and pointed yellow wafery-soled share-bazaar shoes. The women, one of whom was his tired-looking wife, all wore their everyday cotton saris with long-sleeved sweaters for good measure; whether they wore any additional woollens deeper down I of course couldn't tell. On their feet they had cotton socks and thin-soled open *chaplis*. The party started wailing piteously—especially the women—as we crossed in opposite directions, complaining bitterly that they had no idea and no one had warned them that it would be so cold and the journey so tough. They must have thought me singularly hard-hearted when, instead of sympathizing, I roundly told the man off for his silliness in not making proper enquiries and equipping himself suitably before launching on this hazardous pilgrimage from Bombay with the womenfolk. In the circumstances I could only offer cold comfort and advise them to turn back because without proper warm clothes and bedding they would all assuredly perish; I don't know how they fared afterwards. The plight of those poor women was truly pitiable, but that a shrewd Gujarati stockbroker should be so ignorant and so naive as not to know better seems difficult to imagine.

The Tibet trip was one of the rare occasions of which I kept a narrative diary in addition to separate field notes on birds. On most other expeditions I relied, and still do, on companions like Loke Wan Tho, Meinertzhagen and Dillon Ripley—far more punctilious and industrious diarists than I—for happenings during the expeditions. The Tibet trip was full of interest and thrills and novel experiences too long to relate as a connected narrative in this book. But a few disjointed vignettes picked out at random may help to convey some of the flavour of a memorable venture. The notes are as scribbled in my diary at the time, with a slight paraphrasing here and there for the sake of intelligibility.

25.v.45 Khela to Sosa (en route to Garbyang) for overnight and next day in Shri Narayanswamy's hospitable Ashram, 8,300 ft, started in 1936. . . . received kindly, shown over buildings, etc. still mostly under construction. Housed in thatched shed which serves as dharamsala for sadhus and others less holy, mostly jatris to and from Kailas. Narayanswamy a handsome youngish black-bearded long-haired man evidently 35–40 or so; speaks good English . . . a Kerala man from certain clues he let drop, e.g. 'yeggs' and his tell-tale accent on 'continuously'. He seems to know Raihana [Tyabji] well and apparently has some pull in Baroda which he often visits in winter fund-gathering tours to the money-pots of Ahmedabad and elsewhere. At present he apparently has only two permanent associates, a holy man in an off-white 'nightgown' with dark ringlets and beard, looking like a decayed bandit—a Hur I thought—and a less holy retired schoolmaster from a neighbouring village who is the general manager of the establishment's worldly activities such as erecting buildings, obtaining food supplies (of the best) and making disbursements to staff and workmen. Was unsuccessful in drawing out the swami re. his past history and future aims. Place impresses me as a particularly good setting for a sanatorium—grand mountain surroundings and overlooking Nampa glacier to E, but not particularly austere or reverence-provoking. Swami does not appear to be—perhaps he hides it effectively—either very learned or scholarly. Large portion of our conversation centred round the journey to Kailas (of which he claims to have made thirteen) and food. One thing we discovered was that the food they have is simple—but best ghee, best milk, best honey and best everything. So the ashram at least provides plenty of rest and wholesome food for the body. Of spiritual food, if any, we saw no trace except a tiny garret in his detached one-room *kutia*, a cabin in which the swami is said to meditate. . . . The gardening part is managed by the 'ex bandit' and he does it very well with the help of Pocha's seeds and gardening catalogue, rattling off names of flowers as from *Index Kewensis*. Beautiful roses, pansies, poppies, calendulas, snapdragons and pinks now blooming. The snow has only lately gone and in another three weeks everything in this garden should be very lovely . . . according to the swami a large snake—about 18 inches thick (by show of hands)—dwells in a serpent grove on steep hillside above ashram, carrying *mani* on its forehead—like a bright shining star. Swami has seen it with his own eyes on dark nights at about 400 yards range. A local chap once saw it and came running to the ashram, laid himself down at the swami's feet and died. 'It was fright that did it.'

3 June 1945. Garbyang. A fine morning at last and so to Nampa Glacier *c.* 9 miles from here, guided by local tough of forbidding exterior called Gelong. Actually he is quite mild but a good and convincing mimic of a hardened bandit. Nampa lies in Nepal territory, but by some arrangement goats, sheep and cattle are allowed to be taken up there for pasture during the season just commencing. A bit too early as yet. Large areas or grazing meadows are immense snowfields, but already a good few goats and sheep busy on the herbage sprouting up as the snow melts. Azaleas: masses on hillsides just clear of snow; bushes *c.* 4 ft high with clusters of pale pinkish and purplish flowers, and leaves rather like rhododendron. Many other species of flowers including purple irises, buttercups and a mauve flower that grows in clusters (?) already covering considerable patches. In a fortnight the place will be one mass of colour. Glorious view of glacier and surrounding snow peaks.

4 June 45. Called on Thakur Nand Ram re. final arrangements for crossing Lipu Lekh. Weather since yesterday clear and sunny and crossing now possible. Have decided to engage as guide and interpreter stout Gelong who led us to Nampa yesterday. He is recommended as a trustworthy and efficient man. Apparently it is the guide's business to arrange for coolies, tents and transport animals. From Garbyang we are taking 15 seers of 'suttoo' (tsampa) and are planning that henceforth lunch shall consist of this in varied forms. Has been blowing hard since *c.* 11 o'clock, ceaselessly, quite No. 6 of Beaufort scale. Particularly violent about sixish and a peculiar hazy bluish light over the surrounding mountains. At 6.30 a fairly severe earthquake shock *c.* 15 secs. made us rush out of dak bungalow. Resulted in numerous landslides and avalanches. Thick clouds of dust on steep hillsides, as after a cannon bombardment, all around, accompanied by rattle of stones and loosened boulders—some as large as a double-storeyed house—bounding down.

5 June. Had conference at Nand Ram's 10 a.m. and fixed up the following for journey to Taklakot (first village in Tibet) starting tomorrow morning: Gelong, guide interpreter and general manager Rs 3 per day (without food) up to Gyanima; 6 ponies each to carry 30 seers at Rs 10 per pony up to Taklakot, with 2 attendants at Rs 4 each; 1 tent for kitchen and servants, hire up to Gyanima Rs 8. From Taklakot onwards baggage to go on yaks. Gelong to arrange. Plan roughly to reach Gyanima after doing Manasarovar and Kailas around 15 July.

6 June. Garbyang to Kalapani 12,000ft. . . . Temperature at 7 a.m. 39°F . . . Heavy downpour accompanied by thunder and lightning. . . . With every loud peal of thunder stones and boulders come hurtling down the overhanging cliffs. In places you are walking along a narrow ledge—the path—scarcely 3 ft wide with a roaring torrent several hundred feet sheer below on the other side . . . you wonder whether they are going to get you. It would be too bad if they do. But 'What to do, man!'.

7 June. Shangchim. Gelong wishes to start us off for Lipu Pass at 2 a.m. while the snow is hard. Let's hope he will be able to capture and load up the ponies before sunrise! The idea is to get to the top just as daylight appears as path on other side difficult for ponies in the dark. At long last we seem to be on the Edge of Beyond!

8 June. Got up at 1 a.m. Took down and packed up tents and loaded ponies in pitch dark plus one candle and one flashlight torch. Sky ominously overcast. Started at 2.30. There is nothing that will answer to the name of path to Lipu. You just go stumbling and slipping over large stones and boulders that have slid down from the heights and thickly litter the ground. Unpleasant going in pitch darkness and how the pony men kept to the track is a wonder! You climb 3,250 ft from Shangchim to the head of the pass. Fresh soft snow made going difficult for the laden ponies. In places they sank in to the belly and were hauled out with trouble, one man tugging at the head rope and the other literally lifting it out by the tail. Deep clefts in the snow had frequently to be jumped, and serious accidents to ponies and baggage was quite on the cards. Quite a number of times the ponies had to be unloaded and the baggage carried over the bad bits. Exciting but slow work. Great credit to the pony men for boldness and initiative. Head of Lipu Lekh reached about 6.15: temperature 28°F. Heavy freshly fallen snow all over causing unusual delay to the opening of the pass for traffic. Goats and sheep seem to be the most satisfactory form of transport in such conditions. A large flock with laden panniers virtually whizzed past while we and ponies were floundering in the snow. I stood the march very badly, partly due to the altitude and load of sheepskin coat and bulging rucksack (18+ lbs) and partly to no sleep this night and the night before. Climbing over snow most distressing to wind and limb. Character of terrain changes abruptly on crossing the pass. Having trailed the Kali up to its source on the Indian side, we descend following the Karnali down from its source on the Tibet side. Taklakot, the first Tibetan village cis-Lipu, a large and important seasonal mandi (closed in winter) for barter trade between India and Tibet. Halt for procuring yaks to replace the ponies which will return to Shangchim. Helped by Mohan Singh, a merchant from Dharchula with shop in the mandi; engaged a villainous-looking fellow named Lakpha, in coloured felt knee-boots and dirty saya-like robe with a belt round the middle, long greasy hair plaited in a pigtail, and rings in his ears. Hired his four yaks for our baggage each to carry 2 maunds (160 lb) at Rs 40 per yak for 30 days up to Gyanima, plus 30 per month for Lakpha (or Lapha) himself. Part of his job to keep us supplied with fuel, sticks or dried yak-dung for cooking. . . . Gompa or monastery on opposite hilltop (above Taklakot). Entertained by presiding lama, known as 'raja', to salted buttered tea (not at all bad!) and some sugar-coated gram. Raja apparently not too hard on himself: sleek, well-fed, with a variety of eatables within arm's reach without getting up from cushion, with young brahmachari [novitiate] in attendance. Tea in silver Tibetan cup in front and more in kettle in corner. Does not impress as being ascetic or scholarly, but *may* be both and more! Gompa a curious haphazard collection of 'jari-purana' bric-a-brac, including an odd assortment of atrociously stuffed moth-eaten, dust-laden, soot-begrimed animals, e.g. bear, leopard, wild yak, and horns of blackbuck and Schomburgk's Deer hung from ceiling in adjoining room. This with a large admixture of prayer-wheels, prayer flags (perhaps obligingly supplied by Japan!) with some gilt and lacquer odds and ends. Afraid I am very little impressed, in fact rather depressed, at all this weird mumbo-jumbo that goes for religion, and at the blind faith that mankind has developed in things we imagine (why?) will bring salvation in the hereafter. Perhaps a little less dirt on themselves and in the immediate surroundings of the gompa (which function freely as an open latrine) would do more than all the prayer-wheels within the place whirling violently—on ball bearings if you like.

10.6.45 . . . three of the frisky yaks refused to cross two sorry-looking wooden bridges in spite of much beating from back and tugging from fore. They scampered off and threw part of the load. The animals had to be unloaded at the two places, the baggage carried across by the men and reloaded on the other side. The yaks plunged in the icy water and swam across the strong current . . . I like the pace of the yaks, it just suits me: it is leisurely, and gives plenty of time for dawdling, observation and photography. . . . Bought two legs of sheep from chap carrying a slaughtered animal on a pony for Re 1. Good business for both parties. Am told last year a whole sheep cost only Rs 2½! . . . How to dress for a march is the great problem. Sun burning hot but it takes no time to become freezing (under fleeting cloud).

Sekang *11.vi.45* . . . at 3 p.m. the wind sprang up. This is our first experience of the real stuff which has made Tibet justly notorious. For the last 3½ hours the little tent is being battered and buffeted and in imminent danger of being blown off from above our heads. Luckily we have a spare 'kennel-for-two' type of tent for such an emergency, but let's hope we don't have to use it: it will be bad for nerves! 30°F during night. Canvas water-buckets frozen; very nearly also feet! . . . Stout Gelong has started praying loud and long every morning—rather alarmingly so! . . . The furze bushes are paradise for the birds and also for the birdnester. Could happily spend a week of field days here, but 'goodgood' things evidently also wait ahead, so must move on. . . . How I miss Wan Tho! With his energy and enthusiasm we could have worked wonders with bird photography.

13.vi.45 Sekang to Nayeze. At summit of pass (Gurla, 16,500ft)—flat and wide enough for 200 Churchill tanks abreast—are many (votive) piles of stones collected by the pious and demon-fearing. The main pile is surmounted by the usual pole with every conceivable form of rubbish—rags, wisps of dirty wool, and horns and skulls of yaks etc.—dangling from it. Lappha, evidently a demon-fearing chap, burst out into a volley of victorious chanting, mounted the pile and added his contribution to the junk. Gelong, though a Hindu fears the devil none the less. He also erupted in a series of pious grunts and chants which I hope the devil understood. We were warned by Khem Singh, for *our* good here and in the hereafter, that from the top of the pass one must always first look at 'rait shide', towards Manasarovar, and not to 'lep' towards Rakhas Tal. To do otherwise is disastrous. . . . Glorious and unbelievable views of both lakes with the icy dome of Kailas towering in the background. Extraordinary opalescent tints of Rakhas and changing shades of Manas according to time of day and state of sky—from almost snow-white through jade and emerald green to deepest ultramarine blue and purplish black: something to remember! Surface of Manasarovar 14,950 ft; circumference 54 miles; greatest depth according to Swami Pranavananda is *c.* 300 ft. Encircled by mountains of which only the peaks snow-capped at present.

It was near the Thugolho Monastery on the southern shore of Manasarovar that I first ran into Swami Pranavananda, a rational and science-oriented holy man with long experience of exploration in that region. We took to each other immediately, and had a long and interesting conversation on a purely physical plane—therefore in a language I could understand. He has since written two highly informative books on the region— *Kailas-Manasarovar* (Swami Kaivalyananda, 1949), and *Exploration in Tibet* (University of Calcutta, 1950), for which I was happy to lend him some of the photographs and ornithological notes made on this 'pilgrimage'. I met Swami Pranavananda—again ran into him—only after thirty-one years, in 1976, but this time in the very different setting of Rashtrapati

Bhavan, New Delhi, when we were both receiving awards from the President of India, Shri Fakhruddin Ali Ahmed—he the Padma Bhushan and I its elder brother.

I like Lappha more and more. He is cheerful and obliging, but like Gelong prays too loud and long, commencing rather unnecessarily early a.m. Also when urging the laden yaks alongside he is incessantly groaning and chanting aloud something pious I presume, but by the nature of the job in hand it could well be otherwise! . . . Through open fly of tent, from flat on back and head on pillow, watched 8 pairs of Barheaded geese together with several Brahminy ducks grazing unconcernedly within 50 yards of tent at sunset. Delightful sight, but oh for a .22 and roast goose instead of the eternal dal and rice!

17.vi.45 Barkha (or Parkha). Plain along foot of Kailas range. An enormous bare flat (miles and miles in every direction) covered with small shingle and scanty scraggy grass. They say will develop into rich pasture-land in a month's time. This is verily the Roof of the World and as a battlefield would have delighted the heart of Tamerlane and the warriors of old. Several major wars of ancient times could go on here simultaneously without coming in one another's way. . . . When I chased a Fat-tailed Lizard, Lappha, who is some species of Buddhist, admonished me saying that according to them killing one of these lizards is equivalent to a hundred murders. The lizard having taken to a desert life and renounced the good things of this world—eating, drinking and merrymaking—has become a swami or recluse. Therefore, killing it ranks with the murder of one sadhu = 100 ordinary mortals.

A scourge of rats once ate up all crops and started an epidemic of bubonic plague. A swami introduced cats as counterblast and fixed this 'exchange ratio' which remains stable under every kind of world crisis. Many troops and herds (one of over 70) of Kyang by shores of Rakhas Tal. Very wary: difficult to approach within 200 yards, often taking alarm and scampering off with much dust at much longer range. No young foals! What is the breeding season? Total seen today certainly over 300. Yaks delight in dry dung of wild ass, never failing to pick up and crunch a mouthful as they pass along. . . . Tarchan (or Darchan) 15,500 ft is a dreadful place for beggars. The official *parikrama* of Kailas starts from here, which explains it. We begin earning merit from tomorrow. Man's zeal and greed for merit in the hereafter is truly ridiculous and pathetic. Why can't he be satisfied with trying to gain merit in this one and only life which he can regulate, and leave the future (on which he has no control) to look after itself? . . . First leg [to Diraphuk] of official holy circuit [*parikrama*] of Kailas along a rough stony up-and-down footpath but well tamped down with the feet of faith and piety, aided maybe also by those of successful blackmarketeers. About a mile beyond Tarchan met two pathetic looking chaps in filthy rags and tatters—apparently Tibetan— who were busily doing the *parikrama* by the prostrating method. They stood up, clapped hands above their heads and threw themselves face down, hands extended forward in supplication, and so on and on to salvation. Poor chaps: I do hope they will not be done out of their hire at the other end! . . . Above this height (16,500 ft) must depend for fuel entirely on dry yak's dung. This assiduously gathered by eagle-eyed Lappha in the folds of his Tibetan robe all the way . . . It is good that one always has something to grouse about, but on the whole this is proving a very interesting ornithological experience. It should be of great help in giving the finishing touches to my *Birds of the Indian Hills* . . . . [Bivouac at Dirapukh] . . . though there it is, towering above us, Kailas certainly looks far more imposing from a great distance than from its bottom . . . . [Second leg of parikrama] I tried hard to cheat by riding a yak [over the formidable Dolma La, 18,500ft] but there was none to be had: at least this is what I was told by Lappha and Gelong. They were horrified at the idea of my hoping to acquire merit so cheaply, and seemed disgusted at the meanness of my nature in even thinking of such a subterfuge. Visited the local Gompa, one of the well known four on the holy circuit. Was nauseated by the general atmosphere of squalor and filth and mumbo-jumbo humbug about the place. Is this really Buddhism or anything worth the name of religion? . . . Murderous business getting to top of Dolma La through deep soft snow. Completely done up. In distress by the time summit reached: could hardly do 50 steps before stopping to 'admire the view'. Laden yaks sinking in soft snow up to belly then frisking and bucking and throwing the baggage about! Descent on other side over enormous boulders, gradient often 1:2 or steeper. Nevertheless yaks seemed to feel all the merrier for it: extraordinary animals! Reached the next bivouac (Zunthulphuk) at 4.30 dead tired. Lay down in tent and philosophized over expeditions and the perversity of people who under-took them when they could be eating mangoes [then in season in India] and lying in dry, soft and comfortable beds instead of damp hard ground with pointed stones poking odd parts underneath. Expeditioners came off poorly!

25.vi.45. Ding Tso *c.* 15,200 ft a small lake *c.* 6 miles in circumference NE of Manasarovar. Considered by locals to be the head while Manasarovar is the body—therefore more holy. Its E shore most exciting ornitho-logically: a broad belt, in places ¼ mile wide, waterlogged bogland or tundra—a succession of green, spongy, rounded mounds or humps separated from one another by deepish water channels—a miniature archipelago in effect. Many of the 'islets' actually free-floating so that you had to be nippy and on your guard all the time lest the one you had stepped on went deep under before you could jump on to the next. Treacherous quicksands abounding, so extra caution to be exercised. But this zone most promising and productive of good results with nesting birds. Great Crested Grebes, Brownheaded Gulls and about 15 pairs of Blacknecked Cranes around lake and obviously most breeding. Cranes' prancing and leaping dance very like Sarus: also voice and call, the latter slightly higher. One egg taken and scrambled; delicious—a welcome escape from the unchanging dal and rice!

While trying to reach a grebe's floating nest got into serious difficulties and imminent peril of getting swallowed up by quicksands. While on a floating mound at deepest part of bog suddenly realized, when down in icy water to thighs and sinking fast, that there was no other within jumping distance. Panicked wildly. Whipped round and made one desperate leap for last one which meanwhile had floated away further. By sheer luck only *just* made it. A lesson learnt; will heed Gelong's warnings more seriously hereafter!

Gelong, in spite of looks, turns out to be extremely afraid of dying before his time. All morning he was in mortal fear and co-operated as little as possible from a perfectly safe distance, taking no chances in this boggy habitat. He trembles at the distant sight of wayfarers whom he invariably suspects of being 'kharab admi' or bandits on the flimsiest of imaginary evidence. Yesterday he led me a detour of miles (so I felt) to avoid what the rest of our party ascertained to be a family of perfectly harmless individuals from whom there was even a chance of buying some much coveted mutton with tact! (Learnt later that Gelong had good cause to be in constant dread of bandits—who infested the Manasarovar area—having had bitter experience not long before. He had been beaten up, gagged, robbed and thrown by the wayside until rescued by some chance passerby a couple of days later.)

At the time of my visit, before the Chinese walked into Tibet, the Manasarovar area was known to be dangerously bandit-ridden. Helpless pilgrims from India were frequently waylaid by gangs and robbed and beaten up, and sometimes even killed. I had been warned by Gelong repeatedly of the risk of moving around unarmed and alone, but had thought it was only *his* way of making the trip a little more exciting for us.

However, one morning, attended by Gelong while hunting for nests among a patch of furze bushes, I fancied I noticed a slight movement some distance ahead but paid no heed to it. When we got closer to the spot there suddenly popped up from his ambush a grimy ferocious-looking ruffian with an ugly dagger in his belt and a matchlock slung over his shoulder. He promptly started shouting and gesticulating with alarming truculence which it was perhaps just as well I didn't understand. I have never seen a living human turn so pale as Gelong did upon the bandit's challenge; the expression 'white as a sheet' seems no wild exaggeration. He was visibly shivering with fright and begged me again and again in terrified undertones to flee from this '*kharab admi*'. I realized that it was now too late to think of any such action, and in any case it would have been futile as we had an endless open plain before us and no help within thirty miles. Luckily at that moment I suddenly remembered my shooting-stick (a seat, as used by cricket umpires) which Gelong was carrying. In a loud voice I ordered him to hand it to me quickly. I pretended it was a gun and mimicked loading it with a cartridge drawn from my pocket with deliberate ostentation. I take it that the bandit was unfamiliar with a contraption of this kind with its shining metal parts. He looked visibly concerned when I opened and closed the seat with a noisy klick-klacking, loaded the 'gun' and sloped it over my shoulder like the real thing. It was now my turn to shout back sentiments which I am glad (for his own sake) the ruffian did not understand! Fortunately the bluff worked: the man's truculence subsided at once; he turned away sullenly and made off. I marched back to camp with mock bravado, apprehensive all the time of a bullet following us behind, and thankful for a happy ending to a most uncomfortable situation.

. . . For the last 3 or 4 days the weather has been quite exceptionally fine, different to anything so far experienced on this trip. The air is champagne and one is never tired of chasing birds. It keeps light till 9 p.m. The sun is broiling hot but immediately a cloud comes over a sweater is welcome. This is the turning point of the trip. Tomorrow we begin working back towards Gyanima while evidently the Tibetan summer is only just beginning.

26.vi.45. Kyangma. Last night (Ding Tso) full moon and eclipse. Great excitement for Lappha and Gelong; both frantic with loud chanting to their respective makers, lasting over an hour, punctuated by blood-curdling shouts and threats to the Black One to let go of the moon which he was trying to swallow. Apparently lamas in a gompa about 3 miles away on hillside across lake also greatly perturbed at impending loss of moon, and much ghoulish shouting and firing of guns was heard. In the midst of his shouting Lappha shook his knife at the Black One, and this supreme threat no doubt persuaded him to release moon! Was glad to be able to sleep after the rescue. . . . Counted 119 in a herd of kyang . . . Had visitation from a Jongpen, some sort of governor, on his way from Lhasa to Gyanima (where he is posted), with a band of ragamuffin hangers-on. He sat down on end of P's sleeping-bag, physically examined everything we possess—aneroid, compass, cameras, thermometers, rucksacks, aluminium mug, and of course binoculars—which were freely passed round with much enjoyment. Can't quite gauge the calibre of these gents called jongpens. Even if only of tahsildar status surely he can't have seen or heard of many of these things for the first time as without doubt he appeared to! He couldn't get over the needle pointing towards Kailas whichever way the compass was turned. Great merriment among the gangsters. . . . Snow finches of two species (Rednecked and Tibetan) nest in rat holes apparently live together on friendly terms and with occupant mouse-hares. A rat and a finch seen to go down same hole! . . . Large herds of Kyang (one of over 100). The places they frequent have, from time to time (commonly) a drag mark in the sand, something like the track left by a snake, or by a frisky cow that has a log tied round its neck (to prevent it from straying). It is about 2 or 2½ inches broad and often up to 30 feet long (one over 90 feet), not straight but roughly wavy. Locals say it is made by an ass dragging one hoof; but why is the ass *such* an ass?! I wonder if these marks have been observed before and explained? . . . In the clear atmosphere of the boundless Barkha plain everything looks just across the way. But what a way it is! Miles and miles and miles you seem to get no nearer. It is tiresome work . . . Prescribed a mixture of *gur* and tsampa for a species of biscuit for tea. Result: the hardest and most waterproof type of reinforced concrete ever heard of in the toffee line. Fault of course Khem Singh's for getting the mixture wrong. Chewed a block like *supari* for over half hour then gave it up. Would do well as catapult ammunition! . . . Yak moults (from long-haired winter to short-haired summer pelage) in flakes, and patchily: neck and back first, belly and legs last when the season hots up. The belly hair has to be sheared as it does not flake off. The yakmen pull off flakes of hair and begin spinning yarn on a sort of 'takli' while marching alongside the laden animals. This yarn used for making tents and blankets. Black preferred to white as does not show dirt: fetches twice the price of white. Annual produce 1 kg+per yak. Domestic bull and cow yak produce best quality hybrid 'jhibbu': fetches double the price of pure yak, which presently Rs 70 to 140 or so. Jhibbu much preferred generally as hardier and more docile and tractable. Can be put to plough. Although superiority of jhibbu generally recognised, still not bred by everybody as considered unnatural and immoral practice, bringing bad luck. So only the wicked prosper! Yak refuses to enter shed or stable just as it refuses to go over bridge. Produces a single young per year. Gestation 9 months: calfs in spring. Normal life 18–21 years. Full strength at 4 years. . . . When arriving at the stone pile that marks the head of every pass, the yakmen jump and prance about frantically, yelling 'So..so..so..so..' in prescribed rhythm, 'So' apparently being some species of deity. When asked why he did not yell when crossing a minor pass, Lappha said he didn't care for minor deities with whom he can argue and quarrel on more or less equal terms. He only respected the major gods who needed to be kept on the right side of. (The Dreamer whose dreams come true?). Have not been able to make out at all whether the people here take religion seriously or as a joke. Superstition, black magic and devils of numerous species certainly keep them in fear and trembling, but about the rest? . . . The shops in the mandis [Taklakot, Gyanima, Dharchula, *et al.*] carry an extraordinary assortment of stock-in-trade: cloth, cast-off woollens of every description, electric torches, new and secondhand army boots and plimsolls, tea from Lhasa and Beringg, sugar (*misri*), hurricane lanterns, safety-pins and miscellaneous improbable items requiring great ingenuity and imagination to muster. The shop-keepers also carry on barter, trading various articles with sheep's wool, furs, borax, etc. Was shown 2 or 3 beautiful Snow Lynx skins, rough cured but not mangled, obtained by barter. Jaman Singh of Dharchula sells them to a merchant in Peshawar for Rs 130 or thereabouts each.

13

Loke Wan Tho

In a slim little magazine called *Victory* that used to be published in Bombay during World War II for the benefit of transient army personnel, there appeared in 1942 an article entitled 'The Raven who Lost his Temper'. It concerned an incident that occurred while a young bird photographer—later to acquire international fame—was trying to photograph a heron's nest on the sea cliffs on the Pembrokeshire coast, which also had a pair of nesting ravens nearby. The writer of this article was given as Wan Tho Loke. A school master of the Doon School at Dehra Dun, J.T.M. Gibson, then Lieutenant Commander in the Royal Indian Navy, who had volunteered for military service and was temporarily posted in Bombay, saw the name and wondered if this was the same Loke whom he had taught as a boy at an English school in Switzerland some years previously. He contacted the author through the editor of the magazine and found that he was right. After finishing his education at Cambridge and London Universities, Loke, still in his mid-twenties, had returned home to Singapore to take charge of a flourishing business empire built up by his late father, and which was conducted with consummate sagacity and success during his minority and education abroad by his wise and capable mother. This was shortly before the Japanese tide swept over Malaya and converted Singapore into Shonan. In anticipation of that foregone eventuality, Loke, his mother, and younger sister, Peng, were forced to flee Singapore and seek refuge in India, at Bombay. In the course of the escape on I think a Dutch ship, Loke was subjected to a number of harrowing experiences which nearly cost him his life. His ship was bombed by Japanese aircraft and sunk, and he was badly scorched by a blast in the fire it caused on board. His eyesight, feared lost at the time, was fortunately restored only after several weeks in a hospital in Jakarta, where he was taken after being 'salvaged' from the sea by an Australian cruiser. Gibson asked Loke how he proposed to occupy his time during his exile, and what his special interests were, so that he could help with suggestions. On learning that one of Loke's particular passions—apart from English literature and writing—was bird watching and bird photography, Gibson promised to put him in touch with a bird-watching friend, meaning me. The dinner meeting in Gibson's naval quarters a few days later proved mutually momentous and providential for both the guests. It brought me quite fortuitously in touch with a most unusual and lovable character and marked the beginning of a friendship which, through a close identity of outlook and interests, grew in depth and understanding over the years, right until his tragic death in an air crash in 1964. For Wan Tho that meeting with me and his consequent introduction to the BNHS also proved a blessing. It opened up avenues for meaningful and enjoyable utilization of his enforced leisure in India, and saved him from the deadly boredom it could otherwise well have entailed. It helped him to use his talents and opportunities to best advantage and in the process to develop into a highly competent ornithologist and world-class bird photographer. Both the Society and I continued to profit from his grateful munificence during his lifetime—a process that was kept up by his gracious mother Mrs Loke Yew, and by his friendly and charming sister Peng (Lady Y.P. McNeice) after the former's death. In the twenty-two years that this inestimable friendship flourished there was hardly a birding expedition, international bird conference or bird photographing holiday which Loke did not share with me personally or with munificent financial support. Later on he maintained that in this way he derived almost as much vicarious satisfaction as from personal participation; and since pressure of business gave him so little respite for birding expeditions, this was the next best thing.

Being much impressed by Loke's keenness about birds and bird photography I casually asked him if he would be interested in joining me in a birding expedition to Kutch, for which I was just then preparing. Loke jumped at the offer and accepted it at once. In the course of the next four months in Kutch I had ample opportunity to test his capacity for spartan living—for putting up cheerfully with the rough-and-ready existence which low-budget bird surveys involved—living completely off the land, sometimes in bug-ridden *dharamsalas* with loud throat-clearing pilgrims, or maybe tumbledown cowsheds. On such expeditions there was *dal* and rice for lunch and rice and *dal* for dinner, with light provided by smoky hurricane lanterns, and there were sundry other tiresome deprivations then particularly necessitated by Hitler's war. Though at that time I had no inkling whatever of Loke's social status or life-style back in his Singapore homeland, it was obvious that he was unused to such privations, and all credit to him that he bore them seemingly joyfully and with such good humour. Never in all the time we lived together in the field on more or less this pattern in Kutch, and off and on for two or three years thereafter, did he once complain or grumble about the prevailing discomforts, nor drop a hint about his patrician life-style in his own country before being forced out by the Japanese. Outwardly he seemed to enjoy and thrive on these discomforts as though to the manner born; except I realize that with the chronic dysentery he was uncomplainingly suffering from all the time, it can't have been fun running out in the open in the middle of the night looking for a bush!

Wan Tho passed the initial test in Kutch with flying colours. I was happy to discover in him a truly kindred spirit and dedicated co-worker, ever ready to pull his weight and more under all circumstances. His keen sense of humour, unfailing courtesy and quiet good manners, friendly disposition and capacity to mix at all levels, and to remain cheerful and unruffled under a leader not famous for sweetness of temper, made him an ideal adjunct to our field camps. The near identity of our outlook and interests brought us closer together than any other of my latter-day friends. During his forced exile in India, while the Japan war was on, the countrywide regional bird surveys gave him a god-sent opportunity to indulge his passion for natural history and the out-of-doors, and devote his entire time and energy to ornithology and bird photography—and in this he came to be regarded a maestro.

Wan Tho was a great lover of English literature, with a connoisseur's sense of appreciation and criticism. This made him a charming and stimulating companion in camp, when all the mundane chores of the day were over and we sat reading after dinner in the light of a couple of miserable hurricane lanterns. He would break out now and again into reading aloud passages which had specially caught his fancy, sometimes with a chuckle and often with an obvious smacking of the lips. He himself wrote pleasingly in an easy style and with a keen sense of humour. His meticulously kept diary of day-to-day happenings all through our various collecting expeditions together help to recall many incidents I had long forgotten, since my own dry-as-dust notes chiefly concerned birds and ecology.

Most of our shifting from camp to camp across the country had to be done, as in the Hyderabad survey, by privately owned converted buses, usually tired veterans and invariably overloaded. Petrol was scarce and strictly rationed during wartime so that most such jalopies had been converted to run on charcoal gas. When an incline became too steep for the engine to manage on its own, all able-bodied passengers were expected to get out and push. Wan Tho always entered into the spirit of this game with gusto, but on one particularly hot and sultry midday, scrambling back into the bus still panting from an extra vigorous exertion, he casually said 'Sálim, you should really have a station wagon of your own for this sort of work. You will then be independent of all this trouble and can load up your baggage and equipment whenever you wish and go off wherever and whenever you like.' The argument seemed flawless. I agreed with him entirely, but conditions at the time being what they were, financially and otherwise, thought no more about it until most pleasantly reminded of it a few months later.

Japan had lost the war; Shonan had been reconverted to

Singapore as of old, and the widely scattered exiles were being
fast herded and repatriated to the island by the British government in order to rehabilitate its disrupted trade and industry in
the shortest possible time. Wan Tho, who was among the first
batch of businessmen selected for return, had greatly feared
that his business would have been completely ruined and that
he would need to start it all over afresh. It was the pleasantest
surprise of his life to find that, thanks to his Chinese manager's
tact and sagacity, the business had actually thriven during the
Japanese occupation and that he himself was one of the
wealthiest men in Singapore once more! Announcing this
joyfully in one of his first letters to me after his return, he
casually reminded me of that long uphill bus push in Madhya
Pradesh and what he had 'philosophized' to me on the occasion
about a station wagon for my field work, adding 'I enclose a
cheque: buy yourself a suitable station wagon; and remember
there is more where this came from in case this much doesn't
suffice'.

True to his ancestral Chinese tradition Wan Tho had an eye
for beauty—beautiful mountains and natural scenery, beautiful
flowers and birds, beautiful pictures, beautiful porcelain,
beautiful everything else, not excluding beautiful women in
whom, indeed, he was somewhat of a connoisseur! They were
important enough always to find mention in his diary wherever
encountered. His first wife Christina was a very beautiful
woman: unfortunately she herself knew it only too well. She
was never happier than under a constant shower of expected
adulation. I fear I was not popular with Christina because, not
being much of a courtier, I could never bring myself to pander
to her vanity in this blatant fashion. I suspect that at times she
was even somewhat resentful of Wan Tho's intimate attachment
to me—being my *alter ego* as it were—especially when the
three of us were together at international bird meetings or on
motoring or photographing holidays in Europe and elsewhere,
or when I was staying as their guest on my frequent visits to
Singapore at Wan Tho's invitation. It is a pity that Chris should
have banked so heavily on her glamour and good looks. She
had no need to since she possessed many other more solid and

less ephemeral qualities and accomplishments to make her stand out from amongst most of her peers. Although Chris could be disarmingly charming when she chose, in company and as a socialite hostess, their temperaments and outlooks on major issues had seemed to me so different from the very beginning, while we were holidaying together for a couple of months in Kashmir soon after their marriage in 1950—his so quiet and scholastic, hers so flashy and gaiety-loving—that I had feared the partnership wouldn't last. In the event, after ten or so uneasy years of 'terrible storm and treacherous calm' the end came. The deliverance cost Wan Tho £93,000 (or was it 97?) by way of alimony but, as he put it with a sigh of relief, 'it was cheap at that!'

Soon after that bird photographing trip to Kashmir with the Lokes in the spring and summer of 1951, I was invited for a film talk on Kashmir birds at the Bombay University Women's Hostel. Here I met a young female journalist of about 35 who, though not glamorous, did for the first time since Tehmina's death seriously throw me off balance by her charm and intelligence. She spent a couple of week-ends at 46 Pali Hill while Kamoo and Hassan were away on a holiday in Japan. Grapevine rumours revived premature hopes in my dear sister Kamoo who, with my other sisters and nieces, had all along been scheming and trying to get me to settle down once more. AK (as I shall call her) came to spend a week of birding with Wan Tho and me at Bharatpur as the Maharaja's guest, during which we came to know each other better, and I saw more of her again in Delhi and Bombay later. Though I sometimes still think of her with mild nostalgia, it was on the whole lucky for me, and perhaps less doubtfully so for her, that our mutual infatuation was short-lived, because on the touchstone she didn't seem the sort who would in the long run relish the rough-and-tumble gypsy living that was the fate of an impecunious freelance ornithologist. After 1952 or so this apparition vanished into the void, and I have heard no more about her since. In Wan Tho's meticulously written diaries of our expeditions together I find the following entries from that memorable week in Bharatpur, and the sentiments he had confided to his 'Dear Diary'.

October 19. Mrs A . . . K . . . arrived today from Delhi. A dark lady, spare of frame and drawn of visage. A lady with a mission in life. Sense of humour rationed. A vegetarian, arty. Age about 35. About 5'3" and weighing practically nothing. Communist by sympathy . . . October 22. Sat up on roof of Maharaja's guest house until late (11.20) discussing Indian music and dancing. A is more interesting and intelligent than I had at first imagined. . . . Romance is entering in again, late, into Sálim's life: I hope he will not be hurt, but I fear for him.

No need to, it all soon blew over, and just as well!

Between the collecting expedition in Kutch and his return to liberated Singapore we didn't have a chance to do another major systematic regional survey together, though short, casual collecting and shooting trips to different parts of the country were frequent. Both of us had greatly looked forward to, and carefully planned for the 'pilgrimage' to western Tibet in 1945 from which, to our mutual disappointment, Wan Tho had to back out in the last stages of preparation due to some urgent minor surgery. Most of our longer collecting and photographing expeditions after his permanent rehabilitation in liberated Singapore—chiefly in Bharatpur, Kashmir and Sikkim—were comparatively comfortable affairs, specially as regards logistics and commissariat. They were indeed more in the nature of a busman's holiday, though serious enough to be scientifically meaningful all the same.

My *Birds of Sikkim* is based chiefly on two such expeditions of two to three months each, both funded by Wan Tho, and in one of which he participated personally. His diary of the time is replete with evocative anecdotes which recall many long forgotten incidents and details. This was around the year 1955, long before democracy and the Border Roads Organization overran Sikkim and swept it into dubious modernity. Even so-called jeepable roads were non-existent beyond Gangtok then, and leisurely enjoyable back-packing with mule or porter transport for baggage was the normal mode of travel beyond the capital.

Of the Kewzing-Pemionche trail the diary says

The man who wrote that 'it is better to travel than to arrive' clearly had never walked a Himalayan mile! Every time we do a march, I am always happy to arrive.' [Of dak bungalows along the trail]: These rest houses are provided with crockery, cutlery, beds, and mattresses and other necessities, and are therefore very comfortable to live in. I am sitting on the verandah of the rest house (Temi) writing my notes looking at the roses now in full flower, with the blue hills beyond shrouded in mist. I have had a good wash and am now in my pyjamas, although the time is only 5.45 p.m., and with body pleasantly weary and mind content, I look out and am thoroughly happy. A party of Whitecrested Laughing Thrushes have just flitted by making their loud cheerful cackle. Dinner will be served in a short while and by 8.30 or so we shall be in bed. It is a good life, certainly the antithesis of the life I lead in Singapore. I have not read a newspaper for days . . . We get up just after 5 in the morning, lunch at 11, dine at 6 or 6.30 and go to bed not later than 9 p.m. [On the trail to Singtam]: We also met a number of very pretty girls going to market, and I asked permission to photograph them.

One of the guests on duty tour staying at the Gangtok Residency at the same time as ourselves was a Superintending Engineer of the Central PWD in charge of a large district stretching from Calcutta to Sikkim and Assam. He was too precious a subject for Wan Tho's incisive diary to miss.

He was a curious fellow, utterly without table manners as we understand them: thus he would eat off his knife, drink his soup loudly, and blow his nose into his serviette. His speech was peculiar and not edifying. In speaking of concrete roads, which he held were unsuitable for the climate of Sikkim, he said 'They crags (cracks) and sings (sinks): they set hard like i-stone: what is the bloody sense? Must (most?) definitely costlier.' And of oil extracted from Assam, 'it cost us not cheaper, even, I mean to say, into our terra firma. Do you see what I mean?' . . . Rai Bahadur Densappa [the Chief Secretary to the Chogyal's government] on the other hand, is a man of great intelligence with an impish sort of humour. When he heard that I was to be escorted beyond the Inner Line in northern Sikkim by the Tahsildar 'to keep an eye on me' ('a watcher to watch the bird watcher', as Sálim put it) the Rai Bahadur said 'You make use of him. He is the head of his district, and he has only to wink and he gets it. You extract venom from a cobra and make good medicine with it: you do the same with him. But he is much better than a cobra of course!'

In the event the *tahsildar's* company actually proved a boon since it saved us a great deal of logistic and procedural worry.

Of a nest of the Ibisbill photographed at Yakthang, near

Thangu, altitude *c*. 4,000 metres (18 April 1955) the diary reads: 'As a result of leaving the hide in place overnight, the bird was absurdly tame, and Sálim could make any noise inside the hide without frightening it. At one time Sálim got so tired of having the bird perfectly still on the eggs for a long time that he tried every method, short of getting out of the hide, to make it move, including singing "God Save the King" full-throatedly, but to no avail.' Of course I had expected that at least would make the bird stand up!

About the Thangu region: 'Everywhere one sees prayer flags. The prayers are printed on them from blocks which may be had at the monasteries. Do we, who believe in Science, believe in all this, or do we say with Tolstoy "Science, that is the supposed knowledge of absolute truth", or guardedly pray with the Scientist "O Lord, if there be one, save my soul, if any".'

Mention of *The Birds of Sikkim* reminds me of one particularly uncomfortable incident during the ornithological survey of the Chogyal's state around the year 1955. In the time I was camping at Lachen there was a fairly severe earthquake in the area, causing a number of major landslides among the surrounding mountains. A large section of the mule track between here and Chumthang, running along a steep contour, had slid down into the torrential river several hundred feet down, almost vertically below. Porters and pack animals had trampled out a fearsome, narrow alternative footpath across the loose debris some distance below the vanished original—how fearsome I was to discover only when I got on it some days later. As usual I had left the camp all by myself loaded with rucksack and binoculars well ahead of the porters, hoping to do some quiet birdwatching en route. While uneasily picking my way over this terrifying ledge I reached a spot where the loose detritus from the hillside above had slid down to block the narrow path in the form of a scree which was still in ominous motion. Though only a couple of metres wide, this patch would need stepping on to get across. The risk of tumbling down with the debris into the river so steeply below gave me cold feet, with a peculiar feeling of giddiness and inertia that left me rooted to the spot. I could move neither forward nor turn back, so promptly squatted down, resigned to await the arrival of the porters no matter how long that might take! During the half hour or so of waiting, the 'conveyor belt' flow of the powdery earth over the scree and edge of that awesome abyss had a strangely hypnotic effect and was not conducive to self-confidence, and I was mightily relieved to see the first heavily laden porter arriving. He seemed rather perplexed to find me resting in such an unlikely shadeless spot but understood when I pointed to the scree in pantomime. Hauling me up casually by one hand, he stepped nonchalantly on the scree and whisked me across, continuing his march without interruption as though it were all within the day's work. The rest of the laden porters who followed seemed not even to notice that anything was wrong with the path. They marched unconcernedly over the scree simply as if it was not there. In retrospect, it was not an experience of which I can feel proud, and singularly deflating to my ego.

The only other time I have experienced a feeling of similar hypnotic paralysis and complete helplessness to move forward or back was when—in spite of being forewarned—I had rashly persisted, partly in a spirit of bravado, in wanting to climb up the roughly 100 ft tower of Oxford University's Museum of Science to look at the swifts nesting in the ventilators which David Lack and his intrepid wife Elizabeth had been studying since 1948. The results of this classical study are in Lack's fascinating book *Swifts in a Tower*, published in 1956. This Museum tower rises about 60 feet from its base in the upper part of the building. From here the ascent to the floor of the tower is by a steep narrow spiral staircase which is in complete darkness for part of the way. It is followed by a terrifying, almost vertical 30 ft ladder without a handrail, through the first platform. Another 30 feet or so up a slightly less but still sufficiently forbidding ladder brings you up to the second such platform within easy reach of the glass-backed boxes in which the birds can be observed on their nests. I give these details merely to justify my overwhelming temptation to give up after one look down the shaft of the tower from the head of that terrifying vertical railless ladder. This I would most gladly have done had not Dr Lack been apprehensively watching my progress from below. But having unwisely rejected his earlier dissuasion I felt honour bound to grit my teeth and make it to the top—cost what it may—though at one stage I was paralysed with fright and ready to collapse.

14

Flamingo City

Among the Indian princes and princelings whom I had opportunities of knowing a little more intimately than others—chiefly on a naturalist's plane—was Maharao Vijayarajji of Kutch. He was over sixty when he came to the *gaddi*, having been on a patient and seemingly unending probation as Yuvraj for forty years or more, thanks to the robust good health of his father, Maharao Khengarji, who had come to be regarded by two generations of his loyal subjects as an ancient, indestructible monument of Kutch. Both father and son were keen sportsmen and knowledgeable naturalists, the former as a hunter of big game, the latter particularly interested in birds—game as well as in general. Besides being an excellent shot with gun and rifle, Vijayarajji was an accomplished tennis player in his younger days and a 'habitual' entrant in all-India tournaments, which he frequently won since many of the renowned players of the day were only too happy to partner him in the doubles.

I first became acquainted with Maharao Vijayarajji in 1942, soon after he, at long last, ascended the *gaddi*. By then he had lost some of his youthful vigour and assumed a comfortable, portly shape, abetted by lack of exercise forced by an injury to his knee. Though having to cut down on shikar jaunts needing physical exertion and mobility, he still retained an enviable expertise in small-game shooting and a lively interest in watching birds, especially of his own state. Thus it was at his invitation and under his generous sponsorship that I undertook a field survey of the bird life of his fascinating state with a view to producing for him an illustrated book on the birds of Kutch on the lines of my *Book of Indian Birds*, which had caught his fancy. In 1943 World War II was still very much on and petrol was severely rationed in India, bringing private transport virtually to a standstill. As a special sop to the ruling princes, however, an extra quota of petrol was allotted to them which, in the case of Kutch, enabled freer movement for the bird survey and visits to out-of-the-way places otherwise difficult to reach.

In between camps my party usually spent a couple of days in Bhuj for re-fitting, and each time I was in, the Maharao would invite me to accompany him on his evening drives to some scenic point in the environs of the town and 'take the air'. He was usually alone, attended only by a flunkey armed with a thermos, a bottle of 'pegs' and a supply of pistachios and almonds and things of that sort for His Highness to while away his time pleasantly, while listening to or discussing my report on the progress of the survey. One of the things that struck me as singularly odd at the time—especially coming from a man normally so courteous and considerate—was that never in all these outings did he even once offer me any of the things he was stolidly munching away while the replenishing flunkey stood attentively at his elbow. That it should never have occurred to him to do so seems queer and inconceivable, yet there it was.

I am reminded by a note in my diary of that time of a crude manifestation of the anachronistic feudalism that still persisted in Kutch. I felt outraged, while responding to the Maharao's request to meet him at the palace for some discussion, to discover too late that it was mandatory for 'natives' to alight from their vehicles—whether car or horse carriage—at the main palace gate and cover the fifty yards or so up the drive to the entrance porch on foot. This mandate applied uniformly to all *Indians*, of whatever status, whether residents or visitors, official or non-official. The enormity of the *diktat* was that even the Indian *dewan* (chief minister) of the state visiting His Highness on official business had to 'crawl' in this fashion, while *any* European or Anglo-Indian of howsoever dubious a quality could drive straight up to the porch without let or hindrance, and perhaps even with a welcoming salute from the armed sentry at the gate. The 'reigning' dewan at the time of my survey, a highly respected senior Indian civilian, had to submit to this perverse indignity, while the lowly Anglo-Indian Customs Inspector could drive right up to the porch. I got a shock when ordered to alight at the main entrance, created a scene, and later protested to the Maharao in no uncertain terms about this insulting iniquity. I hope it had some effect, but I never had occasion to visit the palace a second time.

A peculiar oddity that amused me greatly when observing the intra- and interspecific habits and behaviour of that now-extinct genus—the maharaos, maharajas and nawabs—in the course of my bird surveys of the various Indian states, was the comic ostentation with which the rulers addressed each other, back and forth, as 'Your Highness' in tête-à-tête conversation, even though they might be old friends and contemporaries or close relations. When talking to one of 'lesser breed' some of them took good care, when referring to a brother Highness, to slip in inconsequentially—as though in parenthesis—such vital information as 'He is 13 guns, you know, I am 17' and thereafter run on with the discourse.

Kutch is a chronically drought-prone area, and a succession of bad monsoons will often inhibit breeding of the flamingos for two or three years. The birds need an optimum depth of six to eight inches of shallow inundation on their breeding ground to generate their mound-building activities. If the monsoon has failed or been deficient, this depth is never attained on the nest site. In that case the water leaves the site high and dry before September or October, when the normal breeding season should commence. If the monsoon has been heavy, as in 1944, the water on the site is too deep, and may take a long time to dry to the acceptable depth. Hence, unlike most nesting grounds in Asia, and in Europe, Africa and the New World, the season in Kutch is a moveable feast and unpredictable. It may range anywhere between September/October and March/April or be completely suppressed. The 'city' itself lies deserted the rest of the year, since after the birds have finished breeding they disperse far and wide along with the newly fledged young in small flocks or large feeding concentrations, frequenting coastal lagoons and salt pans, as at Point Calimere, and in Saurashtra and Sri Lanka. In the non-breeding season they also frequent brackish lakes such as Sambhar in Rajasthan, Chilka in Orissa, and others.

Knowing my special keenness to study the Kutch flamingo and the disappointments I had had on earlier visits to the breeding grounds, the Maharao had a special lookout kept on flamingo movements in the Great Rann. That is how I received an express telegram from him one day in April 1945 while I was in the midst of hectic preparations in Bombay for the birding 'pilgrimage' to Kailas and Manasarovar the following month. The breeding colony—'Flamingo City'—was then at the peak of its activities and I was urged to come immediately. This long-awaited opportunity, coming even at such an awkward moment, was too good to miss. I arrived in Bhuj by air two days later. Air flights were elementary and erratic in the war years and trains were slow and leisurely, involving connections at Viramgam and elsewhere with metre-gauge lines through various Kathiawar principalities, each of which insisted on maintaining a few measly miles of its own railway system, more as a status symbol than anything else. These operated to unco-ordinated timings, no doubt to assert their independent status on neighbouring princelings across the fence. Since the states did not subscribe to the fetish of punctuality you were lucky if you sometimes caught your connections. Then, finally, you had to bivouac for the night on the crowded platform at Navlakhi in Jamnagar—a sort of open air dormitory free for all—to take the motor launch across to Kandla in Kutch next morning, followed by four hours in an exasperatingly sluggish narrow-gauge train before you finally arrived in Bhuj, a total of forty hours or so from Bombay.

In Bhuj I had the pleasure of meeting Sir Peter Clutterbuck, a former Inspector-General of Forests in India who had done a stint as Chief Conservator of Forests in Kashmir State after retirement, and was now in Kutch at Maharao Vijayarajji's invitation to reorganize the Forest Department of the state. Throughout his Indian service, Sir Peter had the reputation of being an exceptionally able forest officer and a dedicated naturalist and conservationist. Though no longer young, he had expressed to the Maharao a keen desire to visit Flamingo City along with me, in spite of the summer heat and physical hardships involved in the journey.

A fairly sybaritic tented camp had been set up by the Kutch durbar for our overnight halt at Nir, which was reached from Bhuj via Khavda, partly by car and partly on camelback (about seventy miles). I recall the acrimonious political key on which my relationship with Sir Peter opened at the tête-à-tête dinner that night—damask tablecloth, silver cutlery, liveried waiters! The years of the World War and the decade or so before, with Mahatma Gandhi and the Satyagraha Movement in operation, had embittered relations between Indians and the British to an unprecedented degree. All the British in India, government servants high and low, as well as the boxwallahs—were scandalized and almost foaming at the mouth over the 'subversive' preachings and mischief of that 'seditionist rat Gandhi', as Meinertzhagen had called him, and his traitorous henchman Nehru—even after the correct education he had received at Harrow and Cambridge. Earlier in the evening Sir Peter had thus gratuitously started unburdening himself on the subject, and now gave me an unprovoked broadside of the pent-up venom of his spleen. As I have confessed before, I have never been famous for the sweetness of my temper, and here was sufficient provocation for jettisoning restraint. I am afraid perhaps I said more nasty things than the occasion called for, but it did help to clear the atmosphere between Sir Peter Clutterbuck and myself for ever after. I made it plain to him that I had no wish or intention to convert him from his firm convictions, nor would it be worth his while to try to change my views—and that was that; we both had a deep common interest in birds and wildlife, so why not confine ourselves to those topics and leave politics to the politicians? After this first unfortunate but decisive confrontation, I found Sir Peter a singularly charming and delightful companion, and the friendship and mutual regard generated on that flamingo trip endured till his death in about 1958 in England, where I was happy to have met him a few months earlier. The catalyst in our bond of friendship was partly also his doting son Brigadier J.E. (Jack) Clutterbuck, R.E., who retired from India in 1948 as Chief Engineer of the then G.I.P. Railway after many years of meritorious service, to start a new life in England—farming in Somerset. Jack was to me a kindred spirit, an altogether lovable and admirable character, mad about the Indian jungles where we had spent many happy days together from time to time camping, shooting, trekking and naturalizing. He was one of my closest and most cherished English friends.

The traditional Flamingo City—the same as used by the birds year after year at least since 1896 when first reported—lies some 10 kilometres north-east of Nir (at the tip of Pachham Island), out in the pancake-flat featureless Rann. To reach the place one has to wade on foot or ride on local ponies or camels which skid and slither alarmingly through the ankle- to thigh-deep water, more or less concentrated brine, of over-soft, slippery slush often overlaid by a deceptive crust or razor-sharp salt crystals like splintered glass. Under the intense desert sun it produces the blinding glare of freshly fallen snow. The fetlocks of the ponies sometimes get badly lacerated as the hoofs sink through the crunchy surface. Thankfully, the April heat felt less oppressive than the 45°C + shown by the thermometer, because a cool breeze blew throughout the day and even made a cotton coverlet distinctly welcome at night in our open-to-sky bivouac. This was, and still remains, the only occasion it was possible to make a fairly accurate physical count of the population of Flamingo City in a peak breeding year, and to observe something of the nocturnal movements and behaviour of the birds, for it was a period of brilliant moonlight with a clear sky and optimal conditions. However, the lack of fresh water at the site, and of fuel for cooking and fodder of any kind for the riding and draft animals, made a longer stay than our two nights 'on location' impossible. This would necessitate elaborate and carefully planned previous *bandobast*. After measuring out the total area of the colony on the ground and randomly demarcating several 'built up' sample plots of about 90 metres × 90 metres each, and allowing for the bald (unbuilt) patches in between the nest clusters, I calculated the total number of occupied nests in the 'city' to be 104,758. On the basis of this figure, and taking two adults to each nest and two young to every three nests, plus the hordes of non-breeding adults and sub-adults around the colony, the total population would probably be of the order of half a million birds. This would undoubtedly make Flamingo City the largest breeding colony of the Greater Flamingo in Asia, and at least *one* of the largest in the world. I have long realized the potential of the Great Rann of Kutch as an area for biological surprises, justifying a full-scale scientific exploration, and regretted not being able to carry out a more thorough and extensive survey myself. On a subsequent visit to Flamingo City I was lucky to discover a colony of Avocets (*Recurvirostra avosetta*) breeding in its 'suburbs'—the first ever record for the subcontinent—and on another visit a few years later a nesting colony of Rosy Pelicans (*Pelecanus onocrotalus*)—also the first—among the worn-down disused flamingo nests on the periphery.

To make doubly sure that the camera he had lent me (to replace mine which had developed a last-minute hitch) behaved as it should in my hands, Maharao Vijayarajji had considerately sent out from Bhuj the state photographer, Ali Mohammad, with complete paraphernalia and a special assistant, whose function was not immediately apparent. The two photographers and their equipment made up two complete camel loads. The vintage apparatus—a full-plate studio camera of solid teakwood, enormous proportions and cumbrousness—looked like some antique piece of furniture from the period of William the Conqueror or thereabouts. It had no mechanical shutter but worked by smartly doffing and donning a cap over the lens with the photographer's hand. In open sunshine, despite the operator's lightning sleights-of-hand, the comparatively slow plates, and the diaphragm shut down to a pinpoint, the negatives were often somewhat overexposed. It was obviously a camera with a history, and quite believably the same as made the original picture published in the *Journal* of the BNHS by Maharao Khengarji in 1896 giving positive evidence of flamingos breeding in the Rann. The apparatus not only needed two able-bodied men to rig it up for action on its

massive wooden tripod, but also for its complicated co-operative
operation. It was worked like a ship, and this is where the
trained assistant became indispensable. The chief photographer
(the Captain) had to enshroud his head in yards of black cloth,
eyes glued to the focussing screen. From this position—the
'bridge'—he signalled orders down to the 'engine room', as it
were, to the assistant in front, to twiddle the focussing knob a
trifle this way or that to get the correct focus. The focussing
knob was out of reach of the Captain himself and only a
specially trained assistant could assist. The camera erected at
the nest colony, 'on location', showed up from afar in the vast
expanse as a fair-sized house, and, when a wind sprang up and
the black shroud round the Captain's head began to flutter and
flap, I thought there could be no earthly chance of getting any
photographs of the birds. I am afraid at that point I also became
rather uncharitably facetious at the Captain's expense, but he
bore it all with surprising good humour. It was not until we got
back to Bhuj and he produced the most unexpectedly good
results from his dark room that I realized the laugh had really
been on me, and that it needs something more than a good
camera to produce a good photograph.

An edition of 1,000 copies of *The Birds of Kutch* with twenty
colour plates by D.V. Cowen, fully funded by the Kutch
durbar, was published by Oxford University Press for the
Government of Kutch in 1945, under severe wartime constraints. It was acclaimed by reviewers in India and abroad.
Five hundred copies of the book were retained by the Maharao
for presentation to his state guests. Unfortunately, these copies
were carelessly stored in a damp cellar where most were
destroyed by white ants. The publication was priced at a nominal
Rs 20 per copy and the edition was soon exhausted, secondhand copies fetching up to $100 thereafter.

One of our camps during the Kutch bird survey was in a tiny
godforsaken desert village of a few down-and-out hovels called
Rapar on the easternmost edge of the state, bordering on the
Little Rann. The only comparatively substantial building within
its mud-walled 'fort' was the police station manned by a couple
of policemen and their camels for patrolling the area, and a

single *puggee* whose main job was to walk round the village in the early morning and at evening dusk, eyes on the ground, to monitor the footprints of any strangers, human or camel, that may have entered or left the village since the last scrutiny. The station house had been cleared for our use by orders from above. It was at Rapar that we first came across this very remarkable tribe of hereditary trackers (*puggee* from 'pug', meaning foot, or footprint). They are as familiar with the footprints of the inhabitants of a village as with their faces, and can tell with absolute confidence whether particular footprints, human or camel, belong to a resident or to a visiting outsider. In desert areas where camel-stealing is one of the favourite local pastimes, this accomplishment is of the greatest help to the police in tracking down not only lost or stolen camels, but also camel thieves and other criminals. One or two such *puggees* formed the normal complement of every remote police out-post. The hereditary expertise these professional trackers have acquired through generations is phenomenal and truly amazing.

Khan Bahadur Malcolm Kothavala, the Inspector-General of Police in Kutch at the time of the survey, who had unmatched experience of *puggees* in the various desert states of Rajputana where he had served, related the case of a camel stolen from a border village like Rapar. This camel had a very slight limp in its left foreleg and its footprints were in consequence distinctive, but only for the local *puggee*. One night the camel disappeared along with a stranger who, as the ground monitoring had shown, had entered the village the day before. The village *puggee* got on the trail and followed the camel led by the stranger for several miles beyond the village till the ground became too hard and stony for any clues, and the trail was lost. Two years later this *puggee* took leave to go to his village miles away but in the same direction as the camel he had followed. While moving around his village, like a busman on holiday, he happened upon a camel's footprints which he confidently identified as those of the animal he had trailed two years before, but the footprints of the man leading it were different. Anyhow, he followed the spoor to its owner's house. On questioning the man it turned out that he had purchased the animal from its former owner a few months earlier. The seller was traced and from his footprints the *puggee* confirmed his identification as the person who had led the camel away from its native village. After the normal gentle third-degree persuasion, the thief confessed. Both he and the purchaser of stolen property got it in the neck, and the camel was restored to its rightful owner in its rightful village. The Khan Bahadur had many other stories of the phenomenal feats of tracking performed by these simple untutored folk, with the skill passed down from father to son through countless generations. It is a pity that, with increasing sophistication in methods of crime detection, the *puggees* are fast losing their importance as well as the skill and expertise they have acquired through the ages— and with it their jobs and livelihood.

In 1945, R.I. Pocock, who was revising the Mammalia volumes of the Fauna of British India series, wrote to the BNHS asking whether it could arrange to obtain a few fresh specimens of the Kutch wild ass for critical study, since adequate material was lacking in the British Museum (Natural History). Maharao Vijayarajji, with his accustomed generosity, offered to provide all facilities to the Society for a collecting expedition in the Little Rann, which is the stronghold of this animal. I was doing the bird survey of Gujarat at the time (March 1946) and was glad to avail of the opportunity for a closer acquaintance with this rare and interesting animal, the ecology and biology of which was so little known. It would also give me a chance to investigate the birds of the Little Rann which I had missed during the Kutch survey, and long suspected to be the only breeding ground of the Lesser Flamingo (*Phoeniconaias minor*) in the Indian region.

A narrative of the wild ass expedition with field notes on the habits and food, etc., of the species, together with measurements and other details of the five specimens collected, is published in the *Journal* of the BNHS 46: 472–77 (1946). To weigh the animals in the field a rough-and-ready beam scale had to be improvised, hung from a tree with a wild ass at one end and three or four domestic ones (i.e. my camp followers!)

at the other. The latter were subsequently weighed individually on a standard weighing machine and tolerably accurate weights of the animals obtained. The trip proved highly rewarding also from the ornithological angle. We fortuitously struck a vast open expanse of shallow brackish water in the debouchment of the Banas river into the Rann, where there was a heavier concentration of migratory ducks, waders and other birds than I had ever seen before or have since—duck by the million darkening the water for miles, the majority apparently Common Teal (*Anas crecca*) with a sprinkling of hordes of Shovellers (*Spatula clypeata*), and doubtless many other species not distinguishable in the distance. Besides these, there were some eighty Rosy Pelicans and three to five lakh Lesser Flamingo (*Phoeniconaias minor*) (*no* Greater), countless thousands of sandpipers, stints, redshanks, greenshanks and others; also thousands of Common and Demoiselle Cranes, all apparently collecting for the outward migration. Unfortunately I never had a chance to visit this place at the proper time again.

15

Bharatpur

Before 1935 I only knew the 'Ghana' of Bharatpur by its reputation as a phenomenal private duck-shooting reserve of the maharajas and their elite VIP guests. That year, at my bidding, my friend Prater, Curator of the BNHS, wrote to Sir Richard Tottenham, ICS, a keen naturalist-sportsman member of the Society, to enquire what facilities would be available from the state for setting up a pilot wildfowl ringing centre at the famous Keoladeo Ghana *jheel*. Sir Richard was the Administrator of the state during the minority of Maharaja Brijendra Singh, and the High Panjandrum whose word was law. That is how I got my earliest introduction to this fabulous wetland which has since become one of my most regular stamping grounds, and in the process developed into the Society's chief centre for the study of bird migration in India. Prior to that time practically no bird ringing had been done in the subcontinent, barring the pioneering experiment in Dhar State (now in Madhya Pradesh) in 1926 by the enterprising ruler, Maharaja Sir Uday Singh Puar. Aluminium rings bearing the legend 'Inform Maharaja Dhar' had to be specially hand-crafted for him by the BNHS (in the proverbial style of the early Rolls Royce engines). It was a slow and laborious job as strips of appropriate sizes had to be cut from the metal sheet, their sharp edges filed smooth, and the legend and serial number manually punched, letter by letter, from steel dies. Under the circumstances the operation could only be on a very limited scale. Despite this the recoveries reported from such distant places as Turkestan, Siberia, and other parts of the USSR were so exciting and encouraging that I was determined to have the BNHS take up bird ringing as one of its major field activities if and when funds and facilities ever made it possible. Using the Dhar success as a lure the Society was able, through the good offices of some of its civilian members in the Sind administration, then a part of Bombay Presidency, to persuade a handful of affluent sporting zamindars to take up the ringing of migratory ducks. But here again the bottleneck was the ring supply. Rings marked 'Inform Bombay Nat. Hist. Society' had still to be manually prepared and were sparingly available. In spite of the modest scale on which ringing was done in Sind the recoveries were gratifying beyond expectation.

It was a long wait, but 'possibility' did drop into our lap fortuitously and unsolicited, via the World Health Organization. Around the year 1957 there erupted an apparently new form of encephalitis in the Kyasanur forest area of Karnataka (South India), affecting villagers and monkeys, sometimes fatally. The tick-borne virus of this encephalitis (known as 'Monkey Disease' or KFD) was reported by the Virus Research Centre, Pune, to be closely related to Omsk Haemorrhagic Fever and the Russian Spring-Summer Encephalitis (RSS) complex. The apparently transcontinental distribution of the virus suggested that it could have reached here through the agency of ticks on birds migrating betwen USSR and India, and the WHO seriously seized upon the problem. In March 1959 I was invited to a meeting in Geneva of a 'Scientific Group on Research on Birds as Disseminators of Arthropod-borne Viruses', with the project proposal prepared at their request for the study of bird migration in Kutch and north-west India. The proposal was warmly approved, and with financial support from WHO the first-ever organized scheme for bird ringing and migration study in the subcontinent was launched. This is the genesis of the Society's Bird Migration Project, a study of which the seed was well and truly implanted in me during the visit to the Ornithological Observatory at Heligoland in 1929.

Up to the mid-sixties the WHO was itself receiving substantial financial aid from the US government for its wide-ranging public health research programmes, chiefly in underdeveloped countries. After three or four years WHO's funding to the BNHS ceased. Because of its massive involvement and commitments in the Korean war the US was obliged to prune its research grants drastically, which in turn brought the BNHS under the axe. The Society's bird ringing project was seriously jeopardized, and it would certainly have collapsed but for the timely intervention at that point of the Smithsonian Institution in Washington. They considerately took over the funding for the interim period of uncertainty, followed fortuitously by the dropping from the blue of a totally unlooked-for source.

At that time the US Army Medical Research Laboratory, a component of SEATO with headquarters at Bangkok, was conducting a massive bird ringing programme known as MAPS (Migratory Animals Pathological Survey) in South-East Asian countries like Japan, the Philippines, Thailand, Malaya, Indonesia and Taiwan. MAPS was anxious to extend its activities to India, where the excellent performance of the BNHS in bird migration study had been commended to it by both the WHO and the Smithsonian. The overall MAPS programme was directed and co-ordinated by the ebullient and dynamic American ornithologist Dr H. Elliott McClure, an extrovert with whom it was a pleasure and an education to work. I have always been a stickler for the utmost economy in the handling of institutional funds. Therefore I was bucked no end when McClure expressed to me later his amazement and appreciation of the Society's performance in terms of birds ringed to dollars spent, as compared with the other South-East Asian countries MAPS was financing.

The bulk of the funds for the MAPS project came from the US Army Research and Development Group (Far East), Japan. MAPS had been following the BNHS's ringing work in India with interest and acclaim, and on learning of the possibility of its having to be wound up promptly offered to step in with the funding on condition that our data and results would be made available to it to complete its own information. That seemed fair enough, and I did not at the time suspect that such a useful scientific collaboration could or would land the Society and me personally as Chief Investigator in so much unpleasantness and adverse publicity.

It seems that an enterprising journalist, styling himself 'Scientific Correspondent' of some north-Indian newspaper, had got wind of the Society's ringing collaboration with MAPS. He came out on his own with a highly imaginative alarmist story, imputing that the Society was in this way colluding with the United States to explore the possibility of migratory birds being used in biological warfare for inducting and disseminating deadly viruses and germs in enemy countries. Since our migrant birds came chiefly from the USSR, and possibly also China, this lent credibility to the report in view of the Cold War, which had hotted up considerably about that time. The report caused a furore in Delhi's political circles and generated much heat and noise among our pro-communist, anti-US 'patriots' in the Lok Sabha. The outcry resulted in two successive enquiry committees, both of which fully absolved the Society and the project director Sálim Ali of criminal intent or subversive action. But the MPs remained unconvinced. In order to stop the noise and clear lingering doubts and suspicion once and for all, the government appointed a third so-called 'high power' committee of three top-ranking scientists, one each from the Virus Research Centre (VRC), Pune, the Tata Institute of Fundamental Research (TIFR), Bombay, and the Zoological Survey of India (ZSI), Calcutta, to review the matter thoroughly and *de novo*. It was not till their verdict fully endorsed the earlier findings that the Society regained its credibility and public image. However, during the two years or so that the hullabaloo was on, our migration study had practically come to an end for want of funds, the MAPS project itself having terminated meanwhile. To avoid a repetition of similar awkward incidents the government decided that the entire funding for all collaborative projects approved by it would in future be undertaken by itself on a request from the American collaborating agency from the counterpart rupee funds held in India under the PL 480 scheme.

With the resumption of funding from this source the Society's ringing programme was resuscitated and expanded to cover the ecology and movements of the avifauna, both resident and migratory. Our bird migration research programme and the practical training in field work it has afforded to the numerous young postgraduate biologists involved in it—some of whom have won higher university degrees in zoology by research in Field Ornithology under the Society's guidance—is among the more cherished satisfactions I have derived from my long association with the BNHS. So far (1983) we have been able to absorb most of our own products as research biologists on this and two other ongoing five-year collaborative projects with the Fish and Wildlife Service of the US Department of the Interior. A third project to study the ecology of the bird strike hazard at Indian aerodromes, also under way, is sponsored and funded fully by the Government of India through the Aeronautics Research & Development Board of the Ministry of Defence. In the three decades of its operation the bird migration project has produced information which enables guesswork to be replaced by solid factual data of great scientific value concerning bird migration in India.

Before the WHO funding for the BNHS's regular bird migration studies became available I had timed my annual visits to Bharatpur to coincide with the nesting season of the resident water birds—storks, herons, egrets, cormorants, ibises, spoonbills and others—which breed in the Ghana in such densely packed mixed heronries. Their movements within the country, and of some even beyond, are little understood. With the friendly co-operation of the Maharaja and the assistance of his shikaris and game guards, I had managed each year to ring several hundred nestlings with our hand-punched rings. Some tell-tale and highly interesting information was provided even by the scanty recoveries, often at unexpectedly distant places. Naturally the tally was not impressive. It was only after we had access to free supplies of rings of assorted sizes from specialist suppliers in Sweden, and to mist nets from Japan, that large-scale ringing got under way. For the first five years or so our attention was mostly confined to land birds, chiefly gallinaceous and passerine, specially the ground feeding forms—the potential hosts of ticks. Serious duck ringing could only be taken up much later, because the locals at Bharatpur and in the other localities of operation were unskilled in catching ducks

and other waterfowl in a sufficiently big way. It was only after
our discovery of the expert Bihari professional trappers of the
Sahni and Mirshikar tribes, and their almost disastrously
successful catching methods, that large-scale waterbird ringing
became possible.

Before it became a waterbird sanctuary and then a National
Park, Keoladeo Ghana was the fantastic private duck-shooting
preserve of the Bharatpur rulers. As long as the present
Maharaja retained his powers there was no question or thought
on his part of voluntarily giving up his shooting rights and
converting it into a sanctuary. Apart from his casual shooting
of a few ducks for sport and the table, he traditionally used to
lay on three or four big shoots every season to which all sorts of
VIPs and some less than V were invited—viceroys, governors,
top civil and military brass, and brother princes from other
states. Numbered butts were allotted to the guns, distributed
in strategic spots all over the lake. The whole operation worked
with the mechanical precision of an army manoueuvre, with
men of the state forces drilled as beaters to keep the birds
moving over the guns and not letting them settle. Enormous
holocausts were 'accomplished' at some of these gargantuan
shoots, and there are several records of two to three thousand
birds killed in a single day, and three records even of over four
thousand. The all-time record bag of 4,273 ducks and geese to
38 guns for Keoladeo Ghana was made in November 1938, with
Lord Linlithgow, the ruling viceroy, as the presiding slayer.
Although the lord sahib's own contribution to the bag was not
impressive, he did distinguish himself by creating what must
surely be a world record, of firing 1,900 rounds of 12-bore
ammunition from his own shoulder on that day. Only one who
has let off even a paltry hundred shots in a morning's snipe
shoot and got his shoulder black and blue will appreciate the
magnitude of this almost superhuman performance, even after
making due allowance for his lordship's considerable weight
and substance.

What gives to the Ghana its unique distinction as a birdwatcher's haunt is not only the fantastic concentration and
diversity of species of both resident and migratory waterbirds

at the appropriate seasons, but the uncommonly extended period of half a year or more at a stretch over which bird-watching can be enjoyed here. In a season of normal monsoon, residents such as storks, egrets, cormorants, etc. commence breeding in August. By November, before the parents and young have evacuated the heronries, the influx of the migrant ducks and geese has begun, which continues till end-November, by when the migrants have completely taken over. The prolonged unbroken period for the watching of water birds is a feature which is perhaps unequalled elsewhere in the world. This is what makes Keoladeo National Park such an ideal venue for the nature tourist and bird photographer—a questionable advantage from the conservation point of view!

The youthful and enthusiastic K.P.S. Menon, ICS, a great friend and admirer of my brother Hamid, took over from Sir Richard Tottenham as Administrator of Bharatpur State in 1936 or thereabouts. I remember how thrilled and delighted he and his twin daughters, then aged about twelve, were to punt out with me on the *jheel* in those wobbly iron 'tubs' to handle and ring the baby storks and egrets in the nests.

Another unique feature which has made Keoladeo Ghana world famous is the fact that it is the only wetland in the subcontinent where small numbers of the rare and exquisitely beautiful snow-white Siberian Cranes winter, in spite of the many other superficially identical wetland habitats with which Uttar Pradesh and the Indo-Gangetic Plain are studded. Whether it is some special food item not found in the other *jheels* that restricts the bird to Keoladeo, or what, is not known. And since the species is now included in Schedule 1 of the Wildlife (Protection) Act 1972 (Totally Protected) it is unlikely we shall ever get to know this from examination of stomach contents. My first meeting with the Siberian Crane occurred in 1937 when collecting mallophaga (feather lice) at Keoladeo with Meinertzhagen for his special study. A flock of eleven birds had arrived, of which I shot one. The bird, unfortunately, had no mallophaga on it, but we preserved its stomach contents, which consisted almost exclusively of the corms of Cyperus grass, of which several species occur in the wetland. These were to be identified specifically at Kew, but the identification somehow never got done. Thus, whether or not the bird is so choosy about its winter habitat due to the food factor remains a mystery. We were also collecting mallophaga from raptors (birds of prey) at the same time, and a note in Meinertzhagen's diary indicates how dramatically the population of this group of birds had declined in the interval since then. The entry reads: 'Bharatpur, 2.3.1937. After breakfast shot 2 Spotted, 2 Pallas's, 2 Imperial, 1 Tawny, 1 *Spilornis*, 1 *Circaetus*. I might have shot a dozen of each if I had wished to.' It is surprising he didn't!

In the deed of transfer of power from Bharatpur State to the Centre at the time of India's Independence, the Maharaja had insisted on inserting a clause that he would be allowed to retain the exclusive right of shooting in the Ghana for himself and his friends. In view of other more important issues involved, this concession was readily conceded by the government. However, the Maharaja's policy of continuing to shoot while denying this privilege to the general public was deeply resented by the powerful anti-maharaja party of the state, which was prepared to go to great lengths to punish him for alleged misdeeds and injustices in the past. They had whipped up an agitation alleging that he was holding on to the Ghana solely for his selfish pleasure and to entertain influential friends at court in Delhi, and thereby wickedly depriving the poor land-starved ryots of good cultivable land and the water they so badly needed for their crops. With the backing of crooked politicians complete physical devastation of the Ghana was plotted, and indeed was imminent, when quite by chance I got wind of the plot. I happened to be at Bharatpur then with two eminent ornithologist friends, Horace Alexander, the well-known Quaker ('Quacker' as one newspaper spelled it), and General Sir Harold Williams, Chief Engineer of the Indian Army at the time. All three of us knew Prime Minister Jawaharlal Nehru quite well and knew also of his deep personal love of nature. We apprised him urgently of what was afoot and craved his immediate intervention to stall the vandalism. And it was Jawaharlal's prompt and positive response that saved the teetering Ghana from the brink. Through Rafi Ahmad Kidwai, his energetic and sympathetic Minister of Agriculture & Irrigation, he had the charges of deprivation of land and water examined and reconciled by experts of his ministry to the satisfaction of all concerned. And in due course the headstrong Maharaja was coaxed and morally pressurized into surrendering his shooting rights. Thus was the Ghana saved from certain annihilation, and it stands today as one of the world's most fabulous waterfowl resorts.

16

Bastar 1949

Bastar and Kanker were two of the tribal states in the Eastern States Agency under the Raj, in an area that was little known biologically up to the time of my bird survey in 1949, and therefore a specially tantalizing blank for the field naturalist. Two years after India's Independence the rajas were still on the *gaddis* which had become decidedly shaky in the uncertainty of their future. It was still very wild country and comparatively unaffected by the processes of 'civilization', 'development' and prudery against female toplessness which was the normal tribal regime. Happily, Bastar then was a very different place from what it has since become vandalized into, especially after the Japanese got scent of the vast iron ore deposits of Bailadila. All-year motorable roads, dusty and untarred, were few and far between, and of a strictly arterial nature. Most of the communication was by a scanty and irregular private bus service, otherwise by bullock cart, over fair-weather forest roads or rutted cross-country tracks that were really *kutcha*, including the straw-and-bamboo makeshift bridges over the forest streams which often got washed away in the flash floods of the monsoon. Except for a few tired army disposal jeeps, four-wheel-drive vehicles were unavailable. When the water in the streams was low, the Loke station-wagon often got stuck in the loose sand bordering them or sunk down to the footboards in mid-stream, whence it had to be pushed and hauled out by manpower if available—usually timber cartmen stranded in like cases. After bitter experience of this sort I learnt to carry with me as standard equipment on the wagon a couple of

shovels and a roll of chicken wire-netting to spread over the
sand and prevent the wheels from churning in. It saved us
many an unpleasant hour of fruitless scouting for help. Another
unpleasant experience taught me to carry a bicycle, by way of a
life-boat, strapped in special brackets on the roof of the vehicle.

It happened one afternoon while driving between a largish
village called Geedam, and Jagdalpur, the capital of Bastar
State, that in negotiating a particularly bad stretch of road with
more than thirty kilometres still to go, the axle gave way and
one of the back wheels flew off, dragging the lopsided truck
almost into a roadside ditch. A single bus belonging to a local
operator used to shuttle past this spot once every alternate day.
We had met it going in the opposite direction earlier that
morning, so expected that as per schedule it would return on the
morrow. It was now late in the afternoon and the only thing
to do was to unload the vehicle and set up a bivouac in a
nearby open plot, make ourselves at home for the night and
hope for the bus to return next morning. After breakfast the
beddings, camp cots, cooking utensils, buckets, lanterns and
everything else were hurriedly repacked while we waited
patiently for the bus to turn up. When there was no bus in
either direction by sunset we knew that something had gone
wrong and opened up everything again and resigned ourselves
to spending one more night in discomfort and some anxiety.

A man-eating tiger had been reported in the area, on account
of which all the bullock-cart traffic had also come to be sus-
pended for over a week. The process of unpacking in the
evening and repacking next morning and waiting patiently was
repeated, but as there was still no bus in either direction till
dusk, no means of sending an SOS to Jagdalpur, and the
prospect of the same uncertainty on the morrow, I decided to
leave the gypsy camp in care of Gabriel and the cook, and
foot-slog to Jagdalpur when it got a little cooler after midnight.
So at two o'clock next morning, taking advantage of the
brilliant moonlight, accompanied by the second skinner,
Anthony DeSouza (a tough young Goan refugee from East
Africa), the loaded Mauser slung on my shoulder, we started to
walk. The road ran through dense mixed bamboo and *sal* forest

known to be the beat of the tiger who had claimed his last victim in that neighbourhood only ten days earlier. I realize now that it was a rash thing to do, as the rifle could have served no useful purpose in a sudden eventuality. It was an eerie and nerve-racking experience as every imaginary movement of a shadow felt like being stalked. But there seemed to be no end to this waiting for some form of transport to turn up, and the sun was so fierce that the prospect of a long trudge during daytime was not appealing. I was sorry for poor Anthony DeSouza whose feet had got sore and were bleeding from shoe bite while still many miles from our destination. But he could not be left behind to follow on his own with the bogey of a hungry tiger around, and he had to be hustled along in spite of his painful predicament. I reached Jagdalpur at about eight in the morning, having covered the distance in about six hours of non-stop marching, no doubt urged on from behind by the imaginary man-eater. The friendly manager of the bus company, one Mr Krishnaswami (or Krishnamurti?) provided us with a breakfast that remains memorable for the delicious home-made *idlees* with honey, which tasted like manna from heaven under the circumstances, washed down with genuine 'by-the-yard' Madras coffee. The manager soon provided a relief vehicle and his expert workshop foreman to tow the derelict station-wagon in, and after a couple of days of tinkering and hammering we were on our way again.

It is small wonder that even at that time, although the forests were in a less mauled condition than now, wildlife of every description had been reduced to such a deplorable state that a spate of man-eating tigers had begun infesting the region. The tribal Bhils, one and all, were expert trackers and all-year hunters with locally made muzzle-loaders and bows and arrows. In addition to this, there are the traditional pre-sowing *parads* or community *battues* every year in which all the able-bodied men from tribal hamlets miles around join to beat out vast tracts of jungle and slaughter everything that moves, big or small, whether mammal, bird or reptile. These hunts are to propitiate the spirits of the forest and ensure a good harvest, and the destructive practice continues unchecked in spite of prohibitory forest laws.

An example of the Bhils's expertness as hunters was given me by a tribal who I had engaged as a jungle guide during the Bastar bird survey. Up till that time the magnificent Great Black Woodpecker (*Dryocopus javensis*) was known to occur only in the Western Ghats south of Belgaum. The distribution given by Stuart Baker in the *New Fauna*, our standard reference book at the time, was 'Travancore to Belgaum on the western coast of South India'. However, since its publication, the Gujarat bird survey had extended the distribution northward along the Western Ghats to the Surat Dangs (adjoining Khandesh). All the same, I was very surprised and intrigued to come across a large black woodpecker in a patch of overgrown secondary jungle in this distant part of central India, and was anxious to collect the specimen to establish its identity. The bird was excessively shy and alert, and kept moving away and from tree to tree, well out of gunshot. After half an hour or so of fruitless and exhausting chase, and afraid of losing the specimen, I offered my Bhil attendant a fortune of five rupees if he brought me that bird. The man took my gun and slunk off through the dense, thorny undergrowth. Within five minutes I heard a shot and in the next two the specimen was in my hand! He assured me that this large woodpecker—locally known as *Bhainsa-khidree*—was not very uncommon in that area and that both the bird and its squabs, avidly robbed from nest-holes, were very good eating—which made sense of the bird's inordinate shyness. Hornbills and other hole-nesting birds were also becoming scarce for the same reason. The extension of the range of the Black Woodpecker, and some others hitherto considered predominantly Western Ghat forms, right across continental India to the Eastern Ghats, is among the significant findings of the Bastar/Kanker bird survey. It makes an important addition to the species with Malayan affinities found in Kerala and humid south-western India, which has a distinct relevance to Hora's 'Satpura Hypothesis' referred to earlier.

The adjacent 'native' states of the Eastern States Agency, which came next in my series of regional bird surveys, were Mayurbhanj, Badrama, Bamra, Korea, Keonjhar, Nilgiri, Dhenkanal, and several others. With their merger and re-organization they had all been absorbed in the adjoining states of the Indian Union, namely, Madhya Pradesh, Andhra and Orissa. In spite of the reckless damage done to the forests, particularly of the smaller states, by timber lessees and over-exploitation by rapacious forest contractors, the forest—mostly *sal*—were by and large in good condition, though large areas had been badly degraded through years of shifting cultivation (*jhoom*) which was the tribals' normal practice in the hilly tracts. Mayurbhanj was perhaps the largest and best organized of the Agency states and contained some magnificent forest with an abundance of wildlife. Simlipal, one of the finest game preserves of the Maharaja, is now one of our best-stocked tiger reserves.

The Maharaja of Sarguja's sole commitment to his subjects throughout a long life seems to have been to slay tigers, not only in his own state but from wherever around that he got *khabar*. He died sometime in the seventies with what must surely be an all-time record of 1,170-plus tigers on his conscience, if any. I recall that once, while I was visiting the Kanha Wildlife Sanctuary before its graduation into a National Park, somewhere in the sixties, this Maharaja, who had taken an adjoining shooting block, drove round one afternoon to say 'howdo', beaming with joy and self-satisfaction, and announced to me that it was the happiest day of his life because he had shot his eleven hundredth tiger that morning. After offering due felicitation I asked how he managed to hold the rifle steady, since I could see he was suffering from some sort of palsy and his hands were shaking like leaves in a storm. His Highness, it seems, got just as much fun in slaying a tiger by resting his weapon on the railing of his *machan*. Truly there is no accounting for tastes. When asked by an admiring visitor some months later how many tigers he had bagged altogether, his Highness replied '1,140 *only*', emphasizing 'only' with some degree of self-pity.

A brother Highness from the same group of states, namely him of Korea (eastern Madhya Pradesh), has earned unenviable immortality by sportingly gunning down all of the three last remaining wild cheetahs in a single night from a jeep, aided by blinding headlights, thus successfully wiping out the species for all time from Indian soil.

17

Motorcycling in Europe

I have been an ardent motorcycle addict ever since I first rode the 3.5 h.p. NSU belonging to a Zerbadi friend, L.M. Madar, in Tavoy, soon after I arrived there in late 1914. My passion for motorcycles and motorcycling has grown with the years. Even after I was finally persuaded to retire from this form of exhilaration in 1964 at the age of sixty-eight, following upon several narrow shaves in the mounting chaos of Bombay traffic, and even after the wrench of parting with my last machine—a 1949 model 500 c.c. twin cylinder shaft-driven Sunbeam—I have never ceased to be thrilled by the sight and music of a BMW streaking past. Alas, owing to restrictions on the import of foreign-made automobiles and motorcycles soon after Independence, it is now rarely that one sees the more aristocratic thoroughbreds on Indian roads, except for an occasional vintage model. The plebeian lesser breeds, the Rajdoots, Jawas, and even their big brothers of the Enfield family, fail to touch the chord. It is therefore only on the rare occasion when I travel abroad that I am able to satisfy the craving, and then I make every effort not to miss any motorcycle shows that might be on. In my callower days in Burma practically all my reading consisted of motorcycle journals and books and periodicals on birds, general natural history and big-game hunting, especially relating to India.

The first motorcycle I actually possessed—at least partly, since it was the property of our Tavoy business firm J.A. Ali Bros. & Co.—was in 1915. It was a 3.5 h.p. twin cylinder 'Zenith', a belt-driven machine without a gear box but with a clever device known as Gradua Gear, advertised as 'Invincible, All-conquering'. The device was intended to reduce the diameter of the driving pulley on the engine, by which a wide sliding range of gear ratios could be obtained between the high and low. It was operated by winding a horizontal arm with a knob situated above the petrol tank in the manner of a tramcar's brake handle. Since then I have had Harley Davidsons (three models of different horsepowers), a Douglas, Scott (twin-cylinder water-cooled two-stroke), a New Hudson, and others for short periods, and last and most beloved of all the Sunbeam on which I closed my motorcycling career. It is my everlasting regret that I never managed to possess a BMW to die happy! I was deeply absorbed in the refinements and improvements in the designs of motorcycle engines from year to year, and avidly followed the specifications and road-test reports in the specialist journals and manufacturers' catalogues. In the early days I revelled in tinkering with my machines, tuning up or otherwise needlessly meddling with the engine instead of leaving well alone, often taking it apart completely on holidays and putting it back again, getting besmeared with grime and oil and grease in the process. And I often wondered in the end, when left with a handful of extra bolts and screws and cotter pins and washers, why the manufacturers had been so generous as to put them in at all when they seemed so obviously dispensable. I prided myself greatly on the maintenance of my machines, both the engine and the exterior, spending long hours every weekend by way of relaxation in the spit and polish of shiny metal parts and waxing the paint, and deriving considerable satisfaction from the envy of less finicky but perhaps wiser fellow enthusiasts.

In 1950 the BNHS, as whose curator and editor of publications I functioned since Prater and McCann emigrated abroad soon after Independence—the former to settle in the UK and the latter in New Zealand—raised a fund from amongst its members to meet the cost of sending me as India's unofficial delegate to the International Ornithological Congress in Uppsala, Sweden. This was the first to be held after World War II, which had badly disrupted international contacts between ornithologists, and the reunion was looked forward to with joyful anticipation.

The Congress was to take place in June in Sweden since it was one of the few European countries that had escaped practically unscathed from the devastation of the War. The venue was the beautiful university town of Uppsala, the birthplace of Carl Linnaeus, the father of the modern system of biological nomenclature. I left Bombay by the P. & O. *SS Stratheden* on 4 May 1950, accompanied by the Sunbeam. On the latter I planned to do a grand tour of England and the Continent, visiting widely scattered friends retired from India, as well as nature reserves and places of natural history and conservation interest, especially related to birds. In spite of the gratuitous advice of well-wishers and the forebodings of doomsayers, the plan proved to be a wise decision, thoroughly worthwhile and enjoyable in every way, and above all a far less expensive and more convenient method of getting around than any other—especially under the rather chaotic post-War conditions of public transport at the time. It left me independent of time-bound itineraries and forward booking of hotels, railways and buses, etc. that render last-minute changes difficult or impossible, and bind one down to the slavery of time-schedules. On steaming into Liverpool Street Railway Station from Tilbury Docks, where I had expected to be met by my ornithological friend and prospective London host, Meinertzhagen, I was positively bewildered by the sea of humanity that surged on the platform to receive the train-load, and was wondering to myself how the two needles would ever find each other in this vast human haystack.

Pushing and elbowing my way rather aimlessly through this motley crowd I noticed in the distance a tall thin figure, erect like a flagstaff, head and shoulders above the jostling throng. With his usual thoughtfulness and originality Meinertzhagen had hired a soapbox and installed himself prominently upon it; this is how we discovered each other! Meinertzhagen lived in a three-storeyed semi-detached Victorian building bordering Kensington Park Gardens, a once aristocratic locality, with his magnificent research collection of several thousand bird skins made in practically every corner of the world during more than half a century. The majority of the skins, prepared with his own hands with characteristic thoroughness and excellence, all meticulously labelled and catalogued, are a joy to handle and study. Meinertzhagen's wife, Annie Jackson, also an ornithologist of some distinction, had died in a revolver accident (evil minds find it thinkable it may have been contrived!) in 1928 or thereabouts, and at the time of my visit he had living with him a very attractive young niece, Theresa Clay, about thirty, an entomologist working in the South Kensington Museum and later to become an internationally recognized authority on mallophaga.

No. 17 Kensington Park Gardens formed part of a row of connected buildings of uniform baroque architecture, a style fashionable in London in the second half of the nineteenth century. Its colonnaded front entrance was on the street and the back entrance led from an enclosed courtyard-like garden, commonly shared by all the residents of the rows of similar semi-detached houses on the other three sides. It was early in the month of June and the famous annual Derby race was imminent. It was apparently a traditional ritual with Meinertzhagen to invite a number of his closest friends to picnic lunch and merrymaking with him at Epsom on Derby Day, and I was lucky to be in London in time to be included. Some twenty or thirty of us, young and not so young, male and female, were driven to Epsom Downs in a chartered charabanc and spent the day in sybaritic feasting and jollity, watching the races fom the roof of the vehicle and cheering and shouting with the thousands of other spectators similarly positioned on bus tops and similar vantage points. There was a veritable sea of vehicles crowded cheek by jowl in the vast parking paddock, and an amusement park was attached, with gambling games of 'skill' and chance of every sort. I wouldn't have imagined till then how light-hearted and jolly Meinertzhagen could be: he led in all the fun, rode on the merry-go-round horses, slapped his thighs in delight and seemed to enjoy himself thoroughly.

One thing about this Derby junket that is vividly fixed in my memory and with a sense of outrage, almost, is the brutally primitive toilet arrangements that were in operation. As can be imagined, on a cold windy day in the open there was a great demand for this facility. There was a large unpartitioned *shamiana*-like marquee tent to which you got admission by paying 6d at the entrance. Within, you were faced with the unedifying sight of twenty or more men all lined up and unbuttoned, no semblance of privacy, and many more queued up behind, along a shallow runnel in the turf, all getting their money's worth of relief. Due to the briskness of business the runnel was overflowing its edges and by midday had already formed a snipe marsh of human urine through which all comers had to splosh their way to the line of action. This would be a disgusting exhibition of barbarism even among the most backward civilizations, and I must admit that it gave me a rude shock to see this in the homeland of the Englishman, who, in India, is usually so snooty about the unhygienic habits of the 'natives'. No, we couldn't beat this in India.

Apart from the superb collection of bird and natural history and big-game hunting books in Meinertzhagen's library—many of them first editions and collectors' items—I was particularly impressed by the unbroken series of his meticulously kept diaries since 1890 or thereabouts, each annual volume uniformly typed in an italic fount and handsomely bound in leather. The diaries record in detail not only Meinertzhagen's personal experiences and adventures as a wide-awake colonial military officer in the British colonies in Africa, but also his lively impressions of his contemporaries, official as well as non-official. The political and social conditions of the period, and candid—often pungent and not always charitable or unbiased—views and opinions on men and matters are also on record here. The diaries, moreover, contain a vast store of scientific facts and data gathered during his long military service, and on numerous scientific and hunting expeditions in Africa and elsewhere, which are invaluable as coming firsthand from an exceptionally keen and observant individual with a distinctly original mind.

These diaries have formed the basis of Meinertzhagen's *A Kenya Diary*, and several other outstanding books. They have been exploited to good advantage by his biographers, for instance by John Lord in *Duty, Honor, Empire* (New York,

Random House, 1970). Meinertzhagen's adventures in Africa and the stories of his bravery and courage earned him widespread fame as well as notoriety. The awe in which he was held by people 'on the other side' is brought out in one of Gavin Maxwell's books. In his boyhood recollections of his uncle, Lord William Percy, himself a keen ornithologist, Maxwell says, 'He [Lord William] was a close friend of Colonel Dick Meinertzhagen whose exploits in Kenya were famous; he was a legendary figure to me, made even more ogre-like by Uncle Willie's reply to some particularly inane remark of mine, "Gavin—Dick Meinertzhagen's coming to stay next week. I wouldn't say things like that in front of him if I was you—*he's killed men with his bare hands!*" '

Meinertzhagen was a close friend and admirer of Dr Chaim Weizmann, the propagator of the idea of a homeland for the Jews. After World War I, when Meinertzhagen was military governor of Palestine for a time, the two were actively engaged in scheming for the implementation of the Balfour Declaration. After Israel became a reality Meinertzhagen visited the country frequently and was an ardent champion of the Jews who had immigrated from all over to settle in the Promised Land, and full of praises of their dedication, industry and 'patriotism'. By contrast he saw little good in the Muslim Arabs, for whom he had an undisguised contempt. The Israelites, it is true, had achieved wonders in the material development of the land during the short period of their occupancy, making the waterless desert bloom in agricutural self-sufficiency and hum with galloping industrialization. In response to one of his panegyrics I had expressed a keenness to visit the country but doubted if with a Muslim name I would be welcome. In a letter written on his return from a visit to Israel in May 1953, Meinertzhagen says:

> I had a wonderful time watching migration of hawks, storks and seagulls on the Gulf of Aqaba, over the Dead Sea and up the Jordan Valley. You need have no doubt about visiting Israel: there is no class distinction, no religious persecution, no political persecution. It is the purest form of communism without any of the objectionable elements of dictatorship. The whole population is loyal to the Israeli Government whether they are

communist or right-wing conservative. I have never seen a country in five years achieve so much under such harmful conditions of encirclement by six Moslem Arab states. The whole atmosphere is one of enthusiasm, progress and patriotism, without a trace of aggressive nationalism or boast. In fact humility, such a rare human attribute, dominates everyone. I believe Israel is the only stable factor in the Middle East. Go there and see! . . . In what part of the world is the worst mess? Is there any part of the world where there is not a mess? Both Africa and Asia are awakening: they have passed the yawning stage and are now getting on their feet, but I wish they would not make such a noise about it.

After a week or so in England, during which I motorcycled out to a number of far-flung friends in the country in the fabulous springtime which is the glory of the English scene, I took a Swedish tourist ship to Gothenburg. After a night with friends of friends in the industrial city of Orebro, I arrived in Uppsala in the afternoon, just in time for the opening session of the Congress, to a mild sensation among the delegates and my friends at my wonderful timing, having ridden out all the way from India! I had fitted out the solo machine with two bulky canvas pannier bags which carried an all-purpose wardrobe—including a black *sherwani* for formal occasions—much of which I realized too late was just redundant ballast. The bags could be unstrapped and carried to the hotel room on the night halts, but while convenient as containers, their weight disturbed the balance and produced a disconcerting tail-wobble which became quite dangerous when travelling at speed on the slippery cobbled road surfaces found in many small European towns and country villages. Among several unscheduled tosses on this account I recall a particularly nasty one before entering war-shattered Münster in Germany. The skid spun the motorcycle completely round and landed me sprawling in the middle of the road, luckily with only minor physical damage, not serious enough to interfere with the resumption of the journey. Luckily also, there was little following road traffic at the time to make matters worse: one of those gigantic delivery trucks, each carrying a dozen or more automobiles from factory to distributor, which always shook my composure as they thundered past on the autobahns, could at that moment of truth well have wound up the enterprise abruptly!

I had been warned against French motorists and their mania for *vitesse* generally, and against French truck-drivers specifically. Of the first I had enough hair-raising confirmation on Paris roads, but luckily escaped disaster more than once. I had ample experience also of some other unlovable traits of the Frenchman—at least the Frenchman of the capital. It happened to me so many times before I decided to quit Paris that I cannot believe it was just individual lack of friendliness and courtesy, but perhaps a crude and deliberate display of the Frenchman's notorious linguistic chauvinism. Paris was new to me, and in spite of a close study of the city's road map before I started out each day, when one suddenly came upon a diversion for road repair, it was easy to get completely lost in that maze of streets and boulevards. Unfortunately I speak no French, and every time I pulled up by a pedestrian for help in the politest English I knew, he just looked at me, then turned his back and walked away without even pretending to be apologetic.

From the time of my first introduction to the fantastic breeding ground of the flamingo in the Great Rann of Kutch in 1944, this has been a bird of very special interest for me. At the Congress in Uppsala I had occasion to meet and exchange notes with several American and European ornithologists who were also flamingo fans and had read of my investigations at the Rann colony. I was naturally keen to visit the European breeding grounds in the Camargue (southern France) and in the delta of the Guadalquivir river in Spain to compare the ecological conditions. The doyen of French ornithology, Professor J. Berlioz of the Musee d'Histoire Naturelle, very kindly gave me letters of introduction to the flamingo warden in the Camargue.

Dr Luc Hoffman, a young Swiss ornithologist, fast oncoming then but internationally established now, who owned a biological research station later to earn international fame as Station Biologique du la Valat, extended hospitality and birding opportunities in the area. He expected me for lunch on a certain day and I had timed myself to arrive at his residence, about a hundred kilometres from my night's halt, around one o'clock. I hadn't reckoned with French truck-drivers, so actually landed up at my destination at 4.30 with a deep gash on my forehead, a smashed headlight and sundry minor dents on the machine, fortunately not serious enough to hold me up. While I was cautiously negotiating a blind curve, a fully laden truck whipped round the corner with French *vitesse* and gave me a very unpleasant near head-on. After sending me sprawling, the driver shouted something in his mother tongue (uncomplimentary, no doubt) and drove on as if it was all in the day's work. A good samaritan in a following car picked me up, clothes covered with blood, and rushed me down to a small hospital run by nuns from a convent a few miles from the city of Arles. Not one of these good women spoke English and it was a trying pantomime (quite amusing in retrospect) trying to explain the circumstances and situation to them and to establish my credentials, and to convey in dumb charade that I *had* had an anti-tetanus injection before, about which they seemed particularly concerned. The kind sisters soon stitched and bandaged me up, and washed the blood off my clothes, but were loth to discharge me in that condition, insisting that I remain as an in-patient for the night. It was a wordless tussle with much gesticulation that finally got me my release, with further pantomiming of gratefulness. I didn't have my host's telephone number and it seemed impossible to explain to the kind nuns what I wanted. But they got me a taxi to the Sunbeam, still on its side, which, with some assisted tinkering, straightening in the right places and hammering into shape, started off without fuss and gave no trouble on the way. My lunch host, worried at my 'no show', was deliberating on further action when I rode in with bandaged head to tell the tale.

Unfortunately, July is not the flamingo breeding season in the Camargue, but it was interesting to visit the site and examine the disused nests which were far more easily approachable than Flamingo City in the Rann of Kutch. In good seasons something like 7,000 pairs are estimated to nest in the Camargue. In 1945 the only tolerably reliable estimate that has so far been made of the Kutch colony on the basis of occupied nests showed approximately half a million birds in the Kutch population, including both sexes as well as downy and partly fledged young. That count did not include unhatched eggs still under incubation. Thus it is quite believable that the Kutch colony of the Greater Flamingo (*Phoenicopterus ruber*) is the most populous in Asia, and may be almost the largest anywhere. For me the 1945 expedition to Flamingo City in Kutch is particularly memorable because it was the only one in several visits before, and many since, that I have been lucky enough to find the colony at the high peak of the breeding activities.

The two post-Congress field excursions from Uppsala I had chosen were to Abisko in Swedish Lapland and Riksgransen near the Sweden-Norway border. It was all a fantastic fairyland of superb scenery, of snow-patched mountains, rushing torrents and partially frozen lakes and tarns. Around mid-June the breeding of birds was at its height, and for me it was particularly interesting to meet some of our wintertime Indian friends—Curlew, Whimbrel, Rednecked Phalarope, Broadbilled Sandpiper, the two Godwits and the two Stints—in their summer finery and on their Arctic nesting grounds.

At Abisko we were billetted in tourists' log cabins, one of which I shared with Peter Scott of the Wildfowl Trust, and Finnur Gudmundson, an Icelander and a giant of a man, perhaps the largest and most massive human in my experience. One of my pet aversions, and my idea of uttermost misery, is having to share a cabin or a tiny high-altitude tent with a robustly snoring companion. I had not met Gudmundson before and had no notion of his vital statistics or his potential as a snorer. Therefore when I first set eyes on him filling our little cabin with his gargantuan bulk my heart sank and I braced myself for a thoroughly miserable night. Happily the fear was belied: unbelievable for one of his size Finnur proved a considerate non-snorer. I found him to be a gentle and friendly soul and an excellent ornithologist, from whom I learnt a great deal about his fascinating homeland and its bird life.

I find that I have missed out much of the latter-day story of the BNHS, with which I have been so closely associated, particularly since my repatriation from Burma in 1924, and more particularly since India's Independence. It has been a period of great intellectual gratification for me personally, and also, I like to feel, of considerable significance in the progress of the Society and the proper projection of its image within the country and abroad. One of our greatest difficulties soon after Independence, during my secretaryship and as stop-gap Curator, was to find a suitable incumbent in place of Prater, and an Assistant Curator to replace Charles McCann—who should normally have stepped into the breach. Both of them had set a standard of excellence that was difficult to match. Thus, it was after a prolonged period of trial and error with several probationers that potentially suitable though inexperienced replacements became available.

This reminds me of a miraculous coincidence that must surely stand as unique. I have recounted the story many times before to all and sundry but it will do no harm to repeat it here. One of the candidates selected was a young zoology M.Sc. from Kerala who, surprisingly, seemed interested in and even eager to undertake field work, which normally involves a fair amount of sustained physical exertion and is thus usually shunned by most who can afford to. In trying to learn something more about this unconventional youth's background I casually asked if he had ever heard of a person called Jeevanayakam in Kerala. This Jeevanayakam had been the member-secretary of a roving committee of educationists (the Statham Committee) appointed by the Travancore government in the 1930s to inquire into the alleged malpractices of state-aided private schools. While touring the state for the bird survey in 1932, I was constantly bumping into this committee in the various dak bungalows or camp sheds we had to share. Jeevanayakam had always shown great cordiality and friendliness to me and a keen interest in our bird work, but after that we had lost touch. Now here was a young man from Kerala: what more likely than his knowing about Jeevanayakam's whereabouts? Jokingly I inquired of Daniel if he had ever heard of such a person in his native Travancore who I had known a mere twenty years before. By a one-in-ten million chance and with almost total unbelief I learnt that this Jeevanayakam was indeed none other than Daniel's own father! True to south-Indian custom and tradition, the intitial J in J.C. Daniel stood for Jeevanayakam. And how naive of me not to have guessed it!

Harking back to my own sorry experience of 1929, when I had wanted to specialize in ornithology for my future career and found no institution or university in India equipped to impart the proper instruction, I was able to persuade the University of Bombay after we had acquired the necessary experience and expertise to supply this deficiency, to recognize the BNHS as the guiding institution for post-graduate research in Field Ornithology, leading to Master's and Doctoral degrees in Zoology. For my first M.Sc. student, Vijaykumar Ambedkar of Poona, I prevailed upon the University as a special case to appoint Dr David Lack F.R.S.* as a foreign external examiner for his thesis on 'The Ecology and Breeding Biology of the Baya Weaver *Ploceus philippinus* (Linn.)'. This was really more for my own satisfaction that my guidance was on the right lines. Dr Lack's assessment of Ambedkar's thesis was reassuring. After making some minor criticisms he said:

> Assuming that the standard for the M.Sc. of the University of Bombay is about the same as for English universities, I am of the opinion that the present thesis is worthy of the award, and well up to the standard required . . . I found the thesis very interesting, very clearly written and presented, with a very good coverage of the literature of the subject, and with a sufficient amount of original research to justify the award fully in my view.

With a nucleus donation from myself, I initiated a fund under the BNHS named the Sálim Ali–Loke Ornithological Research Fund (SALOR). Its corpus of about Rs 300,000 was built up by donations from members and well-wishers of the Society, but chiefly by benefactions from the Loke family of Singapore, in memory of my close friend and fellow-ornithologist, Loke Wan Tho, killed in an air crash in Taiwan in 1964. The interest on this corpus supports two postgraduate Fellows at a time for two to three years each. Latterly, a munificent grant from the Sir Dorabji Tata Trust has enabled the Society to endow an additional Fellow for the period of his study. All this has been a source of great satisfaction to me, since the Society is now capable of producing adequately trained field biologists of a calibre otherwise difficult to find in India.

---

* Director, Edward Grey Institute of Field Ornithology, Oxford.

18

Hamid Ali

A book entitled *Apprentice to Power* by Sir Malcolm Darling, a distinguished Indian civil servant, published in 1966, fortuitously came into my hands a few years ago. It describes the author's first three and a half years in India some sixty years earlier as a newly joined member of the Indian Civil Service, and is based mainly upon the letters he wrote home to his mother and friends in England as well as excerpts from his diary. In the preface he confesses: 'as to myself and India, I arrived there knowing something of its history but nothing about its peoples.' The very first paragraph of the opening chapter of the book describing his arrival in India gave me a least expected thrill of pride. It read:

> On Sunday, November 27, 1904, the *City of Vienna* dropped anchor in Bombay. I was sleeping on deck, and when I woke the sun was rising in a glow of crimson behind the distant hills across a fine open roadstead. It was already hot, and the air was heavy with an exotic fragrance, first met at Port Said. Port Said had given me 'a scare of the East—the natives look so revolting'. Happily there was an Indian on board who gave me a very different impression. Hamid Abdul Ali, a native of Bombay and like myself new to the Indian Civil Service, was widely read in French, German and English, with opinions of his own on all he read and a strong sense of humour. For me he was 'the' most interesting person on board; yet because of the accident which had made him dark instead of fair he stands even more aloof from the ship's company than I do.' It was my first hint of the wide social gulf in the India of those days between East and West.

Hamid was my favourite brother, as he perhaps was of all

my brothers and sisters. I like to presume that I was closest to him—an inferior imitation—in temperament, interests, outlook and likes and dislikes. It is certainly to his influence and direct encouragement more than anyone else's in the family circle that I owe my early initiation and development as a naturalist. Ever since he gave me one of Rowland Ward's egg collecting kits as a present on my eleventh or twelfth birthday, he followed my progress in bird study with sympathy and encouragement, and his helpful comments and advice always acted as a spur to greater efforts on my part. I felt genuinely elated when, after seeing my report of the Travancore Ornithological Survey he wrote (Satara, 20.6.35), 'I have only lately gone through your article on the Travancore Survey in the last number of the BNHS *Journal* [Vol. 37 (4)] and think it right to send off a few lines to congratulate you on the way in which you have tackled the subject. This is, to my mind, the maturest and soberest in expression and the most thorough in content and matter. I felt so happy reading it, I thought I *must* sit down and write to you.' The winter schoolboy vacations I spent with Hamidbhai in camp during his duty tours in Sind were an education by themselves. They were memorable opportunities, not only for fostering my love of natural history and birds but also because they gave me an insight into the secret of the universal popularity and genuine love and respect he inspired among the country folk in his care. Indeed so genuine and deep-rooted was this esteem and affection that when after twenty years or more I had occasion, in the course of my bird work, to visit some of the districts where he had served, I had only to give the 'password' that I was a brother of Hamid Ali to be gushingly welcomed with open arms by the grey beards who had known him personally, and be given lavish hospitality and assistance.

Hamid was a remarkable linguist. Besides scholarly proficiency in English, German and French among the European languages, he was fluent in reading and writing Urdu, Hindi, Sindhi, Gujarati, Marathi, Pushtu, Arabic and Persian, and could also speak most of these languages with fluency.

The case of my maternal uncle, Abbas Tyabji, Hamid's father-in-law, was peculiar but by no means unique in the political turmoil of the times. On his return from England as a barrister, in 1893 or thereabouts, he had joined the judicial service of the Gaekwar of Baroda, and after serving as District Judge for a number of years he rose to the bench and served as a judge of the Baroda High Court until his retirement in 1913. Being my mother's elder and only brother he was thrust into the guardianship of my brothers and sisters on my mother becoming widowed in 1897 or so. However, he was only the titular guardian, and the brunt of real guardianship of the family, soon to be orphaned, fell on the willing and selfless shoulders of another more distant uncle, Amiruddin, and his childless wife Hamida Begam, whom I have mentioned before. It is sad to relate that since my return from Germany in 1930 and continuing joblessness, to the end of his days (he died in 1935 or '36) Abbas remained the most caustic critic among my elders of my ornithological activities, which he thoroughly disapproved. He considered I was merely a shirker and a waster, and that ornithology was just a cover for my indolence and reluctance to do 'honest and gainful' work. It is a pity he did not live to see that the indolence has paid dividends!

However, all this is a different story. Right from the time of his education in England and up to his retirement as a High Court Judge, uncle Abbas was a true-blue loyalist among the loyalists. Though a moderate nationalist at heart, he would stand no adverse criticism of the British as a people, or of the Raj, and even a mildly disparaging .remark about the King-Emperor or the royal family was anathema to him; so much so that if he was ever caught in a discussion where such disloyal or 'seditious' sentiments were being aired, he would get up and walk straight out of the gathering. If he had any strong sentiment about Swadeshi he certainly didn't show it by precept or example. His clothes were mostly made of foreign material and everything about his household and style of living was patrician, truly western and very 'proper'. This being so, he naturally disagreed vehemently with Gandhiji and his methods of political mass agitation—the cult of civil disobedience, of non-co-operation with the British Government in India (non-violent though it be) and militant Swadeshism involving the burning of foreign cloth. In other respects his moderate but simmering nationalism and his absolute integrity and fairness as a judge were widely recognized and lauded, even by leftist Congressmen and anti-British extremists.

Thus it was that after the Jallianwalabagh massacre in 1919, when the Congress set up an independent fact-finding committee, Abbas Tyabji's name as chairman/convener gained solid support. After listening to and cross-examining hundreds of eyewitnesses and victims of General Dyer's brutality with nausea and revulsion, mixed at first with some degree of disbelief at the applause the General's action had won from Raj diehards and English conservatives, Abbas was a changed and thoroughly disillusioned man. He made a complete political somersault overnight, as it were, and soon became one of Gandhiji's most devoted co-workers. He discarded his western aristocratic life-style and took ardently to simple homespun *khadi*. He travelled round the country in unused-to third class railway carriages, halting in unlovely bug-ridden *dharamsalas* and ashrams, sleeping on hard ground and foot-slogging miles in the hot summer sun preaching the gospel of non-violent non-co-operation with the 'satanic' colonial British Indian Government. All this hectic activity and hardship he undertook when well past seventy, including several years aggregately in jail as a political prisoner.

Hamid was Assistant Collector and District Magistrate of Panchmahals district, Gujarat, in 1917. I had occasion, during the 'study break' from Burma to spend a few days with him in camp during his working tour in winter. At that time he had to try a case in which a village *patel* had been charged by the government for 'disloyalty' or 'sedition' or some such political offence which had become a fast-spreading 'infection' in Gujarat since Gandhiji's return from South Africa a couple of years earlier. Gandhiji had come over to give evidence in defence of the *patel* who, after a prolonged hearing, was finally discharged. We were living under canvas a short distance away from the court tent, in a magnificent old mango grove, and I vividly remember Hamidbhai escorting Gandhiji into the dining tent after the trial for a cup of 'tea', which was in fact goat's milk and some roasted groundnuts (or *chewda*?) kept ready for him. Though he had not yet acquired his full Indian aura, I was thrilled to meet the man who had earned such worldwide acclaim for his anti-racial and humanitarian work in South Africa. What impressed me most were his transparent and unassuming simplicity and his quiet sense of humour. Being allergic to pomposity in any shape or form, and a firm believer in the saving grace of humour, I have the highest admiration for one who is not obsessed with his own importance and can sometimes laugh at himself, as Gandhiji obviously could. Indeed, I consider myself fortunate to have had this accidental chance of a family tête-à-tête with Gandhiji, since all my later meetings with him have been impersonal and more or less in the nature of public *darshans*.

Hamidbhai was District Magistrate in the several districts of the then Bombay Presidency, where he was posted from time to time during this period of political turmoil, between about 1915 when Gandhiji returned from South Africa upto the time of his retirement from service with a sigh of relief in 1935, when the National Movement had become uncomfortably hot for him. His position all through this epoch was particularly awkward and unenviable: by conviction he was a wholehearted nationalist, yet as a senior civilian and administrative head of his district he was bound to uphold the letter of the law impartially and deal with political agitators in the manner prescribed. His nationalist leanings and his popularity with political leaders as well as the general public had made him covertly suspect with the rulers, and a marked man from almost his apprenticeship to power. That he did not rise to anything higher than a Collector and District Magistrate during his service, in spite of his tact and quiet efficiency, was quite obviously due to his insufficiently disguised nationalistic out-look and tendencies, and to his popularity with all levels of the Indian public, whether pro-government or anti.

His wife, Sharifa, the daughter of Abbas, was more volubly nationalistic, sometimes rather indiscreetly so, which added to the awkwardness of Hamidbhai's position. She was a strong-willed, dedicated social worker, particularly interested in the education of girls and the social uplift of village women. She was a staunch champion of the Swadeshi Movement, which at the time carried strong political overtones, and she made no secret about it. With a roving father-in-law preaching the naughty cult of civil disobedience and non-co-operation at his doorstep, and such an outspoken wife within, the awkwardness for Hamidbhai was mounting to embarrassment. He pleaded with Abbas to keep away from his district, since, if he came and made an anti-Raj speech within his jurisdiction, it would leave him no option but to arrest him. Uncle Abbas, to his credit it must be said, fully appreciated Hamidbhai's predicament and considerately kept away.

In his last-minute briefing to police parties going off to keep or restore law and order in villages threatened with civil dis-obedience, Hamidbhai always stressed the need for cool-headedness and the use of minimum force even under provoca-tion or threat of physical violence. In one of his districts where the Superintendent of Police was an empire-building young Britisher, a serious forest satyagraha by *adivasis* was threatened and even bloodshed feared. Hamidbhai was naturally greatly perturbed. On his way to the scene of disturbance the DSP with a posse of armed policemen stopped by for the final briefing from the District Magistrate. I heard Hamidbhai plead with him to use as little force as possible, and then only if absolutely unavoidable. And his parting words were 'No firing on any account!' In the event actual force *was* avoided, though at one stage the situation had got decidedly ugly. And the District Magistrate heaved a sigh of relief.

On retirement from service in 1934 or thereabouts, Hamid and his wife Sharifa had settled down at Mussoorie in the charming old bungalow 'Southwood' which he later gifted to the Central Government for the use of officials as a holiday home. Some of his more intimate cronies love to recall a puckish prank Hamid once played on them when well past seventy-five, and after over half a century of happy married life with Sharifa. They were shocked beyond belief one morning, to receive from him without any previous inkling whatever a bombshell curtly announcing that he was getting married and inviting them to be present to witness the ceremony. The Hamid Alis were popular socialites and 'do-gooders' in the hill-station, with a large circle of intellectual friends and admirers. They were well known as a devoted and exemplary couple, and his friends could not believe that he was about to acquire a new wife—and at that time of life! They thought the poor old man had gone off his head, and felt genuinely relieved on learning the explanation later. It seems that according to Shariat law a Muslim may in his lifetime gift away his property in part or in whole to whomsoever he pleases. But once he is dead it is obligatory for his property to go to his legal heirs, however distant or indirect, irrespective of any will he may have made. Being a Muslim, and being childless, the only way in which he could assure his property going where he wished was by getting his marriage registered under the Civil Marriages Act and then executing a will accordingly. So this is what it turned out to be all about!

In Bombay one afternoon, around three o'clock (November 1980), as I was working at my desk comfortably undressed, in sleeveless vest and short sleeping *izar*—therefore least prepared for visitors—in barged a complete stranger, having somehow escaped the vigilance of our normally watchful dogs, straight into my study. He was a thick-set man of around sixty-five, dressed respectably in western style, complete with a necktie. I was naturally annoyed at this unannounced intrusion at such an odd hour and asked him rather brusquely who he was, what he wanted, and why he had chosen this unusual time to call. He apologized and explained that he was a visitor from Gujarat specially come to Bombay on a mission of great personal importance for himself. He had found out my address somehow and had been trying to locate 46 Pali Hill for a considerable time. He said he wanted nothing from me but, on the contrary, had come looking for me simply in order to repay a long-standing debt. He then introduced himself as one Kshirsagar who had recently retired from the registrarship of one of the universities in Gujarat. He explained that his father had been a school master and a dedicated social worker in Satara years ago, in which dual capacity he had come in intimate contact with and developed a deep regard and friendship for my brother Hamid Ali ICS, who happened then to be the Collector of Satara. The father had died some time ago and on the tenth (or fortieth?) day after his death they had performed the customary ceremony of feeding cooked rice to crows for the salvation of the departed soul. It seems that when the rice was put out a number of crows gathered, but they all just sat around in a circle and none would approach the proffered bounty. Seeing this, one canny elder suggested that there was probably some wish of the deceased that his son had failed to honour, or some monetary debt of his still standing undischarged. The son could not recollect any omission of this sort offhand, but he ultimately recalled that at one time, years after my brother had retired from service and settled in Mussoorie, Kshirsagar's father had sent Hamidbhai an urgent SOS for financial help in a critical situation connected with Kshirsagar's impending departure to the USA for education. Within minutes of his taking a vow before the gathering to the effect that he would spare no pains to repay the debt, one of the crows, recounted Mr Kshirsagar, sidled up to the rice and began pecking at it, presently to be joined by his waiting companions. This promptly removed any lurking scepticism his foreign education may have injected in Kshirsagar about the mediation of crows in the saving of human souls; it converted him to a firm belief in the 'superstition' for evermore. All honour to him, however, for repaying a long forgotten ¡debt—unreminded and unasked—after fifty years, even if perhaps for a vicariously ulterior motive. Would that more men like him were born, and oftener!

The fulfilment of that vow was the mission that had now brought Mr K to Bombay. I was one of the executors of my brother's will, but could trace no mention of any such loan among his papers. I therefore refused to accept the payment, but since Kshirsagar seemed so desperately anxious to fulfil his vow I passed him on to S.F.B. Tyabji & Co., the advocates who were handling the estates of the late Mr and Mrs Hamid Ali. The lawyers also could not find any record of the transaction among the estate papers and were likewise refusing to

accept payment till, in desperation, Kshirsagar pulled out a
crumpled old postcard from his pocket written in Hamidbhai's
own hand from 'Southwood', Mussoorie, dated some time in
1934 (or '35), acknowledging the elder Kshirsagar's request,
advising an immediate remittance to him by bank draft, and
expressing his friendly hope and concern for the money
reaching him in time for his son to proceed on his voyage. The
amount involved, we discovered, was Rs 1,000, therefore no
small sum in those days—when rice and wheat were sold at
8–10 seers per rupee and you could buy a brand new Ford car
for under Rs 4,000. But such was the measure of Hamidbhai's
unostentatious generosity and humanism that throughout his
service—having no children of his own to worry about—he
regularly gave away a considerable portion of his monthly
salary to needy, aged relatives and dependants, or for the
education of miscellaneous poor boys and girls, and other
deserving causes, all completely off the record. We only learnt
of some of these benefactions occasionally and accidentally
from the recipients themselves, or from indirect sources.

Talking of superstitions, I must admit that my own congenital
unbelief in all forms of spiritualism, occultism, astrology and
ultra sensory 'magic' of that sort had been somewhat rudely
shaken, albeit temporarily, after what happened to my brother
Aamir in Burma in 1919, less than two months after he joined
us in business in Tavoy. A few miles out of the town there was a
fairly large masonry tank in the beautifully wooded campus of
a Buddhist monastery containing a dense concentration of
carps, many of which were believed to be hundreds of years old
and all of them regarded as highly sacred. They were pampered
on scraps by devout pilgrims and picnickers alike and had
grown enormously fat and 'desirable'. But they were safe from
poachers and vandals because of a traditionally rooted superstition that any person trying to catch or harm the fish was sure
to come to grief. Aamir, like myself, was a complete unbeliever
in superstition and occultism. Out of sheer devilry and as if to
defy the fates he lightheartedly picked up a stone and flung it
purposefully at the seething mass when no one was about. We
had gone picnicking to this beautiful spot early that morning,

Tehmina in the sidecar and Aamir on the pillion of the Harley-Davidson combination. He was perfectly hale and hearty and full of beans when we left, but complained of a slight stiffness in the joints after we returned around lunch time. We didn't pay much heed to this since from a longish pillion ride over rutted *kutcha* roads this was nothing unexpected. But towards evening Aamir felt slightly feverish, with pain in the joints which got increasingly worse, with rising temperature in the next two days. It was then diagnosed as a severe bout of rheumatic fever, and in spite of all such medical aid as was available in that one-horse little township, poor Aamir was dead on the ninth day.* Call it coincidence if you like, but it did give a severe jolt to my rationalism.

* 22 April 1919.

19

Five Other Men

SIDNEY DILLON RIPLEY

One day in 1944 while I was working on the BNHS bird collection, temporarily housed in the Prince of Wales Museum, in dropped a young American, one of the many US Army personnel constantly in transit through Bombay in those war years. He introduced himself as Sidney Dillon Ripley, a post-graduate biology student of Yale University, some of whose ornithological publications I had been impressed with. I was happy to meet him personally, and we both took to each other at once. He had been drafted into the American forces in South-East Asia and was posted as an intelligence officer in Ceylon, a job that required frequent visits to the Joint Command HQ in New Delhi. This was my first meeting with one who was destined to become a lifelong friend and valued colleague, fellow-ornithologist and explorer, and co-author of several scientific papers and books. On this occasion and on his subsequent breaks of journey between Ceylon and Delhi, we discussed the possibilities of joint ornithological fieldwork and specimen collecting in India, and built air-castles about the expeditions we would make together once the War was over, when conditions returned to normal and free movement within the country, specially along our north-east border, became possible. Our first priority was to be the Mishmi Hills in extreme north-east Assam, the ornithology of which had never been properly studied. In the event it took a considerable time after hostilities ceased for conditions to become sufficiently normal for this type of activity: it was not till the end of 1946 that a beginning could be made. Shortage of petrol and vehicles, due to strict wartime import restrictions and as an aftermath of the war, had made road transport, especially in off-beat places, a serious problem. In the case of the Mishmis the problem was less serious since most of the transport in the hills had to be done by pack mules and porters. Although the Mishmi expedition was a joint exercise, the sources of its funding were different. The financing of my part was—as on so many previous occasions—done entirely through the benefaction of Loke Wan Tho, while the BNHS helped with the services of a field collector/skinner, and, later, with the necessary museum facilities.

It was the first time that Italian and Japanese nylon 'mist' nets were tried out in India to catch birds, and their effectiveness, especially of the simplified Japanese type, convinced us that in thick shrubbery and undergrowth, as in the Mishmis and the eastern Himalaya generally, where skulking and secretive birds rarely showed themselves, this is the only way of detecting their presence and securing specimens. It was on this, our first joint expedition to the Mishmis, that the idea was initially mooted between us of doing a revision and updating of Stuart Baker's bird volumes in the Fauna of British India series (published some twenty years earlier), which we and other critical ornithologists had found unsatisfactory in many ways. We also felt that the new edition should be a thoroughly updated publication, not only for the use of professional museum ornithologists but also for the amateur bird watcher, and therefore well-illustrated and with popularly written life histories of the birds—more or less on the model of Witherby's *Handbook of British Birds*. We would split the authorship between taxonomy and ecology, the former being chiefly Ripley's responsibility and the latter chiefly mine. Source material for the general section would come largely from my own field records kept over the last fifty years, plus Whistler's meticulous bird notes from his several years of service in north-west India, and from Ripley's several Indian collecting expeditions. These would be supplemented by critically sifted extractions from all the major publications on Indian birds in the last 150 years. The taxonomic base of the proposed *Handbook of the Birds of India and Pakistan* would be an authentic, comprehensive and up-to-date checklist to be prepared by Ripley and published under the sponsorship of the Bombay Natural History Society. Our *Handbook* was intended also to be an authentic source of complete information about all that had so far been recorded on some of the species, and what aspects were not sufficiently known and needed further study.

The library research and extraction work, subsidized by the Government of India, the US Educational Foundation and the Indian National Science Academy, took about four years, of which I spent six months in the US, mostly at Yale University where Ripley was Associate Professor of Zoology at the time. It gave us a chance of discussing together and trying out alternative formats and write-ups to find the best way of synthesizing the taxonomy section, to be written by Ripley in the US, with the life history section in Bombay by myself. My living expenses in America came from a Seessel Zoological Fellowship of Yale University, obtained through Dillon Ripley's kind intercession, while the round air trip came out of a Smith-Mundt Travel Grant. Work on the manuscript started in earnest only in 1964, by which time Dillon Ripley had moved over to Washington as Secretary of the Smithsonian Institution, and the first volume of the *Handbook* was published in 1968. Thereafter, the rest of the ten volumes followed each other at short intervals. The series was completed in 1974 and the last volume officially released by the Prime Minister, Mrs Indira Gandhi, on 16 November 1974—four days after my seventy-eighth birthday.

From his earliest contact with the BNHS Dillon Ripley has been its fervid supporter, and especially since he took over as Secretary of the Smithsonian Institution. The Society and the Institution have both benefited substantially from their association in numerous ways. Many of the rather elaborate birding expeditions to politically sensitive and unexplored areas in the eastern Himalaya, along our north-eastern frontier, which have yielded such valuable research material and significant

additions to scientific knowledge, could not have been undertaken without the collaboration of the BNHS. Dillon Ripley's
enthusiastic personal participation in these expeditions, along
with his friendly, highly versatile and deceptively fragile-
looking wife, Mary, contributed immensely to the fun of camp
life. I had first met newly-wedded Mary in 1950, all elegantly
attired and spruced up in the civilized social atmosphere of the
International Ornithological Congress at Uppsala, looking a
lot more fragile than now (1984). Immediately thereafter the
couple were due to launch out on a birding expedition into the
wilds of the Naga Hills (or was it New Guinea?), and I
remember how she struck me as a singular misfit for the rough-
and-tumble conditions she would have to face. However, after
sharing several strenuous expeditions with the Dillon Ripleys
subsequently, I realized how sadly I was mistaken: Mary
Ripley amid the elegance of her Washington drawing room is
not the same as Mary Ripley in safari outfit in a dripping
leech-infested jungle camp. The two 'avatars' are irreconcilable.

The Bombay Natural History Society decided to bring out a
Festschrift issue of the *Journal* in commemoration of my
seventy-fifth birthday on 12 November 1971, for which Dillon
Ripley amiably accepted the editorship and offered to obtain
suitable contributions from our international circle of mutual
ornithological colleagues and friends. To a somewhat over-
generous Introduction to the Festschrift (which was later—
1978—published by Oxford University Press in book form as
A Bundle of Feathers) Ripley added in lighter vein a 'poetaster-
ical' panegyric of his own make which cannot be allowed to
escape immortalization. Here it goes:

ODE TO SÁLIM ON HIS SEVENTY-SEVENTH
BIRTHDAY

12 November 1973, in camp, Bhutan
From the Wakhan and the Rann
    To Point Calimere and Kandy
In monsoon rain or sun,
    In dak bungalow or dandy,
Wherever there are birds

You will hear the reverent words:
  Oh Sálim's our hero, Sálim's the man
    Whose knowledge is always on tap.
  The terror of wrens, Finn's Baya's fan,
    A truly remarkable chap.
So ho for the Wedgebilled Wren
  And hey for the tragopan hen;
So ho for the tweet tweet tseep
  And hey for the leopard's cheep.*
Let's squeak like Blewitt's Owl
  And honk like water fowl
  As through thicket, bog and heather
  We hunt for Hume's stray feather.
  Oh Sálim's our hero, Sálim's the man
    Whose knowledge is always on tap.
  The terror of wrens, Finn's Baya's fan,
    A truly remarkable chap.
For our part we know all his knowledge will glow
  For ages to come, his lamp will shine out.
His birthday we sing while pheasants all crow
  And birds of all kinds join in tuneful shout.
Nor Hodgson nor Baker knows more about life
  Nor Coltart nor Inglis have weathered the strife
About bird lore and bird song with steadier light
  Than our hero whose birthday we welcome tonight.
  Oh Sálim's our hero, Sálim's the man
    Whose knowledge is always on tap.
  The terror of wrens, Finn's Baya's fan,
    A truly remarkable chap.

In the event, due to the vagaries of the printing trade, the Festschrift number of the *Journal*—Vol. 71(3), December 1974—saw the light only in March 1976. The Ode was actually presented to me on my seventy-seventh birthday at a celebration

---

*Laboured. This reference is to the man who described the call of Molesworth's race of Blyth's tragopan, from where it sat in the middle of a bamboo clump, as sounding like a leopard! One of our pet jokes.

dinner arranged hush hush by the Dillon Ripleys in camp at Phuntsholing, on the culmination of one of our joint birding expeditions in Bhutan.

JOHN BURDON SANDERSON HALDANE

One of the most remarkable men it has been my good fortune to be associated with, even for the few short years he lived and worked in India, was Professor J.B.S. Haldane—a veritable giant both physically and intellectually. It was a fortuitous coincidence also that my earlier work on the ecology of Indian birds had come to the notice of Professor Haldane before he migrated to India, and had caught his fancy and won special approbation. In many of his popular lectures and talks at scientific conferences and seminars he often went gratuitously out of his way to make flattering references to my work, holding it up as an example of what it was possible to achieve by industry and dedication with no more sophisticated a tool than a pair of binoculars. He was for ever critical of 'foreign-returned' Indian scientists (especially from the US) who kept harping on the lack of sophisticated apparatus here and trying to justify the mediocre quality of the out-turn of most research scientists and laboratories in India. Haldane lost no opportunity to emphasize that no advantage was being taken by Indian scientists of the matchless opportunities for biological field studies available at their doorstep—opportunities that were the envy of western biologists.

JBS's phenomenal memory and powers of absorption and concentration, and the depth and breadth of his knowledge—not only of all the formal scientific disciplines like physics, chemistry, biology, biometry, genetics, etc.—but of ethnology, anthropology, philosophy (particularly Hindu philosophy) and astronomy, was encyclopaedic. He could read the heavens like a book and identify the major constellations and their constituents by their Sanskrit names. The greatest wonder to my mind was how, in the midst of all his multifarious intellectual preoccupations, scientific research and writing, he yet managed to keep himself abreast so profoundly of the latest discoveries, theories and developments and ongoing research in all branches of science and the humanities, and be able to synthesize, discuss and explain them in such meticulous detail. As one of his distinguished colleagues, Professor Sir Peter Medawar, head of the Zoology Department of London University, in his Preface to Haldane's biography *J.B.S.* by Ronald Clark (1968), writes: 'He could have made a success of any one of half a dozen careers—as mathematician, classical scholar, philosopher, scientist, journalist or imaginative writer. To unequal degrees he was in fact all of these things. On his life's showing he could not have been a politician, administrator (heavens no!), jurist or, I think, a critic of any kind. In the outcome he became one of the three of four most influential biologists of his generation.'

The bushy eyebrows, massive head and gruff exterior gave Haldane a deceptively forbidding look to strangers. He could not suffer fools and charlatans for certain, and usually kept them in no doubt about this. But with youngsters, of whose sincerity to learn he was assured, he could be extremely gentle and patient and considerate, and would sacrifice endless pains and time to help them along. While a professor at the Indian Statistical Institute, Calcutta, he picked up several bright and promising students in this way and groomed them into highly original scientists, encouraging them to undertake well-thought-out 'fool experiments' as he called them, even at the risk of failure, but some of which could occasionally lead to unforeseen clues and rewards.

When the visit to India of Queen Elizabeth II in 1961 was first mooted, Haldane was officially asked for suggestions as to what he thought she should see in India. He replied 'If Her Majesty were allowed to choose her own programme after consultation with Mr Sálim Ali, our greatest naturalist, she would perhaps visit Chilka Lake (Orissa), Kaziranga (Assam) and Sambhar Lake (Rajasthan), preferably not killing any animals. She would at once acquire popularity with a hundred million or so Indians who take animals seriously, as Jehangir acquired it.'

I was deeply touched by an impromptu letter he wrote to me in May 1961 on his return from Italy, where he had attended an International Congress on Human Genetics. It said: 'I have

received a monstrous prize of about Rs 160,000 from the Italian
Accademia dei Lincei. Probably you deserve this prize more
than I. It was difficult for you to become a biologist. It was
difficult for me not to become one, with my father's example
before me . . . . If you have a biological job where a few
thousand rupees would help, I should be able to spare them.'

At the Congress held by the University of Malaya in
Singapore in 1958 to celebrate the centenary of Darwin and
Wallace and the bicentenary of the publication of the tenth
edition of Linnaeus's *Systema Naturae*, at which Haldane had
been invited to preside and at which he urged me to present a
paper ('The Breeding Biology of some Indian Weaver Birds'),
he struck sniggerers dumb by the brilliance of his Presidential
Address—'On the Theory of Natural Selection Today'. The
surreptitious sniggering among the European section of the
audience, as yet very 'true blue', booted and suited and
thoroughly 'proper', was due to his occupying the Presidential
chair in the Indian dress he had adopted, consisting of a
(somewhat crumpled) white cotton *kurta* and loose pyjama,
and Pathani *chaplis* on his unstockinged feet. But the most
stunning of his intellectual wizardries came later when he was
chairing the section on Biometry. After introducing a speaker
whose paper involved a great deal of statistics and mathematics,
Haldane descended from the stage and sat down on a classroom
bench in the first row to listen, his elbow resting on the desk
and hand supporting the massive head. He sat still in this
position, eyes closed, for ten minutes or more while the lecturer
reeled out statistics upon statistics, so that many in the audience
thought Haldane was fast asleep, because the paper was indeed
a lullaby for most of us. The listeners nudged each other,
pointing to him. Suddenly the lion sprang to life to suggest to
the speaker that he had probably made a mistake since, if this
figure was this and that figure was that, the result could not be
what he had shown. The speaker got flustered and embarrassed,
and hurriedly rechecking his figures apologetically admitted
that Haldane was right. While the audience was enjoying the
spectacle of a sleeping chairman, as they thought, Haldane was
mentally working out the statistical details for himself. It was a

remarkable demonstration of his power of concentration and left his scoffers completely floored.

Official procrastination and delay in scientific matters was anathema to JBS. Upon learning of the inordinate delay on the part of the CSIR to respond to my application for modest funding to keep two bright young scientists in the field on an ornithological project, he wrote to me with characteristic generosity: 'Barrackpore, May 2, 1962. If you want Rs 3,000 or so to help a hopeful young man, why not apply to me? Even if I say "No" I shall do so quicker than CSIR.'!

RICHARD WATKINS BURTON

Lieutenant Colonel R.W. Burton, was the sixth of nine brothers, all, interestingly, in the military profession. Four (or five?) of them were in the Indian Army, following in the footsteps of their father, General E.F. Burton, also a veteran tiger slayer. In his younger days, right from the time he joined the BNHS as a greenhorn subaltern in 1891, R.W. Burton was an ardent sportsman, developing with experience into an intrepid big-game hunter. He lived through many thrilling encounters with wounded or man-eating leopards and tigers, and survived serious mauling by a wounded bear. As has happened so often to veteran hunters, Burton switched over in later life to wildlife conservation with the same passionate zeal as earlier to shikar. With Independence in 1947, the loosening of firearms controls and laxity in the maintenance of law and order—when most of the conservation-conscious British forestry and administrative officials left the country—India's wildlife fell on evil days. Among the attenuated cadre of Indian officers of the forest administration, which from its inception had borne the statutory responsibility of caring for wildlife, there was only a handful of sufficiently interested or know-ledgeable men to safeguard the wildlife left in their charge. In the context of revenue-earning forestry, which they considered their main commitment, wildlife received bottom priority, and its care was even looked upon by some as an imposition. Wildlife within the forests and outside was disappearing at an alarming rate and many species seemed on the verge of extinction.

It was at this point that Colonel Burton, who, on retirement from the army had chosen to settle in Bangalore and was now on the Society's Advisory Committee, stepped in to lend the full weight of his long experience and concern to the BHNS (of which the honorary secretaryship had willy-nilly devolved on me) in its efforts to keep the subject of wildlife preservation in focus with the government and public. Our principal strategy was to keep up a continuous flow of well-informed articles in the local newspapers, issue educative pamphlets, and direct appeals to the authorities and ministries concerned. Our object was to dispel apathy and create public and governmental concern for the wild animals that were being ruthlessly slaughtered all over the country. It is largely to the credit of the BNHS and of conservation-minded officials like M.D. Chaturvedi (the first Inspector General of Forests of Independent India) and S.L. Hora (Director, Zoological Survey of India), as well as to a thin sprinkling of individual naturalists and sportsmen, and importantly to a few stalwart British sportsmen 'staybacks' like Colonel Burton, R.C. Morris and E.P. Gee— along with the solid backing of Prime Minister Jawaharlal Nehru—that the Indian Board for Wildlife got constituted, paving the way for a better deal for wildlife.

The powerful boost given to the wildlife conservation movement by the masterly address of Mr Prater, the Society's Curator, at the Golden Jubilee celebration in 1933, on 'The Wild Animals of India and the Problem of their Conservation', had marked an awakening of interest in wildlife among the public and a sense of responsibility and concern for its preservation. It led to the high-level inter-provincial conference convened by the Government of India at Delhi in 1935, which made a number of practical recommendations for the better protection of wild animals both inside and outside forest areas. Some of the major recommendations took a long period in gestation, and it was not till after Independence, in 1953, that the Indian Board for Wildlife was born, charged with the responsibility of recommending to the Central Government policy matters and suitable strategies for the protection and preservation of our wildlife heritage. The very well conceived and widely distributed pamphlet *Wildlife Preservation in India—India's Vanishing Asset*, stressing the urgent need for conservation through legislation and practical measures, was one of Colonel Burton's many seminal, timely and effective contributions to the cause he held so dear.

EDWARD PRITCHARD GEE

After retirement from a long innings of tea planting in Assam, E.P. Gee—a 'chronic' bachelor—settled down in Shillong where he assembled one of the finest private orchid collections in Assam, mostly taken in the wild by himself. As a young planter he had been an exceedingly keen sportsman-naturalist and an inveterate fisherman, which he remained to the end. By about 1948, when I first met Gee on the BNHS's survey of the rhinoceros population in Kaziranga Wildlife Sanctuary at the invitation of the Governor of Assam (Sir Akbar Hydari Jr.), he had given up shooting and taken to wildlife photography with a vengeance—a hobby in which he soon came to excel. He joined hands with Colonel Burton and R.C. Morris, who had also turned to conservation with missionary zeal. After meeting him at Bharatpur in 1957, Loke's diary describes Gee as

> a fairly heavily built man, balding, and wears tortoise-shell covered spectacles. Like Browning's thrush he repeats everything twice over, the second phrase tumbling out after the first, 'peeneka pani hai, peeneka pani; He got fed up, he got fed up, so he shot himself, so he shot himself.' Gee is rather hard of hearing, and this may be the reason for the trick of repetition. Sálim, too is pretty deaf, and when he and Gee talk to each other, the one in his high piercing voice and the other in his lower monotone, the world does not have to strain its ears to hear what they are saying!

During World War II Gee had volunteered for service and, since he was used to handling a large plantation labour force, he was assigned to the Pioneer Corps to supervise the building of one section of the famous Burma Road. As it happened, and unbeknown to either, there was another man of the same name supervising a different section of the road a few miles further on, and the superior officers were constantly getting confused between the two Gees. So, since our Gee was rather fond of talking, they aptly dubbed him 'Chatter-Gee'!

In 1961 I was prospecting for suitable ringing sites in the eastern Himalaya for the BNHS's Bird Migration Project. It had been reported by N.D. Jayal, when he was Assistant Political Officer at Tuting in the Siang Frontier Division a couple of years earlier, that this long crater-like valley was a very good place at the proper season for the study of migratory birds to and from Central Asia and beyond, and Gee cheerfully offered to accompany me on a reconnaissance. Before the PSS (perforated steel sheet)-covered airstrip was laid down during the war, the journey to Tuting from the political headquarters at Pasighat took fourteen days of foot-slogging up and down through thickly forested steeply mountainous country: now it took us just forty minutes by an austerely stripped supply plane, as we perched upon sacks of rice and *dal* and *ata*, with drums of kerosene, petrol and oil as fellow-passengers, and a few live goats—mutton on hoof—for good measure. Flying with the doors of the elderly and somewhat tired Dakota wide open, with the wind gushing through, and looking straight down on an endless succession of peaks, ridges and awesome gorges thousands of feet below was a thrilling experience, even though the gigantic snow-covered mountains flanking the route through narrow valley corridors sometimes did seem much too close to the wing-tips for peace of mind! End of November was of course too late for seeing the autumn migration here, but, in any case, the remoteness and logistic hurdles would make ringing at Tuting an impractical proposition for the BNHS. Just a few weeks after our visit to Tuting the Chinese dragon overran the area in our first border war.

During the same reconnaissance we visited Jatinga to check its reported suitability for ringing migratory birds, though here again November was not the proper season. Jatinga is a tiny village in the North Cachar Hills which has, in recent years, acquired notoriety for the stories about the 'mass suicide' of birds—invented by imaginative newspaper reporters—which takes place here at certain times of the year. From local testimony we gathered that under certain weather conditions on moonless nights during the south-west monsoon, when the sky is cloud-overcast and there is a slight drizzle and heavy ground mist, with the wind blowing south to north through the valley, i.e. against the flow of autumn migration, large numbers of birds of numerous families fly into bright lights, put up by the villagers to attract them, and are killed *en masse* for food by the ambushed hunters. The best time of the night is apparently between seven and nine and then again from two to four in the early morning. There seems nothing abnormal in migrating birds being attracted to bright lights on dark cloudy nights when the starry sky is invisible. This is a common experience at lighthouses along regular migration routes. But to me the real mystery of Jatinga is that among the birds on the move during such nights are many diurnal species like the Emerald Dove (*Chalcophaps*), Hill Partridge (*Arborophila*), Whitebreasted Kingfisher (*Halcyon smyrnensis*), and others which have always been considered resident and non-migratory, and which should ordinarily have no business flying at night. However, recoveries in India of such 'resident' species ringed in South-East Asian countries and the USSR suggest that there may well be a migratory element among the local populations behaving in the same way as the true long-distance migrants. Intensive ringing of resident birds in the area will throw more light on this problem.

Edward P. Gee (otherwise EPG) was one of the latter-day breed of cultured, well-educated planters. His dedication to wildlife conservation blossomed after he gave up the gun for the camera, and it became a veritable obsession with him after his retirement. He kept visiting the various national parks and major wildlife sanctuaries on his own to study and monitor in turn the local conditions at first hand, and he wrote extensively and authoritatively in the *Journal* of the BNHS, in *Oryx* (the reputed organ of the Fauna and Flora Preservation Society), and in various other scientific periodicals. He also wrote frequently in Indian dailies to publicize the cause and kept plugging the message of conservation through his own excellent wildlife films, lectures and radio talks, with missionary zeal. As a discerning freelance naturalist and a dynamic member of the Indian Board for Wildlife, Gee's opinions and suggestions were greatly appreciated and respected in official circles. His

book *The Wildlife of India*, published by Collins in 1964 with a
very felicitous Foreword by Prime Minister Jawaharlal Nehru,
is one of the most popular and informative books on the larger
wild animals of India and their status—interestingly and chattily
written for the layman and illustrated with his choice
photographs.

Gee was a very good and understanding friend to me and a
most valuable asset to the BNHS, ever ready to help in its
activities in any way he could when called upon, often at
considerable inconvenience and expense to himself. Would
that the Society had more committed members on the Gee
model. It is tragic for Indian nature and wildlife conservation,
and for Gee himself, that he died while still so active and full of
enthusiasm, and just when his assiduous efforts and the movement for which he had worked so selflessly were beginning to
show results.

HUMAYUN ABDULALI

One of my most promising *chelas* from his early schoolboy
days in the twenties, after my final repatriation from Burma,
was my cousin Humayun, a son of my brother-in-law Hassan's
elder brother, Najmuddin Abdulali. Najmuddin, after a prosperous run of business in Japan, had decided to shift his headquarters to Bombay. He lived at Andheri, which was then a
quiet, well-wooded suburb, the haunt of many of the commoner
birds, some of which nested in his jungly compound. It was
apparently here that Humayun's juvenile interest in natural
history triggered off and he started collecting bird's eggs,
snakes, lizards, frogs and other small creatures. In observing
new bird arrivals and finding nests the youngster was assisted
by a uniquely unusual servant woman, who, though completely illiterate and untaught, had a natural idiosyncrasy for
birds and went about looking for them on her own.

By the time Humayun had done with school and taken up
the formal zoology course at college (St Xavier's) he had already
become an enthusiastic and knowledgeable all-round naturalist,
specially interested in birds, of which he had made a very

creditable study collection for his college museum from the Bombay neighbourhood. This material, together with my own, collected chiefly between 1924 and 1929, formed the basis of our joint paper, 'The Birds of Bombay and Salsette', published in the *Journal* of the BNHS in 1936–7. In the early thirties Humayun spent three long college vacations with me on the Hyderabad and Travancore bird surveys. There he got his first practical introduction to methodical specimen collecting and fieldwork, which he has since developed to such good purpose. As an enthusiastic and perceptive young naturalist with keen observation and an original, inquiring mind, he proved a most useful field assistant: a pleasant, stimulating and amusing companion in camp and on shooting trips, being a tireless and discriminating collector of bird and other natural-history specimens. Humayun was an excellent shot with his 12-bore and usually kept the camp in meat. Moreover, he was somewhat of a dare-devil, ever ready to undertake risky missions in quest of birds, such as scaling up a towering scarp to an eagle's eyrie, or dangling at the end of an uncertain rope a hundred feet up within a cave-shaft to examine swiftlets' nests.

While Honorary Secretary of the Society (1950–62) and its representative on the Bombay State Wildlife Advisory Board, Humayun was actively involved, in collaboration with the Forest Department, in drafting the Bombay Wild Birds and Wild Animals Protection Act of 1951. It was the fruit of critical painstaking study and distillation and adaptation of similar legislation in a number of advanced western countries, and, with slight modifications, it later served as the model for the Central Wildlife (Protection) Act, 1972—acclaimed as the most perfect piece of wildlife legislation we have so far had in India. It was mainly through Humayun's initiative and efforts as Honorary Secretary that the Society's negotiations with the Central Government for a separate building for the permanent housing of its offices, library and invaluable zoological collec- tions were successfully completed—as witness whereof stands Hornbill House today. It is as unfortunate for himself as for the causes he holds dear that in later years Humayun has not always been the easiest man to work with, to the detriment of his own image with many of his former associates, cronies and admirers. His undoubted competence could otherwise have contributed so much of constructive value.

20

Scientific Ornithology and Shikar

In my later days it has somehow been generally taken for granted that because I like birds I am bound to be revolted by the thought of anyone killing a bird, leave alone thinking of killing a bird myself. This assumption is far from correct, and it sometimes puts me in embarrassing situations. It is true that I despise purposeless killing, and regard it as an act of vandalism deserving the severest condemnation. But my love of birds is not of the sentimental variety. It is essentially aesthetic and scientific, and in some cases may even be pragmatic. For a scientific approach to bird study it is often necessary to sacrifice a few. I do not enjoy the killing, and sometimes even suffer a prick of conscience, but I have no doubt that but for the methodical collecting of specimens in my earlier years—several thousands, alas—it would have been impossible to advance our taxonomical knowledge of Indian birds—as the various regional surveys have done—nor indeed of their geographical distribution, ecology and bionomics. However, I believe a stage has now been reached when the *ad hoc* collecting of Indian bird specimens is no longer essential, except for special studies such as moult, or in the case of a few remote and unexplored pockets of the country, or of a few little-known species that are rare in museum collections. There is sufficient research material available in the BNHS, the Zoological Survey of India, and the great natural-history museums abroad, for solving most taxonomical problems. Thanks to international understanding and co-operation among scientists and scientific institutions, and to speedy air transport, the problem of borrowing supplementary material for comparative studies has been simplified. Even from the time, until not so long ago, when birdwatching was rather looked down upon as an amateurish, time-killing pastime of the idle rich, and only morphology and taxonomy regarded as 'scientific' ornithology, my own principal interest has centred on the living bird in its natural environment.

I have bothered myself little with taxonomy except as an academic exercise. From the sidelines I have watched with dispassionate amusement, sometimes with distinct amazement, the wordy and often acrimonious battles among taxonomic giants as well as pedants and charlatans whose only acquaint-ance with the birds in question has been with musty museum specimens. The glib and self-assured manner in which some play the taxonomy game reminds me strongly of one of the immortal Omar Khayyam's quatrains—'Hither and thither moves and mates and slays, and one by one back in the closet lays'. And this is often what it really amounts to. After a full circle we are usually back in square one, where we started. The exercise fails to give me a thrill: so it has always been, and so will it always be, I fear. Happily, the overall emphasis has been shifting, particularly since World War II, from taxonomy to the field study of the living bird—Ecology and Behaviour. The scientific respectability and public recognition birdwatching has acquired within recent years was greatly boosted by the award of the Nobel Prize for Biology in 1973 to two (of the three joint) winners—Nikolaas Tinbergen and Konrad Lorenz—who had both started their careers as amateur bird-watchers.

Having grown up in an era when hunting for sport in the British tradition was regarded as almost a status symbol by the upper middle-class Indian—*the* thing for every young man of consequence to cultivate, or at least be able to talk about—I naturally became an ardent shooter under the inspiration and tutelage of our father-uncle, Amiruddin Tyabji. Amiruddin was a popular socialite among the élite and on intimate hail-fellow-well-met terms with sundry sporting rajas and nawabs of his day. His amiable nature and his prowess as a shikari were well known, and made him a frequent invitee to their hunting forays. The stories of the regal tiger hunts and big-game adventures which he brought back fired my youthful ambition to become an inveterate big-game hunter. As a schoolboy I waited eagerly for the winter vacations—the shooting season—when I would often foist myself on some kindly upcountry relation, preferably a district officer doing his official winter tour and, incidentally, providing convenient shooting opportunities for himself and his guests. Most of my shooting as a vacationing schoolboy consisted of small game such as duck, snipe, partridge, quail and hare, which were abundant everywhere in the days before World War I, and decreasingly so even up to World War II. The bags were occasionally supplemented with an odd chinkara, blackbuck, hog deer, barking deer or pig, depending on the country. These shooting galas were usually shared with other Christmas house-guests and a number of schoolboy cousins more or less my own age, and there was a good deal of friendly rivalry amongst us youngsters in the number of rounds fired per bag obtained. As our quota of cartridges was carefully doled out to us, everyone naturally strove to excel.

During his service in Sind, then a province of Bombay Presidency, my second eldest brother, Hamid, was the most regular and uncomplaining victim of these schoolboy invasions. Perhaps the most productive period from the point of view of my shikar experience and natural history, and also for Hamidbhai himself and the several young cousins, was while he was posted as Superintendent of Land Records, and later as Manager of Encumbered Estates in Sind. His official duties were then light and left plenty of time for sport. Moreover, his winter tours then covered the entire province, and thanks to his thoughtfulness on behalf of his guests, the itinerary was contrived as far as possible to include the best shooting localities during the three or four weeks we were with him. Hamidbhai had taken to shooting fairly late in life, soon after joining the ICS in 1904 and being posted to Sind, where most of his British colleagues were ardent shikaris. Sind was reputed to be, and indeed was, a paradise for small game in those days, and it remained so at least up to the time of Partition. He soon became an excellent shot with gun and rifle, and it was seldom that any of the younger members of the party could better his daily record. He discouraged us from aspiring for record bags, whether of duck or partridge or any other game; and being a keen naturalist and bird student himself, insisted on the bag being vetted each time and the species properly identified before being consigned to the kitchen. This early exercise has stood me in good stead. Though we never shot in excess, there was hardly a day when there was no game on the table, and often at all the major meals.

Those who have never ridden a well trained, repeat well trained, riding camel can have no idea of what a speedy and comfortable mode of travel it is in sandy semi-desert country. Hamidbhai had two specially good riding camels in his regular establishment, one for himself, the other for his wife Sharifa, on which most of their winter season touring was done. When there were camp guests, extra animals were hired for the duration from all-too-willing-to-please zamindars, many of whom prided themselves on being breeders and connoisseurs of pedigree camels. Hamidbhai usually went off by himself early in the morning before the rest of us were up and about, either on his beautiful bay gelding or on his favourite riding camel, to do his official inspections and other field chores, attended by a motley crowd of zamindars and local gentry and revenue officials mounted on ambling ponies of assorted sizes and quality, who often found it difficult to keep up with his camel. Its driver, the trusty and bearded Jan Mohammad, took puckish delight in showing off the paces and performance of his mount, and in the discomfiture of the retinue struggling to keep up.

Shifting camp every three or four days was a complicated exercise, but the fuss-free efficiency with which it was accomplished was, and still is, a standing marvel to me. The several large and cumbersome Swiss tents, furniture and baggage, including *durries, charpais,* folding chairs and tables—dining, dressing, office, wash, and others—thunderboxes, galvanized iron bath tubs, buckets and kitchen utensils, had all to be transported. Crockery, glassware, reading lamps, hurricane lanterns and other fragiles were packed in specially designed wooden chests with concave backs which fitted snugly pannier-wise, one on each side, on 'freight' camels. The baggage train consisting of maybe fifteen or more pack camels tied nose to tail one behind the other jogged along all night, led by a camelman, and usually arrived at its destination in the early hours of the morning. So expert was the routine packing that in spite of the heavy and continuous jolting received, specially on the more frisky and recalcitrant animals, hardly ever did any lamp or crockery suffer damage. By the time the sahib and his guests arrived in the forenoon of the following day, everything was ship-shape—the various tents for the office, mess and guests were up and ready for occupation, the furniture and articles on the dressing tables and in the bath room, even an inadvertent safety pin, exactly in the same position as in the previous camp. The relay cook had been in action and lunch was ready on time, so that it was difficult to realize that you had shifted camp at all. The little army of *khalasis* or tent crew responsible for the operation were expert at their jobs, and the termite-like speed and orderliness with which the cumbersome tents and their furniture were handled at both ends was truly impressive. Of course for most of the basic equipment, such as tents and furniture, two sets needed to be maintained to allow one set to leapfrog to the next halt while the other was in use. Conditions have altered, alas, and in these days of hurry and bustle, of jeeps and motor trucks, of black-topped roads and furnished dak bungalows, of electric lighting and easy accessibility by telephone to departmental Secretaries and Ministers, combined with the inordinate increase in paper work at headquarters—the operation of Parkinson's Law—a district official's tour is no longer the leisurely idyll it used to be. As to shikar, in addition to the regrettable loss of its public respectability, the prohibitive cost of services and goods, of ammunition, and above all the tragic disappearance of game, large and small, from most of the country, has put an end to all legitimate sport. No vacationing schoolboy can ever more hope to enjoy the sort of outdoor opportunities that we had!

My first meeting with the Taloor or Houbara Bustard

(*Chlamydotis undulata macqueenii*) was during the first of such shooting vacations in Sind, in 1910 or thereabouts. I had read a good deal about protective coloration in animals and how it helps them to elude their enemies, but until I received a practical demonstration of this device from the houbara I could never have believed the perfection of its efficiency. The taloor is cherished by gourmets, and it certainly has its points as a table bird. But taloor shooting from camel back, as is usually done in Sind and as was laid on for us, is poor sport—a vicarious exercise at best. However, it involves consummate skill and judgement in the preliminary manoeuvring of the camel on the part of its shikari-camel driver. The eyesight of these desert dwellers is truly phenomenal. To pick out with the naked eye a houbara in its native sandy environment at a distance of maybe 500 yards is a feat that few can perform, even with binoculars, without considerable previous experience. After the shikari sights a bird the strategy is to circumvent it by a wide detour in a series of narrowing circles without arousing its suspicion until you are within gunshot range of the quarry. At one point in this manoeuvre you suddenly realize that the bird you have been watching slowly walking away while surreptitiously following your movements, has magically vanished. In the twinkling of an eye it has squatted flat at the foot of a diminutive bush, neck stretched out on the ground. The shikari pulls up the camel and nudges you excitedly to shoot, but for you the bird is simply not there. In desperation he points to that dried cow pat at the base of yonder bush and urges you to fire at that, which you reluctantly do, more in order to allay his disgust. It is only when the pat turns over with the shot that you notice the outspread wings and recognize it as your quarry! This is how I got my first houbara and also my earliest object lesson in the value of protective coloration for survival in animals. Elsewhere—as in Kutch—houbara shooting is usually done from the ground by having the birds driven over the guns. This method is somewhat more 'sporting', and on a cold and windy day when the birds really move, the shooting can be quite difficult and exciting.

But the houbara is pre-eminently and *par excellence* a quarry for the falconer. Small wonder that the indiscriminate activities of sheikhs of the Gulf Emirates, who are chronic falconry addicts, are threatening to wipe the houbara out of existence in many of its pristine habitats. In the winter of 1967–8, for instance, one enterprising sheikh alone accounted for 915 birds in Pakistan in about four weeks' hunting. And this vandalism continues to increase year by year.

21

The Books I Wrote

Field notes on birds, about their occurrences and abundance, their habits, behaviour, associations, and other facets of their ecology and life history recorded over a long period of years, as in my own case, tend to become so much useless—more correctly, unusable—junk unless they have been maintained in a methodical way, properly indexed, and kept scrupulously up to date. For the greater part of my bird watching life, before the cassette type of mini tape-recorder and suchlike sophistications were born and became fashionable, the taking of detailed notes while actually working in the field was a comparatively slow and tiresome affair. A method that I had satisfactorily evolved for myself was to carry in my shirt pocket a small notebook and pencil and keep hastily jotting down on the spot. Besides making a list of the birds seen, I kept a running commentary of any interesting characteristic or unusual observation about them—of their general behaviour, calls and songs, food, nesting, social and interspecific activities or whatever, in a sort of hieroglyphic shorthand of my own. Back in camp and as soon as possible—before the nuances were forgotten—these syncopated notes were 'decoded', suitably amplified, and transcribed into a special loose-leaf ledger, each species under its own 'account head' in the style of commercial book-keeping. Each entry, even when no more than an individual sighting, was posted up with its date, locality, altitude, etc., so that in course of time upon opening the ledger at the required page I found spread before me everything I had ever observed anywhere about that particular species. Thus, when assembling material for a report or book the job was vastly simplified and expedited.

In September 1935 I was formally commissioned by the BNHS to write the long-discussed book on some of the commoner birds of the Indian countryside in simple non-technical language for the layman. It would cover some 180 selected species and use the colour illustrations, one bird to a plate, from the Society's wall charts which had proved popular with English-medium secondary schools in India. Terse descriptions of about 350 words each would cover such topics as Field Identification, Distribution, Habits, Food, Calls and Nesting, together with a few general chapters on Migration, Flight, Bird Watching, Usefulness of Birds to Man, in addition to the Preface and Introduction. The current format of four birds to a plate was first adopted from the fifth (1955) edition onward for reasons of economy, when new plates had to be prepared to replace the old and worn-out four-colour blocks from the wall charts, and additional species introduced. I had received these details informally from my friend and colleague, S.H. Prater (the Society's then Curator) much earlier, and had in fact prepared rough drafts of much of the text while refugee-ing in my joblessness at Kihim in 1930.

Talking of preparing the text at Kihim reminds me of an extraordinary experience with which I cannot resist interrupting this narrative. The family seaside cottage at Kihim consisted of a small all-purpose ground-floor room surrounded on three sides by a fairly wide open verandah, where most of our day was spent, and where stood my writing desk with files of notes and papers and rough drafts of the various chapters. Tehmina and I slept in a tiny garret-like bedroom upstairs. On coming down one morning I found, to my horror, all my papers in disarray, badly mauled and some of the loose sheets torn and lying scattered on the floor around the desk, some even in the garden several yards away. It was a puzzling situation for which no immediate explanation was thinkable. Nothing happened for the next two or three days, then the spook struck again with more papers destroyed, leaving me still more mysti-fied. On the following night after the mischief was repeated I realized that the man or beast or whatever it was, was turning into a malignant addict and it was time to take action. So I sprinkled some wood ash on the floor round the desk to see what the pug-marks would reveal. Sure enough, the culprit proved to be a dog; though why a dog should be so deeply interested in my notes as to repeat the unrewarding exercise time after time and chew up and carry off the loose sheets was difficult to guess. As there was no knowing when the next raid might occur, and at what unearthly hour of night, I worked out a suitable strategy. Dharma, our deaf old *mali*, slept in a cabin a few yards away from the main cottage. I tied one end of a string to his big toe and the other to a cow-bell at the head of my bed, where also stood in readiness my 20-bore shot gun. For this medium of communication we devised a special code of action so that I could be silently alerted while the culprit was *in flagrante delicto*! Two or three days later at 3 o'clock, pre-dawn, the cow-bell tinkled. I got out of bed quickly, clutched the gun and crept quietly down the creaky stairs. On detecting my presence the mongrel hastily jumped off the desk and was slinking away shiftily with a self-condemning guilty look—tail between hind legs and surreptitious backward squints from the corners of his eyes. To make sure of keeping the miscreant out of further criminal mischief I shot him dead, with no regret whatever. But to this day I wonder at his extraordinarily aberrant behaviour: what had that miserable cur found so rewarding in raiding my desk and ravaging my indigestible papers, not once but again and again?

The drafts of the various chapters were tried out on Tehmina, who was of the greatest help in moderating the language. She had a remarkable 'feeling' for colloquial English prose style and ironed out stilted passages to make for pleasanter reading. Readability is a feature that many reviewers and readers of *The Book of Indian Birds*, and my later books, have frequently gone out of the way to remark upon, to my very special gratification.

Among my favourite and most admired naturalist writers are W. H. Hudson and E. H. Aitken (better known as EHA). Their writings are models of how even prosaic dry-as-dust factual information can be made pleasurable reading with a little extra attention to honing and polishing, which EHA at least was known invariably to pay before publishing his facile, seemingly effortless, essays. I set great store by readability, and consider the extra time and effort involved in achieving this well worthwhile.

Since this was the pioneer of colour-illustrated books on Indian birds in the now-popular Field Guide format, and is acknowledged as largely responsible for creating and fostering much of the interest in birds and birdwatching seen in the country today, it may interest the reader to know some of the vital statistics of the publication. The first edition of 3,000 copies appeared in August 1941; it was printed throughout on imported art paper at the Times of India Press, Bombay, with a published price of Rs 14. *The Book* dealt with 181 species of the commoner and more familiar birds of the countryside; the number of included species increased progressively with each edition, as unfortunately also the price. The latest (eleventh) edition of 10,000 copies published in July 1980 covers 280 species and is priced Rs 60. The total number of copies published in all the previous ten editions together was 46,000—each edition averaging about 4,500 copies.

The Book was lucky in getting off to a flying start, since the war with Japan was on at the time and large numbers of British and Allied troops were constantly in transit through Bombay on their way to and from South-East Asia. They included many keen birdwatchers seeking just the kind of introduction to unfamiliar tropical species that the book provided. Among the distinguished earliest users of the book have been Pandit Jawaharlal Nehru, an ardent nature-lover, who got a copy autographed by me while lodged in Dehra Dun jail (*c.* 1942) to send as a birthday present to his daughter Indira, then herself in Naini jail. In her Foreword to *Our Birds* written for children by Shri Rajeshwar Prasad Narain Sinha (published in 1959), Mrs Gandhi recalls the circumstance, saying, 'Like most Indians I took birds for granted until my father sent me Shri Sálim Ali's delightful book from Dehra Dun jail and opened my eyes to an entirely new world. Only then did I realize how much I had been missing.' Later still, as Prime Minister of India and Patron of the BNHS, Mrs Gandhi, in her inaugural speech at the Society's centennial (15 September 1983), again referred to this incident, saying, 'I had always loved animals but I didn't know much about birds until the high walls of Naini prison shut us off from them, and for the first time I paid attention to bird song. I noted the songs, and later, on my release, was able to identify the birds from Dr Sálim Ali's book.'

I discovered that Maulana Abul Kalam Azad, while imprisoned in Ahmadnagar jail as President of the Indian National Congress, following the Quit India session in 1942 and Gandhiji's call to Do or Die, had also consulted the book, borrowed from his fellow-prisoner Jawaharlal in a neighbouring cell, for certain details of his truly classic story about the irrepressible pair of House Sparrows that had chosen to nest in a hole above his bed. *The Book* has been translated and published in Hindi and Punjabi and an Urdu translation is in preparation.

Upon the final winding up of the Tavoy business concern of J. A. Ali Bros. & Co. and a splitting of the liabilities between the two partners, my share of indebtedness to various parties for interest-bearing loans and investments in the firm had been startling. During the several years practically without income after my return to Bombay, and the slow rate of liquidation of such assets as I had inherited from the business, the interest continued to mount alarmingly. At one stage it looked desperately unlikely that at the rate of repayment which I then found possible my liabilities would ever be cleared. The backlog kept rocketing from year to year in spite of some of my creditors having considerately agreed to waive the interest, and some even to whittle down the quantum. Even so, my liabilities continued to give me sleepless nights now and again, and I despaired of ever getting the millstone off my neck. It was at this point that *The Book of Indian Birds* came like a godsend. From the royalties of the first four or five editions I was able to pay off all the creditors in full, to my eternal mental relief.

After the success of *The Book of Indian Birds* and *The Birds of Kutch*, which followed it in 1945, summer-vacationing friends suggested my doing a similar colour-illustrated guide to the birds commonly met with at and around the popular hill resorts in the Himalaya, and the Nilgiri and other peninsular hills. With encouragement from Oxford University Press, of which R.E. Hawkins was then General Manager of the Indian Branch and who had published my *Birds of Kutch*, and with the ready compliance of G.M. Henry (the well known Ceylon bird illustrator) to paint the plates on a royalty-sharing basis, an edition of 10,000 copies of *Indian Hill Birds* was printed in the UK in 1949 by the photo-offset process. Henry's illustrations were superb, and altogether the book received flattering reviews in scientific periodicals, Indian and foreign, and encomiums from users within the country. In spite of this the sales were disappointing for the publishers, and the first edition took over twenty-five years to sell out! The book remained out of print for five years, during which, however, there was a marked build-up of interest in bird watching within the country as well as a spurt in ornithological and wildlife tourism from abroad. The demand for bird books shot up in consequence, and OUP felt impelled to bring out in 1979 a straight reprint of *Indian Hill Birds* in its original format, pending a revision for the second edition, followed soon after by third and fourth impressions. A measure of the worldwide monetary inflation and rise of costs in the interval is seen from the fact that the original published price of the book, Rs 20 in 1949, had shot up to Rs 140 for the 1984 reprint! But then, the plates are still printed in nine colours from the original film separations.

Sir C.P. Ramaswamy Aiyer, a reputed Sanskrit scholar and leading lawyer of Madras, was Dewan of the princely state of Travancore in the 1950s, and by virtue of this office also Chancellor of the University at Trivandrum. He was apparently impressed by my scientific report on the ornithology of Travancore and Cochin, which had appeared serially in the *Journal* of the BNHS between 1935 and 1937, and decided to get it published in the form of a 'popular' colour-illustrated book for the benefit of zoology students, foresters, tourists and others, and granted a subsidy to Oxford University Press for the purpose. The excellent illustrations were commissioned from D.V. Cowen (Mrs V. Gardner Lewis), a keen and competent bird watcher whose reputation as a bird painter already stood established through her work in *The Book of Indian Birds*. Five hundred copies of an edition of 1,000 were taken for distribution by Travancore University (published price Rs 35), and the rest ran out of print within a very short time, leaving a considerable unsatisfied demand, albeit perhaps not large enough to warrant immediate commercial reprinting. The book thus remained out of print until 1969, by which time in the linguistic realignment of the Indian states Travancore and Cochin had absorbed the adjoining Malayalam district of Malabar and emerged on the map as Kerala. Meanwhile, the demand for a second edition of the bird book had also been building up, and again through financial assistance from the University a revised and enlarged edition of the book to include Malabar was published, this time as *Birds of Kerala*, priced the same as before. This was exceptionally good value at the time and, like its predecessor, this edition also soon sold out. After a few years in the wilderness the Kerala Forest Department has recently supported OUP in a third printing of the book in commemoration of the Golden Jubilee of the Periyar Wildlife Sanctuary in March 1985.

My first casual experience of a tropical rain-forest had been in Tenasserim during the early Tavoy days, and ever since then I had longed for an opportunity to look closer at this type of evergreen forest and explore more intensively its birds and natural history. The Travancore bird survey, in part, had fulfilled that ambition, and in the event proved perhaps the most enjoyable and rewarding of all my regional surveys. Writing up the scientific report had given me special pleasure because of the non-traditional approach I adopted, with stress on ecology rather than systematics throughout. For this departure the report had received felicitous notices from all sides and I was happy to be able to present it to a wider circle of bird students and the public in a more convenient book form. Indeed, in many ways I consider *Birds of Kerala* the most ego-satisfying of all my books, no less so than *The Book of Indian Birds*.

As a result of my several bird-collecting and field-study expeditions in Sikkim in the 1950s sponsored by Loke Wan Tho (about which I have spoken earlier), Oxford University Press, with financial assistance from the Chogyal's government, published in 1962 *The Birds of Sikkim*, priced at Rs 30, with colour plates by the internationally reputed artists Paul Barruel (France), David Reid-Henry (UK) and Robert Scholz (Germany). Of the edition of 2,000 copies, half went to the Sikkim government for complimentary distribution to state guests and others, and the rest sold out within a year or so, and thereafter the book remained unobtainable. A second impression was contemplated, but meanwhile the Chogyal's state got pitchforked into the Indian Union and that was the end of that! By way of advance publicity for the book, which had been suffering an inordinately prolonged gestation, OUP brought out a slim *Picture Book of Sikkim Birds* containing all the seventeen colour plates, together with short write-ups about the birds. These booklets were very good value at Rs 5, and were popular among Sikkim schools and visiting bird watchers.

A thumbnail sketch of the genesis and history of the *Handbook of the Birds of India and Pakistan* by myself and Dillon Ripley is given elsewhere. An amusing sidelight on publishers and publishing strategies when I was prospecting for a possible publisher for the book is interesting to recall. I had offered the book to Oxford University Press, who had published most of my earlier work, and they were clearly interested. However, since a ten-volume work with over a hundred colour plates would be a major long-term undertaking involving an unusually heavy editorial and financial outlay and more than normally heavy business risk, they were dragging their feet on a final decision. It was expected that the book's biggest market would have to be the country itself, since Pakistan was out of bounds for Indian exports, and India was as yet not sufficiently bird-minded to bear the entire brunt. It was feared that the foreign market would not amount to much for a restricted title like this one, and could not be relied upon. In the midst of all this uncertainty the telephone rang one afternoon. It was Mr William Collins, head of the famous British publishing house, who had arrived from the UK that morning, asking if I would come and see him at the Taj Mahal Hotel. He had apparently got word from his sleuths that I was working on such a book and wanted to know if this was true, and whether I had found a prospective publisher for it. I told him the OUP, my usual publishers, had expressed interest but were dithering as it meant a heavy and speculative financial commitment. Collins said, 'I want you to know that we would be definitely interested to publish the book should OUP decide to turn it down.' This news, conveyed to OUP, clinched their decision with exemplary promptness and our contract was signed almost overnight! It was a bold step on the part of Mr Hawkins, but I am glad the publishers have had no cause to regret their decision. In the event it has proved well worthwhile for OUP, both as a commercial proposition and as a matter of publishing prestige. Second editions of each volume are gradually being published, and the imaginatively conceived *Compact Edition*, which incorporates all ten volumes within one cover, appeared in 1983. I cannot escape the feeling, however, that it was really that timely phonecall from Mr Collins that set the hesitant ball rolling!

A couple of years after the *Handbook* was completed, in September 1976, I received a questionnaire from one Shri Narayan Dutt, Editor of *Navneet Hindi Digest* of Bombay, who was preparing to publish a biographical sketch of me. One of his questions was 'How many hours a day did you devote to its [the *Handbook's*] writing and did you write in your own hand or dictate it?' Since several inquirers have also asked similar questions from time to time, my answer to Shri Dutt will hold for all. I said,

I usually worked from 10 to 12 hours a day (sometimes 14 or 15) with short breaks for meals, etc. After the preliminary work of library and museum research, which started before 1953, the actual writing of the volumes took about ten years. . . . I prepared all the first drafts in my own hand (no dictating) and devoted a great deal of time to chopping and changing, rephrasing passages and altering words, and compressing sentences as much as possible so as to be terse and to the point. I firmly believe that besides providing factual scientific information to the reader it is just as important to make the account pleasurable reading. . . . I then had the mauled handwritten draft typed out in triple spacing and subjected it to further scrutiny and the same vetting and polishing process, often getting it re-typed a second time before feeling sufficiently satisfied to have it finally fair-typed for the printer. It was thus a lengthy and time-consuming process—but I found that it pays!

The bird survey of Sikkim had whetted my appetite for a more intensive exploration of adjoining Bhutan than had been possible for Frank Ludlow and George Sherrif in 1933 and 1934. The lack then of roads for wheeled traffic and of bridges over torrential streams and awesome gorges had restricted their movements in this wild and rugged terrain to mule and porter transport, and given to their expeditions the aura of real adventures, which in fact they were. A fascinating narrative of them may be found in *The Ibis* for 1937. In the 1960s I was invited by His Majesty the Druk Gyalpo Jigme Dorji Wangchuk, a discerning shikari-naturalist, keenly interested in wildlife conservation, to study the birds of Bhutan. I agreed to produce for him as *quid pro quo* thereafter an illustrated bird book like the one for Sikkim which he ardently wanted. He laid on all facilities in the way of transport, camping and commissariat through the Border Roads Organization—a semi-military engineering force of the Indian government which was then aiding Bhutan to build a network of arterial roads up to and along its northern international border. They had succeeded in constructing terrifying roads that teetered on the brink of precipitous, impossible-looking contours of rugged mountains, with tight twists and turns and awesome hairpin bends with sheer vertical drops of hundreds of metres, down which many vehicles had rolled during the construction. They reminded me forcibly of a notice on a mountain road I had once read about; it said 'No entry. Road in dangerous condition. Survivors will be prosecuted.' To escape possible prosecution even here in Bhutan we strictly followed those instructions!

These roads are masterpieces of skilful engineering and alignment. Though often blasted out of solid vertical rock, the gradients are so cleverly maintained along the contours that they are never too steep for heavily-laden motor trucks and armoured vehicles. The calamitous drawback of not having strategic roads to the Tibetan border through a friendly 'foreign' country like Bhutan for defense in time of need was dramatically realized when in 1962 the Chinese marched into NEFA (now Arunachal Pradesh), astraddle our only approach to the frontier via Bomdila, leaving no alternative route by which their incursion into Indian territory could have been stemmed.

Six separate collecting expeditions were mounted in Bhutan between 1966 and 1973, of four to eight weeks each, covering the eastern, central and western parts of the kingdom fairly thoroughly. Some of them were jointly conducted with Dr and Mrs Ripley, and the eminent Indian ornithologist, Dr Biswamoy Biswas, of the Zoological Survey of India. As would be expected, the birdlife did not prove significantly different from Sikkim or Arunachal, and it therefore seemed redundant to produce a separate bird book for Bhutan when there was already a comprehensive one for adjacent Sikkim. The king, with characteristic reasonableness, readily agreed with my suggestion that it would be far more realistic to alter the format of the proposed book to that of a conventional field guide for the entire Eastern Himalaya, i.e. the section extending from east-central Nepal to easternmost Arunachal Pradesh, which formed a single physiographical unit. In addition to meeting much of the cost of painting the plates, the Druk Gyalpo committed his government to purchase 500 copies of this *Field Guide to the Birds of the Eastern Himalayas* by way of publishing subsidy to OUP (unbecomingly repudiated by the successor government after the death of the king because the name 'Bhutan' did not specifically appear in the title!). The Chogyal's government had likewise undertaken to purchase 300 copies 'to start with', but by the time the book got published the Chogyal's government had gone with the wind. Despite these unexpected reverses the publication of the *Field Guide* in 1977 was gratifyingly received by users and reviewers alike. By 1983, even with the published price raised to Rs 130, the book had gone through three reprints, and is still going strong.

The National Book Trust, India, was set up in 1957 by the Government of India on the initiative of Pandit Jawaharlal

Nehru as an autonomous organization, primarily with the object of creating a movement in the country to make the people increasingly book-minded. The Trust would produce and encourage the production of good literature in Hindi, English and all the major Indian languages, and make it available to the public cheaply. One of the series of books it had planned was 'India—the Land and People'. The books in this series were to be written by acknowledged authorities in their respective fields in simple non-technical language for the general instruction of the 'common man', well printed and attractively got up, and available at a price the common man could afford. In 1965 or thereabouts I was requested by Dr B.V. Keskar, the Chairman of the Trust, to do a book on Common Birds, more or less on the lines of my *Book of Indian Birds*, which had proved its effectiveness in rousing public interest in birds and birdwatching but whose price was somewhat beyond the range of the average low-income reader. The book would be translated into all the major Indian languages so that its message could receive the widest circulation. I was fully preoccupied with the *Handbook* at the time, but saw the NBT's point, as well as the need and the opportunity, and was loth to turn down the request. So I offered to produce such a book, but jointly with a competent co-author. My niece Laeeq (Mrs Zafar Futehally), a keen nature lover and an imaginative freelance writer in English with a pleasing fluent style, had been in her earlier years among the coterie of my enthusiastic little *chelas* in the birdwatching game, and had become quite proficient in the process. Laeeq was now persuaded to take up the assignment, and with minimal technical help and scientific guidance from me she soon produced a highly readable text fulfilling all the Trust's objectives. *Common Birds* has in fact proved to be one of the most—if not *the* most—popular titles in the 'Land and People' series. Its popularity is evidenced by the fact that between 1967 and 1978 the English edition ran through four reprints. This was followed by a completely new English edition in a somewhat modified format using new plates— several species on each—specially painted for it by the upcoming young bird artist of Rajkot, K.P. Jadav. It has been

translated into Hindi and nearly all the major regional
languages—Marathi, Gujarati, Punjabi, Oriya, Malayalam,
Tamil, Telugu, Bengali and Assamese—in most of which it
has run through two or more reprints. *Common Birds*
continues to enjoy the same popularity in the linguistic
regions as the English edition does overall.

22

Prizes

When I was a boy, and even until fairly recently, zoology in India meant chiefly anatomy, physiology and taxonomy taught in the classroom or laboratory. Life history studies of animals under natural conditions out of doors hardly counted, and ecology and ethology—words now fashionable and on every aspiring lip—were seldom heard. Extra-mural work consisted chiefly of collecting and preserving zoological specimens for classifying, dissecting and describing, which seemed to be the main field activity. Perhaps one of the few honourable exceptions but at a somewhat later date was Sunderlal Hora, the eminent ichthyologist who ended up as Director of the Zoological Survey of India. Hora's researches on the biology and ecology of Indian freshwater fishes, their adaptation to specialized life conditions and the curiously interrupted geographical distribution of Indo-Malayan species were refreshingly unconventional and earned him international renown.

My own chief interest in bird study all along has been in the living bird, its ecology and biogeography. Whether in scientific papers or books, my main thrust has been ecology—a 'contagion' reinforced and given direction by my contact in Germany with such pathfinding ornithologists as Erwin Stresemann and Oskar Heinroth. One of the few Indian biologists to recognize and appreciate the merit of this 'new' ecological trend in the presentation of my scientific field survey reports would of course be Dr Hora himself. And it was on his appraisal of my work-style that the Asiatic Society of Bengal awarded me its coveted 'Joy Gobinda Law Gold Medal' in

1953, during Hora's presidentship, 'For Researches in Asiatic Zoology'—as the citation read. This medal was the first of several such recognitions that have since come my way. While some of these awards may be more prestigious in the inter-national and scientific context, e.g. the gold medal of the British Ornithologists' Union in 1967, which I was the first non-British person to receive, I attach greater sentimental value to the Asiatic Society's medal because it is the first recognition for ornithology to an *Indian*. Also because I consider the first award of a series is always given after an independent and more critical appraisal of merit, and often serves as a convenient trend-setter for others that may follow. By the same token I regard my science doctorate (*Honoris Causa*) from the Aligarh Muslim University as sentimentally more prestigious since it was based on the first critical appraisal of my work. Though ranking no less in my esteem, the honorary doctorates that came to me subsequently, namely from Delhi University in 1973 and Andhra University in 1978, need not necessarily have been altogether so.

The Bombay Natural History Society, with which my destiny seems linked in one way or another, and more closely since the 'retreat' from Burma in 1923, has spearheaded the movement for the preservation of wildlife in the country and been res-ponsible, directly or indirectly, for practically all the game laws and wild birds and animals-protection legislation during the century of its existence. I have been a keen shikari from early boyhood but have felt increasingly concerned at the all too rapid and dramatic depletion of our forests and wildlife, particularly since World War II. This has accelerated with the repatriation of conservation-minded British forestry officials, the slackening of law and order and the disappearance of the princely states—which were most effectively keen on the pre-servation of wildlife. To maintain the BNHS's time-honoured tradition of nature conservation I did whatever was possible under the circumstances in my capacity as Honorary Secretary of the Society and Editor of the *Journal*—positions I had willy-nilly inherited—to keep the good work going and propagate it in every possible way.

The World Wildlife Fund (WWF), which had come into being through the initiative of a group of eminent nature conservationists in the UK, Europe and the USA in 1961 with the object of raising funds through international appeals for financing the nature conservation projects of the IUCN (International Union for Conservation of Nature and Natural Resources), had succeeded in interesting Mr J. Paul Getty, the super-wealthy American oil magnate, to institute the international J. Paul Getty Wildlife Conservation Prize of $50,000. This ranks in prestige with the Nobel Prize for other disciplines. In due course I received a request for nomination of an individual or organization to be chosen for the first award, in 1974, by an international jury of thirteen outstanding conservationists of world stature. I felt happy at this opportunity of publicizing the sterling achievements of the BNHS in the cause of wildlife conservation and nature education in India, which, by default, were unfortunately so little known abroad. It was disappointing that my nomination drew a blank that year, but at least I had the satisfaction of bringing the Society's work into focus with the international jury. That was that. The 1974 Prize went to Mr Felippe Benavides of Peru for his outstanding achievement in saving the gravely endangered South American vicuna. Then, first thing before breakfast one morning in January 1976, the telephone rang. It was the unlikely post master of the Bandra sub-post office asking if I would please come over about a telegram he had just received from Washington. Asked why he couldn't have it sent over to my residence in the normal way, he said he would like to deliver it to me in person with his congratulations as it announced my winning a prize. I was greatly puzzled since I wasn't expecting any prizes, and felt certain there was some mistake. The telegram, handed to me by the post master, bubbling with friendliness, bore my address all right. It read: 'Please keep confidential you are recipient of J. Paul Getty Wildlife Conservation Prize for 1976. Details will follow in a few days. Thomas Lovejoy [Co-ordinator for the Award Jury] WWF-US'. I still felt it was obviously a case of mistaken identity—Sálim Ali for BNHS—because if anyone had nominated me personally I should certainly have known.

It took some time to discover how it all happened. It transpired that my nomination had been filed by a member of the American Senate, Mr Charles McC. Mathias Jr. of Maryland, suspectedly inspired by a mutual friend intimately familiar with the activities of the BNHS, and my connection with it, and a constant well-wisher and supporter. A felicitous citation accompanied the prize, also looking suspiciously inspired by the same source!

On discovering the identity of my 'godfather' I wrote to Senator Mathias to thank him for his unostentatious courtesy and to express my joy and utter surprise at the award. His charming reply dated 8 March 1976 said, 'It was an honor for me to be able to nominate you for the second J. Paul Getty Wildlife Conservation Prize. I want to thank you for winning and thereby causing my judgement to be confirmed by the distinguished international jury. This honor is well deserved and I am pleased it has come to you. . . . Congratulations!' I was doubly pleased to learn later that the choice of the jury was near-unanimous. The Congressional Record of the US Senate of 25 March 1976 carries a report of Senator Mathias's address to the President reading:

Mr President, several years ago, when on a visit to India, I was asked by Prime Minister Mrs Gandhi whether I had met the noted Indian ornithologist, Sálim Ali. When I replied that I had not, she immediately arranged for me to do so and thereby opened the door to one of the most pleasant and interesting experiences that I can remember. As a result I spent a day with Sálim Ali in the national park near Bombay. The privilege was not only in having him open my eyes to the beauty of nature in the jungle, but in sharing his experiences and observations on all aspects of Indian life as he has seen it in a dramatic period of history. I learnt something that day about the birds of India, but even more about the qualities of human nature that are shared by all mankind everywhere. When the World Wildlife Fund requested nominations for the J. Paul Getty Conservation Prize I was happy to propose the name of Sálim Ali. I was of course delighted when Vice President Rockefeller announced that Dr Ali had been chosen to receive the $50,000 award—the largest such award given today for distinguished achievement in conservation. . . . Dr Ali has been credited with being a 'creator of an environment for conservation in India'.

Within hours of the announcement of the award in the Bombay morning papers there was a flood of telephone calls from bankers, investment brokers and miscellaneous gentry of that breed, all giving gratuitous advice on how to invest for highest returns, preferably in their own excellent concerns! Also from inquisitive nosey parkers wanting to know what I proposed to do with all that money. My uniform answer to all such, short and sweet, was that I was meaning to eat it all up quietly by myself, but now I saw there were too many people looking! In the event the lion's share of the prize money went to the BNHS—a long-cherished dream come true—to form the nucleus of its proposed Sálim Ali Nature Conservation Fund, later handsomely augmented by munificent donations from the Loke family of Singapore in memory of Loke Wan Tho's regard and admiration for the Society.

Due to the short notice, I had been unable to attend the award-giving ceremony at New York in February (1976) to receive the Getty Prize in person. It was accepted on my behalf by our Ambassador, Mr T. N. Kaul, with a felicitous speech which was much applauded. Later that year I was at San Francisco for another WWF function. I recall my first meeting there with my Getty Prize predecessor, Felippe Benavides, amusingly described by him as 'the $100,000 handshake'!

For the purpose of keeping a record, and to prove to Doubting Thomases like some of my late lamented elders that even such a seemingly futile occupation as birdwatching is not entirely barren of rewards if pursued with persistence and dedication, this chapter must close with a checklist of the awards and distinctions it brought to me over the years.

1953 Asiatic Society's 'Joy Gobinda Law Medal' for 'Researches in Asiatic Zoology'

1958 Padma Bhushan by the President of India for 'Distinguished Service to Indian Ornithology'

1958 Doctor of Science Degree (*Honoris Causa*) by Aligarh Muslim University

1967 Union Gold Medal of the British Ornithologists' Union

1969 John C. Phillips Memorial Medal 'For Distinguished Service in International Conservation' by the International Union for Conservation of Nature and Natural Resources

1970 Sunderlal Hora Memorial Medal by the Indian National Science Academy for 'Outstanding Contributions to Indian Ornithology'

1973 Doctor of Science Degree (*Honoris Causa*) by Delhi University

1973 Pavlovsky Centenary Memorial Medal by USSR Academy of Medical Science

1973 Insignia of Officer in the Order of the Golden Ark by H.R.H. Prince Bernhard of the Netherlands

1976 J. Paul Getty International Prize for Wildlife Conservation

1976 Padma Vibhushan by the President of India for continued distinction in ornithology

1978 Doctor of Science Degree (*Honoris Causa*) by Andhra University

1979 C.V. Raman Medal of the Indian National Science Academy

1981 Asiatic Society of Bangladesh Gold Medal 'For Distinguished Contribution to Ornithology of the Indian Subcontinent'

1981 Rabindra Nath Tagore plaque of the Asiatic Society, Calcutta

1982 National Research Professorship in Ornithology by the Government of India

1983 International Conservation Award of the National Wildlife Federation, USA

1983 National Award (gold medal) for Wildlife Conservation of the Government of India

23

The Thrills of Birdwatching

One of the standard questions I have inevitably to face is about what thrilling adventures I have had in a lifetime of exploring for birds. My standard answer must seem disappointing to those who expect to hear tales of derring-do. Ornithology as a hobby or profession or persuasion, whatever one may choose to call it, though full of adventures and rewards and disappointments, is by its very nature one of the most peaceable pursuits of the out-of-doors. It is certainly not lacking in excitements and thrills, though these may be of a different kind from what the normal enquirer expects. The excitement lies in ferreting clues and then following them up step by step to the discovery or confirmation of a fact or facts, of which one has obtained a suspicion or hunch. It was while living jobless in the seaside cottage of the Latif family at Kihim in 1930 that I got one of my most rewarding thrills of this kind when I fortuitously hit upon the first correct interpretation of the extraordinary breeding biology of the Baya Weaver bird.

I had grown up only on the traditional accounts of the nesting habits published in literature which had come down to us from book to book. These were interesting enough in themselves for a keen bird photographer, as I was, to want to record on film. But while concealed in a canvas hide perched ten feet up on a step-ladder, a few feet away from the nests, I noticed some unorthodox goings on in the colony which clearly showed that the birds had not read the text books. A few hours in this hide each day, and copious notes and diagrams of the proceedings in the colony, gave me a pretty good hunch of what was probably happening, till at the end of a few weeks it was possible to piece together with some confidence the general pattern of the bayas' breeding biology. Since then the new interpretation has been tested and re-tested and confirmed by myself and other researchers, and with further refinements is now accepted as what might be called the 'authorized version'.

In brief, the findings are that the male baya, who in his breeding livery is a handsome little sparrow-like bird, largely brilliant golden yellow, is an artful polygamist. He may acquire any number of wives, from two to four, sometimes even five—not all at once in the harem style but one by one progressively, depending upon his capacity to provide them each with a home. The male alone is responsible for building the nest; the female has no hand in it. Males select a *babool* or palm tree to hang their compactly woven retort-shaped nests, and several males build together in a colony which may sometimes contain a hundred nests or more. At a particular stage in the construction, when the nest is about half finished, there is suddenly, one fine morning, an invasion by a party of females prospecting for desirable homes. They arrive at the colony in a body, amidst great noise and excitement from the welcoming males, and deliberately visit nest after nest to inspect its workmanship, as it were. Some nests are approved, others are rejected. While the examination is in progress the builder clings on the outside, excitedly flapping his wings in invitation and awaiting her verdict. If the female is satisfied with the structure she just takes possession of it and accepts his impetuous advances. A hurried copulation takes place on the 'chinstrap' of the helmet-like half-built nest, and the pair bond is sealed. Thereafter the male resumes his building activity and soon completes the nest with its long entrance tube. The female lays her eggs within, incubates them and brings up the family. This is entirely her responsibility, and it is rarely—and only after his building impulse has finally subsided—that the male takes a hand in foraging for the chicks. Having completed this nest the male proceeds almost immediately to start a second one a few feet away. At the appropriate half-built stage, another house-hunting female may in like manner take possession of this second nest, and the whole process is then repeated. Thus the male baya may find himself the happy husband of several wives and proud father of several families at practically one and the same time. It sometimes happens that for some feminine foible, female after female fails to accept a certain nest. Undeterred, the male abandons the half-built structure and promptly tries again. In every baya colony there are usually to be seen a number of such half-built abandoned nests. This is the prosaic explanation for them and unfortunately not the more popular lyrical one that they are for the use of the male to swing himself and sing love songs to his incubating spouse nearby!

With the richness and variety of bird life in India, exciting discoveries of a similar kind are awaiting to be made by any birdwatcher who has the requisite enthusiasm and perseverance. Although as yet its devotees here are limited, it is refreshing to find that birdwatching as a hobby is growing rapidly in popularity, along with other civilized outdoor pursuits.

While the field study of birds, 'birdwatching' as it is popularly called, is a peaceful enough occupation, it is not entirely without occasional physical thrills and even hazards. In elephant-ridden jungles in South India for instance, I have frequently found myself in uncomfortably disturbing situations. A wild elephant, suddenly come upon at close quarters—a situation by no means uncommon in parts of Karnataka and Kerala—can be an unnerving experience, almost invariably resulting in the undignified spectacle, for the elephant, of the ornithologist in full flight in the opposite direction. In actual fact there is little danger from a wild elephant unless it happens to be a rogue or a female with a small calf. However, it is bad diplomacy in close-up situations, especially with the wind in the wrong direction, to wait for this to become apparent before taking the only discreet action. For it may well be that in tall grass country, in even the most innocent stampede of a frightened herd, the ornithologist may become an unscheduled casualty. Discretion and not valour is what such situations demand.

The diminutive Cochin Forest Tramway was proudly acclaimed in its time to be the cheapest run railway system in the country, or was it the world? I can well believe either. Its guard, complete with a once-white uniform, the regulation white (once) sola topee, and whistle and flags, drew a salary of Rs 25 per month after his ten years of approved service, and its German-built engine (2 ft gauge) ran on fuel wood cut from the surrounding forest, often as it chugged along. In the 65 kilometres or so of its length from Chalakudi to Parambikulam, the track lay through some magnificent hilly country covered with bamboo and dense mixed moist-deciduous forest with pockets of wet evergreen here and there in the valleys and along streams. The tramway, originally laid by the Cochin Forest Administration for transporting logs from the interior, worked on a combined system of wire ropes, capstan pulleys, weights and counter-weights. The locomotive hauled the train along the flats and gravity did the rest on the inclines, some of which looked terrifyingly steep. The loaded down-coming trucks hauled the up-going empty ones by counterpoise, regulated by a brake drum at the head of each incline, of which there were seven or nine, as far as I remember. Normally the train carried no passengers, but when a forest officer on duty or some visiting VIP was travelling up the line a corrugated iron wagon like a horse van was attached, with chairs placed within.

This is how our Survey party travelled in 1933 to Kuriarkutti, where the government camp-shed stood close beside the track. The train was halted alongside the entrance to the compound and the baggage and equipment unloaded and transferred to the bungalow. It was great fun being hauled up the inclines with wire ropes that hadn't been renewed since the tramway was installed twenty or more years ago, and therefore provided an element of adventure that varied with the steepness of each slope. I remember how every now and again live cinders from the engine would come flying in with a cloud of smut and wood smoke and land on our baggage and clothing. Tehmina's sari and my shirt had several holes burnt through in this way before the journey ended. Forty miles in eight hours was good going; the next station beyond Kuriarkutti, Parambikulam, about eight kilometres away, was the terminus of the tramway, with a forest depot and timber yard, where all the logs were assembled and stacked for transport to Chalakudi.

My next journey by the romantic Cochin Forest Tramway was in February 1946, shortly before it was dismantled, alas, to make way for the gigantic Parambikulam hydro-electric project, with its huge dam and reservoir, which has completely submerged Parambikulam and all the lovely country around it. Enquiry confirmed that we were being hauled up the inclines by the self-same wire ropes as thirteen years earlier, which knowledge made the journey feel distinctly more adventurous. We reached Parambikulam just as it was getting dark. In the verandah of the forest bungalow by the side of the tramway station I found a large squatted congregation of the local *adivasis* (Kadar), and in their midst, sprawled in one of those standard dak bungalow Victorian armchairs with legs splayed out on the extended arm rests, a bare-footed 'topless' European male of sorts in crumpled khaki shorts.

We soon introduced ourselves. He was an Austrian anthropologist, Baron Omar Rolf Ehrenfels, incidentally a recent convert (of convenience?) to Islam, who had escaped to India just before Hitler's famous Anschluss, and was camping in the area to study the tribals. He claimed ornithology to be his second love and expressed great keenness on accompanying me when I went out bird collecting next morning. Led by a forest guard, armed with a .410 collecting gun and dust-shot ammunition, and followed by Omar, we were stalking single file along a narrow animal trail through dense tall grassland about five feet high—the right kind of habitat for the Broad-tailed Grass Warbler (*Schoenicola platyura*), on which my thoughts were bent. Upon turning a bend in the path the forest guard suddenly ducked, excitedly pointing in front. I just glimpsed the head of a tusker elephant striding down the same path from the opposite direction, and turned to flee as fast as I could, motioning to Omar, who was ten yards behind me, to do likewise. I don't know what he made of this gesture, but I have not seen anything react more quickly. He spun round with the agility of a cat and sprinted as fast as his long legs could carry, looking neither to right nor left. The baron soon outdistanced me by a hundred yards, and it looked as if he would never stop running. He did so finally another hundred yards further, and it was only when I got up to him hot and panting that he breathlessly ejaculated in suppressed undertones, '*What was it?*' It was an amusing incident of which, as of the baron's speed and stamina, I am always reminded whenever I see a wild tusker looking at me! In this case the poor elephant had perhaps never noticed our presence. He veered away into the grass before reaching the bend and was not seen again.

Ornithology may sometimes even entail hazards of a different kind. I recall one particularly hair-raising incident along the Himalayan trail from Almora to the Lipu Lekh Pass on my way to Lake Manasarovar and Mt Kailas in 1945, a few years before the Dragon swallowed Tibet. It was at a particularly narrow part of the trail with a thousand feet of vertical scarp on one side and the roaring Kali river some 300 feet vertically down on the other. I had walked ahead of the porters while they were striking camp and was all by myself. Just at that moment a tiny bird—how well I remember that Yellownaped Yuhina!—got up to the top of a bush, some yards away on the flanking hillside. Just as I got it in the field of my glasses, it hopped a bit further up, so to get a better view I took a step back, with the glasses still glued to my eyes, and entirely unmindful of where I was standing with my back to the abyss. As I did so, I felt a small pebble slip from under my heel and heard a faint continuing clatter as it went rolling down the hill. Still unmindful of anything untoward I casually looked back over my shoulder to see what it was all about. What I saw literally made my hair stand on end. In a flash I realized that I was on the very edge of beyond—two inches more and I would have followed that rollicking pebble. The great leap forward I made at that instant would have done credit to Mao's reforming zeal. I am wondering to this day what my porters would have made of my mysterious disappearance when they reached the end of the day's march and found me missing, since finding any trace of a vanished ornithologist in that rocky gorge of the tumultuous river would indeed have been purely accidental.

As a boy I had found it far pleasanter to be chasing birds in pleasant places than doing ridiculous sums in elementary mensuration in the classroom. Since then I have watched birds through half a century and more, chiefly for the pleasure and elation of the spirit they have afforded. Birdwatching provided the excuse for removing myself to where every prospect pleases—up in the mountains or deep in the jungles—away from the noisy rough and tumble of the dubious civilization of this mechanical high-speed age. A form of escapism, maybe, but one that hardly needs justification.

Epilogue

'The advantage of doing one's praising for oneself is that one can lay it on so thick, and exactly in the right places'—so observed Samuel Butler. In writing my autobiography I have tried to keep this wise dictum constantly in view to avoid the temptation of laying it on too thick even in the right places, but with what success I cannot tell. Most of my correspondence, especially from the field, was largely hand-written, and copies were seldom kept; therefore in laying it on I had perforce to rely largely on memory jogged by a judicious extrapolation of the one-way-traffic correspondence, such as has managed to survive through the years, and from faded syncopated shorthand scribbles in field notebooks and specimen registers. I did not keep a regular narrative diary myself but, wherever possible, have drawn eclectically on the recordings of more industrious diarist friends who shared my various expeditions from time to time. These have supplied the keywords, as it were, but many interesting and noteworthy episodes, experiences and personalities have doubtless escaped mention. In a narrative spanning over eighty years this was inevitable. Apart from my natural history interests, perceptive interviewers have often been curious to probe deeper and into the other 'non-professional' facets of my life—my general outlook on things, my interests and hobbies, my views on various mundane matters, and my spiritual faith and beliefs. The answers to some of the questions put to me that border on the metaphysical may be taken as my Articles of Faith.

Q. But for your being English-speaking you may not have been the Sálim Ali that science knows. It has been said that without English, India would be 'an archipelago of nations in a non-navigable sea'. Would you agree that it would be a good thing to foster English as a link language for India? Given time and planning could not English form an all-India linguistic grid that occasions no regional resentments and keeps us in step with modern thought and progress?

A. Placed as we are today, nationally and internationally, I am convinced that in order to keep abreast with modern thought, concepts, science, technology, etc. it is not only desirable but imperative for us to foster English as a link language for India. This is not to say that all possible encouragement should not, at the same time, be accorded to the local languages and to Hindi, meaning the simple colloquial Hindustani that Gandhiji surely had in mind when he advocated Hindi as the common link language, as indeed it had and has become without anybody's special trying. In fact I consider, as many must do, that English is one of the most—perhaps *the* most—important and beneficial legacy the British have left us. It has been the chief factor in the unification of the country, in such integration as we have so far achieved, and in India making a mark in the international sphere. Indeed it seems astonishing to me that even people whom we are otherwise prepared to recognize as wise and intelligent, and to accept as our leaders, should be so blinkered and short-sighted as not to perceive what seems so abundantly obvious to us 'lesser breeds'!

Q. Was religion a factor in your upbringing, and does it play a role in your life now? Has the Sufi tradition influenced you?

A. Like all Muslim children at the time when I was young, and in many Muslim families even today, we were taught from an early age to read and recite the Koran parrotwise, without understanding a word of the Arabic in which it is written, and to go through the prescribed genuflections of formal prayer (*namāz*). I am sorry to confess that all this not only failed to elevate my spirituality but on the contrary rather put me off *formal* prayer for all time as a meaningless and even hypocritical performance. Critical observation in later years of some of my own ostentatiously sanctimonious elders—of their precepts vs. practices—has not helped to alter my views.

Q. Does your association with the study of a species of non-human life—birds—lead you to repudiate man's separateness from the rest of nature? Or do you believe him to be apart from the rest of nature, fulfilling instincts other than those of hunger, procreation and self-preservation?

A. I must confess that I am an out-and-out philistine and non-believer in anything that savours of the ultra-sensory or occult. Therefore I firmly believe that man is no different from any other animal—endowed with the same basic instincts, impulses and behaviour patterns as other animals—only with a more highly evolved brain which enables him to think and act rationally while at the same time presuming to arrogate to himself, by Divine Right as it were, a dubious superiority over lesser creatures. The superb film-classic *Ape Super Ape* illustrates in a beautifully graphic way how man's emotions, instincts and behaviour are basically the same as of lower animals, only somewhat refined, as we choose to consider them. I'm afraid I'm a babe in the woods where philosophy is concerned and deem it futile, for instance, to sit cross-legged on a mountain-top and contemplate the navel, or worry about the Hereafter, or about concepts for which there is no rational basis for believing or disbelieving. I believe with the philosopher George Santayana that 'There is no cure for birth or death save to enjoy the interval'. What I strongly realize is that our present life is the *only* time when we are at the driving wheel, as it were, when we have the power to consciously regulate or control our own actions, and I consider it a gross misuse of that potential to waste our life in pondering over abstruse conjectures and abstractions for which we (at least I) find no satisfying basis. In short, I am what some would call a 'dyed-in-the-wool' materialist, but not necessarily a wicked one! From the tangible scientific evidence around me I see no difficulty in believing that man has evolved from lower beings through the process of natural selection as postulated by Darwin and refined by sub-sequent scientific discoveries, and that essentially he remains a Super Ape.

Q. Would you not concede that there is a non-material factor in man that marks him out from the rest? How would you place man's aesthetic and moral faculties? Would you say they arise in his more highly evolved brain?

A. Not being of a philosophic bent, I must admit that I have never given specific thought to whether the higher faculties of man, such as the aesthetic and moral, arise in the brain. Although I believe that the brain is the main centre of all perception and sensitivity—the ultimate *fons et origo* of all our faculties which in turn are moulded by it—I do not maintain that this is the *only* moving force. There is certainly, it seems to me, something like Conscience (or Inner Voice, as I think Gandhiji called it), of whose origin I will not presume to seek or offer a rational explanation. Unless we are much mistaken there is a similar aesthetic and moral sense also in animals, not often outwardly perceived by humans until it shows up visibly, as for instance in the Bower Birds of the Australian region. Here the male scrupulously clears a piece of ground, builds upon it a bower of twigs, and decorates its interior with deliberately chosen bright-coloured objects, often collected at considerable distances from the structure, obviously for the delectation of the female. Or, take our own Blackthroated Weaver Bird: at a given stage of the nest-construction (by the male only)—the stage at which the female exercises her choice from among several competing nests—the male daubs a little wet mud on it and sticks petals of gay coloured flowers, manifestly to appeal to the aesthetic sense of the prospecting female and attract her to the nest.

Q. Consider Nehru's observation: 'there is no natural conflict between free will and determinism. Life is both. Life is like a game of cards. You have no control over the hand that is dealt you. The hand corresponds to determinism; the way you play the cards corresponds to free will.' Would you exclude belief in the 'dealing of a hand'?

A. While the question of 'a hand being dealt out' goes a little over my head, I do believe that a hand *is* dealt out to each one of us, the outcome of inherited genes, I suppose, over which we have no control and which, for convenience, we call destiny or kismet. But being possessed of free will, I believe it is possible for humans to give direction to this destiny to a limited, though still considerable, extent. In other words (again using the analogy of the dealing of a hand), **to play our** cards to differential effect.

To a somewhat similar question I once put to a like-minded friend, Sahebzada Mahmud-uz-zaffar Khan, he pithily replied in sentiments that might be my own, as follows:

> Life is neither sensuous nor saintly, but multicoloured and evanescent. To enjoy it one needs a fine palate; to understand it common sense. Religion and philosophy are therefore neither applicable nor necessary: yet paradoxically enough they persist. Hence life is also a paradox.

Another question I have frequently had to face is how I reconcile my loud advocacy of wildlife conservation with my views upholding the shooting of game for sport. To those who have never done any sport shooting it naturally seems a contradiction in terms. As I have admitted elsewhere, I have been an avid hunter in my time and gave up not as an act of contrition but for a more pragmatic reason—namely, the all-round deterioration of the wildlife position in the country, with many species pushed to the verge of extinction. A distinction must of course be made between shooting for sport and killing anyhow, merely for the sake of so many kg of meat. The former entails the scrupulous observance of time-honoured ethics, such as no shooting in the Closed Season (when the animals are breeding), the sparing of females and young, keeping within the prescribed bag limits, no shooting from vehicles at night with the aid of blinding lights or at waterholes where the animals come to drink, and so on. These are the very methods of the professional poacher. It is through his despicable activities and not through controlled legitimate hunting that wildlife has reached its present sorry plight. The presence of a legitimate sportsman in a forest other than a sanctuary or national park (which usually has, or should have, its special protective staff) is the most effective deterrent to the poacher, as has been recognized throughout the world, and a statutory ban on all shooting is definitely not the answer. When the poacher knows he is unlikely to meet a sportsman in the course of his nefarious activities, he has a perfect field day to himself. As the tiger reserves have clearly demonstrated in the last ten years, the total protection of a forest ecosystem benefits not only the tiger but also the entire habitat, enabling the prey of the tiger—the deer and pig—to increase proportionately and maintain a natural balance. If areas that have no controlling predators like the larger cats are given proper protection, the ungulates would increase to a number beyond what the habitat can support by way of food, and unless the population is reduced by culling (why not through sport shooting?) the excess animals are bound to perish naturally through malnutrition or disease. A valuable protein-rich renewable food resource would thus be prodigally wasted. For me wildlife conservation is for down-to-earth practical purposes. This means—as internationally accepted—for scientific, cultural, aesthetic, recreational and economic reasons, and sentimentality has little to do with it. I therefore consider the current trend of conservation education as given to the young on grounds of *ahimsa* alone—something akin to the preservation of holy cows—unfortunate and totally misplaced: the interest on the capital *must* be used, while leaving the capital itself intact. This is how I interpret wildlife conservation, and believe that future generations should enjoy the same fun with it that I have had.

Hugh Whistler's Suggestions on How to Run a Bird Survey 1931

'We are all rather agreed that certain recent surveys, particularly those of the Americans and Germans, have been examples of how *not* to go to work. They send a collector to an area and their aim is simply accumulation of a vast number of specimens, largely in order to get new forms and to get duplicates for exchange. They make no endeavour to furnish information of general or biological interest, they teach us practically nothing and their reports are merely critical remarks on skins. The result has been chiefly discredit. I want you to work on much more general and useful lines and I know that that is your own particular bent. You are a biologist and not merely a dry-as-dust closet worker, so I feel sure that we see eye to eye in this matter.

First of all we want actual specimens (1) for identification of the forms which occur in the state (2) in corroboration of your field notes (3) for record and comparison with specimens in other areas (4) for studies of plumages and moult. With Henricks as a skinner you are relieved from the manual drudgery and expense of time that the preparation of skins implies. On my own trips I always have to waste my own time in skinning which therefore lessens my time for more important work. You will be free.

Half an hour round the camp in the morning will therefore suffice to provide Henricks with work on the series of common birds. Anyone who can fire a gun can produce half a dozen birds for him to get on with, pending the arrival of more important things. You will then be free to work the surrounding terrain properly to make sure that no species are overlooked. In Ladakh I used to get out early and get home about noon; and generally have a short evening turn as well. If the common stuff is dealt with by an underling at the camp you yourself can confine your own attention to bringing in more important things. If you are doing a five-mile round it is waste of opportunity for you to be getting the babblers and bulbuls which are common by the camp.

On arrival at a camp you want to study a large-scale map very carefully and see what types of terrain are in the vicinity. Most birds are distributed according to terrain—especially the more interesting ones—so if you only go the same old round again and again you will miss half the interest of the neighbourhood. The map will show you perhaps that in one direction there are low rocky hills, in another an open wide river bed, two miles off is a large *jheel*; a reserved forest and open cultivation fill in the other areas. Each of these terrains will hold certain special species in addition to the generally adapted forms which are capable of flourishing in all the types of terrain. It is important therefore to establish for each camp (1) which species are able to flourish throughout the area (2) which species only inhabit certain parts of the area. You are then in a position to start to establish the biological factors which are responsible for the differences of distribution. Everyone knows for instance why the Snipe will only be found along the margin of the *jheel* but there are innumerable similar factors which regulate the distribution of other forms—food, cover, special adaptations, breeding requirements, etc. etc. Each type of terrain requires to be worked until you are satisfied that you know all about its inhabitants. Watching and thought are of as much importance as killing. I propose in my next letter to give you suggestions as to the points to consider, species by species. Here I am only generalizing, so I will not say more about this study of terrain than to give the larks as an example. Round your camp in a five mile radius you will perhaps find 4 forms of Lark irregularly distributed. Now there must be an explanation behind the irregularity of their distribution. Its ultimate basis is probably food, but food will express itself in external form—one lark may be confined to black cotton soil: another may need open ground under *sal* trees: a third may only be patchy because from some ecological reason it is numerically scarce and so there are not enough individuals, and its numbers never increase, to populate the region. We do not therefore want merely on the American model a report:

Mirafra cantillans.   Abundant.   75 specimens   Camps A B C D
Mirafra assamica.   Very rare.   1 specimen   Camp B
Alauda arvensis.   21 specimens   Camps A & B

We want some hint of the factors which induced their comparative abundance and their difference in distribution. That is what should lie behind ornithology—the specimens and the correct name should only be means to an end.

I realize of course that in the time at your disposal you will not be able to settle all these points, but we want *your* ideas and *your* observation both as a contribution to the problems and as a stimulus to workers in other areas who can then proceed to corroborate or disprove your suggestions.

All the time ask yourself the question WHY. Why is the distribution patchy? Why is the bird in the sandy dry river bed and not in the cultivated plain alongside? Why is it in the roadside avenue and not in the forest? And why has it special modification? Any bird with special modification, the scimitar-bill of *Pomatorhinus*, the racket-tail of *Dissemurus*, the heavy beak of *Pyrrhulauda*, must inspire you with a desire to see why it has the modifications which separate it from others of its family. All such points will occur to you naturally as the survey progresses.

Let your notebook be just as important as your gun. I should recommend you to keep several notebooks. First of all you should have a large general diary to be kept day by day after the lines of those kept by Hume in his Sind trip (Vol. I *Stray Feathers*) and Scully in his trip to Eastern Turkestan (Vol. IV *Stray Feathers*). This will describe the localities, terrain, chief forms met, with special points of interest. At the end of the Survey it can then easily be polished up as an introduction to the Survey report.

Then I personally keep another notebook under species heading. This I run through daily noting each date and place where each species is met with and all points of interest. Each new species is given a space and heading as it occurs. Running through the pages daily serves to ensure that nothing is forgotten. It also gives one the distribution clearly. It was annoying often in the E. Ghats survey to have nothing to show whether common birds did or did not occur at a camp—the absence of skins often probably really meant that the bird was not collected as sufficient had been obtained at other camps—there was nothing to show whether it did or did not occur. The amount given under these species headings varies of course. The Jungle Babbler for instance gets off with 'May 2–31 Camp Hylakandy common and general in all types of terrain'; whereas with a migrant or irregularly distributed species there are daily records with full details. I have daily records extending over years for the migratory species in the Punjab which show the waxing and waning of their passage periods.

Then I should keep a small notebook for soft parts of specimens. Do not write the colours of soft parts on the labels. With each fresh species obtained start a separate page for it in a notebook: write down very carefully the soft parts of the first specimen with the serial number of the skin. Each fresh specimen would then be compared with that entry, the similarity or the differences being noted under its serial number. This will ensure uniformity of description and then when the skins are worked out we can see if differences in the soft parts are correlated with sex, age and seasonal differences. The usual hackneyed formal writing label by label takes far more time and gives far less value—the specimens are divided up, the results are never correlated, and if the colours given on two labels differ one does not feel sure that the difference is not merely two different days' versions of the same colours. This of course implies that your first act in bringing in the day's specimens is to list them up in your serial register of skins and fit each bird with its serial number before it is skinned. The soft parts should of course be noted as soon as possible. This little register may well go out in your knapsack to the field. Be sure to include the colours of the inside of the mouth, which are usually quite neglected but often tell one a great deal.

Don't trouble to measure birds in the flesh. It is however of interest to weigh the larger forms.

Your labels should give information on the following points (1) The state of the organs (2) State of skull (3) Fat (4) Moult.

Regard correct sexing as the most important part of the preparation of the specimen. Henricks will not be able to sex every specimen—shot marks, heat, immaturity, off season, will all make it impossible to sex certain specimens. But it is essential for me to know that when you mark a bird as male you do so because you have had absolute proof *by dissection* that it is a male. Do not guess from the plumage—I can do that, and also the plumages are far less safe a guide than you may realize. Because people have guessed or sexed wrongly for 100 years many facts about the sequence of plumages have been unknown to us. Describe the organs as you find on the label—give a drawing of the size of the testes or of the ovaries where possible. If you are doubtful say so—'organs obscure but apparently ♀'. The more importance you attach to this point the more value I shall be able to extract from the skin in due course. Mark the presence of incubation patches. Say if shot actually *off* a nest— we don't know which sexes incubate the eggs.

With regard to the skull an experienced skinner can say whether a bird is juvenile or adult (within certain limits) from the degree of ossification of the skull. In the juvenile the skull is very soft, hardly more than cartilage—it takes 3 to 4 months to ossify fully. Ossification starts at the base of the skull by the insertion of the vertebral column and also behind the eye—the two areas advancing to meet each other over the brain pan. After the post juvenal moult there is still a patch of unossified skull showing as a little window in the centre, gradually decreasing till the window fades out. If notes are made in the skulls about ossification—and an experienced skinner soon knows it well—between the breeding season and November (after that it is too late) it gives tremendous help in plumage studies, as incomplete ossification at once betrays the immature bird, whatever the plumage.

Presence of Fat in excessive quantities shows that the bird cannot be breeding and that it is probably on migration. Presence or absence of moult if noted helps in plumage studies. Details are not necessary.

I should like you to pay a good deal of attention to food, not of course the hackneyed remark 'insects' or 'seeds', but to any special foods which are obviously being favoured by particular species and which may help to explain their distribution. It is advisable to take a good supply of small test tubes and then stomach and crop contents can be preserved in weak spirit for later identification.

Such small test tubes are also useful for preserving small chicks. You should preserve for down studies 1 or 2 chicks of every species of which nests are found—regard chicks as more value than eggs. Downy nidifugous chicks and larger nidicolous species (e.g. birds of prey & eggs) are better skinned. Be careful to establish the identity of your chicks.

You will say to yourself in reading all this long farrago that there is nothing new in it and that all the directions are obvious. I agree, but my experience is that 9 out of 10 collecting trips and collections lose a huge proportion of their value from a neglect of these obvious details. Carry them out and we shall be able to write a first class report on the birds of Hyderabad State which will be of far more than local interest.'

Ragbag

Of Some Evocative Excerpts from a Few Surviving Letters.
(Remarks within square brackets are mine)

1. Hugh Whistler to SA: 'Battle, 13 September 1938. I am
   most interested to hear that you are an antiquarian—so am
   I—on the Committee of our Sussex Archaeological Society
   of which my grandfather was Vice President. But my
   interests in this line have to be curbed so that the birds
   shan't suffer.'

2. Richard Meinertzhagen to SA: 'London 16 December
   1938. . . . When you hope Hitler and Mussolini will get
   what they want, do you mean war? If so, it looks as though
   your hopes will be gratified at no distant date. I have
   seldom seen such madness. War is the only remedy for
   such maniacs. They understand nothing beyond force.
   But next time there will be a complete dismemberment
   beyond any risk of recovery. We cannot have these shocks
   every few years. I do not mind a good shake-up once a
   century, but every ten years is a nuisance, and it seriously
   interferes with ornithology and my work. Stresemann was
   over here this autumn. He's a good fellow but talks more
   than he should [about Hitler and Nazi politics] and may
   get into trouble. He disapproves of Hitler but cannot
   suggest an alternative. The wretched Jews are having a
   ghastly time and everyone here is doing what they can, but
   it is very difficult as the German Jews are really most
   unsavoury people. One loves them and sympathizes with
   them as long as one does not come into personal contact

with them. They have made themselves a sort of European Untouchables and we now want a European Gandhi to fight for them.' [At the 1954 International Ornithological Congress in Basel I was sharing a room in the University Students' Hostel with my friend the eminent ornithologist Herbert Friedmann—himself a Jew and one of the nicest Americans I know. We got talking about the plight of the German Jews under Hitler during the War, and I remember Friedmann's telling remark 'If the Jews in Germany are all like the Jews in America then I have full sympathy with Hitler'—which was aptly eloquent!]

3. Erwin Stresemann to SA: (After his return from a stay with our mutual friend Col. Meinertzhagen in London in the period between the Munich Appeasement and the outbreak of World War II.) 'Berlin, 1 January 1939. It's the first day of a new and probably fateful year. It is Sunday and the sun shining on snow-covered roofs opposite our little flat on the 4th floor—and let me use this peaceful morning to write you that letter which had constantly been in my mind for one long year since I had Tehmina's and your charming and detailed news about Christmas 1938!! It will be a retrospect on the turbulent active period, full of hopes, achievements and disappointments. Unfortunately I cannot enter into all its details, instructive as it would be to you, but I don't think it would add much to the picture you made yourself already [Of Hitler, the Nazis and Jew-baiting] .... After the Rouen International Ornithological Congress I followed an invitation of Col. Meinertzhagen to be his guest in London together with my sister (the mother of Helmut Bayer) and we spent there a delightful fortnight, devoted to some work at the British Museum but even more so to simply enjoying life in a very pleasant surrounding. . . If you visit the deserts of India you will surely collect ground-living birds together with soil, proofs *a la* Meinertzhagen to show adaptation of the colour of the birds (especially the larks) to environment. This scheme worked very well in SW Africa where I had suggested it to Dr Niethammer. Always be on the lookout

for differently coloured ground—red, black etc. Think of the Crested Larks in the Nile Valley. . . . I think I haven't expressed yet my thanks to you for having so very kindly added—through Mr Whistler's intervention—to our Indian stuff by presenting us with an additional lot of very welcome, and in part even very rare, birds from Travancore. I certainly did appreciate it with great gratitude. What excellent labelling!'

4. Hugh Whistler to SA: 'Battle, 6 April 1939. Confound Hitler. I had arranged to go to East Poland again towards the end of the month. Now I daren't leave England in case of a war. Life is short and that damnable maniac is keeping the whole world in turmoil just for his own personal ambition of being a conqueror surpassing Alexander and Napoleon and all the rest of them. If ever there was a case for political assassination!—one can't help feeling—one life might save millions. The idea is that if we get through April the danger is over temporarily until after the harvest—and then I suppose he will stop me from going to Algeria. What a world!'

5. Hugh Whistler to SA (at news of Tehmina's death on 9 July 1939): 'Battle, 3 August 1939. The break in our correspondence made me wonder uneasily if anything was wrong and today your sad letter of 26 July has brought me your tragic news. I can't tell you how sorry I am for you and how full of sympathy I feel. It had not been my privilege and pleasure actually to meet your wife but it was impossible to have a constant correspondence with you over many years without realising that you were a very very devoted couple and that she was one of those rare companions with which few men are blessed and helped. I can therefore have some slight idea of the desolation and heartbreak that is now yours, and how difficult you find it to believe in the inscrutable designs of Providence. No words of mine can help you. You have got to suffer and win through alone, and you will win through because you know that that is what she would wish. But while you fight your fight, get what tiny help and crumbs of consolation

you may in the knowledge that your friends are feeling and sympathising for you. I am so very very sorry. All kindest regards.'

6. Hugh Whistler to SA: 'Battle, 20 September 1939. My own feeling is that it will not be a long war, and if I am stuck here the arrival of parcels [of survey bird skins] to work at will be a perfect godsend. You don't know the joy of the sight of a parcel of Indian birds waiting on the table—with its thrills all unknown!'

7. Hugh Whistler to SA: (In preparation for the Mysore Survey) 'Battle, 26 September 1939. Herewith a list of birds which you might meet in Mysore State, and what I should like from the systematic point of view. The field notes *you* must pay attention to—our preparation of the new handbook has shown up what little information there is about the field notes of most species, even quite common birds. As a general matter I very much want the distribution inland of species peculiar to the Eastern and Western Ghats. You will also need to work out the Wet and Dry zones in the State. Betts's Coorg notes showed how very local these may be.'

8. Hugh Whistler to S.H. Prater: (Curator BNHS, remarking about the Mysore Survey) 'Battle, 5 February 1940. We really are beginning to get the distribution of Indian birds worked out at last—and this is largely due to your enthusiasm and "push" in getting all these surveys done! Ornithologists have need to be grateful to you.'

9. Hugh Whistler to SA: (Regarding some Mysore Survey skins I had asked him to send to Stresemann as a gift from me) 'Battle, 26 April 1940. About a dozen were marked for Stresemann but of course it is impossible to send them to him [the War was on]—he must just content himself with the rape of the collections in Warsaw which has been reported in the press!'

10. Hugh Whistler to SA: (In response to a political harangue) 'Battle, 29 August 1941. This much is certain. There is both right and wrong in both the Indian and the English points of view, and both sides would be the better for

appreciating a little more of the opposite point of view. So I will leave it at that and I can only hope that however much you hate and loathe the English you can still feel friendly towards an ornithologist H.W. in spite of his belonging to the hated race. I for my part feel that I have a good friend in Sálim Ali who is a very fine ornithologist: to him my kindest regards.'

11. Hugh Whistler to SA: (After Ticehurst's death) 'Battle 5 October 1941. It is a pity that yours and his relations were not very cordial. However, it is too late to repine now. . . . I have been getting all the soil samples out and wedded to their respective larks, and it seems to be working out in a most interesting manner. With some species such as *Lullula* [Black Lark] there is clearly no connection between colour of the lark and colour of the soil. With others—*Calandrella, Ammomanes, Galerida*—there appears to be a very close connection: *Galerida theklae* [of the Nile Valley etc.] *for* instance. I have now collected six races with their soils, from the black-looking bird of Portugal to the bright red bird of the Sahara—each race very accurately reflects the colour of its soil.'

12. E.H.N. Lowther to SA: 'Allahabad, 2 August 1942 [a week before the passing of the Quit India Resolution by the Indian National Congress]. In your letter of 7 April you *almost* became political in your views! I was sorry Sir Stafford Cripps failed in his mission, and though I love India and have many very dear friends, I don't think Gandhi's attitude to the Europeans is ever going to settle a very difficult question. First there *must* be understanding between Hindus and Muslims, and between all classes and Europeans. This latter will I believe never come about until Indians and Europeans marry, freely inter-marry, among the better classes. There must be an understanding on both sides. It means an entirely new approach to the question, but take it from me, the colour bar *has to go*—it will be one of the things that will go when we have peace again. And why shouldn't it? What right has the European to think he is a better man than an Indian? He isn't and he

knows it. And he will have to give up thinking of the children of a mixed marriage as "little black bastards" as he so often does now.'

13. Honourable (Mrs) Joan Whistler to SA: 'Battle, 9 August 1943 [in response to my condolence on HW's death on 7 July 1943 of cancer]. I should like to tell you what a very very high opinion Hugh had of you and all your knowledge, and how much he too appreciated your friendship—and how much pleasure all your wonderful letters gave to him. He was so pleased with your book [*The Book of Indian Birds*] and the very kind way you talked of him in the Preface. I know there was no feeling of competition or rivalry ever between you—nothing to spoil your friendship, and therefore I am just going to ask your advice [about revising HW's *Popular Handbook of Indian Birds* for the fourth edition which was published in 1949. HW's bird collection, including H.W. Waite's, consisting of some 26,000 skins, together with all his meticulous bird notes, are now in the British Museum (Natural History)].

14. In 1968, while I was temporarily away from Bombay on field work, a letter of condolence came to the Society from a friendly Russian fellow-ornithologist Dr A.I. Ivanov of the Zoological Institute, Leningrad, on 'the sad demise of my dear friend Salim Ali', reported to him by an Indian visitor—one Prof. Singh (?) of Osmania University. The letter was replete with exaggerated eulogy of virtues such as are usually discovered only post mortem! Few men are given the satisfaction of realizing in their lifetime how excellent and indispensable they were, and I happened to be one of the lucky ones, not once but in two separate resurrections. I was shown Dr Ivanov's letter on my return to Bombay and lost no time in convincing him that he was grossly misinformed.

(a) Dr Ivanov to SA: 'Leningrad, 9 July 1968. I cannot express how glad I was when I read your letter that the information I had was absolutely wrong! According to Russian omen [*sic*] you have to live now as long as possible for a human being. My friends were very glad to learn the good news.'

All went well while I was fulfilling the Russian omen, and up to August 1974 when both the International Ornithological Congress and the International Council for Bird Preservation were held in Canberra (Australia), which I had expected to but could not attend.

(b) Guy Mountfort, President of the British Ornithologists' Union to '*Mrs* Salim Ali' [who had died in 1939]. 'Black-boys, Sussex, 21 August 1974. The news of your husband's death [origin a mystery!] was announced at the International Ornithological Congress in Canberra last week, and caused great consternation. He was one of the world's most famous and distinguished ornithologists, and his passing will sadden his many friends throughout the civilized world. I had the privilege of knowing him for nearly forty years. On behalf of the Members and Council of the British Ornithologists' Union I send you our deepest condolences. My wife also wishes to join me in expressing our personal sympathy for your sad bereavement.'

(c) Guy Mountfort to SA: 'Blackboys, Sussex, 4 September 1974. I am more pleased than I can say to receive your cheerful letter informing me that the announcement at the I.O.C. of your death was, as you say, "somewhat misleading" . . . Every one is going to be delighted. You are, of course, not the first famous man to disprove such a rumour, and I hope you will make good use of it in your autobiography. It even happened to me during the war, when I read my name in the list of casualties!'

Another friend, Dr Yoshimaro Yamashina of Japan, President of the Asian Section of ICBP, had also heard the same grapevine news.

(d) Dr Yamashina to '*Mrs* Salim Ali': 'Tokyo, 11 September 1974. . . . my most sincere condolence for the sad occasion of the bereavement of your beloved husband . . . Ever since I had met your husband for the first time in 1958 at Helsinki, he had been giving me his kind help . . . I had always been paying great respect to him as my teacher and my father. On 19 August, however, I learnt most distressingly of his sudden demise. At the beginning of the Executive Committee meeting we observed one minute silent prayer for the repose of his soul. We could not, however, in Canberra get any news on when and by what illness he had passed away, which news we all are still waiting to get . . .'

(e) Dr Yamashina to SA: 'Tokyo, 1 October 1974. Thank you very much for your letter of good news dated 16 September 1974. I do not know how the false news got around, but anyway no news can give me greater joy than your telling me that you are in good health. We have an old saying in Japan [apparently universal]: "He who by mistake is said to have died lives longer." So I am convinced that you will from now on keep fine and active as ever for a long time to come.'

15. Erwin Stresemann to SA: 'Berlin, 26 May 1972. This morning Volume 5 of your *magnum opus* arrived, adorned on the first page by your personal dedication which I greatly value. This volume, like its forerunners, is sure to prove of great importance to my further studies. Thank you very very much. We both will be in Tring on July 29, attending the reopening there of the B.M.'s bird collection [moved from South Kensington]. The first time I stayed in this rustic town was in 1910 before I sailed to Bali and the Moluccas, welcomed and trained there by Ernst Hartert [his guru]. Long, long ago!'

* * *

. . . TO SEE OURSELVES AS OTHERS SEE US

Candid Opinions of an Expedition Leader who Started Off
with Damaging
Reservations and Ended Up as a Valued and Understanding
Friend.
Revealing Excerpts from the Diaries of Colonel
Richard Meinertzhagen, D.S.O.

14th April 1937 Ghorbund Valley, 6500 ft., Afghanistan.
'Pitching camp was a long and tedious business as Sálim is quite
useless at anything of that sort and none of the servants knew
anything about tents or camping. Sálim is so accustomed to be
waited on by an army of servants that he is impotent when he
has to do something himself, and yet he advocates that his class
is capable of governing India. They must first learn to govern
themselves.'

15.4.1937 'I'm not enjoying this at all. I find Sálim trying. He is
inefficient and cannot bear being told how to do anything and
must always do everything in his own way, which is often
wrong. His ignorance of camp life and his helplessness in camp
are pathetic. He tells me he has never had to fend for himself in
camp and has always had masses of servants before. The
pleasure of camp life so much depends on ones companions.'

30.4.1937 'I am disappointed in Sálim. He is quite useless at
anything but collecting. He cannot skin a bird, nor cook, nor
do anything connected with camp life, packing up or chopping
wood. He writes interminable notes about something—perhaps
me. . . . Even collecting he never does on his own initiative.
Like all Indians he is incredibly incompetent at anything he
does; if there is a wrong way of doing things he will do it, and
he is quite incapable of thinking ahead.'

20.5.1937 'Sálim is the personification of the educated Indian
and interests me a great deal. He is excellent at his own theoretical
subjects, but has no practical ability, and at everyday little
problems is hopelessly inefficient, yet he is quite sure he is right
in every case. His views are astounding. He is prepared to turn

the British out of India tomorrow and govern the country himself. I have repeatedly told him that the British Government have no intention of handing over millions of uneducated Indians to the mercy of such men as Sàlim: that no Englishman would tolerate men being governed by rats.'

9 Jan. 1952 Sikkim (post-Independence). 'I find Sàlim very touchy about India and Indians. He resents any trace of criticism and is extremely bitter about South Africans' treatment of the Indian question. My experience of Indians both in Kenya and S.Africa is that they introduced disease, dishonesty and sedition.' [Then follow violent views on Gandhi, 'the rat Gandhi', and present conditions in India of inefficiency, dishonesty and squalor, as compared with under British rule!]

Glossary

adivāsi	tribal forest dweller
ahimsa	non-violence
almirah	cupboard; cabinet
Ameer	Muslim ruler; nawab
anna	⅟₁₆ of the old rupee; about 6 paise
ashram	seminary
askari	African soldier or policeman
ātā	flour of wheat etc.
avatar	incarnation (of a deity)
băbūl	a thorny tree, *Acacia nilotica*
băndobăst	management; organization
băra	big
băzār	market
bēgār	forced labour
bēr	drupe or plant of *Zizyphus* species
bhēlpūri	an Indian snack
brăhmachāri	initiate (celibate) monk
chăpāti	unleavened bread
chăplīs	sandals
chăprāsi	peon
chārpăi	rude bedstead
chauri	travellers' rest shed
chawls	single-room tenement buildings
chēla	disciple
chēwda	snack made of dried rice, gram, peanuts, etc., fried together
chhota	small

choola	stove
chowkidār	watchman; sentry
dak bungalow	rest-house for travellers
dāl	lentils
dărgāh	shrine
dărshăn	audience
dăstār	regal headgear
dewān	chief minister or finance minister of Princely State
dhărămsāla	travellers' dormitory
dhoti	loose (wrapped) Indian nether garment
durries	floor rugs (woven)
făkīr	mendicant
fătwā	diktat; authoritative pronouncement
găddi	throne
gāthiā	dry eatable made from gram flour
Ghana	literally: dense forest. Applied to Bharatpur wetland (bird sanctuary)
ghee	clarified butter
gompa	Buddhist monastery
gŭr	jaggery
halāl	lawful; usually throat-cutting of animals by Muslims for consumption
hubshi	Abyssinian
Hūr	a once rebellious tribe of Sind
idlees	leavened rice cakes (south Indian)
imli	tamarind (*Tamarindus indica*)
intekhab	anthology
izār	loose pyjama
jāgirdār	owner of government-gifted land
jări-pūrana	discarded worthless junk
jātris	pilgrims

jheel	shallow lake
jhoom	shifting cultivation
jongpen	Tibetan governor of province
jowār	Sorghum
kāfir	non-believer
kăndi	a tree, *Prosopis spicigera*
kărwanda	a species of berry, *Carissa carandas*
khăbăr	information; news
khāchăr	a type of 'passenger' bullock cart
khādi	homespun cloth
khāki	yellowish brown colour, as of army field uniforms
khălāsi	tent crew
Khān Băhādūr	a British-Indian honorific title, usually for Muslims
khărāb ādmi	literally 'bad man'; dacoit
khud	ditch
koita	a heavy curved knife
kūrta	long shirt
kutcha	raw; rough, unmetalled (road)
kŭtia	hut
Laibon	African tribal chief
lota	water jug, usually with spout
măchān	platform, usually on a tree
maidān	open field
māli	gardener
măndi	market
măni	gem
măsāla	condiment
maund	measure of weight, c. 40 kgs
mehmāndār	'guest keeper'; host
misri	crystallized sugar
mofussil	up-country (non urban)
mugger	crocodile
mūntăzim	manager; warden

mŭrghi	fowl (chicken)
mushaira	meeting where poets recite their poems
nālā	watercourse; ravine
năllāmăddi	a tree, *Terminalia tomentosa*
nămāz	formal Muslim prayer
năwāb	Muslim ruler or nobleman
Năwāb Hăr Dăm Shikār Jung	mock title for a 'chronic' shikari
nizām	former ruler of Hyderabad State
părād	tribal community hunt
părikrăma	circumambulation
patel	village head in Gujarat
peenēka pāni	drinking water
puggee	tracker
pukka	opposite of *kutcha*, q.v.
pulao	a gourmet rice dish
purdah	curtain; drapes; also, veil
Rai Bahadur	British-Indian honorific title, usually for Hindus
Raj	usually applied to the old British-Indian government
raja	ruler
Rāshtrapati Bhavan	The residence of the President of India
sādhu	a mendicant
sāhib	a title of respect
sămpān	a type of canoe
sărdār	chief; headman; leader
sărdārji	an honorific title applied to Sikhs
sāri	Indian woman's dress
satyagraha	'soul force'; passive non-co-operation with authority
sāyā	robe
seer	a measure of weight, *c.* 1/40 maund
shāmiāna	a marquee-like tent or shelter
Shăriăt	Muslim law

shērwāni	long coat
shikārgāh	game reserve
shikāri	hunter
shikwa	plaint
shōla	a forest formation in south-Indian hills
sola topee	a pith or cork sun hat, fashionable in British-Indian days
sooar ka bacha	literally: 'son of a pig'
Sufi	a Muslim sect
supari	betel nut
suttoo	roasted gram flour
Swadeshi	indigenous; also, movement to boycott goods of foreign manufacture
swāmi	holy man
tăhsildār	a petty revenue official
tăkli	a yarn spinning spindle
tālūka	a division of district
tālūqdār	see *jāgirdār*, q.v.
tăttoo	shifting cultivation; *jhoom*, q.v.
taungya	a small pony
tikka gharry	a horse carriage for hire
tsampa	*suttoo*, q.v.
vakil	lawyer
Yuvraj	heir apparent of Indian ruler
zămindār	landholder
Zērbādi	Indian Muslim × Burmese cross breed

Index